FREDA LIGHTFOOT

Ruby McBride

CANELO

First published in the United Kingdom in 2002 by Hodder & Stoughton

This edition published in the United Kingdom in 2020 by

Canelo Digital Publishing Limited
Third Floor, 20 Mortimer Street
London W1T 3JW
United Kingdom

A CIP catalogue record for this book is available from the British Library.

Print ISBN 978 1 78863 796 1
Ebook ISBN 978 1 78863 665 0

Look for more great books at www.canelo.co

Printed and bound in Great Britain by Clays Ltd, Elcograf S.p.A.

Chapter One

21 May 1894

'Rise and shine, chuck, kettle's on.'

Ruby stretched blissfully, then lifted her arms and wrapped them about her mother's neck in a tight, warm hug. Even if she was nearly eleven, she hoped never to be too old for a morning cuddle. 'Is this the special day you promised us, Mam?'

'It is, love, and if you don't shape yourself, you'll miss out on a very special breakfast an' all. I've saved a bit of jam to go on us bread and marg this morning.'

The thrill of a day's holiday from school made Ruby want to shout with joy, and jam on her bread took it into the realms of fantasy. She'd known too many mornings when there'd been no breakfast at all. Inside, she felt a bit sick with the wonder of it, and prayed she wouldn't disgrace herself by not managing to eat the promised treat.

Molly McBride kissed her daughter and tweaked her snub nose. 'See you wash yer lovely face and hands especially well this morning. We don't want Her Majesty to see the McBrides looking anything less than their best, now do we, chuck? Not when she's come all the way up from London to see us, eh?'

Ruby giggled as her mother gave a huge wink then, one hand at her hip and the other lifting her long cotton

I

skirts, she sashayed away, nose in the air, just as if she were the Queen of England herself. Oh, she was a laugh a minute, her mam. But then she leaned over the table, clinging on to the edge as she started coughing, which quite ruined the effect.

Ruby felt the familiar jolt of panic but said nothing, knowing how her mother hated a fuss or any show of sympathy. 'I won't let it rob me of me sparkle,' she would say, but the cough that had got worse all winter was a constant worry at the back of Ruby's mind. She felt thankful that summer was almost here, for the warmer weather would surely ease it. And Mam didn't want her to worry about anything today, not with the Queen herself coming to open the Manchester Ship Canal that had cost millions of pounds to build. 'The big ditch', they called it. Folk had been putting up flags and bunting for days, and there was to be a band.

Apart from Molly McBride's tuneless singing after her nightly glass of stout, there wasn't a lot of music in Ruby's life. And when the opening ceremony was over, there would still be cocoa and bun-loaf to look forward to, out in the back yard here. Mam had told her nothing about this, no doubt wanting it to be a surprise, but Ruby had heard about it from the other tenants. It was to be a sort of party, all of their own.

After a moment or two the spasm abated and Mam turned to wink again at Ruby, handkerchief pressed to her mouth. 'You waken our Pearl and Billy, while I see how far I can make this jam stretch. We'll want some butties to take with us, so it'll be nobbut a scrape. Now look sharp.'

'I will, Mam.' Pearl and Billy were curled up beside her like a pair of puppies, keeping each other warm. Ruby gave her sister a little shake but she only grunted and sank further under the blanket and old coats that served as covers, her dandelion-bright hair the only sign of her presence in the bed, the fronds intermingling with Billy's light brown locks. If Ruby hadn't known that 'they all came from a different seed though grown out of the same pod', as her mam liked to explain their different fathers, she would have wondered how it was the McBrides could be so unalike. Billy, at four, was an impish ball of mischief. Pearl, at six years old was plump, pretty and a bag of nervous energy with not an unselfish thought in her silly head. And Ruby herself, long-legged and scrawny with nut-brown curls that fell to her shoulders when not in their usual braids, eyes to match set in a pale face beneath winged eyebrows, and with a square chin which proved, according to Mam, that she was obstinate as a mule. Oh, but they were as happy a bunch as any family could wish to be. How else could they have survived?

There was no doubt in Ruby's mind that her mam more than made up to her children for what they lacked in material possessions, or in food for their empty bellies, by filling them instead with an endless supply of love and laughter.

'A kiss don't cost anything,' she'd say and, however hungry and bone weary she was after a long day's work, she'd always find the time to pull the three of them on to her lap, pour herself a drop of stout to keep up her strength, and relate some tale she'd learned from her old dad. He'd drowned at sea when Molly had been quite a young girl and nothing, as she would carefully explain, had ever been the same since. 'That's why we're in this pretty pickle today, because me mam hadn't anything for us to

3

live on after that, once me da's wages stopped coming in, and died of a broken heart, bless her,' she would say. 'So I never had a chance, see? Me brothers and sisters all went their separate ways, God alone knows where. I married the first bit of dish rag who offered to put a roof over me head, and look where that got me.'

Billy, being the baby of the family, would be asleep in no time during this story telling. Pearl would soon grow bored and wriggle down to go off and play with the rag doll Mrs Bradshaw from upstairs made for her, but Ruby would listen with rapt attention, and smile at the familiar tale which changed very slightly with each retelling. 'But you loved the bones of him, Mam, didn't you?' she would prompt, since she adored to hear about this unknown person who was her own father.

'Eeh, didn't I just! He was the kindest, dearest man on God's sweet earth. So handsome, he was, that all the girls were chasing him.'

'But you were the one who hooked him.' Ruby didn't entirely understand what this phrase meant, but her mother used it often and she loved to see the shine of happiness light up Mam's hazel eyes at the words.

'Aye, I did that. The minute I clapped eyes on him, and him on me, we knew we were destined for each other. Destined, that's what we were. Toby McBride and me were meant to be together. Two peas in a pod, Romeo and Juliet, a pair of star-crossed...'

Ruby interrupted, since she knew this description could continue indefinitely and they were coming to the part, which puzzled her the most. 'Then why did he leave, Mam, if he loved you so much? Why did he go back to Ireland without you? And without me?'

Here, her mother would hug her tight and smother her with teasing kisses. 'Now how could you go anywhere without me? You were still in me tummy at that time, bless you.'

'Was Da happy for me to be in your tummy?'

'Of course he were. Said so the minute I told him. Nay, I'm sure he meant to come back, for he loved me right enough. Said as much before he flitted off across the Irish Sea. "Know that I'll always love you, Molly," he said. "There'll never be another colleen as pretty as my sweet Molly."'

Ruby would frown at this, a familiar ache of disappointment starting up in her tummy at the puzzle of it all. 'But he didn't come back, did he?'

'No, drat him, he didn't. Some chit must have waylaid him. But that's how it is with fellas, d'you see? Responsibility and commitment are not words to be found in their dictionary.' Ruby would watch, wide-eyed, as her mam refilled her glass, worrying whether she should suggest she have her tea before she drink any more but not liking to say so, in case there was nothing to eat.

'Like all men he was not to be trusted, the lying, thieving, no-good piece of... Oops, hearken at me, about to use a foul word in front of me own childer. He just couldn't resist any bit of skirt what danced by, and I've no doubt that's what happened. He went chasing after another bit of skirt.'

Ruby would struggle to picture the shadowy figure of her father running after a long black skirt as it danced alone down an unknown street in Ireland, and failed miserably. It didn't make sense. 'How can a skirt dance, Mam?'

'Oh, believe me, precious, there are some what'll dance to any tune, given half a chance. That's life, Ruby precious. Nothing lasts forever. Not the lovely Toby, nor either of the good-for-nothing wastrels who took his place. You remember that, girl. Love you and leave you, that's men all over. So make the best of it while it lasts, because come the first drop of rain, they'll be gone.'

Seeing the tears spilling down her mam's pale cheeks and hearing the racking cough start up again, the conversation would be swiftly brought to an end and Ruby would be filled with shame. It was ever a mistake to talk about her da, for it always had the same effect. She really should be more considerate.

Now Ruby put these concerns to one side and scrambled out of bed, hastily rubbing the sleep from her eyes as she started pulling on a few more layers of clothing over those she'd slept in. There was always a raw chill here in the cellar which comprised their home. Not that this troubled her overmuch, for she'd long since grown used to a bit of discomfort. They'd lived in a dozen places over the years but Ruby didn't care how many times they moved, so long as the family were together, the three of them with their lovely mam. She splashed cold water on her face and scrubbed at her teeth with a salt rag, just as Mam had taught her, then hurried back to the thankless task of waking her brother and sister.

Grasping her sister's shoulder Ruby shook her again, more firmly this time. 'Wake up, Pearl. Morning has come, at last.' Hardly having slept for excitement herself, she couldn't see why her sister wasn't equally eager for the day to begin.

Pearl's blue eyes blinked open, then closed tight again, as if she couldn't bear the morning light, though very little penetrated the grime of the single window. 'Leave over, Ruby. I'm stopping here a bit longer, in the warm.'

Ruby ran her hand beneath her four-year-old brother and sighed with relief that for once he hadn't wet himself. The sooner she got him to the lavvy, the better. Gathering him in her arms, she lifted him from the bed and carried him out to the back yard where she sat him on the cracked wooden lavatory seat. She'd learned the importance of getting to the one privy early, before the rest of the tenants in the building started queuing for it. Still half asleep, he proceeded to do his duty while Ruby held on to him, making sure he didn't fall down the long drop of the tippler lavatory as some small children had been known to do.

'Is it today we see the ships, Ruby?' He started to scratch the rash of eczema on his knees and Ruby gently stopped him. 'It is, Billy.'

'I mean to go on a big ship meself, one day.'

''Course you do, love.'

Back in the cellar Ruby gave him a thorough scrubbing with carbolic soap, paying particular attention to behind his ears, making him yelp in protest, before quickly dressing him and leaving him to pull on his own socks and clasp his clogs while she turned her attention to Pearl. 'Aren't you up yet, you lazy tyke? Our Billy's up and dressed already. So am I. Come on, breakfast is nearly ready. And there's jam!'

'I'm coming, so stop yer nagging.'

When still she made no move, Ruby half dragged her from beneath the covers and Pearl let out a yowl of indignant protest when a wet flannel was slapped on her face.

Giggling, Ruby shared a conspiratorial glance with Mam, who was carefully scraping margarine on to thick slices of bread at the old wooden table which they grandly called 'the kitchen', though there was no stove and anything they needed to cook had to be taken down to the bakehouse on Clarendon Road. Ruby didn't mind the closeness of their living quarters because she never felt alone there. The cellar might smell of boiled cabbage and bad drains, be running with damp, thick with cockroaches and the peeling wallpaper someone had once optimistically put on alive with fleas, but it was their sanctuary and she felt safe in it.

This was because Mam guarded her precious charges every minute of the day, save for the hours when she worked on the fish market and left them with Nellie Bradshaw, the old woman who lived directly above and spoiled them something wicked, though she'd scarcely two ha'pennies to rub together for herself. Nevertheless, Auntie Nellie, as she liked to be called, was a soft touch for a gob stopper or sherbet dab. If she'd no money for such a treat, she'd give them a crust of bread to chew on till their mam came home and, for this special day, had managed to get some flawed loom ends of cheap cotton from the mill and helped Mam to dye and make them up into brand new frocks for the two girls, the first they'd ever had in their lives, which proved that something important was going to happen. Ruby had sensed this anyway from the whispered conversations between the two women as they'd cut and stitched and made their plans.

'I must have 'em looking decent,' her mam kept repeating, over and over. 'I can't let 'em go if they don't look respectable. And I'll not have any toffee-nosed official think I don't look after 'em proper.'

'No one would think such a thing, Molly, just look at their little faces. Picture of health they are – unlike you, chuck. A good long rest is what's needed to set you right. Anyroad, we're probably wasting us time when they'll only be given summat different the minute they get there. Eeh, but I'll miss you when you've all gone.'

Puzzling over this mysterious conversation, Ruby wondered if perhaps the Queen herself might be handing out new clothes down by the canal, though this seemed unlikely. And why should Auntie Nellie miss them? They'd only be gone for a few hours, wouldn't they? But then it was probably just that Mam had been planning this day for weeks, and seemed feverishly determined that all must go smoothly. She absolutely insisted that no matter what the cost, both her girls should be dressed up to the nines for the day and although Ruby might protest that it was unnecessary, she was secretly delighted with her dress.

It was navy blue, fastened down one side with shiny brass buttons they'd bought on the Flat Iron Market, and with a white sailor collar trimmed with a paler blue braid. Once she'd finished her breakfast, Ruby was at last allowed to put the dress on, smoothing the crisp new cotton with awed reverence. Then Mam set about braiding her long brown hair. It was always worn this way so she didn't catch anything, but, in honour of this day, the plaits were fastened with stripy ribbons, of which Ruby was inordinately proud. So pleased was she with the effect, she didn't

9

even wince or complain whenever Mam pulled the hair tight on her scalp.

By the time this onerous task was completed, Pearl too was up and dressed in a sailor frock identical in every way save for its being a paler blue, because pastel colours suited her fair colouring.

Billy looked a proper little sailor boy, Mam said, in a carefully darned navy jersey and cut-down trousers that covered the worst of the scabs on his knees. The minute he put on the sailor collar and smart blue sailor's hat, he kept saluting and barking out orders, just as if he were captain of a big ship and they were his crew.

'Aye, aye, Cap'n,' Ruby would laughingly reply, pleased to see her little brother so happy.

As for Molly McBride herself, Ruby thought she'd never seen her mother look more beautiful. She wore a wide-brimmed straw hat smothered in artificial flowers atop her knob of brown hair, tilted to an angle that would shade the purplish stains beneath her eyes. She had on her best blue-and-white-striped blouse above her Sunday skirt and Ruby felt quite certain that the McBride family could be taken for royalty themselves, so fine were their outfits. She could hardly wait another minute for the celebrations to begin.

Chapter Two

The grey clouds and threat of rain did not in any way detract from the excitement of the day so far as Ruby was concerned. By eleven o'clock they'd found themselves a spot among the crowds on Salford docks and settled to wait the long hours until the royal train carrying Queen Victoria was due to arrive at London Road Station. Mam explained how the royal procession would be led by the Duke of Lancaster's Own Yeomen Cavalry as well as mounted police, and would include the Lord Mayor, the Lord High Sheriff and other civic dignitaries. They'd make their way along Moseley Street, Stretford Road and Trafford Road for the opening ceremony. The Royal Standard already flew above the town hall in readiness.

Ruby loved to see the dull, grey, cobbled streets all trimmed up with bright bunting, flags of the empire and dozens of Union flags, as well as being filled with people eager to see the Queen. Even the sun peeped out from behind heavy clouds from time to time, as if doing its utmost to play its part but not quite managing it. She could hear the band playing marching music and people joining in with a song or two, whenever they knew the words.

After they'd eaten their jam butties Molly agreed to allow Billy to go off and explore the docks with a group of older boys, with strict instructions that he behave and not get up to mischief.

'See you stick hold of Cally's hand.' Cally, being an older boy of fourteen, could, in Molly's opinion, be trusted.

'If you get lost, you'll end up a vagrant in the work-house, like them poor mites over there.'

She indicated a nearby stand filled with children from the Salford Workhouse. They looked strangely silent and forlorn in their institutional garb and with their solemn, wizened little faces, quite at odds with the jovial attitude of the people around them. Billy tossed them a withering glance, spat on his hand and said, 'Cross me heart, hope to die, I'll be good as gold. I promise, Mam.' Filled with self-importance, and thrilled to be allowed to go off with the big boys, he would have agreed to anything.

'Can I go too?' Pearl wanted to know.

'No, you can't. Why would girls want to look at ships?'

'I don't, but why should our Billy get all the fun? Anyroad, it's better'n sitting here, doing nothing.'

'Cuddle yer dolly,' Mam told her as she turned up the cuffs of Billy's jersey sleeves, which were rather long, and fondly kissed his cheek. Embarrassed by this show of affection, he rubbed at the offending spot. 'Aw, Mam.'

'See that yer back here by three o'clock, and not a minute after.' Molly worried a good deal about her youngest child. He'd been sickly as a baby and now caught every cough and cold going, as well as suffering badly from eczema. She constantly had to wrap his chest in goose fat and brown paper, not that it did the slightest bit of good.

'I will, Mam.' He was already wriggling free of her clinging hold.

'Think on, or I'll murder thee meself,' she called to his rapidly retreating back. 'Here, you've forgotten yer ship.' She waved the wooden toy in the air but Billy paid no attention. He was far too busy looking at real ones.

Mam had insisted that they all bring something with them. Ruby had brought *Robinson Crusoe*, her favourite book. Being the only one she had, she'd read it a dozen times from cover to cover, and never tired of the tales of adventure within. Pearl had chosen her rag doll, Sally Ann, which she'd been happily clasping in her arms until her mother told her to play with it, after which she tossed the doll aside, as if it had personally offended her, then sat frowning and pouting in a heavy sulk.

Ruby paid little attention either to her sister's sulks or her own book for, despite the long wait all through a gloomy afternoon, there was far too much going on to be bored. There was the procession of ships on the Ship Canal, hawkers plying their wares, selling toffee apples, monkeys on sticks and little flags to wave at the Queen. It didn't matter to Ruby that she'd no money to buy any of these things, for there was sufficient bustle of activity amongst the patiently waiting crowds to keep her amused. Even when there was nothing much to see at all, she was content just to sit quietly, with her hands in her lap, and feel very grand in her smart new frock.

By mid-afternoon a thin drizzle started and it was then that Molly began to cough. It made her double up with agony and she strove to stifle the sound in her pocket handkerchief, not wanting any fuss, as was her wont. Ruby cast anxious, sideways glances in her direction, then up at the obstinately grey sky. If only the sun would come out and stay out, and warm them all up! Instead, they began to shiver after the long wait on the cold cobbles. After a while Molly stood up, straining to see over heads and catch a glimpse, not of the Queen as everyone might assume, but of her absent son.

'Where is our Billy? He should be back by now. Didn't you hear the clock strike four, Ruby? I'll swear it must be gone four.'

'I think it was only three, Mam.'

'He'll be all right. He always is,' Pearl snapped.

'Don't you give me any of your lip, girl. You know nowt about the agonies of being a mother.'

'How could I? I'm only six. Is there anything more to eat? I'm hungry.'

'Want, want, want, that's your trouble, miss. Allus asking fer summat! Where is the little blighter? Is that him, dangling over the edge of that dry dock? Heaven help me if it is, I'll wring his bleedin' neck with me own fair hands.'

For one split second Ruby thought Mam was about to launch herself through the mass of people and off the end of the quay to do just that, but suddenly a shout went up and, as one, the crowd surged to its feet and began cheering and waving flags, scarves and hats with abandon.

The Queen and her entourage had finally appeared on the scene and there was no hope now of mother and son being reunited until the opening ceremony was finished and the crush had abated.

–

It was all over. Queen Victoria had made her little trip in the Admiralty yacht the *Enchantress*, sailing a short distance down the Ship Canal from Trafford Wharf to Mode Wheel Locks. The three McBrides had caught an enticing glimpse of the royal party as they'd clattered past afterwards at a brisk pace in a stream of carriages. Now they'd disappeared completely, presumably with other duties to perform before departing from Manchester Exchange Station at about eight o'clock. The huge crowds were starting to disperse. All day they had waited and within minutes the excitement seemed to be over.

But at least Molly had recovered her recalcitrant son. She held him now in a vice-like grip and even while showing him the full measure of her fury with a stream of verbal invective, was happily stroking his hair and checking every limb for fractures and bruises. Satisfied that he was in no way harmed by his adventure, she gave his bottom a little smack, just to show how frightened she'd been.

Billy opened his mouth as wide as it would go and wailed at the top of his voice, though he could hardly feel the smack through the thick fabric of his trousers. A trail of snot spurted from his nose and, unable to bear the sight of her miserable son for a second longer on this gloriously special day, Molly pulled out a clean bit of rag from her pocket and scrubbed his face till it shone as red and bright as a polished apple. Then she enveloped him in a suffocating hug and swore she would never let him out of her sight again.

Later, this was a promise Ruby would ever remember. For now, she could only laugh at the antics of her mischievous brother, her own eyes like stars as she kept repeating, 'Eeh, weren't that grand? Did you see the Queen? And the Prince and Princess? Oh, weren't it grand?'

'They went too fast to see them properly,' Pearl complained.

'They can't hang about for one little girl when they've a whole city to visit,' her mother told her, softening the words with a smile. 'Come on, time to go.' For a moment Molly McBride did lose her sparkle and stood absolutely still, gazing down at her three children, looking for all the world as if she were about to burst into tears for no reason that Ruby could see, for hadn't it been a smashing day. The best she could ever remember. But then, following another fit of coughing, Mam blew her nose and fixed a bright smile on her face.

'Are we going home for the cocoa and bun-loaf now, Mam?' Ruby wanted to know.

But Mam only said, 'Best foot forward. We're off somewhere very special, though it's a bit of a route march.'

And so indeed it proved. They walked for what seemed like miles, not back to their own buildings but past Buile Hill Park, out towards Brindle Heath and into the countryside beyond. Several times one or other of the three children would stop to wail or whine, to complain of a stitch in their side or to enquire about where, exactly, they were going.

'Aren't we going home yet, Mam?'

'When do we get us cocoa?'

'Has our Pearl pinched it all for her dips?' This was a favourite treat for them all, a mix of cocoa and sugar in a twist of paper to take to school, but Pearl had a knack of helping herself to the cocoa tin when she'd a mind. But then Pearl was good at making sure she didn't miss out on whatever was going. On this occasion she vehemently denied doing any such thing. Molly said nothing, allowing them to rest for short periods and then urging them on again, giving no answers to their many questions.

They finally came to a stop when they reached twin gate posts set into a high wall. Beyond, Ruby could see the grey stone walls of a large house. 'Where's this, Mam? Where have you fetched us?'

When no reply came, Ruby glanced up at her mother and her heart gave a little thump of fear to see Mam's pale face awash with tears. What was wrong? Why was Mam crying? She usually only cried when they talked of the useless men in her life. Ruby couldn't ever remember seeing her shed a tear for any other reason, particularly not when they were out enjoying themselves. The skin on her mother's face had gone a sickly grey-green colour and Ruby began to feel truly frightened. Something must be dreadfully wrong. Was she ill? Had her cough grown worse, just in the course of one day, and Ruby hadn't noticed?

Molly McBride pushed open the big wrought-iron gates and ushered her three children through. The drive was long and straight and by the time they reached the end the last of the light had faded and dusk had fallen. She ordered Pearl and Billy to sit on the step in front of the massive front door, then taking Ruby's hand led her a short distance away.

'I want you to be a brave girl and listen to what yer mam has to tell yer. It's very important, so don't say a word, just listen carefully.'

Ruby was so terrified by what her mother might be about to say that she couldn't possibly have found her voice, even if a gun had been held to her head.

Mam's face was now on a level with Ruby's own as she hunkered down before her. 'I've got to go in the sanatorium, for me cough. You understand, love? And I'll not get out next week, nor next month. It's going to be a long job, months at best, so I must ask you to look after our Pearl and Billy for me. Can you do that?'

Ruby, mesmerised by the tears welling up in her mother's eyes and yet not spilling over, could only nod.

'I've fetched you here to this lovely house, to be looked after proper. You'll be safe in this good, clean place, with fresh air and...' She gave a little sob, as if the effort of holding back her tears was almost too much for her. 'I want you to promise me to be a good girl, to eat up everything they put before you...'

But she could go no further. Her words became lost on a choking gasp of anguish and mother and daughter fell into each other's arms, clinging together in a tight embrace as if nothing and no one could ever tear them apart. So terrible a sight did they make that Pearl and Billy sat like stone, too horrified to move or even shed a tear themselves. Paralysed with fear, they sat and watched the awful spectacle before them as if witnessing the end of the world, which in a way they were, their world anyway.

With a superhuman effort Molly McBride regained control of her emotions, smothered each of her children in a flurry of kisses and hugged them to within an inch of their lives.

'When you sees me again, I'll be a different woman. Fit and well and...' Emotion overwhelmed her and, turning, she walked quickly away. Only Ruby could tell, by the way her mam's shoulders were shaking, that she was still crying.

It was then that the big oak doors opened.

Chapter Three

Ruby stood shivering in flannel petticoat and knickers. She could hear Pearl's loud, hiccupping sobs as she pulled on long black woollen stockings, though even her sister's complaints had been silenced by the uncompromisingly stern expression on the woman's face. She was so tall that Ruby had to tilt back her head in order to see it properly, scarcely visible beneath the wide folds of black and white fabric which comprised the nun's headdress. Her long, flowing black skirts were protected by a large apron, and around her neck hung a silver cross. Ruby thought this quite beautiful and, as her mam had been at pains to teach her good manners, she smiled politely at the nun and asked if she might please have her best frock back.

'Indeed, you may not. And you'll address me as Sister Joseph, if you please.'

Ruby thought it rather silly for a woman to be given a man's name, but decided it would be rude to say so. Instead, she watched with sinking heart as their precious sailor frocks were taken, folded and shut away in a drawer. She felt instinctively that would be the last they would ever see of them and felt a raw grief, not so much for the loss of these garments as for the effort her mother had put into them, into ensuring that her little girls were dressed in their best when she delivered them to Ignatius

House. Now, all of those dreams had come to nothing. The McBride children had been stripped of their identities and given new ones, the kind which made them look exactly the same as everyone else. Even at ten years of age, Ruby understood this stark truth. The nun's next words confirmed her worst suspicions.

'Your number will be 451, and your sister's will be 452. See you don't forget them.'

Ruby gulped on the hard lump that came into her throat. 'What about our Billy?'

'He will be 453, of course,' she was tartly informed.

'I mean, where is he? Where have you taken him?'

The night before, as soon as they'd arrived, the three children had been bathed in something, which had made their skin and hair smell funny. Too much hair was, apparently, disapproved of and so Pearl's and Ruby's long curls were cut sensibly short while Billy's head had been shaved completely as he was found to have nits. After a supper of bread and dripping, they'd each been presented with a bag in which they were to keep a comb, a toothbrush, tablet of soap and a face flannel. They were then put to sleep in cold narrow beds in a room as small as a jail cell with the stern reprimand that they'd arrived far too late for them to join the other children in their dormitories, which seemed like yet another black mark against them.

When the nun had gone, leaving them alone in the dark, Pearl had crept out of her bed to come and curl up beside Ruby. Even so the pair wept together at the dreadfulness of their situation. Where was Mam? When would they see her again? Would she ever get well? And what would happen to them if she didn't? They didn't care to think too much about this awful possibility so

Ruby cuddled Pearl close while she told her one of mam's stories.

Billy was denied the comfort of a cuddle as he hadn't been allowed to sleep with them and it had broken Ruby's heart to listen to his wailing cries as he'd been half dragged, half carried away down the long echoing corridor.

This morning, before they were allowed anywhere near the other children, they'd been brought here, to this tiny changing room, where they'd been stripped of their precious belongings and presented with new clothes: a strange assortment of undergarments, a dark green dress and a cotton pinafore, all marked with their individual identity number in black thread.

Sour-faced Sister Joseph cast a critical glance over them, sniffed with an air of disapproval and instructed them to fasten their pinafores in a neat and tidy fashion. 'And make sure you keep them clean. We don't want any slovenly behaviour here.'

Ruby was delighted to be reunited with Billy. He bounced up into her arms at breakfast then whispered that he'd wet his bed and that the lady had removed it and given him a straw pallet instead. 'She told me she'd give me a cold bath if I did it again, to cure me, but I don't like cold baths our Ruby.' The shame and fear the little boy felt was plainly visible in his wide and terrified gaze.

''Course you don't, love.' Over my dead body, Ruby thought, on a surge of protective rebellion. She kissed him, smoothed the tears from his wet cheeks, as Mam would have done. 'Don't worry, I'm sure it won't come to that. They won't expect no different till you settle in.'

The three were seated together at the end of a table that ran the length of the room which seemed to be packed with children, all of them entirely silent, save for when they chanted grace in a singsong chorus. Each of the McBride children was presented with a plate, a spoon and a tin mug before being served with a portion of thin porridge. When a kindly nun came to pour warm milk on their porridge, she whispered that talking at the table was not permitted. Billy, however, was bursting with questions which he desperately needed answering.

'I want to know where me mam is. When is she coming to fetch me? Where's me mam?' His high-pitched, protesting voice rang out in the silence of the dining room and dozens of pairs of shocked eyes turned in his direction. Ruby was horrified, and embarrassed on her brother's behalf. Utterly oblivious, he asked the question again. 'Where is she, our Ruby? I want me mam.'

Even strict Sister Joseph failed to silence him. He kept on asking the same question every few minutes. Ruby did her best to hush him, and to console and comfort the little boy, without giving him any explanation. But then how could Billy, at four, understand that his mother was very ill indeed, and couldn't take care of her own children any longer?

Following the dish of lukewarm porridge, slice of bread and margarine and mug of milky tea which the McBride children ate with hungry relish, they were ordered to remain where they were until everyone else had filed out of the dining hall and gone to their lessons. Once more Sister Joseph stood before them.

'You must stay here until I come and fetch you,' she instructed the two girls, then, grasping Billy firmly by the hand, proceeded to march him away. He dragged his feet, let out a great wail of distress, then wrenched himself free

and ran back to Ruby to bury his head in her lap. He
burst into tears and Ruby wrapped her arms tight about
him, holding his quivering little body close, just as Mam
would have done. Sister Joseph's face, normally the colour
of sour milk, turned an odd sort of puce but, despite the
shivers of fear running down her own spine, Ruby was
determined to get an answer to her question this time.

'Where are you taking our Billy? I need to know where
he's going.'

A sharp indrawn breath, and a narrowing of the gimlet
eyes rewarded her courage. Unmoved by the animosity in
the gaze glaring at her from beneath the nun's headdress,
Ruby continued gently stroking Billy's shaven head with
one hand, while keeping a tight hold of Pearl with the
other, just in case anyone should try and take her away
too.

'Naturally, being a boy, your brother will be in a
different section of the house from you girls.' The venom
in the woman's tone sliced through her like a knife.

'Which section? Where? Will he be in the baby class?'

'Dear me, questions, questions! You've got far too
much to say for yourself 451. Did no one teach you to
speak only when spoken to?'

'I need to know where he is. Mam asked me to look
after him. She was most particular about that.'

'Your mother doesn't care one way or the other what
happens to you.'

Ruby felt all the blood drain from her face. 'That's not
true. She *does* care. And she made sure we were properly
dressed up for when she fetched us here.'

Sister Joseph gave a loud snort of disdain. 'Don't think
you can fool me with those fancy frocks you arrived in.

Far too good for the likes of you. I can recognise stolen property when I see it.'

'They were *not* stolen!' Ruby cried, appalled by the very idea that this woman from a religious order should think such a thing about her mam. But her interjection seemed to inflame the nun's temper all the more and she was now wagging a furious finger in Ruby's face.

'Don't lie to me 451. Your mother abandoned you. She was clearly no better than she should be. Utterly feckless, like a hundred others of her ilk. Fortunately, that task falls to more responsible guardians now and Billy will be taken proper care of, at last. As for you, 45l, you'd do better to curb that curiosity of yours. If you don't want it to get you into further trouble.'

Ruby's brown eyes seemed to blaze with jagged spears of gold. 'It's not true what you're saying. Mam *didn't* abandon us! She *never* would! She were poorly and had to go in the sanatory.'

'The sanatorium, you mean?' Sister Joseph blinked, as if this information were new and rather unexpected. She did a swift genuflection. 'Then we can but trust in the Lord that she will recover. Either way, she is in God's hands now.'

Alarmed by the depressing turn in the conversation, and moved by her little brother's distress, Pearl too suddenly dissolved into tears. 'Is me mam going to die?'

Ruby wished herself a million years older and wiser, but Mam had always told her to stand up for herself, and hadn't she sworn to look out for their Pearl and Billy, so she certainly wasn't going to let a bad-tempered old nun put her off her stride. She grabbed Pearl and held her close in a fierce hug. 'No, she ain't going to die, Pearl. And we ain't going to be orphans.'

'No, indeed, you are *vagrants*, which is worse,' Sister Joseph tartly informed her, as if it were all their own fault that their mother was sick and hadn't been able to provide for them.

'What's a vagrant?' Ruby could have bitten off her own tongue almost the moment the question popped out of her mouth. Just seeing the acid smile beneath the wimple warned her that the nun would take great pleasure in telling her.

'In this instance, it means you are the offspring of a destitute, in dire need of discipline and obedience.'

Both girls looked bewildered, as well they might. For the benefit of their improved education, Sister Joseph continued with her explanation as she resolutely hustled them out of the dining room and down a long, empty corridor, which smelled of beeswax polish and sawdust, mingled with something far less pleasant. 'It is our task to inculcate these essential traits into rough, urchin children such as yourselves. To teach you to respect your betters and combat the delinquent lifestyles you have so far been subjected to. What we do not need here at Ignatius House are unruly, naughty little guttersnipes with too much to say for themselves. Our aim is to produce quiet, orderly and well-mannered children who understand the meaning of moral rectitude. It is our Christian duty to rescue you from the life of crime and the corrupt environment you have hitherto known in order to rehabilitate you. In short, we will turn you into newly reformed, Christian boys and girls.'

Ruby had understood little more than one word in ten, nevertheless she felt outraged by the lecture. She might only be a child but she knew when she was being insulted. 'We didn't lead no life of crime. Mam allus did her best for us. Give us a right walloping, she would, if we did owt wrong. But she loved us. And she allus said we should mind our manners and say our prayers every night. So we don't need to be reformed, thank you very much.'

This outburst caused Sister Joseph to halt in her tracks and stare down at her charge open-mouthed. The long, terrible silence which followed seemed to stretch into eternity before she found her voice. 'Never, in all my years at Ignatius House, have I encountered such gross insubordination. Indeed, I fear the task of salvation is going to be more difficult than I imagined. Your defiance, 451, will be curbed. And I shall personally see that it is.' Whereupon, she plucked Billy from Ruby's grasp and carried the little boy away, kicking and screaming.

–

Ruby did her utmost to conform, if only for the sake of her brother and sister, but it made no difference. As punishment for her insolence on that first day, she was denied any opportunity to see her brother, even at play-time in the afternoon. At least she and Pearl could be together, but Ruby knew Billy must miss them dreadfully, and worried about him all the time. He would be sobbing his heart out every night, probably wetting his bed even more than usual, and feeling desperately alone and unwanted. Ruby worried over how his chest was, or if his eczema was still troubling him. She asked the other children if they had seen him but nobody had. Boys were only allowed to stay at the home until they were ten, and were kept in a separate wing of the house although they were generally allowed to visit their sisters during recreation hour.

But not Billy!

One night in the dormitory when Ruby was on her way to the bathroom with Pearl, who was afraid to go alone in the dark, a hand grasped her shoulder, making her squeal in alarm.

''Ere, are you the sister of Billy McBride?'

'Yes, I am. Why, have you seen him?'

'Don't tell anyone I said so, but the other boys are giving him hell. My brother Sam's in the same dormitory and he told me. Billy's the littlest, see, so they're making him do all the work, and making him suffer summat shocking if he don't do it right.'

'Are you telling me our Billy is being bullied?' Ruby was appalled, a rush of anger flooding through her at the thought that anyone, particularly boys bigger than him, could bully her little brother who would never hurt a fly. She must do something to stop it, at once. But what? What could she do? Her mind was in such a turmoil of emotion, Ruby hardly heard the girl's next words.

'Aye, and our Sam says he's had three cold baths this week already for wetting his bed. If he don't get "cured" soon, he'll catch bloody pneumonia – that's if he isn't beaten to a pulp first. Either way, he's a right mess. Getting worse, not better.'

'How is he worse? What do you mean, a right mess?' But her informant had gone, slipping away in the darkness as quietly as she had come.

Ruby decided she could wait no longer. She saw little point in asking the nuns for help. They'd done nothing so far and Sister Joseph never would, not in a month of Sundays. Besides which, she'd already branded her as a liar. Instead, she went on a hunger strike. For dinner that day it was pork and potatoes, followed by sago pudding. Ruby refused, absolutely, to eat so much as a mouthful. She could feel Sister Joseph's eyes upon her the full length of the dining room.

Guessing what Ruby was up to, Pearl was so concerned that she broke the no-talking rule and begged her to eat. 'Don't do it, Ruby. You'll only make things worse.'

Sister Joseph was approaching, bearing down upon them like a ship in full sail, her boots beneath the flowing skirts of her black robes click-clacking on the polished wooden floor. 'Were you talking?' she demanded of Pearl. Girls instantly bent their heads and applied themselves diligently to their food, hoping to avoid trouble themselves. 'Do not attempt to deny it, 452. A lie is a thousand times more sinful, and I distinctly heard you speak. Stand up. Let everyone see the girl arrogant enough to break rules.'

Pearl scrambled to her feet, the tears already spilling over and running down her cheeks. As she stood up, the rag doll, which she always carried with her, fell to the floor. Sister Joseph pounced. 'What is that doll doing in here? Give it to me this minute.'

'*Leave it alone!*' The words had burst out of Ruby's mouth before she'd had time to give them any thought. The effrontery of her daring to issue an order to Sister Joseph brought an instant and terrible silence. Not a sound in the long dining hall could be heard as every knife and fork stilled its clatter, every breath was held. Yet even that didn't stop her. 'That doll is all our Pearl's got to remind her of our Mam. Don't you dare take it away.'

'I beg your pardon?'

'I said, leave her alone. And leave me little brother alone, an' all. Someone is bullying him. For all I know, it could be you what's put 'em up to it, 'cause you're the same. A great big bully! Well, you can save yer nastiness for me. I'm big enough to take it, and I've no intention of eating another mouthful in this damn place until I get to see our Billy. So you can stick yer sago pudding!' Whereupon she turned the dish upside down and tipped the resulting mess all over the table. A gasp went up, echoing shockingly around the room.

For a moment Ruby thought Sister Joseph might explode. Her face went from pink to white to a dark red, very like the colour of Auntie Nellie's best chenille tablecloth, her thin lips almost disappearing in a tightly folded pucker of fury.

Sister George, a gentle soul who hated confrontation of any sort, saved the moment. She scurried over, picked up the fallen doll and ordered Pearl to sit down and get on with her dinner. 'I shall mind dolly for you until you've finished. It isn't appropriate that you bring her into dinner, 452. Sister Joseph is quite right in that. She will also speak to 451 later about her insubordination, will you not, Sister?' And, swivelling around, she smartly clapped her hands together so that with one accord hundreds of girls picked up their knives and forks and continued with their meal. All except for Ruby.

Acutely aware of Pearl weeping silent tears as she struggled to eat the food set before her, and of Sister Joseph standing behind her in a mute, condemning silence, yet she made no move to pick up her own knife and fork.

When the meal was finished and grace said as usual, the other girls all trooped out to begin their afternoon lessons. Ruby was instructed to stay behind. She sat with the untouched meal in front of her, staring at the slops of sago pudding spilled all over the board table throughout that long afternoon. More plates were set before her at supper and again she was left seated at the table throughout the evening right up to bedtime when, finally, she was sent to bed. The next morning at breakfast, the plates of food were still present at her place, joined by the morning dish of porridge and slice of bread and marg. Ruby didn't touch a morsel. She felt ill and light-headed yet had no intention of giving in.

'Are you going to eat that food 451?'

'Not unless I can see our Billy! And have you given our Pearl her doll back?'

'Certainly not is the answer to both questions. You are a bad influence upon him, and set an equally bad example to your sister with this outrageous behaviour. For a little guttersnipe such as yourself to have the effrontery to question the judgement of your betters almost beggars belief.'

For four days she held out. The routine changed some-what. It was decided that missing classes would only inflame her obstinacy, so the food was removed and Ruby was sent to continue her work as usual. Each mealtime, the same congealed dishes were set before her.

When this didn't work fresh food was brought, and it was true that the more appetising aroma almost weakened her resolve, but then she thought of Billy's sad little face, his frightened eyes at being made to sleep on a straw pallet and threatened with the horror of being dumped in a cold bath by way of a 'cure'. Ruby found it hard to imagine a more dreadful punishment for a very human failing. Wasn't it enough that his mother was sick, possibly dying? She thought of his misery and sense of isolation at being kept from his sisters; the fear he must feel at being bullied by the older boys, and held on to her resolve. She would not eat until she could see him, and know that he was well.

Chapter Four

It was kindly Sister George who finally broke the dead-lock. One afternoon during the hour when the children were allowed to play games she brought Billy to see his sisters. He flew straight into Ruby's arms and the three McBrides hugged and sobbed and clung on to each other as if they might never let go.

'I am not in any way condoning your bad behaviour,' Sister George sternly informed Ruby, 'but we cannot have you fading away before our eyes. And I do understand your concern for Billy. I have recently discovered that you were right, he was being put upon by the older boys, which is not at all pleasant, though I doubt he has come to any real harm.' She wagged a finger in his face. 'It was very naughty of you not to tell us, Billy. If we had known, we could have done something.'

Ruby put a protective arm about the little boy's shoulders. 'How would he find the courage to tell when he gets punished for the silliest of mistakes, like wetting his bed when he's upset?' she challenged before starting to examine his arms and legs, much as Mam might have done. She found several scratches and any number of bruises, which she showed to Sister George with a flush of triumph.

'Little boys are always falling down and hurting themselves. As I said, I'm sure nobody meant him any real harm and I've spoken to the boys concerned. As for the bed wetting, all children must learn one way or another. It may sound cruel but this method generally works in the end.'

But Ruby wasn't satisfied. 'If he'd been allowed to see us, his family, regular like, he might well have told us that he was being badly treated. Then we could've made sure he was happy and content, so that he wouldn't wet his bed.'

Sister George fingered the silver cross that hung about her neck, looking uncomfortable. 'I think I've heard enough on this subject 451. I will speak to Sister Joseph and make sure you are allowed to see Billy once a day during recreation, so long as you strive to curb this tendency of yours to defiance. I can in no way condone such behaviour. For your part, you must apologise to Sister Joseph for your obstinacy and carry out whatever punishment she deems appropriate. Is that clear?'

Pearl kicked on her ankle, and Ruby bit her tongue. 'Yes, Sister.'

–

The punishment was to scrub out the girls' lavatories every day for a week. Ruby had to carry out this task on her hands and knees on the stone floors, as well as scrubbing the wooden seats of the earth closets, which smelled strongly of urine and vomit. She did it gladly.

Sister George kept her word and Billy was allowed to see them every day after that. Little by little the pinched look eased from his small, anxious face; the tired bruises caused by countless sleepless nights faded, though he never quite returned to the lively, boisterous little boy he had once been. Something had changed in him, and Ruby didn't know how to get it back.

From that day on it became perfectly clear to Ruby that she had made an enemy. Sister Joseph was infuriated by Sister George's intervention, but it was on Ruby that she took her revenge.

Never, for one moment, was she permitted to perform a simple task if a worse one could be found. Every question she was asked in class seemed to be a thousand times more difficult than the ones required of the other girls; every sum more complicated. Ruby's spelling had to be correct in every detail, her lettering perfect, or she would be made to copy her work out again. If she were one minute late for morning mass, she would be forced to polish the dormitory floor, another task largely conducted on her hands and knees, which Sister Joseph considered to be highly appropriate.

Religious studies took up an increasingly large portion of Ruby's life, as if Sister Joseph had decided that she was more in need of it than the other girls: chanting prayers, singing hymns, listening to readings, or endlessly reciting dozens of Hail Marys as penance for her failings. There were lessons on the meaning and interpretation of the catechism, and she would be regularly examined and interrogated on every aspect of the scriptures to prove that she fully comprehended their spiritual message. And woe betide her if she got any of it wrong! Punishment would follow, swift and sure. This strict regime demanded unquestioning obedience, a state of mind Ruby struggled hard to achieve.

Morning showers at Ignatius House were always cold and, because of the large number of girls, necessarily short. Each was allowed four minutes and Sister Joseph would time them to the second on a fob watch, which dangled, together with a large bunch of keys, from her belt. If a girl overran her allotted time, she would march over and turn off the tap. Ruby considered herself fortunate if she was allowed three minutes and generally managed to wash herself in half of that time, just to make sure she was gone before the nun reached her. Otherwise, she might very well find the soft skin of her backside rapped by the bundle of watch and keys for being dilatory and slow, and poor Ruby would feel the stinging blows for hours afterwards. But then, the slightest misdemeanour seemed to bring down the wrath of Sister Joseph upon her head.

Even for something as relatively minor as not being able to find her handkerchief when it was time to hand it in for a clean one. She would be given a thorough scolding in front of everyone and made to manage without a clean one for a whole week. And always she had to keep smiling or Billy started to worry.

'Are you sick, our Ruby?' he would ask if her spirits faltered.

'No, Billy. Just tired.'

'You won't be going to the sanitary, will you?'

'No, Billy. I shan't be going to the sanatorium. I'd never leave you.'

'Mam said she'd never let me out of her sight, but she did, didn't she?'

Ruby's throat tightened on a shaft of pain. 'Mam couldn't help it. I can. I'm not going to be ill, so stop worrying.'

She could tolerate anything in order to see Billy every day, and keep a careful eye on him and Pearl. So long as they could all stay together, Ruby felt certain she could cope.

But the worst part about living at Ignatius House was not the amount of work they had to do, the stark routine, or even the severity of the punishments. It was the lack of love and absence of emotion of any kind. The children were adequately, if plainly, fed on three meals a day. They were certainly kept clean and healthy with much outward scrubbing from the seemingly endless ablutions in the bowl-room, and the inner purging with castor oil of what the nuns called 'impurities'.

They could benefit from the fresh country air that Mam had set such store by since they were taken on regular Sunday walks as well as being given work to do each day in the gardens. There were lessons in reading, writing and reckoning, a library of books at their disposal, games and toys to amuse them, and a play room for the babies.

But nothing was provided beyond these practical considerations. Rarely was there even a kind word of approval, let alone a warm, loving hug.

It was true that not all the nuns were as stern and sour-faced as Sister Joseph, or as ineffectual as the more reasonable Sister George, but Ruby thought that even the gentlest and kindest could not compensate in any way for the loss of a mother's love.

On the rare occasions when Sister Joseph did appear to soften slightly towards Pearl, who was her favourite, Ruby's trust in the nun was so low that she never felt comfortable about it and would watch her like a hawk.

What the McBride children missed most of all, and grieved for day after day, was their mother. Gone were the nightly story times, the teasing and tickling, the fun and laughter, the kisses and cuddles. Some of the children had visitors from home, whom they entertained in the parlour on a Sunday afternoon. But there were never any for Ruby, Pearl and Billy.

Then one day they got a letter. They knew Mam hadn't written it because she couldn't even read, but one of the nurses in the sanatorium had found the time to send them a short note, telling the children how much Molly loved and missed them, how she thought of them every day and how she would do her utmost to get better and come to collect them.

'Read us Mam's letter again, Ruby,' Pearl would say, clutching her doll tight to her chest.

Billy's eyes would shine. 'She'll be coming for us soon, won't she?'

Ruby too treasured the letter. She kept it safe under her pillow and read it so many times that it was soon falling apart at the folds. Whenever the three children met up at recreation time, they would talk about their mother, huddle together in a corner and watch with keen attention while Ruby wrote down their carefully chosen words in her best handwriting. They liked to tell Mam what they were up to, what they'd had to eat for dinner, which book Pearl was reading and how many marks clever Ruby had got for her composition. Most of all, they needed to give her their love. When they were quite satisfied, they would each of them sign the letter, Pearl and Ruby with their cursive, carefully learned script while Billy, tongue stuck out in fierce concentration, might manage a large B and several sticks, so long as Ruby was guiding his hand.

Then Ruby would hand the letter over to Sister Joseph for posting, as instructed. They did this every week with hope in their hearts, and never received a single reply to any of them.

As the months of waiting turned into years, a sort of acceptance crept over them. Ruby decided that her mother didn't want to worry them over the length of time it was taking for her to get better, and that was the reason there were no letters. She acquired the art of avoiding Sister Joseph, even managing to curb her natural urge to break the rules and stand up for herself.

Ruby's body too began to change. She became aware of budding breasts, of hair growing where it never had before, of strange emotions pulsing through her. Yet not once was she able to view her own nakedness. The girls were instructed to undress each night with all due modesty. Not a scrap of flesh must be glimpsed as layers of clothing were removed, most of it wriggled out of under cover of a voluminous nightdress. Having grown used to sleeping fully clothed in the cellar, at first Pearl and Ruby had left most of their undergarments in place, in order to keep warm in the large, draughty dormitory. But when Sister Joseph had found no neatly folded pile in place on their chair, they'd been taken to task for disobedience and unseemly behaviour.

Since then they'd grown used to the nightly ritual but the odd glimpse of herself, which was all Ruby was privy too, left her with the strange misapprehension of being ugly; of lumps and bumps, aches and pains, which didn't seem quite normal. Did all girls feel this same disillusionment for themselves? Did they too get belly ache, and have this mysterious bleeding which never seemed to be stemmed by the pads of rough cotton Sister George gave her? When it had first happened, she'd felt certain that she was bleeding to death, but Sister had assured her she would live. After a brief initial instruction on how to wash the cloths, no explanation or further mention had been made. The subject was never referred to again. If only someone would speak of it, then she wouldn't worry so much.

Pearl and Billy too were different. Billy had certainly grown taller under the nuns' care. His eczema had cleared up and his hair grown back strong and healthy. But ever since the bullying episode, he hadn't been the same lively little boy he'd once been. He'd become oddly quiet, almost withdrawn, rarely seeming to pay any attention to the activities going on around him. And there were still occasions when there were mysterious marks on his legs and arms. She would ask him if everything was all right, if he felt sick perhaps, or if the big boys had started on him again. But he would simply shrug his shoulders, or lay his head on his arms and say nothing. He hated to be questioned about anything, and Ruby worried about this a great deal. In her heart, she suspected the bullying continued, though felt at a loss to know how to stop it since she couldn't prove anything.

Once, she'd asked him what had happened to his little wooden boat, the one Mam had made for him, and he'd swung round in a fury and shouted at her.

'Wooden boats are for babies, our Ruby, and I'm a *big* boy now!'

She was stunned by this outburst, so unlike the cheerful little boy he'd once been.

''Course you are, and getting bigger every day. By heck, you'll be growing out of them boots in no time.'

Ruby suspected one of the bullies had deliberately broken the toy, and Billy was pretending not to care. The thought made her feel sick.

As for Pearl, she made constant demands upon the nuns who were her teachers, begging for their help and sympathy whenever she didn't understand something, but would then forget what they'd said or refuse to do the work. She could be vexing and manipulative, selfish and utterly brutal. She became ever more clinging and dependent, rarely leaving Ruby's side. If Ruby were to speak to, or play a game with, any girl other than her sister, Pearl would exhibit every sign of jealousy even to giving the unfortunate interloper peevish little nips to make her go away. Yet the same rules didn't apply to her own friends, whom she picked up and abandoned with regular and heartless callousness. One minute she would be all over them, being silly and giddy, the next she would toss them aside and refuse even to speak to them.

Ruby wisely guessed that perhaps her sister wanted to make sure she was the one to end the friendship before they grew bored and abandoned her. That way, she might not be hurt quite so much. Sometimes Ruby would be driven to say something. 'Try not to be unkind to your friends, Pearl. You should treat them as well as you'd like them to treat you. I know it hurts, losing Mam, but it's not right to take out your pain on others.'

But these sessions always ended in the same way, with her younger sister in tears asking if it was because of her being naughty that Mam had gone away. Ruby assured her that it wasn't.

Losing Mam had, without doubt, affected them all very badly.

There were days when Ruby could scarcely concentrate on her work, she missed her mother that much. The pain of it at times was almost unbearable. She missed her smile, her laugh, her silly way of making a joke about everything and not taking life too seriously, even her own state of health. She missed the warmth and smell of her, even the little sips of stout she'd let them taste, and her rollicking laughter when Ruby had pulled a face.

The responsibility she felt for her younger siblings became a heavy burden. Perhaps that was why she would readily make promises, which were impossible to keep.

'Mam will get better soon and come and fetch us, won't she?' Billy would beg.

''Course she will.'

Pearl would be equally certain that the latest letter they'd written would be the one to bring the much longed for reply. 'Won't it, our Ruby?'

'She'll write and tell us that she's fine and dandy, then she'll waltz in that door with a great grin on her face, like always,' Ruby would agree, and they went on writing and hoping.

Ruby was carrying just such a letter in her pocket one morning on her way to breakfast with Pearl when they happened to pass Sister Joseph's office. 'I'll put it on her desk now, rather than after breakfast,' Ruby said, 'so there's no risk of my being late for lessons.'

'Ooh, don't go into her office, our Ruby. Not without permission. What would *I* do if anything happened to you?'

Ruby laughed. 'Pearl, you're a treasure, you really are. Never one to think of others before yourself, are you, love?'

After a quick glance over her shoulder to check that the corridor was empty, Ruby sped into the office, her eyes seeking the wire basket in which the girls' letters were stacked.

'Ooh, do be quick!' Pearl whispered from the door, dancing from one foot to the other in her agitation. 'What'll I do if she comes?'

Quite by chance, just as she turned to leave, Ruby happened to glance down into the waste paper basket, which clearly hadn't been emptied for some days. There was something about the writing on one of the envelopes, which made her bend and pick it out. Ruby stared at it transfixed, her brain unable to take in the implications. Yet it was all too clear. The answer came to her with a slow, dawning horror that chilled her to the bone. The writing was her own. The envelope still contained the letter she'd written the previous week, at her brother and sister's dictation, though instead of being posted, it had been torn up and thrown in the waste paper basket. Did this mean that none of their letters had ever been posted? That they had ended up in this way.

'*Ruby!*'

Pearl's frantic cry from the door brought her out of her numbed state and Ruby slid the torn pieces into the pocket of her pinafore and quickly followed her sister into breakfast.

Despite being hungry, Ruby found it quite impossible to eat the porridge. She could feel the ruined letter in her pocket, like a lead weight. When she heard the click-clack of Sister Joseph's boots, and the swish of her long skirts, she felt herself stiffen and wished she could be a thousand miles away from this heartless, unfeeling place.

'Not on another hunger strike are we 451?'

'No, Sister.'

'Is the porridge not to your liking perhaps?'

Ruby could sense the atmosphere in the dining hall gradually still and quieten, as if a storm were about to break. 'I'm too upset to eat, that's all.'

'Dear me, and who has upset your tender feelings this time?'

'You have!' A gasp rippled around the dining hall. Ruby ignored it. She looked up into Sister Joseph's face, as hard and unyielding as granite, and quietly taking the torn envelope from her pinafore pocket, laid it on the table top for all to see. 'To accept letters, week after week, month after month, pretending that you're posting them and then throwing them away in the wastepaper basket is the wickedest, most cruel thing any person could do, let alone a nun. How many more did you tear up?'

'All of them,' Sister Joseph told her, without any sign of emotion. 'Telling your brother and sister that your mother is going to answer those silly letters was nothing less than a lie, a sin against God. Why you insisted on continuing to write them is beyond me, since it was always perfectly obvious that she wasn't ever going to answer.'

'You didn't know that!' Only the rage Ruby felt at the injustice of the nun's harsh words held her tears in check.

Sister Joseph snorted. 'Of course I knew it. A woman of her ilk can't even read and write. She abandoned you, and no doubt by now is dead.'

It was as if she had been smacked in the face. Ruby went numb. The world itself seemed to stop turning. Even the familiar sounds in the dining hall of countless plates being stacked, knives and forks collected up, died away as though this familiar routine took place in some far-distant place.

'Dead?' How she managed to get the word out, Ruby would never afterwards know. She blinked, cleared her throat, tried again. 'I d–don't understand. What are you saying?'

'For goodness' sake, stop making such a fuss 451. Everyone knows that your mother will be dead by now, and no amount of writing silly letters to her week after week, or telling fairy stories to your little brother and sister will alter that fact. I ripped them to pieces to save us all a deal of trouble, putting them in the wastepaper basket where such rubbish belongs.'

It was in that moment, burning with a hatred which left her speechless, that Ruby made her decision. She wasn't stopping in this dreadful place another day, another minute. They would run away. She would take her family and go. No matter what it cost them in pain and anguish, somehow they would find Mam and prove Sister Joseph wrong.

45

Chapter Five

Ruby wasted no time in putting her plan into action. They made their escape the very next Sunday as they walked in crocodile formation back from church. She'd given Pearl and Billy careful instructions, ordering them not to do anything, which might jeopardise their chances of success. The whole thing worked like a dream. Sister George collected up their prayer books and as Sister Joseph was impatiently ushering her charges out of the churchyard along the road, the three McBrides slipped quietly out of line and managed to duck under the hedge without anyone noticing, just as the crocodile of children turned the corner. None of them moved a muscle after that, scarcely daring even to breathe as they waited for the last of the stragglers to vanish from sight. Once the road was empty, they grinned triumphantly at each other.

If Ruby had known it could be this easy, she'd have done it years ago. 'Come on,' she said. 'Let's find the sanatorium.'

This proved to be more of a problem than they antici-pated. They made their way back into Salford unerringly, as if it hadn't been nearly three years since they'd left it. None of them spoke throughout the entire journey, not wishing to remember the joy of that day when the Queen herself had come to open the Manchester Ship Canal, and

Mam had looked pretty as a picture in her wide-brimmed straw hat with the artificial flowers on top, nor their last sight of her walking away sobbing from Ignatius House.

But once back in the maelstrom of the city, they became disorientated and confused. Which way to the sanatorium? They hadn't the first idea, then Ruby remembered their much loved neighbour. 'Auntie Nellie! We could go and ask Auntie Nellie. She'll tell us the way, and she'll probably be able to tell us how Mam is.'

'Oh, yes,' Pearl said, and set off at a run, Billy galloping along excitedly beside her. In no time Ruby was running too, skipping and jumping with them, the three of them laughing as if this were nothing more than a jolly picnic. Ruby could almost hear Mam saying, '*I'll not lose me sparkle.*'

-

Nellie Bradshaw stared at them in wonder, almost as if they'd dropped on her doorstep straight from heaven. 'By heck, how did you three land up here? On the back of a dust cart?'

'Where's Mam?' Billy blurted the question out before either of his sisters could get a word in. He wanted it made plain that he was the man of the family, for all he was the youngest. And that he would have an answer to this most vital and frequently asked question, come what may.

'Eeh, lad.' The round, apple-cheeked face took on a mournful expression, and Ruby's heart plummeted. It was plain that the old woman did indeed have news, though not any that she relished telling.

'She's not – she's not dead, is she, Auntie Nellie?' Pearl asked, a tremor in her voice.

'We can't talk here love, on the doorstep. Come on inside and have a bite to eat. You look fair starved, the lot of you.'

With a mug of tea in one hand and a jam butty in the other, the children might have been forgiven for putting off the inevitable for a while longer. But Billy decided otherwise. He fixed their old neighbour with a fierce expression and bluntly told her that he was fed up with folk who wouldn't answer his questions. 'Is she dead or not? We want to know.'

'He means we've a right to know,' Ruby quietly added.

The old woman wasn't in the least bit fooled by Billy's aggressive stance, but sadly shook her head from side to side as if giving the matter deep thought. 'I hate to be the one to give you this news lad, but she passed over before the year were out. She were a goner from t'minute she took sick. Why else would she have given you three childer up? Loved the bones of you all she did, but knew she weren't long for this world. She's in a better place now, love.' Adding more hot water to the brown tea pot, the old woman generously refilled their mugs to the brim.

Three silent children sat unmoving, unblinking, before her. Ruby felt strangely calm, almost as if she were detached from the little scene, though a small part of her was relieved that they'd been told the truth at last, and in as kindly a way as possible.

She cast a covert glance across at Billy, his small face looking pinched and set in a familiar, mutinous expression and, if it were possible, Ruby's spirits sank still further. She was well used to his mulish obstinacy. Billy clearly didn't believe a word of it. He'd set his mind on finding their mam and not for one minute would he entertain the prospect of her being dead.

Pearl's reaction was entirely different. She sank her face into her hands and burst into noisy, gulping sobs.

'Now then, lass, don't take on so,' the old woman said, clucking sympathetically over the child and offering her a bit of clean rag for a hanky. 'Yer mam's at peace, and with the Good Lord and she wouldn't want you blubbing over her, not now. You has to eat yer jam butty and grow into a big, healthy lass.'

The kindly words made no impression and, much later, after Pearl and Billy had fallen asleep under a pile of old coats in the corner, since Auntie Nellie didn't have a spare bed in the one room she called home, she and Ruby were finally able to talk.

'You've grown into a fine young woman, lass,' Nellie told her. 'How old are you now – thirteen, nearly fourteen? Your mam would be right proud of you. Nay, but it's a sorry business, is this. D'you like it then, at Ignatius House? Are they good to you?'

'Some of the nuns are kind. Some aren't. But it's a sad place to bring children up. There's no – no love there.'

Nellie Bradshaw nodded. 'I'd heard as much. Right funniosities are some of them nuns. It ain't at all normal not to have a chap. But then I'm a Baptist meself, so how would I know owt about nuns?' Having made a fresh pot of tea, she refilled Ruby's mug. 'Sup up. It'll give your strength. So, what's yer plan then? How come they let you out?'

Ruby looked away, avoiding her old friend's probing gaze, but Nellie guessed. Very slowly she set down the teapot. 'Nay, don't say you've run away? Eeh, heck, that were a daft thing to do. Where are you going to live, eh? You can't stay here, I'm afraid. There's no room.'

'I know, Auntie. We'll find somewhere. Don't worry. They'd soon find us here anyroad. We'll be off first thing in the morning.'

'Nay, lass, go back. At least you get regular meals there.'

'No, I'm not taking them back there. Our Billy was being bullied. Sister George thinks she's put a stop to it, but I know different. I've noticed marks on his legs and he rarely says a word to anyone but me. There's something wrong with him. And our Pearl is not what she was. She's either too clingy, or that daft and giddy she hurts folk without a second thought. It's doing them no good at all living in that place. I'll find work, look after them meself. I can do it, so don't say I can't.'

The old woman didn't ask Ruby how she was herself, she could see it all too clearly in the haunted look in the young girl's eyes, the face that had grown mature before its time, for all she was still no more than a girl, and lovely with it. She let out a deep sigh. 'I'll not quarrel with yer decision, lass, made from the best of motives, I'm sure. But things never turn out quite as you expect. Remember that, love. And think on, if I've a crust of bread on me table, you and yours are welcome to half of it.'

Ruby's eyes filled with tears. 'Oh, Auntie, I've missed you.'

'And I've missed you too, love. Eeh, I have that.'

–

It was around suppertime the following evening when they heard the knocking on the door. And, as a flustered Nellie delayed answering the wrath of God in the shape of Sister Joseph for as long as she possibly could, Billy, Pearl and Ruby slipped out of the back door. They ran pell-mell down the cobbled back street, dived into the first alley and fell headlong over a humped sleeping figure sprawled across it. Several dustbins toppled, spilling their contents everywhere, and a lid rolled noisily away, taking a frighteningly long time to stop spinning and finally fall silent.

'What the 'ell...?' a voice rang out in fury above the din.

It seemed there was not one but several bodies bedding down for the night in the alley. Within seconds mayhem had broken out. Having been so rudely disturbed, the gang of youths came to with a jerk, fists raised, eager to fight. Billy was knocked to the ground, Pearl grabbed by one bruiser who seemed set on nothing short of murder. Ruby flew at the boy she assumed to be the ring leader with a cry of outrage before suffering a blow to her head that sent her flying. Finding herself flat on her back, she was vaguely aware of the weight of someone pinning her down, of fists pummelling her chest and stomach. And then, miraculously, the beating stopped and the weight lifted as her attacker was dragged away.

'Leave off! Let 'em be. They're nobbut kids and soft girls.'

Ruby got slowly to her feet, her head spinning almost as much as the dustbin lid as she pulled cabbage leaves and other stinking refuse from her hair.

Before her stood a boy a year or two older than herself, legs astride, hands in pockets. He was dressed in coarse, ragged trousers and waistcoat over a collarless shirt that might once have been white. On his head was a slouch cap, tipped well back above a thatch of black curls. But it was his face, which captured her attention. It shouted defiance in every insolent line: the flared nostrils, the quirk of the dark eyebrows, the cynical twist of the mouth. It was pugnacious, arrogant, reeking of self-importance, expressing a well-practised carelessness, as if the boy wished to make it clear that he was accustomed to witnessing violence in all its forms and nothing could ever shock him. It declared that he was entirely in control, sure of his place as leader of the gang rolling in the dirt about his feet, and of the rat-infested back alleys of Salford which comprised his small kingdom.

Nevertheless, it was the most fascinating, most intriguing, most exciting face Ruby had ever encountered. There was about it an attractiveness that had nothing to do with the accepted rules of good looks. The eyes were brilliant, the bluest she had ever seen and Ruby realised, with a slight shock, that right now they were regarding her with some amusement.

Brushing down the green uniform dress and pinafore that proclaimed all too clearly what she was and where she came from, Ruby saw his eyes flick assessingly over her, recognising this fact instantly and bringing a flush of humiliating colour to her cheeks. But there was no time for explanations since less than a second later there came a cry from an all too familiar voice behind them.

'It's Sister Joseph with a copper!' Billy's small face was a picture of horror.

The air suddenly seemed to be filled with police whistles, and the sound of running feet.

The boy grabbed her hand. 'Quick, this way.'

In that moment her world tilted and changed. Ruby knew, instinctively, that nothing would ever be the same again.

They squeezed through a hole in a nearby fence which led to the railway embankment and ran along it as fast as their legs could carry them. The police whistles faded into the distance but not for a moment dare she risk stopping to check how safe they were. There was a pain in Ruby's side but nor did she pause to ease it. The boy plunged into a honeycomb of back alleys and cobbled streets and Ruby went with him, dragging a white-faced Billy with her. Even Pearl was silent and uncomplaining as she did her best to keep pace.

Then suddenly the boy opened a door in a tenement block and, thrusting them through it, banged it shut behind them. It was pitch black inside, stank of urine, damp and rotting food. Ruby shuddered as she followed him up the rickety stairs. Once, she'd been used to places like this. Now, after three years with the nuns in Ignatius House, she was more used to stark cleanliness, a scrubbed, ascetic purity. In that instant, doubt assailed her for the first time. Perhaps leaving the home had not been such a wise move after all. Mam was dead. Where could they go? What could they do now? Despite the relief she felt at being free of Sister Joseph, a part of her grieved for what might have been and worried about her brother and sister, about whether she'd done the right thing by them. Hadn't she promised Mam to take care of them, and here she was leading them into possible danger.

The boy pushed them into a small room that seemed to be filled with children. A woman sat breastfeeding one, which was alternately crying and suckling in a fretful, lethargic sort of way, whilst the rest lay tumbled about the floor and the one bed that filled a good half of the floor space.

'You get home some time then?' The woman's hair hung down in lank strands about a face that had once been pretty, and the baby she held so lovingly in her arms seemed exhausted by the effort of trying to gain nourishment from the flaccid breasts. Ruby guessed the woman was equally worn out, and years younger than she appeared.

'Sorry I'm late, Ma. I got held up.'

'What 'ave you got fer us? Summat good, I hope. These childer are fair starved.'

Having been reminded of their hunger, the children all seemed to fling themselves upon the boy at once, clinging to him, searching his pockets, hanging around his neck and all asking the same question.

'What've you got fer us, Kit? Is it summat good?'

He tolerated their attentions with mild good humour. From out of various pockets he drew half a loaf, four stale buns and a packet of broken biscuits, all of which he deposited in his mother's lap. To Ruby it seemed a pitiful amount of food to satisfy all these hungry mouths yet the woman smiled up at him, all animosity gone from her weary face. 'I thought you'd copped it this time, love.'

'Never!'

Her faded eyes looked over the head of the suckling infant and past her eldest son across to where Ruby stood by the door, her own arms tight about Billy and Pearl, holding them protectively close. 'Who's yer friend?'

The boy grinned, blue eyes lighting with that already familiar twinkle. 'We haven't yet found time for introductions, Ma.'

When Ruby had given their names and politely declined the offer of food which was shared out with scrupulous care, the boy introduced himself as Kit Jarvis. He told her he was fifteen and the main breadwinner in the family. He said this with a wry sideways smile, although Ruby saw nothing amusing in the sight of these starving children licking the few remaining crumbs from their fingers and squabbling over the last bit of crust. In her head she had a sudden vision of sago pudding splattered all over a dining table and felt a keen blast of guilt.

Kit didn't explain what had happened to his father and Ruby knew better than to ask. It was none of her business. Nor did she relate their own history. He next drew from his pockets several small packets of tea, which brought forth shouts of excitement from his siblings.

'How did you get them, our Kit?' asked one youngster.

He simply grinned. 'They're free samples from Willy Pidgeon's corner shop.'

'He gave them to you?' Ruby was astonished. Usually such benefits were saved for a shopkeeper's best customers.

'After I'd bought the biscuits, which just happened to have suffered a catastrophic accident earlier in the day, after some idiot knocked over a tin outside his shop. Anyroad, I did some free deliveries for him so he let me have a bag cheap.' Again the grin, and Ruby had to laugh. She didn't ask how such a catastrophe had occurred in the first place to the biscuits, nor why Willy Pidgeon should be so generous, free deliveries or no. It was enough that the treats were all shared out, together with several mugs of weak tea laced with tinned sweetened milk. Best of all she was able to see the colour return to Billy's cheeks.

Much later, from another pocket deep inside Kit's waistcoat, emerged two long sticks of liquorice root which, laughing, his mother proceeded to chop up and hand out to her children. They'd happily chew on those for hours which would help to stave off any remaining pangs of hunger, even if it might result in some loosened bowels.

The McBrides slept that night wrapped in yet another collection of old coats, except that these smelled fusty and damp. Not that it mattered. With Ruby's arms wrapped cosily about Billy, and Pearl's head resting on her sister's shoulder, they felt warm and safe, content to be together. It was almost as if they were back home, and they half expected Mam to appear and tell them one of her old yarns. They slept the clock round and although they awoke to the sad knowledge that they'd never see Mam's cheery smiling face again, at least Sister Joseph wasn't waiting to pounce with her cold showers and list of chores and penances.

But what would this new day bring? And this new life?

Chapter Six

The changes became all too clear on that very first morning when Ruby discovered that little time would be spent hanging around indoors, and that life wasn't going to be easy. Kit, not hanging around waiting for a breakfast which would never appear, had already left the house hours earlier to go to one of his many part-time jobs down at Salford docks.

'He'll be working on how to get food fer us dinner, and then there's the problem of supper. Endless it is. Vicious bloomin' circle,' his mother explained. 'But he does his best so we don't complain, do we, me lovely?' She kissed the baby's head, making him chortle with pleasure, and beamed around at her other children. There were four, including the baby, though there seemed more, perhaps because none of them could be much over six.

'He fetched us a banana once,' one wide-eyed toddler announced.

His mother laughed. 'Not that you knew what to do with it, Henry, so hush up, Mr Clever Clogs.' But she tickled him under the chin, to show she was only teasing, and Ruby felt the prick of tears at the back of her eyes as she experienced a spurt of envy at the family's closeness.

Nobody troubled to wash since there was no tap in the room and most of the children were already dressed, having slept in every item of clothing they possessed to keep warm, a habit the McBrides fell back into with practised ease. But everyone seemed perfectly content. No one appeared surprised or in the least concerned that those who were old enough were expected to get themselves off to school as best they could. Their mother trailed around after them, picking up socks, tying boot laces and issuing instructions, the baby propped on one hip throughout the whole performance. Ruby thought Sister Joseph would probably have died of apoplexy at the sight of all these unclean bodies.

'What about them two youngsters?' The woman jerked her chin in the direction of Billy and Pearl. 'Let them sleep in today, eh?'

Ruby nodded, relieved that she wasn't to be questioned further.

After the older children had gone, leaving only a three-year-old and the baby, a pot of tea was brewed and Ruby gratefully accepted a mug. 'You said he had one or two part-time jobs, Mrs Jarvis. What is it Kit does, exactly?'

'Call me Marie. I don't rightly know what he does. A bit of this, bit of that. Cleaning windows, delivering, sweeping anything he can find. Right now he's down at the docks helping with the stacking and loading and, with a bit of luck, will pick up summat to eat while he's at it, and a nip of rum happen,' she said, her face brightening. 'At best, he might earn a copper or two.'

'I see.' It all sounded a bit vague and Ruby's mind was in turmoil. It would be sensible to spend one or two nights here, but she couldn't depend on handouts. They'd have to learn to stand on their own feet. Somehow or other she must find employment, but would anyone take on a thirteen year old with no experience whatsoever? She suddenly felt very young and vulnerable.

A flicker of pain crossed the woman's face and her eyes filled with tears. 'My Mick died. He was killed in an accident down in the loading bay twelve months ago.'

'Oh, I'm so sorry.'

'Aye, well, I'll spare you the details. Mick was the nearest Kit had to a dad, but he's never complained once. Just left school, found himself work and got on with it. He's a good lad. To his mam anyroad,' she added by way of qualification.

'I shall need to find work too. How should I go about it, do you reckon?'

'Finding work is easy enough, lass, so long as you look smart and clean and as if you don't need it.'

'Oh!' Ruby didn't quite know what to make of this advice.

'Nay, don't worry, love. You look well enough.' Marie studied her more carefully, taking in the full measure of her youthful appearance, the telltale uniform, then glanced across at the sleeping Pearl and Billy, curled up together in their favourite fashion. Her gaze now was thoughtful and filled with pity. 'How old are you, love? If'n you don't mind me asking. I'd like to help you look after them babbies but, as you can see, me hands is a bit full already. And once I've weaned this little 'un, I'll have to get back to work meself. Old Maggie upstairs'll watch childer fer me in return for a few handouts.'

'Oh, that's all right. I can manage, thank you. I'm nearly sixteen,' Ruby lied.

Marie's eyebrows lifted slightly in disbelief, then she gave a gentle sigh. 'Well, you're welcome to stop on till you find yer feet, but even if you finds a proper job like, getting paid a living wage that'll keep a family is well-nigh impossible. Make you old before yer time bosses do, allus clipping a bit off here, cutting a penny off there. Just when you think you're sorted you find you can't afford to pay the rent and eat. Not both at the same time anyroad.'

'We'll manage. I'm sure we will.'

'Happen so.' The sadness in the woman's voice expressed a weary lack of conviction, despite her efforts to inject enthusiasm into her voice. 'I can see yer a lass with a bit of gumption about her.'

Or impulsive, rebellious stupidity, Ruby thought.

At that moment the door burst open and Kit strolled in to place a cabbage and a couple of pennies on the table in front of his mother. 'Best I could do.'

'That's grand. I can buy some tatties and onions, and make us a bit of soup. Bless you, luv. It might even run to a gill of milk for the little 'uns, though I'll need a penny for the gas soon, come to think of it.'

'Don't worry, I'm off now to do me bit of delivering for Willy, then I'll see what else is going.'

'All right, chuck. Take care.' There was warmth in her tone as she addressed her eldest son, and pride shining in her eyes.

'I allus do.' He didn't glance at Ruby until he'd reached the door, almost vanishing from sight, then he popped his head back inside and said, 'Are you coming or not?' His voice was impatient, just as if he'd been waiting hours for her to make up her mind.

His mother chuckled. 'Go on with yer. I'll see to these two nippers,' and seconds later Ruby and Kit were out on the streets of Salford on a cold, autumn morning, and somehow, against all odds, everything seemed right with the world.

–

Life on the streets with Kit Jarvis was an education for Ruby. In the days and weeks following, she discovered that it might be precarious but certainly never dull, even at times quite exciting. She often accompanied him on his delivery round and was amazed to find that at many of the big houses where he took the boxes of groceries, he'd be given a halfpenny, a newly baked cake from the oven, and once a few broken eggs which they took straight back to Marie. They all fed like kings and queens that dinnertime on scrambled eggs and milk.

'Are people always so generous?' Ruby wanted to know.

'Them that aren't can fetch their own groceries,' came his cutting reply.

Ruby didn't dare risk sending Billy and Pearl to school, in case too many questions were asked or Sister Joseph had reported them missing, so most days they came along too. She was always nagging them to behave, afraid they might run off. Not that Billy would, he stuck to her like glue, but Pearl was perfectly capable of doing something daft. 'You do what I tell you, remember?' she constantly reminded them.

'What, me an' all?' Pearl would ask. 'Even though I'm ten now, and not so daft as our Billy?'

'You an' all, madam. You haven't a sensible notion in your pretty head, so let me do the thinking.'

Pearl purred with pleasure, taking this as a compliment. The other boys who made up Kit's gang joined them

61

during the course of that first week. One, introduced as Jackdaw, apparently had a knack of finding useful stuff for them to sell. Charlie and Clem were brothers and hard to tell apart for all they weren't twins. They also had a habit of finishing each other's sentences.

Charlie said, 'I'm eleven, but he's thirteen and shouts all the time. He can't hear proper and got a club foot so he walks funny.'

They both giggled and started pushing and thumping each other, just as if life were some silly jape.

The last of the group was Pongo, so named, he explained to Ruby, because he had a good nose for sniffing out which dustbin was worth exploring for food that had been thrown away, yet was still fit to eat.

'It's all in the nose. Yer know what I mean?' he said, tapping it and giving her a huge wink.

Ruby didn't care to consider how hungry a person needed to be to scavenge dustbins for food. They wouldn't find much in the bins behind Ignatius House, she thought, trying not to show her revulsion, or the fear of what lay ahead that was curdling her stomach. She wasn't concerned in the least on her own account, quite certain she could survive by her wits as Kit did, but Pearl and Billy were too young to suffer such deprivation. They deserved better. Oh, what had she got them into?

All the gang seemed to be shabbily dressed in trousers of varying lengths, any slack taken up by a wide leather belt in addition to braces. Some wore jerseys, others a jacket or waistcoat. They all had clogs or boots, of course, and an identical slouch cap tugged ruthlessly into place or tipped rakishly to the back of their head. And every one of them would have had Sister Joseph reaching for her scrubbing brush and a bar of carbolic soap.

Without exception, Ruby liked the entire gang and, as the weeks passed, only hoped they wouldn't prove to be too bad an influence on young Billy who was hanging on to their every word, even copying the way they swaggered along, sparking the irons on the soles of their clogs every five minutes. It made her laugh just to watch him trying to appear as grown up and manly as them.

Most days the whole gang would go off scavenging leftover vegetables from the allotments down by the River Irwell, or picking mushrooms or blackberries by the canal. When dusk fell, they would move on to the slagheap to pick coal. In no time at all they would be covered in dust and soot. Everyone seemed used to this, so Ruby said nothing. Billy was always happily enthusiastic, the nuns never having allowed him the opportunity to get dirty. Pearl, however, complained bitterly about the state of her pinafore, her pretty face streaked with black tears, and her dandelion hair clouded with black dust.

'How will I ever get clean again?' she'd groan.

'Why would you want to?' Charlie asked. 'We like getting mucked up.'

'It's more important to keep warm,' Kit told her, without a trace of sympathy.

'Is this how you survive?'

'In these streets you learn to get by on your wits. We barter, exchanging our time and skills for a copper or two here and there doing whatever odd jobs come our way. When that doesn't work, we buy and sell any odd bits Jackdaw finds fer us – bits of rags, metal, nuts and bolts. And we scrounge whatever's going begging, like coal and tatties. We ain't criminals, that's for sure.' For a moment his eyes blazed, fists clenched, and his whole body became tense with anger.

'I didn't say you were.'

'So long as you understand! We happen let off steam now and then, do a bit o' fiddling, but we aren't violent. Not like the Napoo who carry cut throats and lop off girls' plaits. We don't hurt or attack anyone, Ruby, not like them what went for you. "Street barbarians", "slum monkeys", that's what some folk call us, yet we have our standards, our code of honour. We only do what's fair game, enough to get by. If the government won't help us, we have to help ourselves, see?'

'Oh, yes, I do see,' Ruby agreed with feeling.

'Property, jobs and money only goes to them what already has plenty. It's the toffs' way of keeping us down. 'Tain't right, so we have to look after our own as best we can. How else can we survive? I mean, when did you last see anybody coming round with any handouts?'

Ruby was gazing up at him, drinking in every word. Only a few inches taller than she and eighteen months older, yet he seemed so much wiser in the ways of the world, so much more in control of his life. 'So you hang around shops hoping for cheap stale bread or free hand-outs? Not forgetting broken biscuits.'

Kit gave a careless shrug. 'Accidents will happen.'

'What about the poor shopkeeper?'

'We only take what's due to us, from them who can afford to spare it, and allus share equally with the rest of the lads in the gang. It's vital that everyone plays fair. Right?'

'Right!'

'Aye, well, so long as that's understood. You're either with us or against us.'

'I understand.' Ruby felt a shiver of apprehension at the stark anger in his face. He obviously liked things to be done his way, a message that had come across loud and clear. She swallowed a spurt of anxiety and offered him a radiant smile, which, unknown to Ruby, made her look suddenly pretty. 'What else do you do?'

He tapped one finger on the tip of her nose. The gesture made her blush bright pink. 'Questions! Questions! You'll find out soon enough, if you hang around long enough.'

The chill of her reservations melted under the warmth of his grin, and the prospect of hanging around with Kit Jarvis for any length of time brought a burn of excitement to Ruby's heart, a sensation quite unlike anything she'd experienced before.

–

The days passed in a whirl of activity. There always seemed so much to achieve and so little time in which to do it. Finding sufficient food for them all to eat, and fuel for the fire so they could keep warm, was a relentless, all-consuming task. And since there were so many of them in the Jarvis household, Kit's share had to stretch further. Ruby, still fearful of becoming a burden, was not surprised when one morning, over their usual cuppa together while Kit was at the docks, Marie asked how much longer she would be staying. It was gently done, with shamefaced reluctance, but the meaning was clear.

Quick as a flash, and without giving it a moment's thought, Ruby answered. 'We're leaving today, s'matter of fact. Meant to tell you but I forgot.' She could feel her cheeks growing warm at the lie but Marie didn't notice, or if she did, chose not to question the decision. 'It's long past time we moved on but thanks for your help. We've really appreciated it.' She kissed the baby's cheek, hugged Marie, and then ordered her somewhat stunned brother and sister out of the door. Billy as always blindly obeyed, having made up his mind that so long as he stuck fast to Ruby, he'd be all right. Pearl was not so easily budged. She stood on the steps in a sulk.

'Do we have to go now? This minute?'

'Yes, Pearl. Come on.'

'But where will I sleep?'

'You'll sleep with us, as always. Come on, Pearl, we haven't all day.'

'But where are we going?'

'We'll talk about that later.'

'What if I get cold or hungry? What will I do then?'

Ruby felt close to panic, not having a single idea in her head as to where they should go or what they should do, yet desperate not to be a nuisance to anyone. Pearl's selfishness wasn't helping. 'Stop saying I – I – I as there's three of us here! We're all in this together.'

'You don't have to rush off this minute,' Marie said, having followed them outside. 'Wait till our Kit gets back at least.'

'No thanks, best if we get on our way.' Now that she'd made up her mind to accept the inevitable, Ruby knew that seeing Kit again would only undermine her resolve.

–

Coping alone on the streets proved to be every bit as dreadful as Ruby had feared. She did her best for her family, but somehow the tricks she'd learned from Kit didn't seem half so much fun on her own, or half so easy to accomplish. They were chased off the allotments by an angry old man when he caught them pulling carrots, and Pearl nearly fell in the river when they tried, and failed, to catch fish. Billy found what might have been mushrooms but since Ruby wasn't sure, she made him throw them away in case they were poisonous toadstools. The little boy didn't even have the energy to cry.

Unfortunately, not even exhaustion kept Pearl quiet. 'I'm hungry,' she'd wail, or 'I need a rest,' at what seemed to be half-hourly intervals throughout the long days and nights.

'Oh, Pearl, do please shut up. We're all hungry and tired. Your constant complaining doesn't help.' Ruby grew increasingly afraid, felt exhausted much of the time, as well as freezing cold, her clothes never quite drying out from one rain shower to the next. And, worst of all, Billy began to cough.

They slept in doorways, under railway bridges or in back alleys, with nothing to cover them but dirty sacks and any old newspapers they found lying around. Sometimes even this relative shelter would be denied them by one or other of the marauding gangs who roamed the area and proved to be far less obliging than Kit's lot. So they would move on, further and further away from the territory they knew well.

One night they were trailing sadly about under the labyrinth of railway arches and the Bridgewater Viaduct that spanned Castlefield, the slap of water in the nearby

Rochdale Canal hardly noticeable above the rumble of trains thundering overhead. Somewhere in the distance a whistle blew. No doubt a gang leader calling his lads together, a common enough practice. Ruby paid no heed. She felt light-headed with hunger and fatigue, shivering with cold, and was desperately searching for a safe place to sleep which wasn't already occupied, or wouldn't leave them vulnerable to intruders when a figure stepped out from behind a pillar right in front of them. Ruby's heart seemed to leap into her throat.

'What way is this to treat a friend, to buzz off without so much as a goodbye?'

She flung herself into his arms and kissed him full on the lips. For a precious moment Kit responded and she felt herself held tight and warm and safe, his body hard against her own. She was a child still, yet somewhere, deep inside, the woman she was to become stirred into life and Ruby became all too aware of the masculine scent of him, the warm strength of his young body. And she recognised too, in that magical moment, that he was equally aware of hers.

He let her go abruptly, with a casual shrug of embarrassment, avoiding direct eye contact as he thrust his hands deep in his pockets, as if keeping them from further mischief. 'I don't know where you thought you were going, rushing out of Salford like that, but you don't seem to be making much of a job of it.' His scathing glance took in the bedraggled appearance of the other two, and Ruby gave a sheepish smile.

'We don't have your skills.'

He gave a slow smile that turned her heart right over. 'Then you'd best come home with me and have some more lessons.'

Whether she would have gone with him or not, Ruby was never to discover. At that moment Charlie and Clem, who had obviously been acting as lookouts, burst upon them like a pair of harbingers of doom falling over each other to speak.

'It's the Coal Wharf Gang, they've heard we're on their patch.'

'Scarper!'

Before any of them had time to think, let alone make a run for it, they were set upon from every direction. Fists and clogs were soon flying, shouts went up, blood flowed, teeth were broken, jaws cracked. Ruby grabbed Billy and Pearl, her one thought to protect them, and the three clung together, shaking with fear, as the battle raged between the two rival gangs. It was terrifying to watch, and the fear she felt for Kit and his lads grew, for they were seriously outnumbered.

Then a shout went up. 'It's the rozzers!'

'Look out, they're after you, Kit, and mean business.'

But it wasn't Kit the police were after, at all. The three McBride children were suddenly plucked from behind the arch where they were hiding, and found themselves caught up in the arms of the law.

They soon learned that Sister Joseph, having remained obstinately persistent throughout these long weeks, had pestered her tame constable to keep a lookout. So it was that on this night when sheer exhaustion had driven the children out into the open, they'd finally been spotted.

As boys ran in all directions, most making an escape but many failing to do so, Kit too was taken into custody, along with Charlie and Clem. Ruby's last sight of Pongo and Jackdaw was of them haring away down the canal towpath. She felt glad that they, at least, had got away.

They were all brought before the magistrates where their punishments were issued with no trace of leniency. No one was interested in listening to their stories, or wished to hear how they'd been desperate to find out the truth about their dying mother, how Billy had been bullied and that they'd wanted only to earn an honest crust and live a normal family life together. Nor did anyone give a thought to how Marie and her four younger children would manage without Kit's help and the money he brought in.

The three McBrides were accused of delinquency, as well as gross misconduct and ingratitude to the sisters of Ignatius House. It was decided that they needed to be protected from the evils and degenerative influences of city life, and that the only recourse was for Ruby and Pearl to attend the Girls' Reformatory for a term of four years. Billy was to be sent to a farm school to learn a trade. Charlie and Clem were likewise condemned to the reformatory. Kit Jarvis, a well-known hooligan in the eyes of the magistrates, was to be consigned to the rigours of the reformatory training ship for a period of three years where a final attempt at reformation would be made. It was made quite clear to him that if this didn't work, his next place of residence would be in Her Majesty's prison.

Kit cast one final glance in Ruby's direction, and although the blue eyes glittered with outrage rather than good humour, his grin was as cocky and insolent as ever. Ruby suddenly found herself grinning back, her eyes silently begging him to understand that although they could do what they liked to his physical person, they could never crush his spirit. She certainly intended that to be the case so far as she was concerned. But as he was led away, her heart was aching, for she held little hope they'd ever meet again.

Chapter Seven

After almost four years in the reformatory, Ruby was to be allowed out on licence. She was eighteen and could hardly wait. It meant that although she would still be under the watchful eye of Miss Crombie, the superintendent, she could at last get a job and start a new life. Strict rules would be enforced such as a monthly report from her employer and, should she lose her job for any reason, she would be obliged to return to the reformatory.

This was not the first time she'd been allowed out on licence. It was, in fact, the fourth. Each of her other prospective positions had lasted less than a month, one of them barely a week. The trouble was that Ruby had never quite acquired the necessary degree of obedience and subservience. What was worse, the more those in authority attempted to mould her to their rules over the years, the more fiercely she'd held on to her own strong will.

There had been the case of the woman who had tested her honesty by placing a sovereign clearly in view on her dressing table. Ruby had handed it back to her employer together with her resignation, saying she wouldn't work where she wasn't trusted.

Then there'd been the jealous wife, so certain that Ruby was sharing her husband's bed that one night when Ruby had gone out to fill the coal-scuttle, she'd found herself locked in the coal shed as punishment for her supposed sins. After hammering and knocking on the door for an hour to no effect, Ruby had squeezed out through the back window and walked the seven miles back to the reformatory. The woman had been furious, accusing her not only of depravity but of absconding from her duties as well.

It was common to be employed by those who wished only to exploit reformatory girls by promising them respectable employment while having quite other requirements in mind. And then there were the snobs who were quite happy to get a reformatory girl as they were cheap, so long as the neighbours never found out. Ruby, naturally, was not prepared to lie about her past, nor keep it a secret.

'I'm not ashamed of what happened to me. I've committed no offence save to be poor. The worst thing I ever did was to run away from the nuns,' she would say to anyone who cared to listen. 'I did it to find Mam for our Billy, and because he was being bullied, only I was too late. Mam was already dead of consumption and nobody had bothered to tell us. So if you don't like it, you can always send me back.' Which was generally what they did.

It choked her up whenever Ruby thought of Billy. If only they hadn't been too late and Mam had still been alive, everything would have been so different. Memories of that moment they'd torn him from her arms to take him to the farm school would torture her for as long as she lived. His cries and sobs still echoed in her head. She'd thought nothing worse could ever happen, but then less than a year after that, he'd been packed off to Canada. His big chance, he'd told her in his letter. A wonderful country with acres and acres of land, thousands of trees and limitless fresh air, as Mam had wanted for him. There was even a family ready to take him as one of their own, so could Ruby agree to let him go?

She'd seriously thought about objecting, although whether the Board of Guardians would have listened was another matter. She and Pearl had talked about it for hours but, in the end, had agreed that it might well be a new beginning for their little brother. What did Salford have to offer to the likes of Billy McBride? It might at least be better for his health.

They'd been allowed one final meeting to say goodbye, at which they'd all wept copious tears and clung together, reluctant to let go for this last time. Ruby had made him promise to write every week and he'd kept his word, at first. Now they were lucky if they got more than half a dozen letters a year. This year they'd had two. That first family hadn't worked out and he'd been moved on, but he sounded happy enough, always looking on the bright side. Ruby could only hope this increasing silence between letters was a good omen and meant that he was well, busy working and enjoying life.

There were times too when she thought of Kit Jarvis, the boy who had tried to help them, and she'd feel an odd sort of ache inside, a longing to see him again. She could remember every exciting detail about him: the masculine scent of his skin, the warm hardness of his young body, the brilliant blue of his eyes. How had he fared in the training ship? She'd heard those places could be pretty tough, far worse than Ignatius House and the reformatory put together.

But all of that was in the past. Today, a merchant who apparently owned a fine house close to the Duke of Bridgewater's at Slate Wharf was considering Ruby for the post of housemaid. Ruby wasn't too clear where exactly that might be, nor did she recognise his name, Barthram Stobbs, but then it was many years since she'd last visited the area and she'd been but a child at the time. Besides, if he was offering escape from the reformatory, he'd need to have two heads and a hunchback before she refused anything he offered.

Even Miss Crombie was doing her utmost to get her the job by painting a rosy picture of her, despite Ruby being considered as one of her most troublesome inmates. 'The girl has an individual, determined nature and although she has in the past been somewhat wilful, is nevertheless capable of being agreeable, when she puts her mind to it. And she is most certainly clean. Oh, dear me, yes, Mr Stobbs. As are all our girls. What's more, she is a hard worker, I'll give her that.' The woman's expression clearly stated that she might wish for more success in other directions.

Ruby became aware that Barthram Stobbs was studying her with surprisingly close attention, and felt herself grow pink under his scrutiny. What was it that he found so fascinating about her? She began to wonder if she had a smut of soot on her nose.

He was noting the flutter of dark lashes against her flushed cheeks, the way her eyes seemed haunted by some sort of need. To his great astonishment he found himself unaccountably mesmerised by the sight of this chit of a girl who stood so proudly before him. He paid particular attention to her mouth, full and sensual and slightly parted, as if begging to be kissed. Yet the institutional clothes, her scrawny, childlike figure, were not only sad but pathetic. What in God's name had got into him? He ached with pity for her, yet he wasn't normally a man with room in his heart for such emotions. He scowled. 'And what have you to say in your own defence, over this "individual, determined nature" of yours?'

'Do I need one?' Ruby asked, quick as a flash.

He was startled by her swift response, and intrigued by it. For all her years in the reformatory she couldn't in any way be described as cowed. 'Individual is the word, ma'am. A rare prize indeed.' Then he put back his head and roared with laughter.

Ruby frowned with displeasure. What right did this man have to treat her with such mocking contempt? Admittedly he wasn't half so old as she'd expected, though he must be well past thirty if he was a day, and no doubt some might call him handsome. He was nowhere near as good-looking as her lovely Kit, not with his high cheek bones, florid complexion and long nose. He was also oddly and inappropriately dressed in what could only be described as a loud checked three-piece suit, as if he'd just returned from the races rather than Castlefield. He wore a starched white collar and blue spotted silk necktie, and sported a white carnation in his buttonhole. Looped across a surprisingly rotund stomach for one so tall, hung a watch chain that was unmistakably gold. A pair of white kid gloves and bowler hat, both of which he'd taken off and placed on the superintendent's desk during the interview, completed the ensemble. The whole effect was rather dapper and sporty, if somewhat incongruous in a businessman.

Miss Crombie seemed to be utterly captivated by him, and was as simpering and sweet as she always was with men who entered the portals of her grey, untidy office and offered her the least little bit of attention. On the other hand she could well have been on the gin, it being well past lunchtime, which would account for the glazed expression in her eyes and why the jowls of her several chins wobbled so alarmingly. Ruby wondered if she was even giving the matter proper attention, save for hoping to be rid of a girl who had become something of a nuisance. To be fair, she did express mild alarm over the fact that the gentleman had not brought his wife with him.

'I would have done so, good lady, were I able. Sadly, I am a widower. My wife died several months ago from a heart condition. I am comfortably placed, though not a rich man, and therefore don't want any silly young miss. I need a girl with common sense and acumen, if you take my meaning, as she will be required to carry out varied duties on her own initiative.'

The superintendent was nodding most sympathetically. 'Indeed, yes, I understand perfectly, Mr Stobbs. How very sad.' She responded warmly to his smile, poured more tea into the china cup she'd set before him, offered a slice of seed cake, and then seemed to recollect her duties. 'Nevertheless, I should remind you that if Ruby turns out not to be suitable and you have need to return her, then it must be in the same condition as she left. If you take my meaning?'

He looked shocked, and then adopted a wounded air. 'Madam, I am surprised you should entertain any doubts on the matter. How could it be otherwise? I am a gentleman after all.'

Flushing bright crimson, Miss Crombie became quite flustered. 'Indeed, sir, indeed! That is perfectly plain to see. As your excellent references from this reverend gentleman so clearly state. I'm obliged to you for being so frank and understanding, and for having come so well prepared.' She gathered up the collection of letters and papers he had supplied as proof of good character in a flurry of breathless embarrassment and handed them back to him with an apologetic little smile which sat oddly on her round, fleshy face. 'I hope you will not take offence at my speaking so plainly? Although it is clearly quite superfluous in your own case, I am duty bound to consider the proprieties. The Board of Guardians would not deem it at all proper for me to allow one of our gels to leave the premises with a male person without making the necessary checks.'

'Of course, dear lady. I understand perfectly.'

'Besides, in some instances these gels are known to have light morals, one must remember that. In Ruby's case, although there was one slight incident it was of no moment, and we have no reason to doubt her honour, I do assure you.'

He seemed to consider Ruby with keener interest, as if this possibility had not previously occurred to him. 'I trust you are correct, madam.'

'Oh, indeed.'

They seemed to have forgotten she was even in the room. Ruby hated it when she was spoken of as if she were not present but bit down hard on her lip, willing herself to keep quiet. She must remember that it was vital she get out of here, at whatever cost.

Thumbs in his waistcoat pockets, Barthram Stobbs circled Ruby where she stood stiffly on the shabby rug, giving a thoughtful little whistle between his teeth as he did so. 'I'll admit there's a show of insolence in those flashing brown eyes, not to mention the tilt of that chin, although it reveals strength of character nonetheless.'

He put out a hand and drew his fingers over her cheek, unable to resist touching her. She possessed the kind of tantalising beauty that any man would love to own. Her skin was pale and translucent, satin smooth beneath the flat of his hand as he traced the line of her jaw before moving instinctively downwards over her throat and shoulders. Her eyes met his, blazing with defiance, silently demanding he stop his wandering hand forthwith. He did so, chuckling softly. 'The girl appears healthy enough. Does she have all her teeth?'

'I believe they are quite white and straight, Mr Stobbs,' Miss Crombie assured him. 'Open your mouth, girl.'

For an instant Ruby considered refusing but then bared her teeth in a parody of a smile, her eyes challenging him to dare ask her to demonstrate any more of her attributes.

'My word, what a difference when she stops scowling,' he mildly commented.

After that came a long, drawn-out silence while he examined her with a shrewd, narrow-eyed gaze that had a dangerous glint to it. Ruby found herself again flushing beneath his scrutiny, wishing she could acquire the art of subduing these flashes of defiance. Wasn't she putting her entire future at risk?

For the first time to his recollection Barthram Stobbs was wrestling with his conscience. It was true that he'd come here today seeking a girl, one who wasn't too particular about where she lived so long as she escaped the reformatory and who would do as he asked without question. The interrogation he'd been subjected to by the superintendent had perhaps led him to embroider his situation somewhat, which was unfortunate, but Ruby McBride was not at all the compliant sort of girl he'd had in mind. She would undoubtedly be a challenge. At the same time, she may well suit his purpose admirably. The trouble was, his thinking was being clouded by baser needs. He felt captivated by her, enchanted almost. Lord, he was acting like a love-sick fool. He gave a soft, throaty chuckle at the thought.

'Your earlier summary was most astute, Miss Crombie, and, I believe, correct. We might make something of her yet. But anyone would think you were anxious to be rid of the little hellcat.' These words, and the broad wink he bestowed upon Ruby, brought a bubble of laughter into her throat and, against her better judgement, she giggled.

Barthram Stobbs grinned. 'Dash it I'll take her. I'm sure we'll suit each other very well.'

Ruby felt very much as a horse might when bought at auction.

The superintendent expelled a huge sigh of relief and at once proceeded, together with Ruby's prospective employer, to discuss such essential matters as wages and living conditions. The girl's wages would be ten pounds a year and her uniform provided, all found, with one half day off a week.

Miss Crombie said, 'The money will be paid directly to me, naturally, and I will supply the girl with whatever she needs for personal items, clothes and such like.'

Again Ruby ached to protest at the unfairness of still being tied to the reformatory and to working for very little reward, but she'd tried objecting to this system before and it had gained her nothing. Her complaints had been treated with open contempt, as if her wishes were of no account, and the prospective employer on that occasion had walked out of the office, declaring she would not offer work to a mercenary little madam who didn't know how to show gratitude. So now Ruby simply prayed for deliverance. Survival was everything.

Looking back, she wondered how she'd survived at all.

If life in Ignatius House had been harsh, the reformatory had been a thousand times worse. Gone were the lessons given by patient nuns. There were few, if any, books for them to read beyond worthy moralising tomes, and the only games they were allowed to play were of the home-made variety such as hop scotch and skipping which demanded little more than a rope, ball or piece of chalk. Not that there was any time for games or relaxation for older girls like herself who were instructed in the arts of needlework, cooking, housewifery and knitting. They were trained for domestic service, nothing more.

Ruby and Pearl had spent much of their time working in the steaming heat of the laundry with the large and cumbersome hot irons, or winding the handle of an ancient mangle. Any surplus energy was expended on doing endless physical drill and exercises, which Pearl quite enjoyed, as she said it developed her bust line.

'One day I'll find meself a good-looking chap who'll appreciate this figure of mine. Don't you reckon, our Ruby?'

And Ruby would laugh and agree. She generally found it easier not to quarrel with her sister, and Pearl certainly was growing into a voluptuous and attractive young woman, one who was most particular about her appearance.

Ruby couldn't have cared less how she herself looked, and since these drill exercises took place while they were still dressed in the regulation heavy calico skirts and long-sleeved blouses, she found them hot, tiring and uncomfortable. Made worse by the fact that for much of the time her insides were churning with hunger, and energy was something she sadly lacked.

She thought of Pearl now. There was nothing more to be done for Billy, but she must never forget her sister. Ruby longed to have her family all together again under one roof but, for the moment at least, this was no more than a fanciful dream for the future. She cleared her throat and took the plunge. 'I have a sister. I wondered if you might have a job for her too, Mr Stobbs?'

Miss Crombie made tut-tutting noises through her teeth while Barthram Stobbs raised a pair of golden brows in mild surprise at her temerity. 'Though I may consider myself comfortably placed, I'm not made of brass, you know.'

The mocking tone was sharp and the Lancashire expression seemed at odds with the rest of his careful diction. Ruby wondered if she'd caught him off guard, but for some reason the change in him gave her pause for thought. Perhaps she should think again before accepting his offer. There was something not quite right about him. Those odd clothes, the interrogative stare, a certain ambiguity about his manner. Then she told herself sternly that perhaps this only showed he'd come up the hard way and made good, as she intended to do one day. She pressed on with her request.

'I wouldn't expect you to take her right away, she's not quite fifteen, but I'd hoped to go somewhere large enough to offer her employment later, perhaps in a month or two.' In normal circumstances they would each have left school by now and been free to find employment. The reformatory, however, worked to its own timetable and set of rules.

Barthram Stobbs appeared to give the notion serious consideration. 'We'll see, we'll see. Perhaps Miss Crombie has an opinion on the matter?'

He smiled enquiringly at the superintendent who, Ruby knew, couldn't have cared less one way or the other what happened to Pearl, or to any girl in her charge for that matter.

Few of the reformatory staff stayed longer than a few months, a year or two at most, as infections were rife here and ill health the norm. Miss Crombie had stayed longer than her predecessors, being now in her third year, but the way she was hitting the gin told its own story.

The pressures and difficulties of the job were beginning to take their toll, which Ruby didn't wonder at. The place was infested with vermin, suffered from defective drains, had moths in the cupboards and fleas in the beds. The sick room was generally fully occupied by sufferers of all manner of illness from diphtheria to scarlatina, chicken pox to consumption. Not to mention common diseases such as ringworm, eczema, impetigo and diarrhoea. The staff here did not have the nuns' obsession with hygiene.

In a dormitory of fifty girls, they'd be lucky if there was more than half a dozen toothbrushes, which they must share between them, and even fewer face flannels. No wonder infections spread. In comparison with the reformatory, Ignatius House seemed like a foretaste of heaven and, set against Miss Crombie, Sister Joseph an absolute angel. Ruby was desperate to get away, and to rescue Pearl too, at the very first opportunity.

'You will at least give her due consideration? She's a good worker and no trouble at all. I couldn't come otherwise.'

'That sounds very like an ultimatum.' Again he regarded her with that dangerously assessing glint in his golden-brown eyes, and suddenly Ruby doubted she wished to go anywhere with this man, not simply because he refused to take Pearl but because he had an unsettling and disturbing effect upon her, and she didn't know why. Nor did she quite trust him. Who did he think he was, eyeing her up and down and running his hands all over her? Having arrived at this conclusion, Ruby lifted her chin, smiled her most winning smile and blithely continued, 'Besides all of that, I'd want twelve pounds a year, not ten, and the money to be paid direct to me.'

Miss Crombie gasped.

Barthram simply laughed, as if she had made a joke, showing teeth as even and white as Ruby's own. Collecting up his hat and gloves, he turned from her and walked to the door. 'I shall give your demands due consideration and return tomorrow with my answer. And perhaps you, Ruby McBride, would do well to reconsider your own situation. I doubt you are in a position to refuse any reasonable offer.'

'Oh, indeed she is not, good sir. Indeed she is not!' Miss Crombie echoed. 'I shall speak to her directly about her lack of manners, you may be sure. Apologise at once for being a greedy girl, Ruby McBride. You really do not know when you are well off.'

Ruby remained mutinously silent.

'Well? What is it to be?'

'Good day to you, sir,' Ruby said, and stalked past him, head held high, managing to quit the office before he did.

—

'Oh, I shouldn't have done it. I always lose me temper and go steaming off in some sort of paddy.' She was sitting on her bed in the long dormitory. It was one of fifty identical iron bedsteads lining the room in four solid rows, but this small amount of space represented Ruby's sanctuary. She put her head in her hands and groaned. 'If only I'd been more polite, he might've agreed. Oh, Pearl, I've blown my last chance, and yours as well. He'll not have either of us now.'

'Well, you should've thought of *me* for a change, instead of what *you* fancy.'

Ruby looked at Pearl and said nothing. She felt too tired to argue that everything she'd ever done had been in her sister's best interest. Instead she said, 'There's bound to be someone else, someone who'll take us both on. We'll just have to be patient.'

'For how long? We'll be grey-haired and ancient before we get out on licence at this rate. I'll never find a fella in here, never have a chance to get wed and have a bit of you-know-what.'

'For goodness' sake, Pearl, there are other considerations in life.' Whatever the two girls had lacked in knowledge of the facts of life while at Ignatius House, had been more than made up for since, in the reformatory, thanks to the other girls. Pearl in particular was obsessed with the subject of sex.

'I don't want to die a virgin, our Ruby. I want to know what it's like, how it feels to be loved by a chap. Don't you?' Indeed she did, and deep in her heart Ruby knew exactly which chap. But she'd no wish to think about Kit Jarvis just now, it only upset her.

'Oh, I don't know why I said what I did. It wasn't that I didn't like him – not exactly, anyway. He's obviously a bit of a character, an eccentric, but not bad looking in his way. You couldn't help but be fascinated by him, but there were something fishy about him. I couldn't quite put me finger on what it was only he didn't seem right. And he could hardly keep his hands off me, the cheeky beggar! Oh, hecky thump, no, I'm not sorry I refused to be his housemaid.'

'Except that he lives in a fine house and you'd be better fed than this,' Pearl pointed out as they both sat contemplating a dish of watery soup that evening at supper.

Ruby took a mouthful, and screwed up her face in distaste. 'It tastes funny. I think they've given us the washing-up water by mistake.'

Both sisters giggled, though not with any great sense of amusement for the meal was even worse than usual. The soup was followed by stringy stewing beef, more fat and gristle than lean meat, and tough as old leather, served with a couple of floury potatoes.

'This meat's raw,' Ruby stoutly protested, making eyes turn in her direction. 'We shouldn't be given food like this.'

'Aye, it's rubbish, that's what it is,' a girl beside her agreed.

Miss Crombie, making her way down the length of the table, her unsteady progress indicating all too clearly how she had spent the rest of her afternoon, hiccupped gently. 'You should consider yourself lucky to have any food at all on your plates. If you gels weren't shafely in the reformatory, being well taken care of, you'd be begging in the shtreets, eating pig shwill.'

'Give this to the flaming pigs then,' shouted another. ''Tain't fit for humans, that's fer sure.'

A potato flew through the air and smashed on to the table, followed by another, and then another. One hit Miss Crombie smack in the middle of her flat chest and she squealed in dismay, pleading with them to be good girls and behave. When they took no notice, she picked up the dinner bell and began to ring it, loud and long. One girl shouted 'Fire!' and all the others roared with laughter.

'*Stop it! Stop it!* Please don't be naughty. You know how it upsets me.'

Sadly, this only made everyone laugh all the more. There wasn't a girl in the room who didn't recognise the desperation in her tone of voice, the expression of sheer terror in the superintendent's bloodshot eyes. She might beg them to be good but Miss Crombie, as every girl present knew only too well, no longer had the power to make them.

Within seconds the dining room was in uproar. Food was flying everywhere, girls were jumping up and down on the benches, singing and dancing, yelling and screaming, and poor Miss Crombie and her staff were becoming ever more demented, running around ineffectually blowing whistles and clanging bells, achieving nothing very much at all. It was not surprising that, in view of their hunger, the girls' good humour rapidly deteriorated and serious fighting broke out. Crockery and windows were broken before finally the riot was brought to an abrupt end by the arrival of the constabulary.

Chapter Eight

Several days later Ruby once more stood before Barthram Stobbs. Miss Crombie was not present on this occasion as she had handed in her resignation on the evening of the riot and departed, clutching her carpet bag, without spending another night in the place. Many of the girls had been brought before the Board of Guardians or, worse, the magistrates' bench. Pearl and several other girls who had taken no direct part in the riot were nevertheless accused of provocation and ordered to spend three days in padded cells, meant to cool their hysteria. Pearl didn't go quietly. She'd been dragged away screaming that it was all Ruby's fault.

Ruby was utterly devastated. Of course it had been her fault. It had been *she*, yet again, who had made a fuss, a reckless complaint about the state of the food, and poor Pearl who had suffered in consequence.

The interview was this time conducted by the chairman of the governors himself, his bloodshot eyes entirely unforgiving, even the pimple on his bulbous nose seeming to nod a warning that no protest would avail her. Barthram Stobbs's offer had apparently changed and the chairman was telling Ruby what a very fortunate young woman she was.

'You are to be spared from sinking further into immoral depravity through the sanctity of holy matrimony.'

'Holy hell?'

'Hold your tongue, girl! Haven't you done enough damage already? We've lost Miss Crombie and must now find a new, less beneficent superintendent to keep the girls in order.' The chairman sighed heavily as he glowered down upon her and Ruby would not have been in the least surprised to see fire breathed from those wide, hairy nostrils. Turning his back upon her, he addressed his next remarks directly to his visitor. 'Immorality is ever a problem with these reformatory girls. Along with disobedience, rudeness and impropriety. They are drawn from the lowest stratum of society and it is a well-nigh hopeless task to redeem them from those depths.'

Barthram Stobbs said, 'This girl has potential, I believe, and I am, as I have explained, in need of a wife. I really do not have the heart to seek more than a good housekeeper and helpmeet. My dear late wife was all to me, and without her I cannot imagine ever...'

He could hear the quiver of insincerity in his own voice, felt certain the dratted man could guess that this was all a lie, that he was no widower, never had had a wife, nor ever felt the need for one. But he did now. Dear God, he must have her. He meant to make Ruby McBride his own, one way or another, and if the price was matrimony, so be it. It was one he would happily pay.

The chairman cleared his throat. 'Quite, and I understand perfectly. I admire your Christian charity, sir, and trust you will not live to regret this amazing act of generosity.'

'I'm sure I will not.'

'The necessary arrangements have been made?'

'Indeed they have. I collected the special licence this morning. We can be wed today, without fuss or delay.'

'Very wise, I'm sure.' The chairman turned to Ruby, who was listening in a state of complete shock. 'Well, there you have it, girl. Redemption offered to you at the eleventh hour.'

'I'm not marrying *him*. I don't even know the man.'

'Watch that sharp tongue of yours, girl. You'll have ample opportunity to get to know him.'

'Never!' Ruby's defiant stance was not having at all the effect she had hoped for. Barthram Stobbs was clearly highly amused by her spluttering protests, and the chairman showed not the least concern.

'You are being given the opportunity to achieve respectability and security. Are you saying you would prefer to go to jail? If so the alternative is three months' imprisonment for inciting a riot. Is that what you would prefer?'

Ruby fell silent, all rebellion draining from her at this awful prospect. She'd heard about the inside of the Bridewell, and once having suffered incarceration there, the slide into the gutter was generally unstoppable.

Taking her silence for agreement, the chairman pulled out his watch to check the hour, as if to indicate that he was a busy man with better things to do with his time than listen to silly girls. He beamed upon her beneficently. 'What's more, you can now expect to be invited to take part in the annual treat on the first Monday of the New Year, to partake of tea and bun-loaf and to collect your ten shillings reward money in return for producing your wedding certificate. How very splendid! These moments of success are what make our reforming task worthwhile.'

'Success? But I...' Ruby began.

'Enough! You are, I repeat, a most fortunate young woman to be spared incarceration and would do well to show proper gratitude. Say thank you to Mr Stobbs for his generous offer, and to us for our efforts on your behalf.'

Silence.

'Say it!'

Ruby pressed her lips together and glared mutinously at the floor.

The chairman grunted his disapproval. 'You see what we have to contend with? Complete obduracy. I wish you every success, sir, in your Christian endeavour. Every good wish.' And the two men shook hands, thus acknowledging that the deal had been struck.

–

'What's this when it's at home?' Ruby stared in stunned disbelief at the sight which met her eyes. 'This don't look like no big fancy house. Pardon me if I've been struck blind, but I'd say there's some mistake here.'

'No mistake, Ruby.'

'It's no more than a scrubby old wash tub!' This was, perhaps, an unfair description of the steam tug lying at anchor on a quiet stretch of the Duke of Bridgewater's Canal. It gleamed with varnish, its wheelhouse encased in oak-grained planking, a funnel painted in high gloss black, and steam pipe and whistle plated with polished copper. Inscribed in shiny brass lettering on the side of the boat was its name: *Blackbird*. Behind the tug, and obviously in tow, lay a pair of filthy barges, currently empty but stinking of household refuse, cotton waste and coal dust. In no way could the entire rig be taken for a house, nor to be in need of a housemaid.

'Is this some kind of joke?' Ruby asked. 'Because it doesn't tickle my funny bone one bit.'

'You wanted to escape the reformatory and you have, so stop complaining, get on board and put the kettle on.'

Ruby realised that not only had she been married against her will, to a complete stranger, but she'd also been hoodwinked into believing there would be a comfortable house at the end of the day. She'd hoped at least for some sort of respectability and security, as the chairman of the governors had indicated. Now it would seem even that had been a trick.

Barthram Stobbs's expression would have given weaker spirits pause for thought before tackling him head on about the situation, but Ruby stubbornly stood her ground. 'You can't get away with this. The Board of Guardians will want to know how I'm doing as your "good wife and helpmeet" in a proper house, not on a flippin' boat.'

'Then they're going to be disappointed, as are you. And even if they come looking for you, which I doubt, they won't be able to find you since I gave a false address. Your Miss Crombie should've paid less attention to her own personal comfort and more to her charges'. As for the chairman, he was simply relieved to have another reformatory girl successfully placed and off his hands.'

Both facts undeniably true, Ruby silently conceded.

She tried a different approach. 'Why did you do it? And why me?'

He was beginning to wonder the very same thing himself, beginning to doubt his own sanity. Perhaps that was the answer. She'd sent him mad with lust. Just to look at her standing on the docks, legs astride, hands at her slender waist and a delectable expression of pouting fury on her lovely face, told him all too clearly why he'd lost his reason. 'Why not you? Most red-blooded males would find you appealing, Ruby McBride, despite your sharp tongue.'

To her dismay, Ruby found herself blushing. 'So that's it. You think reformatory girls are easy meat, like most other chaps with mucky minds.' She tossed back her hair and met his laughing eyes with defiance. 'Well, if you think that putting a ring on my finger will get you a bit of what you fancy, you can think again. No one takes advantage of Ruby McBride, I can tell you that for nothing.'

'I'm sure they don't Ruby. I'm quite certain of it.'

'So there'll be no wedded bliss.'

'Indeed I didn't expect any.'

'No wedding night!' She felt the need to make her position clear.

He seemed not in the least put out by this declaration. 'Matters of this sort have a way of resolving themselves in due course, I've always found.'

His words confused her. He sounded so calm, so in control, yet speaking in riddles so that his meaning wasn't entirely clear. Was he saying that he agreed to leave her alone, or that she'd give in to his demands in the end? Ruby tried once more to make her own views on the matter plain. 'I want no hanky-panky. None at all!'

He had the temerity to laugh. 'I wouldn't dream of it. Hanky-panky, as you call it couldn't be further from my mind.'

Now she was even more confused. 'Then what's on your mind? What is it you want me *for*?'

'You'll find out what your duties are Ruby, when I see fit to tell you.'

She watched in dawning disbelief as he calmly took off the white kid gloves, and after carefully tucking them into his pockets began to uncoil ropes and make ready to slip anchor.

'I'm not getting involved in anything illegal.' The tension between them at these words was palpable. It was as if she had issued a challenge.

He looked at her out of narrowed eyes. 'Are you suggesting I'm a crook?'

'You might well be, for all I know. What happened to your first wife, for instance? Was it really her heart what killed her, or was that a lie an' all?'

For no reason she could fathom, he seemed to find this funny and laughed out loud, yet little humour showed in his eyes which were a strange, golden shade like rich brandy that matched the colour of his tousled hair. Unusual for a boatman, who were more commonly dark and swarthy. 'I like a girl with spunk. You remind me very much of myself at your age. But yes, you're absolutely right. That was a lie too.' He did not explain in what respect and Ruby shivered on a frisson of fear as he leaned closer, dropping his voice to a low hiss. 'You're forgetting one thing – *I'm* in charge here, not *you*, so *I'll* make the decisions. Right? I think you'll find it to your advantage not to question me too closely Ruby McBride, nor to dispute my authority too strongly.'

Leaving her with her mouth hanging open and, for once, at a loss for words, he climbed aboard, strode the length of the two barges and began to check their towing hooks. Back on the tug, he opened the valve to start up the steam engine. Ruby stood rooted to the spot throughout the entire operation, having immense trouble accepting the reality of her situation since it was so totally unexpected. She felt as if she were living some sort of nightmare, one from which she kept vainly hoping she might wake.

'Well?' He stared across at her from the tug, clearly impatient for her to make up her mind. 'What's it to be, marriage or jail? The choice is yours.'

Fury and fear warred for supremacy, making her limbs twitch so badly Ruby could barely keep still. Yet if she dashed off into the wide blue yonder, what good would that do her? He could have her brought back, as if she were an errant, foolish young bride. She belonged to him now, almost as if she were his property. Besides, where would she run to? She couldn't return to the reformatory, since it was unlikely the Board of Guardians would allow her back in view of the fact they considered her well placed: a success story. More likely they'd send her to the workhouse, or, as they'd already threatened, to prison for inciting a riot. She'd also be adding absconding while out on licence to her crimes. Oh, she was in a right pickle.

Neither did Ruby have any wish to end up living rough on the streets where she'd no doubt either starve to death or be picked up again by the police; her only crime that of destitution. If only their Billy had never been bullied and they'd never run away from the unfeeling nuns and Ignatius House. If only their mam had never fallen ill. No, she'd been down that road once too often. She had to live with whatever cards life dealt her. Billy was in Canada. Pearl was confined in a padded cell, and Ruby herself must somehow survive until the day they could all be together again. Which meant exercising her wits, not giving way to self-pity.

At the back of her mind, ideas and plans for this long dreamed of future began to take shape. Barthram Stobbs had said he might be prepared to offer Pearl a position. Perhaps, in time, she could hold him to that, with or without a house. In the meantime, some matters couldn't be ignored and must be made clear from the start. Nor dare she risk doing anything which might spoil her chances. It was a fine line she must tread with care.

Ruby smiled at him, soft brown hair falling seductively over her cheeks as she gave a careless shrug, as if she'd had her say and was content to go along with his scheme. Her tone of voice was calm, even sweet, yet somehow uncompromising. 'You lay one finger on me without my say so, wife or no, and I'll kill you with my own fair hands. D'you hear me, Barthram Stobbs? I don't care if I do swing for it, I'd see you dead first.'

A moment of thoughtful silence and then came that now familiar answering chuckle. 'I knew I'd chosen well. Get on board. I'm a patient man, Ruby McBride. You're young and I'm willing to wait to enjoy the fruits you have on offer, delectable though they undoubtedly are. In the interim, I shall make good use of your clever mind and fiery spirit. I'm hoping such an irresistible combination will make me a deal of money.'

Several hours, and numerous locks later they reached the Bridgewater Viaduct. Ruby was surprised by this. She'd expected them to head for the main docks where the big ships discharged their cargoes and took on fresh loads and supplies. Having tied up the tug for the night, Barthram explained to Ruby over a supper of pie and peas, how he was known locally as "the baron". She assumed this was because of his superior skills as a carrier, transporting coal, cotton and other goods the length of the canal, often as far as Liverpool and back. He did not disabuse her of that assumption.

'But you can call me Bart.'

Ruby couldn't imagine ever being so familiar. 'Right, Mr Stobbs,' she said, with deliberate insolence.

He didn't rise to her challenge, his smile mocking, eyes shrewdly assessing. 'I have many attributes, which you'll learn about all in good time. Perhaps you'll warm to me, in the end.'

Despite a show of stubborn persistence on Ruby's part, he refused, absolutely, to give any indication what these so-called attributes might be. Nor did he offer any further explanation of her duties, claiming there would be time enough the next day. 'You can have a trial run. See how you shape up.'

'Trial run? What sort of trial run?'

He stood up and wiped a dribble of gravy from his chin, a sardonic smile twisting full, sensual lips. 'It's time to turn in. When you've finished washing up, you can bunk down forward, where the cabin boy usually sleeps. As I said Ruby, I'm a patient man. The marriage will not be consummated until you're good and ready.'

'Which will be never.'

He gave a lazy smile. 'I'm sure that after a good night's rest, you'll feel much more amenable in the morning.'

He then removed the check jacket and trousers and, standing before her in his long-johns, folded the suit with care and laid it away in a large battered trunk, together with the cravat, watch and chain, and the crisp white shirt. Finally, he removed a layer of padding from around his stomach, shedding years from his age in the process and becoming, upon the instant, a different man entirely. His body suddenly appeared lithe and lean and firmly muscled. He pulled on a silk dressing gown and tied the cord about his slim waist before giving her a wry, crooked smile and withdrawing to his spacious cabin aft. Ruby had watched the entire performance in enthralled silence, astonished and utterly captivated by the transformation.

Who and what was this man? He was her husband.

–

Lying in her cramped quarters, Ruby tried the word out in her mind, over and over, attempting to accustom herself to the unaccustomed sound of it as well as the reality. It all seemed unreal, as if this marriage had no connection with her. Again she considered making a run for it, even got so far as trying the door, only to find it locked and bolted. She was a prisoner, which made her feel sick with fear and filled her with a new surge of anger.

Ruby wondered if she would ever be free to make her own way in the world. Oh, but she meant to be one day, of that she would make certain. Then she'd do as she pleased. Wouldn't she just!

But even if she had been able to escape tonight, where could she have gone? Who knew what terrors lurked in the shadows beneath the railway arches of Castlefield. The last time she'd been in this area was that fateful night when they'd been taken back into custody, just as if they were criminals.

In her head, Ruby could still hear the whistles and the shouts, smell the panic and the fear of the running boys, and feel Pearl and Billy's shuddering sobs as the three of them were dragged apart. She could recall all too clearly the gnawing hunger of life on the streets. The bitter cold, the damp seeping into her bones, the constant fear of attack, and the warm, exciting pressure of a young boy's body as he consoled her for failing to survive without his help.

Chapter Nine

The next morning, when breakfast and chores were out of the way, Ruby was confronted with yet another Barthram Stobbs, one dressed in the uniform of a police constable on the beat. She blinked, startled by this unexpected sight. Despite smelling oddly of mothballs, he again looked completely different from the suave, lean man in the dressing gown of the night before, and remarkably convincing. Ruby recalled having glimpsed the brass buttons of uniforms and other items of apparel inside the chest, including a clerical collar. All of which seemed strange, and Ruby didn't care to imagine how he had come by them.

She opened her mouth to ask why he was thus attired but, on seeing the harsh set of his jaw, thought better of it and closed it again. Ruby had already learned that Barthram Stobbs was not a man to cross.

He checked that all was secure on both tug and barges, no work having been done overnight on any of the vessels so far as she could tell. He then ushered her out on to the canal towpath and made them all secure.

'Do as you're told and you'll come to no harm,' he tartly informed her, reading the questions in her hazel-eyed gaze. Ruby could only hope this was true. She'd hardly slept a wink the night before, her mind turning over ways to get out of this muddle. No solution had presented itself but now, after seeing his box of tricks which looked for all the world like disguises, it didn't take a genius to work out that whatever he was up to wasn't within the law. After her time in the reformatory Ruby was left with the constant fear that the least step in the wrong direction and she could be sent down for years, married or no.

Minutes later, they were just two anonymous faces in the lower reaches of Deansgate. Barthram Stobbs strolled the length of the street, making his leisurely way through the shoppers and then back again. Ruby trailed close behind as instructed. He made a most convincing police constable, even to giving directions when one woman stopped him to ask the way to somewhere, and picking up and dusting off a child who had fallen in the gutter. What would he do if there were a real emergency? she wondered, and almost wished one would occur, just to test him. However, all remained quiet and at length he drew her up a side street and told her to listen carefully to his instructions.

'In a moment, I'm going to go into that pawnbroker's shop over there to speak to the shopkeeper. I shall ask to check the large notes in his till or cash box, on the grounds that they might be counterfeit. Then I'll insist that he accompany me to the local police station where the money, which I will carry for safe keeping in a special bag, will be checked and examined by experts.'

Ruby was staring at him, bemused. 'You don't imagine for one moment that he'll just hand it over, do you?'

'Oh, yes, he'll hand it over all right. I shall offer him a reward for carrying out his civic duty. It's a ploy which has always worked in the past, and I see no reason why it shouldn't work today, so long as you play your part well.'

'Me? No, I've already told you. I'm doing nothing…' He didn't even wait for her to finish speaking but pushed her back against the wall, one hand pressing down hard on her shoulder as if giving a troublemaker a good telling off. Many people glanced in their direction as they passed by, but everyone seemed perfectly satisfied that this was simply a police constable carrying out his duties.

'When you see me come out with him and start to head off in that direction,' he carefully pointed up the street with one finger, 'you dash up, all in a state, and claim there's a fracas going on in Whitworth Street, that somebody's being attacked by rabble-rousers and a constable is needed right away. Do you understand? And do as I say?'

Ruby saw quite clearly now why he was called "the baron". It was a fitting nickname for a clever and superior conman whose sole task in life was to separate people from their hard-earned money, no doubt with exemplary speed. Well, he wasn't using her in his nasty little schemes. 'Why would I?'

'Because I insist upon it,' he replied, giving his familiar, crooked smile. He could feel the skeletal thinness of the girl's shoulder beneath his hand and even as he barked orders at her, Bart was mentally noting that she was in dire need of good food to put some flesh on her bones. 'Don't worry he'll not touch you. He'll believe every word that falls from your sweet lips, because you'll make sure that he does. Right?'

Ruby pressed her lips together in mute rebellion. 'Do your worst, and see if I care. You can't hurt me any more than Sister Joseph did, or the flippin' reformatory.'

'Ah, so that's the way of it, I see.' He gripped her arm and gave her a little shake. 'I should point out, Ruby McBride, that I have friends and contacts everywhere, even in reformatories. Your sister is still detained in one, I believe? And who knows what might happen to a young girl when she no longer has an older sister to protect her.'

Ruby felt all the blood and fury drain from her veins, leaving her weak with anguish. 'You wouldn't hurt our Pearl?'

He momentarily widened his eyes in a helpless sort of gesture. 'You know I'm very fond of young girls, sugar and spice and all things nice. But my appetites are normal. I prefer my women to be willing and mature enough for loving. Some men's tastes, however, are less orthodox. I'd hate to see any harm come to your Pearl, when she'll soon be going out into the world. I wouldn't recommend you do anything rash.'

He recognised naked fear in her lovely eyes and felt an inner loathing of himself that he must speak to her thus, yet she undoubtedly thrived on defiance, and he needed to be able to depend upon her complete obedience at all times or more lives would be in danger than one young girl's. 'Do we understand each other?'

Ruby longed to challenge his assumption that he could reach Pearl, wherever she might be, yet somehow didn't quite dare. Even though he'd already shown himself to be an habitual liar, his tone had hardened, and she heard not a hint of compromise in it. In that moment she could only wish herself a thousand miles from this spot; that she could step on board one of the great vessels that came daily into the Ship Canal and disappear forever off the face of the earth, or at least from the clutches of Barthram Stobbs.

Perhaps it was this thought which put the idea in her head. Daring, risky, but one which might see her safely out of the country and on her way to finding Billy. It would be a laugh to play the baron at his own game but it would take careful planning, of that she was certain. Nothing could be done in a hurry, as there was still Pearl to rescue from the reformatory. Ruby realised that she must learn to bite her tongue and do as he asked. For the moment at least, as she must give the impression that all was well, that whatever he asked of her she was willing to go along with. 'All right, all right! Keep your hair on. I'll do it.'

His grip slackened and the chilly smile thawed slightly. 'Good girl! All you have to do is hold your nerve, and carry out my instructions to the letter. Perfectly simple.'

It felt very far from simple so far as Ruby was concerned. Long before he'd entered the shop premises, she could feel her limbs start to shake. How she would ever manage to walk, let alone run, she didn't care to consider. The wait, while he was in the shop talking to the proprietor, seemed endless, as if it would go on forever, and she had a sudden urge to visit the lavatory. But how could she? He might walk out of the door at any minute.

And then there he was, with the shopkeeper in tow, the pair of them chatting in a friendly enough fashion.

For a moment she felt frozen to the spot, but Ruby had believed him when he said he could hurt Pearl. Barthram Stobbs was clearly a clever operator of which there was no doubt. He'd not only fooled Miss Crombie and herself, but also the Board of Guardians by winning over the chairman of the governors and trapping her into matrimony that was anything but holy. She began to run.

'*Help! Help! Police!*' Somehow a torrent of nonsense about gangs and fights came bubbling out, perhaps dredged out of the banks of her memory.

'My dear, my dear.' In her nervousness she barely heard his next words so that he had to repeat them, urging her to be calm and explain where, exactly, these rabble-rousers were.

Ruby hadn't the faintest idea. Everything he'd told her had gone from her head and she simply stared up at him, her mind numb, completely blank. Barthram Stobbs rested a hand on her shoulder, as a proper police constable might, and patted it gently.

'Take your time, my dear. You've had a shock. Now, which street were you in when you saw this attack?'

'Whitworth Street!' The answer came out on a gasp and she knew it was the right one because one of his eyes flickered briefly into a wink. No one but herself would have noticed since he had bent down towards her, his face inches from her own and a mask of concern. Barthram turned to the pawnbroker beside him, and mildly suggested he go on ahead to the police station.

'I shall join you there shortly, sir, the moment I have dealt with this poor little miss and her attackers.'

Amazingly, perhaps dazzled by Ruby's beauty, the shopkeeper seemed quite happy to do so, making no protest as Barthram Stobbs, in his policeman's guise, dashed off in the direction of Whitworth Street, hustling Ruby before him, the bag of notes still in his hand.

The moment they turned the corner he dived quickly down a back alley, under a railway bridge and through a maze of streets down by the River Medlock. Only when they were again at Castlefield in sight of the canal did he stop, lean back against a wall and start to laugh. 'Which is the last that gullible fool will ever see of this particular constable!'

Ruby bent over and vomited into the gutter.

–

Over the weeks and months following, Ruby discovered, to her great frustration that as Barthram Stobbs's wife she was as powerless as she had ever been in the reformatory. He cared not one jot for her opinions, or her feelings, only for the state of his own finances. The money he had conned out of the pawnbroker he stashed away in a tin box, before hiding it in his cabin. The next evening he received several visitors, all rough-looking men, and Ruby watched through a crack in her door as he counted and shared out the notes between them.

'What has that poor shopkeeper ever done to deserve being robbed?' she asked him later, over supper.

'One – he is very far from poor. Two – he's a pawnbroker, not simply a shopkeeper, and three – not an honest one either. He thinks nothing of robbing folk blind of their last halfpenny should it suit him to do so. He had it coming to him. Shed no tears over the fellow, Ruby.'

She was, however, expected to shed many tears on numerous other occasions. He would have her wait by some fancy house or by the dock offices to waylay Manchester Ship Canal Company officials after a board meeting, and claim to have been abandoned by a cruel uncle/husband/stepfather, without even the wherewithal to get home. It proved amazingly easy to persuade these toffs to part with tram or cab fare. Sometimes, if they got a good look at her lovely face, they'd toss her half a crown and ask if she had any more favours on offer, at which point Ruby found it more prudent to dissolve into further tears than to stalk off in high dudgeon. Seeing her distress left them riddled with guilt at the improper suggestion they'd made, and they might well add another half crown to go with the first.

'It's all down to those wistful hazel eyes of yours,' Barthram would say as he pocketed the cash.

And look where wistful hazel eyes got me mam, Ruby would think. With three children by different men, a fate that would not be repeated by her daughter.

'It's small change to them,' Barthram Stobbs was saying. 'Meat and drink to those less fortunate.'

'It's still wrong to steal, and you can't claim to be starving.' Nevertheless Ruby found herself required to play many parts and became quite certain she must have heard every lie under the sun, seen him in every possible disguise from undertaker to solicitor's clerk, military man complete with monocle to idle vagrant. Though she was utterly convinced that the baron was a fraudster, yet she learned he also possessed the skills of an artist and the charm of a rake. He was, without doubt, master of his craft and she couldn't help but admire his fertile imagination and gift of the gab, for all she neither approved nor understood the necessity for either.

'Why do you do it?'

'The whys and wherefores needn't concern you, Ruby McBride. You'd be well advised to keep your nose out of my business.'

'What you make me do is my business. I need to understand *why*. She did nothing to disguise the contempt in her voice, meeting the answering fury in his blazing eyes.

For his part, he wanted to protest, to object to her prying too closely into his affairs and demand to know why she always thought the worst of him, but then he would bite back the words unspoken. She was right. He did push boundaries to their limits, and he couldn't explain, not to her, not right now, why he did so. Not till he could trust her completely. 'What is it exactly you object to, Ruby McBride?' His voice was savage in its harshness.

'The way you treat people, for one thing. Why do you play these cruel tricks? It's dangerous, for another. If you got caught, you'd end up in t'clink.'

'I won't get caught. The people who contribute to my fund, as you might call it, wouldn't welcome the publicity any more than I would.'

'Oh, I know you think you're mighty clever, but it'd take only one mistake, one person to spot you thieving, and that'd be it.'

'You underestimate me.'

'That's what they all think, except in your case maybe I do,' she agreed with a weary sigh. 'But you must admit you're hard to fathom. You have brains and intelligence, and although you're getting on a bit, you're not that old.'

'I'm twenty-eight Ruby. No age at all.'

She was momentarily startled. There was such a sadness to the planes of his face, handsome though it might be, a bitter twist to the sensuous mouth, that he appeared older than his years. What had made him so? Ruby wondered, before briskly brushing the thought aside to be considered later, at her leisure. 'Well then, why don't you find something more worthwhile to do, instead of fleecing folk?

You could make good money out of these barges that you drag around, if only you'd put your mind to it.'

He pulled a face, as if there were a bad smell under his nose. 'You're saying I don't work hard enough?'

'I am.' She tilted her chin, challenging him to dispute this damning indictment in an effort to persuade him that honest labour was good for the soul. 'It wouldn't be too bad a life. I'd be prepared to do my bit.'

'I suppose you're right in a way. It's true that if I put more effort into the barge work, I could build myself a good business. I'd have no objection to that, so long as it was done in a way to suit me. In the meantime, the boats are a good cover for my other interests shall we say, and I've no intention of dirtying my hands with heavy toil and sweat for a pittance, not if I can avoid it. That would be a waste of my resources.'

Ruby rarely understood the fancy words he used, yet still she struggled to grasp how his clever mind worked. She couldn't help but be intrigued by him, despite the fury he invoked in her. He'd robbed her of the freedom to marry where she chose – Kit Jarvis – if she'd had her way, and sometimes this resentment boiled over into pure hatred. 'I've seen you stashing away all your ill-gotten gains so, go on, tell me, what are you saving your brass for? What's it all in aid of?'

'I need my comforts, Ruby.'

'What for, yer old age?'

'I think we might start dipping into it before then. My living expenses are modest at the moment, but I aim one day to surround myself with the luxury I deserve. A fine house by the river perhaps, and the money to pay for it without too much effort! Would you like that,

Ruby? Do you dream of a place of yer own some day?' he teased, mocking her Lancashire twang, and she found herself flushing.

His voice, generally speaking, showed no trace of an accent. Where did he come from? Who was he? She was becoming curious about him but, young as she was, Ruby understood how dreams could be magical, dangerous fantasies and sympathised with anyone who harboured them. 'Aye, happen I would, if pigs could fly.'

She wanted a home of her own very much. It needn't be big, just roomy enough for Pearl and Billy to share it with her. She loved to indulge this particular fancy along with the sweeter one where Kit Jarvis turned up out of the blue, announced that he'd loved her since the first day he'd clapped eyes on her, and asked her to wed him. That one had kept her going for four years in the reformatory. It turned to bitter ashes; all hope destroyed on the day Barthram Stobbs had forced her to become his wife. Which brought her back to her current problem: staying on the right side of the law.

'I don't think you should achieve your dream at other folk's expense.'

He laughed. 'Ruby McBride, champion of the underdog! I like that. But it is possible to be too honest, don't you think? Fortunately we don't all possess your high moral scruples. Nevertheless, I would recommend that you keep your nose out of my affairs! I don't pay you to argue, or ask a lot of damn fool questions over matters you don't understand.'

'You haven't paid me anything at all yet,' Ruby spat back, rigid with temper. 'Not that I've noticed.'

'As my wife, I don't have to. Clever of me, don't you think?'

'Because you're a selfish git, more like.'

He seemed amused by her invective. 'I may pay you something, in due course, out of the kindness of my heart. In the meantime you have a home of sorts, food in your belly, and you're not being ill treated, are you?'

The calmness of his response made Ruby incandescent with rage. It was difficult for her to mumble an agreement that she was not.

Stroking her tilted chin with the ball of his thumb, he trailed it onward down the curve of her throat to withdraw it only seconds before it dipped into the enticing shape of her neckline. 'Well then, I'd start thinking of ways to offer a return on my good will if I were you, or I may change my mind about saving your little sister from the yawning jaws of the factory system where she is almost certainly bound. I'm sure you'll find it worth your while to be generous, in the long run.'

Then he walked briskly away, leaving Ruby both disturbed by the bold caress, and oddly insulted that he could resist her so easily.

Chapter Ten

Ruby's life had changed beyond recognition. A committee of reformers no longer strictly controlled the ordinary, everyday tasks she now carried out. She could choose what food she wished to eat, which clothes she wore, even borrow whatever books she fancied from the mission library. Yet still she did not feel that she had any real control over her life. What had gone wrong? She'd expected to be mistress of her own fortune once she'd left the reformatory but seemed to be more trapped than ever. Barthram Stobbs, husband and conman, was very much in charge of both their lives. Why didn't she stand up to him as she used to stand up to Sister Joseph and Miss Crombie? But then Ruby knew why.

She didn't dare take the risk, for Pearl's sake. Not until she was good and ready, until she had all her plans in place and was quite certain Pearl was safe. Ruby had never feared punishment on her own account but it grieved her to think that it was her sister who was suffering for her latest burst of rebellion. The reformatory regime would be even tougher as a result of the riot, Miss Crombie's replacement no doubt as stern and austere as the Board of Guardians could find. All because she'd stupidly taken out her irritation over Barthram Stobbs by complaining about the food. What was it about institutional food that brought out the worst in her? Being left starving hungry, no doubt.

Pearl was now lost to her, temporarily at least, and Ruby herself married to a man she loathed. She'd failed her sister, failed Billy too. In trying to save him from the bullies, she'd somehow caused her little brother to be sent to a far-off land, and taken proper care of him. Tears of grief rolled down Ruby's cheeks. She'd broken her promise to her mam. Let them all down badly.

Perhaps it was too late for Billy, but there was still Pearl to think of. Ruby wished that she could believe that Barthram Stobbs would help her to save her sister, but she couldn't trust him. All she knew for certain was that if she couldn't alter a situation then she must somehow find it in herself to tolerate it, and not confront every problem with reckless defiance. Hadn't she learned that much during the harsh years of her childhood?

From time to time she would hear of a ship heading for Canada and Ruby would make up her mind to be on it. She longed to go there and find Billy, to reunite her family and give them the love they'd been denied in their miserable lives. She was surely old enough to take charge of them both now? Ruby went over and over her plan. She would cut her own hair, and Pearl's, dress them both as cabin boys. A wild scheme, admittedly, but hadn't she learned the art of disguise from a master? Or they could simply stow away in a lifeboat. Somehow, it must be possible to get on board.

What they would do after that, she hadn't quite worked out. She certainly couldn't afford the passages home. Ruby hoped they would find employment in Canada. It was a big country, after all. Billy had said so. There must be plenty of work there, not like here in Salford where a job was increasingly hard to come by.

Night after night she would adjust and add to these plans, and then come morning she'd wake to discover that the latest ship had sailed to Canada and she was no nearer to putting them into effect. She still hadn't found Pearl, which somehow must be achieved before they could begin to look for Billy. Ruby would weep sorrowful tears into her pillow, then console herself that it had all been nonsense anyway. How could she possibly stow away on a big liner, travel to a far-off country on the opposite side of the world? Lot of nonsense, she'd sternly scold herself, and for a while manage to put the whole notion out of her head.

And then another Canada-bound liner would steam into port and the same old dreams would start up all over again.

Ruby concluded that until the happy day arrived when these dreams could be fulfilled, the only way to survive, and ultimately achieve her freedom, was to play along with Barthram Stobbs's scams. For now. She would do her best to please him so that he wasn't watching her every second of the day. She would fool him into thinking that *he* was in control, when really *she* was the one in charge.

So, although she gave every impression of trusting him, Ruby remained very much on her guard. What other choice did she have, if she was to do right by her sister?

Her first task each morning was to clean the tug from stem to stern, tidying and sweeping out the cabins, scrubbing the board table and paintwork with washing soda till they glowed like new. She'd fill the water barrel and coal bunkers, trim the lamps, and, of course, it was her task to cook the meals. There was a tiny stove with a chimney, meant to keep them warm though its effectiveness was limited. A cupboard in the main cabin held their few provisions: tea, sugar, bread and butter and a tin of condensed milk. The hinged door would fold down and double as a table, where they ate breakfast and supper.

Fortunately, more often than not and to Ruby's immense relief, Barthram left her to her own devices for much of the day, while he went off gallivanting with his docker cronies. Sometimes he wouldn't come home until quite late and she would hear the rumble of their whispered conversation through the thin cabin walls, well into the small hours.

She didn't ask where he went, or what they got up to, or pay attention to whatever issues apparently absorbed them. Nor did she want to know, simply glad to have some time to herself. Ruby was only too relieved that he wasn't involving her quite so often in his nefarious schemes these days.

While he was away she would pretend the boat belonged to her alone. Ruby would take pride in scrubbing it clean, in touching up any varnish which had got scuffed or scratched, redoing the paint work, even to painting flowers and other pretty designs on the walls of the vessel. She didn't mind the hard work, the cold, or the cramped discomfort of life on board. She'd come to love the tug. She loved her tiny cabin with its narrow bunk, the shelves where she stowed away her clothes and the precious copy of *Robinson Crusoe* that Mam had given her all those years ago. If it weren't for missing Pearl and Billy, and pining for Kit Jarvis, she'd be happy as Larry here.

So long as her husband stayed away!

When she'd got everything ship-shape and gleaming, she'd gossip with the other boat women. Depending where they were on the canal, this might take place at one of the little shops that had sprung up along the towpath selling hot pies and mugs of tea, soup, meat and other provisions to the boat people, since they weren't always welcome in normal shops. A favourite place to meet was at the Boatmen's Mission. Some of the women occupied narrow boats with very limited facilities, and stopping off at the mission for a cup of tea and the chance to escape their claustrophobic living quarters for a bit of crack while they caught up on news was always welcome. The mission also provided laundry facilities, a small lending library, which Ruby cherished, newspapers for the men, games for the children, and the opportunity for her to write long, loving letters to Billy.

The women would tell her how fortunate she was in her husband. 'Good man, Barthram Stobbs,' they would say. 'Do anything for anybody will Bart.'

'Aye, proper toff is the baron.'

'Never has a thought for his own safety,' said another.

'That's true, whatever yer problem, Bart'll sort it out for you.'

Ruby would frown and listen to these words of praise, thinking maybe the women were talking about someone else entirely and not the man she'd married at all.

–

On the days when he was home, they'd visit a grubby wooden hut on Trafford Wharf where for a couple of pennies they could buy a bowl of thick pea soup and a slice of bread and butter each for their midday meal.

Ruby would concentrate on the delicious food while Bart would talk with the dockers. She didn't trouble to listen too closely as it involved people she didn't know, officials of the company, secretaries and union leaders. But it was clear that the men weren't too happy with their rates of pay, which she didn't wonder at. Times were hard, what with another cotton slump and a lot of folk in Lancashire being on short time. Ignorant as she was of business matters, even Ruby realised that this state of affairs didn't help the dockers one bit as there was less cotton and coal to transport on the canals if the mills weren't fully operational.

'Bleedin' slave labour it is. And some of these bags contain dangerous stuff,' one man complained. With typically Lancashire irony he was known as Sparky Joe because of his constantly doleful expression and slow way of speaking.

'Aye, Sparky, you're right there.'

'He is. We should be paid danger money for handling bags of lamp black,' another cried. 'It comes in paper sacks that split soon as you touch 'em. Then you get covered in black powder from head to bleedin' foot. They ought to pay us extra for the flippin' washing, if nowt else.'

'The company could at least provide us with showers, and give us time to clean up before we go home. Sometimes the conductor won't let us on the bus as we're that filthy we'd mucky his seats.'

Bart frowned. 'Ask the foreman for a meeting and put these points to him.'

'We have, but he won't take them to the superintendent.'

As so often in the past, Bart felt infuriated by their apathy, wanting to take them by the throat and shake them, make them stand up for their rights, though he understood and sympathised with their vulnerability. 'Well then, your only recourse is action.'

'That's fighting talk, man.'

'Why not?' Bart struggled to remain calm, knowing they needed support and encouragement, not bullying tactics. 'If reason doesn't prevail, you have to force people to listen to you, not buckle under. Isn't that what gets results?'

'Aye, listen to the baron, he's right.'

'Hear, hear.'

'All you have to do is get your union man to call a halt to work whenever he spots a dangerous cargo.'

The men glanced at each other, sheepish expressions on their weary faces. 'We haven't joined no union, not us unskilled workers. We leave that to the seamen and the craftsmen. We dockers are a casual labour force, with no rights to call us own.'

'Rubbish! It's time you did join. For God's sake, unions are for all, skilled and unskilled alike.'

There were mumbles of agreement, while others put forward excuses, names of employers who had strong objections to union activity among their workers, no matter what the law of the land might allow, and then one name emerged above all the rest: Giles Pickering.

Sparky said, 'He owns a whole fleet of barges, tugs, ships. You name it, it bears his name on the ticket some-where. And I've a family to feed. It's more'n my life's worth to stand up to him. You tried it once, Tom, didn't ya?'

'Aye, and he made sure I got no work for weeks because I'd complained about the haphazard way some hessian bags were stacked. I kept me mouth shut after that.'

Then they all leaned closer, putting their heads together to plot and plan. Ruby paid no attention. She was far too busy eating her custard tart.

—

As Christmas approached, Bart grew increasingly restless, sometimes sitting for long hours staring at Ruby in reflective silence, at others endlessly fidgeting, almost nervous in his demeanour. She observed this strange behaviour with covert interest. What might he be planning?

This was what she feared most of all: the fact that even after months of living under the same roof, she was no nearer to understanding him. Who knew what he was chewing over in that overactive brain of his, perhaps with one of his cronies downtown. He was as much a mystery to her as ever and Ruby worried where his agile mind might lead them.

But then she'd long since decided that Barthram Stobbs was a strange character: the kind of man who gave no indication of what he was thinking or feeling. A man who liked to be in complete control which was perhaps why he'd wed her, to be sure that he had a woman firmly in his grasp. Even so, Ruby believed that she could deal with his idiosyncrasies. There was no evidence of violence in him, and for that she was grateful. He'd never struck her, nor yet attempted to interfere with her in any way despite his having the right, in theory, as her husband.

Not that she expected this state of affairs to go on indefinitely. There were times when he lapsed into a

120

brooding silence, watching her with a raw intensity, openly appraising her. Just as if she were a piece of merchandise and he were assessing her value, Ruby thought, outraged. This 'stripping-me-off look', as she termed it, worried her a good deal, but she'd learned to make herself scarce when he was in one of his moods. She'd also insisted on being given the key to her cabin door which, to be fair, he'd agreed to, albeit with an amused, rakish smile. 'Don't you trust me, Ruby?'

'I don't think about you at all.'

'I suspect you do. I believe you think about me a good deal more than you care to admit.'

Night after night Ruby's sleep was indeed disturbed by dark imaginings, quite certain that this would be the night he'd come to claim his rights. In her dreams she would see his handsome face loom close, sense his warm breath against her cheek, imagine that she felt the brush of his lips touching hers, then she would wake in a lather of hot emotion. Or she would be quite unable to get to sleep at all, listening for his step upon the wooden boards, a tap on her door and the soft echo of his voice calling her name.

'Ruby. Aren't you ready for me yet?'

She would bury her head under the pillow, her heart pounding in her ears as she tried to quench the images that flooded in. What would it feel like to have Barthram Stobbs make love to her? Would he be tender, passionate, caring or brutal and touch her heart? How could that be possible when it already belonged to Kit Jarvis?

Exhaustion finally claimed her and Ruby woke to the bright sunlight of another day and the knowledge that she was safe for a while longer. But from his expression at breakfast, she recognised the very real pleasure he derived from playing this game of cat and mouse. The twisted smile proclaimed all too clearly that he would have her in the end, but in his own good time.

Chapter Eleven

Queen Victoria died on 22 January 1901. On a cold, clear day in February her son Edward VII opened his first Parliament, thus ushering in a new age. Sad as the people were to lose their treasured monarch, yet the change represented a new beginning for a new century. For Pearl, the coming of spring that year brought little change in her own circumstances, nor offered any hope of rejoicing. She knew herself to be an outcast, an untouchable, just one among countless others who had spent their childhood in an institution and was now somehow tainted by it.

But she'd discovered ways of making life bearable, even exciting.

Her first position as scullery maid had not worked out. She'd been returned to the reformatory on a charge of 'impudent conduct', simply because she'd told her employer to keep his hands to himself when he'd attempted to fondle her breasts. Pearl was very proud of her figure and certainly no prude, but being mauled about by a whiskery old man with bad breath was not her idea of a good time.

Dallying in a grassy meadow behind the cabbage patch with Sam, the gardener's boy, at this, her second position out on licence, was another matter entirely. He was a good few years older than herself at twenty-two but quite a looker with those dark brooding eyes of his. Pearl had no objection to him fondling her any time he liked. Rather as he was doing now as she lay sprawled beneath him with her blouse all unbuttoned, her plump breasts spilling out and his young mouth suckling her like a babe, sending thrills of desire rippling through her. Like hot wine, she thought, rather fancifully for one who'd never tasted it.

Today was a perfect day for loving. The sky was a pale blue streaked with smudges of white cloud that looked as if they'd been painted by some artist's brush. The smell of damp, loamy soil mingled with the more cloying scent of May blossom in the hedgerow behind them and somewhere, not too far off, she could hear chickens cackling and scratching. She really should be getting back. The housekeeper was a dragon who didn't take kindly to scullery maids who skived off. Oh, but she didn't want to go, not just yet.

'Lift up your frock, Pearl, and let me have a feel. I won't hurt you, honest.'

'Give over, what do you think I am?' She was burning up inside with the need for him to touch her but didn't want him to think her cheap. That would never do. This sensation of power to reduce a man to a quivering wreck with one tantalising glance, one kiss from her luscious mouth, was utterly intoxicating.

It had been drummed into them all at the reformatory not to respond to a wink or a whistle, nor to embark upon even the mildest of flirtations. Admirable advice, Pearl had to admit, although sadly not the sort which she could abide by. Up until now there'd been no opportunity for any fun. It had been nothing but work the whole time, with not a man in sight.

Once out in the big wide world, however, it was a different story. The chance for a bit of slap and tickle, as it was fondly called, seemed to be available at every corner, and Pearl found that she simply couldn't resist a handsome face, a strong arm, or a teasing word of love, however insincere it might be.

She knew Sam didn't love her, any more than she loved him. Pearl adored the pungent aroma of male sweat on him, the scent of warm sunshine in his fair hair, the muscles that rippled through his young, lithe body, but not for a moment did she allow these distractions to lower her guard one inch. She had every intention of falling in love with someone who had pockets full of brass, not with a poor gardener's apprentice on five bob a week. But until a suitable candidate chanced along, there was no reason why she shouldn't enjoy herself in the meantime.

She drew up her skirt slowly, inch by tantalising inch, to just above her knees, giggling deliciously as he ran his hands up her long, smooth limbs. Then he was eagerly pushing them apart, groaning as if he were in some sort of agony.

'Oh, Pearl, yer that beautiful, I can hardly believe yer letting me do this.'

Pearl wished he would stop talking and get on with it. Within seconds, her flannel drawers were somewhere around her ankles. He'd unbuckled his belt and unbuttoned his trousers but she wasn't paying the slightest attention to any of this because she was far too intent on wanting his fingers to go on sending small explosions of delicious sensation through her body. Once she'd redirected his attention to satisfying that need she lay back unresisting, her hair a sunburst of colour in the sweet-scented grass, eyes closed and her arms flung out, wanting it to go on and on, until the burning need in her was finally quenched.

'You're a naughty girl, Pearl. Did no one ever tell you that?'

She giggled. 'That's why they sent me to the reformatory, I suppose. Don't you like naughty girls, Sam?'

'Oh, yes, Pearl. I certainly like you,' he said, his breathing ragged with excitement.

Something warm and hard was being pushed against her private parts, seeking entry, and Pearl gave a little startled squeal, as if she hadn't intended him to go so far. But then she began to help him, drawing him into her, all pretence abandoned as she succumbed to that driving need. 'Oh, and I like you, Sam. Give us a kiss.'

As she reached up to put her arms about his neck, mouth parted to receive his kiss, he pushed her back, pinning her arms down while he thrust into her with long, hard strokes, quickening to a powerful surge of energy as he came swiftly to a climax. The sensation of pleasure that cascaded through her brought that pitch of excitement Pearl had come to crave, almost as a daily necessity, to prove that she was alive. It was, in her estimation, the only joy she had in life, and surely everyone deserved a little pleasure? But it was over far too quickly, leaving her with an ache of disappointment, a sensation of being slightly cheated. She was the kind of girl, Pearl decided, who needed a lot of loving.

'Ooh, please don't stop. I want more,' she groaned as he slumped upon her, all energy spent. Now it was his turn to chuckle. 'Give a lad a minute to draw breath, and then you'll get more, love. By heck, you will.'

By late summer it became apparent to Pearl that she was pregnant. It amazed her that such a thing could happen so quickly, after only four months in service. It must be because she was so young and fertile, she thought, with some degree of pride. Not that she'd bargained on getting caught. She'd certainly no wish for the encumbrance of a child.

Terrified of being found out, she dosed herself daily with castor oil and essence of peppermint, hoping to rid herself of the problem, so far to no effect.

Pearl knew only too well that were she discovered, she'd be in dead trouble. Immoral girls were a great trial to the reformers, who considered them to be filled with wickedness and moral corruption. They certainly wouldn't be in the least interested in her tales of romance: of how she'd been abandoned by the traitorous Sam in favour of an upstairs maid. And how she'd found consolation in the arms of a handsome young groom who'd promised undying devotion, but had turned out to be married already.

In the short time she'd been free, Pearl had taken every path she could in the pursuit of pleasure and had enjoyed herself hugely. Now it seemed she must face the consequences.

Summing up the possibilities, she surmised that she very likely faced incarceration in the workhouse, if she was lucky, for it could be somewhere far worse. She'd even heard of a girl being sent to a mental home with the lunatics. She might still be there so far as anyone knew. Another had been forced to spend hours in solitary confinement on her knees in penitence for her 'crime'. When the poor creature had been considered sufficiently remorseful for her promiscuity she'd been thrown out into the streets, still not having given birth and with little hope of help or even adoption for the baby as the church did not approve of her behaviour. The child was apparently her responsibility and she must take care of it, come what may. Pearl knew only too well that once out on the streets, if the girl didn't die giving birth, the child certainly would, of starvation, cold or sickness.

Every one of these prospects filled her with terror.

'Thank your lucky stars you haven't got the clap.' Her new friend Elsie broke into her gloomy thoughts with these few comforting words, having been thoroughly put in the picture and asked if she knew of some other remedy worth trying. 'Then they'd send you to hospital, all dressed up in a purple frock, so everyone would know why.'

Pearl shuddered. 'How can you tell if you have it?'

'Yer bits and pieces drop off.'

'Oh, crikey! Blast you, our Ruby, for getting me into this mess.'

'Why were it your Ruby's fault?' Elsie wanted to know, eyes wide with wonder.

'If she'd thought of *me* for a change, before setting off on that hunger strike, riots and whatnots, we'd be out of this Godforsaken rat hole, that's why.' Pearl was even more convinced that if they'd stayed at Ignatius House, instead of running off on that hare-brained escape, they might have survived much better. Hadn't she told Ruby so a dozen times?

What if their Billy *had* been knocked about a bit by the bigger boys? What of it? It wouldn't have done him any real harm, him being a lad and not a soft lass. And Sister Joseph hadn't taken out her peevish temper on Pearl half so much as she had on Ruby. In fact, every now and then she'd given her a boiled sweet in return for a bit of a cuddle. What was so wrong in that? It was all Ruby's doing they were in this mess, all because she was such a rebel.

It was then that the pains started, and on a blast of searing fire that shot down her spine like forked lightning, Pearl knew she'd got away with it. This time. So long as she managed to live through the next few hours, she'd be as good as new.

But, by heck, there was so much hate in her, it was a wonder it didn't burn her insides out. Burn her sister to a crisp, more like. Wherever she was, blast her!

–

The baron led Ruby along Byrom Street not far from the skin hospital where stood a fine terrace of houses, many occupied by doctors, lawyers and other professionals. Dressed as a very ordinary-looking knife-grinder, he selected a spot from which they could observe the comings and goings on the street, then settled down to watch and wait. Ruby had learned that he was good at waiting, it was one of his most useful skills, but it helped if he had something to occupy him while he kept an eye on things, and sharpening the odd knife now and then would do very nicely. She made the comment that it would also allow him the opportunity to chat to the pretty housemaids who brought them.

He smiled into her eyes. 'You aren't the teeniest bit jealous, Ruby, are you?'

'Of course not!' She could feel her cheeks start to burn as she staunchly lifted her chin. 'Why should I be?'

'Why indeed? I shall talk to the housemaids, of course, for it is immensely useful to be a good listener. I learn a great deal that way.' The smile he gave her would, on any other man, have been considered heart stopping. Ruby dubbed it smarmy.

She'd no idea what their purpose was in being here this morning because despite having lived with him now for almost a year, he was still the most secretive, unfathomable, uncommunicative, infuriating man she'd ever met.

And the most intriguing!

The next day they were again in Byrom Street, the baron this time dressed as an insurance clerk, complete with satchel, his rugged good looks hidden behind round spectacles and a neatly clipped moustache. He excited no interest from passers-by, not even from a police constable who stood on the corner of Liverpool Road, since he looked very much the kind of man one might expect to see in the city at this time of day, hurrying back to his office, or out on his rounds collecting weekly payments from clients.

And so it continued, day after day.

As he worked and smiled and talked with the maids, every movement in the street had to be noted: the hour a husband left for work in the morning and the one in which he returned each evening. Which particular morning or afternoon the lady of the household chose to visit her friends, or do her shopping at Kendal Milnes.

He was clever enough to choose a new location from time to time, St John Street or Quay Street, which afforded him a different viewpoint. He would change his disguise completely on each occasion, becoming a window cleaner, street sweeper or hot pie seller; putting on a moustache here, blackening a tooth there, colouring his hair, wearing spectacles and wigs. Even Ruby became dazzled by the variety of roles he adopted over the course of a week, and by his clever cunning and endless patience.

Sometimes she would be dressed in similar rig and given a specific role to play; at other times he would insist she remain hidden and simply observe. She found this the most boring part and said so. 'I don't want to hang around a back alley all day. What is it, exactly, that I'm supposed to be watching out for?'

'I know it is dull, Ruby, having nothing much to do, but I want you to stay out of sight, to keep your eyes and ears open for any comings and goings in the street. One man alone arouses much less attention than a man and a girl hanging about together. Besides,' he stroked her cheek in a lingering caress, 'I'd hate anything to happen to you.'

Ruby didn't believe for one moment that it was for her own safety that he hesitated to use her, only his own. And she hated him for that hypocrisy too.

A pattern soon emerged and each night, back on the tug, he would question her to test her out. He loved it if she had missed some detail that he had spotted.

'Didn't you notice that the man from number one hundred and forty-nine is always late home on a Thursday?' he challenged her as she stood stirring the stew on the stove one evening. 'You must pay particular attention to him, Ruby.'

'Why must I?'

He reached into the pot, tasting the gravy with the tip of his little finger, and smiled his approval. 'Will this be long? I find that I am ravenous, though not only for food.'

His gaze upon hers was steady and Ruby felt her limbs turn to water. Why was it that she could live quite comfortably with this man, but whenever he came too close he filled her with the jitters? He put his hand upon her waist, drew her ever closer, and she was afraid that he might hear the rapid beating of her heart.

'Happen he has a mistress,' she gasped, saying the first thing that came into her head.

'Who?' He seemed to have lost track of their conversation. 'Ah, of course. Why did I not think of that? The value of a woman's viewpoint. Such details could prove most useful.'

He moved smoothly away from her, poured wine into his tankard. Even his choice of drink was different from other men's.

'I'll follow him for a bit then, shall I?' Ruby suggested, snatching at the chance to have some time to herself, to escape from his dominating presence for an hour or two. He seemed to be giving the matter careful thought, shrewdly weighing the suggestion from all angles while his brandy-gold eyes fixed upon her lovely face with an unreadable expression in their depths.

'Very well, but no prancing off and pleasing yourself, as I have eyes and ears everywhere, Ruby. Remember that.'

'As if I would! I'll find out where he works, shall I, and what he does on that particular day of the week?' She beamed cheerfully, hugging to herself the pleasure of seeing him thrown off balance by this show of initiative on her part, plainly unsure if he could trust her, but in the end deciding to risk it.

'I know a good deal about him, where he works and so on, but anything you can discover about his social life could be most valuable, Ruby. Most valuable indeed, and if it turns out that he does have a mistress, follow her too. Anything you can find out about such a creature can only be of benefit to our cause.'

'And what cause might that be?' she cheekily enquired, and he playfully tweaked her nose.

'Perhaps, once I'm certain that I truly can trust you, Ruby McBride, I will tell you everything about myself. Until then you must simply do as you are told, difficult as that may be.'

His hand circled her neck, gently smoothing the nape, and Ruby again began to experience that strange tightening about her ribs, a feeling that left her fighting for breath. 'When have I ever let you down?'

'Just remember, I'll stand no nonsense. Not from anyone. Not even you, Ruby McBride.'

She let out an exasperated sigh. 'Why do you insist on still calling me that after all these months as your wife? When do I become Mrs Stobbs?'

He smiled, though there was sadness still in the intensity of his gaze. 'When you become a proper wife to me, Ruby.' Caught in a trap of her own making, she said no more and concentrated on dishing out the stew.

Chapter Twelve

Pearl was feeling decidedly sorry for herself. She'd satisfactorily disposed of the encumbrance of an unwanted child but had again lost her job as a result. Now she sat on the edge of a kerb, her arms wrapped about her knees, soaking wet and shivering with cold in a cutting December wind, and cursed her blessed sister with every nasty swear word she'd ever learned in the reformatory over the years.

'Happy bleedin' Christmas,' she muttered to herself with feeling.

Had it not been for Ruby's stupid rebellion, she'd never have got into this mess in the first place. It was her sister's fault entirely, and what on earth Pearl was going to do about it, she hadn't the faintest idea.

Somewhere in the distance she heard the hooting of a ship, the sound echoing down the alleyways and empty streets, haunting, melancholy. Pearl shivered. It made her feel as if she were all alone in the world. And then she realised with a shock that this was true. She was alone. She had no one at all to call her own now that she'd lost Ruby and Billy. Where can I go? What can I do? Not back to the reformatory, that much was certain. Pearl hadn't eaten for days and she was ravenous. If she didn't get help soon, she'd starve to death. That's if she didn't die of pneumonia first.

'Are you working, love?' So absorbed had she been in the depths of her own miserable self-pity, she hadn't even heard the man approach.

'Do I look like I am?' she snapped, and then heard the jingle of coins in his pockets and her interest quickened. 'Why d'you want to know?'

'It's a cold night, chuck. Bit o' comfort wouldn't go amiss.' She looked at him more closely. He was a seaman, quite young and not bad-looking, no doubt with a week's wages burning a hole in his pocket. Pearl slowly uncurled herself and stood up, smiling directly into his eyes. 'What is it you fancy?'

—

Once Ruby discovered, to her own satisfaction at least, that the man in question owned Pickering's Wharf which had started up around the same time as the Ship Canal opened, she pursued him no further, fully prepared to tell Bart that he worked late on a Thursday. She made no efforts to discover whether or not he had a mistress. Where was the point? She had more important matters on her mind. She'd heard no word of Pearl, nor any more news of Billy, so she eagerly snatched at this opportunity to set about asking around. She spoke to the people she met in and around the docks, skippers on tugs and barges as well as the dockers who worked on the ships, asking if they'd seen her sister.

'She's only young, just a kid really, quite pretty with yellowish-blonde hair, blue eyes and rather plump. She might be working in a factory or warehouse perhaps, or in service at someone's house.' Ruby checked out every local address suggested but other places could have been on the moon for all the hope she had of getting there.

Sparky Joe ponderously promised to keep an eye out for her, though he didn't hold out much hope of success. His gloomy voice held its usual note of pessimism as he explained just how many factories, mills and warehouses there were in the canal basin, let alone in Manchester as a whole.

She got exactly the same reaction when she asked about Billy. 'Do you know which liners carried orphans and destitute children out to Canada a few years back, and to which part of the country they might have gone?'

Heads would be shaken, lips chewed in quiet contemplation. Nobody knew anything for certain although various possibilities were mentioned by people trying to be helpful, which left Ruby more depressed than ever as her dreams of starting a new life across the seas in a faraway land seemed doomed to failure.

And what if she ever did manage to reach Canada? That would mean she'd never see Kit Jarvis ever again. This was such a bleak prospect that it made her feel sick inside. It came to her with a jolt that for all these months, while she'd been asking after Pearl, she'd also been secretly keeping a sharp lookout for Kit too. Hoping for one glimpse of his cheery face, his twinkly blue eyes. Oh, it would be so good to see him again. He couldn't be too far away, surely.

It was perhaps a forlorn hope but he may be able to help her find Pearl, then they could all travel to Canada together, which would be grand. What would it matter then if she was still married? Even the baron couldn't follow her to the other side of the world, could he?

Ruby felt more buoyed up with hope than she had in months. She set about her enquiries without wasting another minute, and to hell with the flippin' baron and his schemes. What did it matter if one of his scams didn't come off for once? Serve him right. She had more important matters to attend to.

–

On their third visit to Byrom Street, the preparations were entirely different. This time there was no disguise, no subterfuge, not for the baron. Today he walked the length of it bold as brass.

Ruby kept well back, hidden in the shadows of an alleyway, with strict instructions to keep a weather eye on the goings on in the street and to call him instantly should she see any sort of trouble or disturbance. What shape this might take he didn't say, and Ruby didn't ask. She really didn't see it as her concern, any more than what he'd been talking about in hushed undertones half the night with his docker cronies, well into the small hours. Ruby was determined not to get involved in anything remotely illegal, and would very much like to have refused to accompany him today, had she not known that he was perfectly capable of dragging her here in ball and chain, if necessary. Now she watched in mutinous silence as he knocked on the door of number one hundred and forty-nine.

She saw him speak quietly to the maid who answered, doffing his hat courteously to her. She couldn't hear the words exchanged between them but after a short discussion the maid disappeared inside to return seconds later, smiling, to invite him in. Bart didn't even turn to glance in Ruby's direction, he simply smoothed down his slicked hair and stepped over the threshold.

Ruby was flabbergasted. 'What a cheek!' And what was she supposed to do now, besides keep a lookout for this imaginary disturbance? No doubt a tale he'd made up to be sure she didn't wander off and enjoy herself. The more Ruby thought about him dallying with some pretty housemaid while she stood about on a cold winter's day, the angrier she got. It was not simply because of the inclement weather. What sort of behaviour was this for a married man? She very nearly marched right over and hammered on the front door to ask him. No doubt he would be inside for hours, up to goodness knows what mischief.

Ruby flounced a few paces further up the alley, resolving to pay no attention at all to what might be going on behind the lace curtains of number one hundred and forty-nine, nor to his carefully spelled out instructions about disturbances. If the police came, let them discover his conman disguise, arrest and lock him up in some dark prison and throw away the key. Serve him right. She'd be the first to dance at his trial, and on his grave if it came to that.

She became so consumed with dreaming up these satisfying images that it was some long moments before the unusual noises in the street penetrated her consciousness. Only when the sound grew to the unmistakable clatter of hundreds of pairs of feet on cobbles did she run to the end of the alley and gaze, dumbstruck, at the sight that met her eyes. It wasn't a made-up tale after all!

A band of dockers were marching along, carrying banners. In bold lettering these proclaimed such statements as: *A man's pay for a man's work. No more slave labour.* And: *A living wage for all.* What were they saying? Were they threatening to strike?

She was aware of bitter grievances among the men, knew that they felt themselves grossly underpaid. Now it seemed their patience had worn thin. But if they went on strike what would that achieve? They'd only irritate their bosses, could well lose their jobs as a result and then their families would starve since there was no work to be found elsewhere.

But they weren't alone. A pace or two behind marched the women. Wrapped in their shawls and tattered working frocks, some carrying babies or dragging children by the hand, they were bravely displaying their solidarity with their menfolk. They weren't shouting or even singing, the only sound they made that of their clog irons on the setts: a bleak hollow clatter with a sad echo in its wake.

Ruby hovered in the shadows while she watched their silent approach in an anguish of indecision. Could this be what Bart had meant when he'd asked her to warn him if there was trouble? Surely not. How could he have known that they might come along the street today?

There came a far more forbidding sound, one that chilled her to the bone. It was that of police whistles, and booted feet running down the street. They seemed to come from every direction to confront the procession of dockers. Ruby saw the men stop marching and grow instantly tense. She recognised the grim expressions in faces gaunt with hunger as they set back their shoulders as if mentally gearing themselves for a fight.

Ruby went cold with fear. She'd let Bart down by not keeping a proper lookout. What should she do now?

At the same instant, the door of number one hundred and forty-nine burst open and a man stormed out into the middle of the road. It was the very same gentleman Bart had asked her to follow. Giles Pickering. Now she wished with all her heart that she'd carried out Bart's instructions to the letter, certain that she'd failed everyone in some way that she didn't quite understand.

Pickering stood side by side with the approaching police, shaking his fist at the band of dockers. 'I'll have no trouble here. Go home this minute, if you know what's good for you.'

While he shouted and raved at the silent group, Ruby saw another figure slip out through the door of the house behind him. Bart himself. She thought he meant to make his escape, to vanish quietly before the police or the householder decided to investigate what mischief he'd been up to in there: either seducing the parlour maid or stealing the silver. Instead, he sauntered into the middle of the road, positioning himself in front of the leading docker, then turned to confront the other man who was by now seething with rage.

Bart's voice rang out, clear and strong. 'You can't say I didn't warn you, Pickering. Haven't I been telling you for some time that there was the threat of just such a demonstration taking place?'

Pickering's lean face, with its little goatee beard and neatly clipped moustache, showed not a trace of emotion. Only the tension in his voice revealed his deep anger. 'And I've told you, Bart – baron – or whatever you call yourself these days, that I'll not negotiate with agitators, yourself included. I refuse to be blackmailed into…'

Bart didn't wait for him to finish before insolently interrupting, 'No one is blackmailing you, but you'll have to start listening soon. These men have a right to put forward their case, to make a silent protest.'

'Not on my street they don't. You can play your damn silly games of subterfuge, make out you're not bent on stirring up trouble, but I know that you are, as do the police here. I'll not risk my business being ruined by unions, nor tolerate strikes of any sort, for any reason. Not in *my* yard. Involve yourself in this sort of socialist, reactionary mischief and your card is marked. I'll see you finished, boy, for inciting this sort of violence.'

'Don't call me that. I'm nobody's boy. And I've witnessed no sign of violence here. Even the police constables are, I think, satisfied on that score, since they are standing patiently by doing nothing. And you can't "mark my card" because I'm not employed by you, not any more. I'm not employed by anyone, praise be. Unlike these poor souls here. All they want is for their union rights to be recognised, a fair day's pay for a fair day's work. What is so wrong in that?'

'Aye, that's all we want. It's our right.'

'Hear, hear.' A murmur of agreement rippled through the length of the procession.

'These people are suffering from genuine privation, and are simply attempting to demonstrate that fact in a respectable and mannerly fashion.'

Pickering spoke through gritted teeth. 'Utter poppycock! They're naught but troublemakers, and you're encouraging them, damn you!'

'It is not poppycock when a man is compelled to pawn the clothes off his back in order to feed his children, or when he must choose between a roof over their heads or food on the table – assuming he hasn't had to pawn that too.'

'Aye, true enough,' Tom Wright's voice rang out, and a rumble of voices agreed.

Ruby saw how the police pushed forward, lifting their truncheons in a menacing fashion.

'I'd take care if I were you,' Pickering warned, wagging a finger in Bart's face. 'You know the House of Lords ruling as well as I do. If these union members of yours go out on strike, they'll be liable for any financial losses the company sustains. I'd take that into account if I were you, before advising them of their so-called rights.'

Despite the threat, Bart pressed on undaunted. 'That was a crazy judgement, and one we'll continue to resist. As it happens these men are not on strike, not yet, so nothing they are doing here today is unlawful. I live and work side by side with these dockers and they're not troublemakers. They are desperate men. They work from dawn till dusk shovelling coal or heaving cotton, carrying goods on your barges, and earn coppers at the end of it. And that's no one's fault but their employers', of which you are one. You were the ones who negotiated uneconomic rates for haulage but *they* are the ones to suffer. They don't work for you out of charity, or a sense of loyalty, but from fear. Fear of sickness and starvation, fear of debt and homelessness, and worst of all, fear of losing their jobs.'

'Which you are risking by encouraging them in this sort of lawlessness! However, since you seem to be the only one they'll listen to, tell them to go home, now, before it's too late.'

Watching from the shadows, Ruby recognised and understood the dilemma the men found themselves facing. They were valiantly attempting to stand up for their rights yet did indeed fear for their jobs. She could see it in their haunted eyes.

Sparky's lugubrious face loomed up out of the crowd. 'We're going nowhere till we get satisfaction.'

Twin spots of colour like ripe plums had appeared on the ashen planes of Pickering's flat cheeks. 'How dare you! I'll not be threatened by my own workers, nor tolerate this manifestation of civil disorder. It's inconceivable that such a blatant display of anarchy should take place in my own street, before my own front door. My wife is upstairs cowering in fear, and no wonder. You would never see me and mine involved in this sort of despicable behaviour.'

'That's because you've no need,' cried a woman's voice from the back of the crowd which had gathered to watch events. 'Since you know where your next slice of daily bread is coming from.'

'Hush up, Aggie. Don't make things worse,' Sparky yelled back at her.

While the two men had been arguing, the police had quietly split into two groups, lining the street on either side in an almost threatening way. On hearing the woman call out, a policeman advanced upon her, looking for all the world as if he meant to strike her with his truncheon. Despite her brave words, she cowered before him, a child held tight in her arms as she began quietly to weep.

Without pausing for thought Ruby ran out into the street. 'Leave off, you great bully. Can't you see the babby in her arms?' She wrapped her arms protectively around both woman and child and glared up at the constable, her face a picture of defiant insolence. The air was suddenly charged with danger, yet Ruby held on, unrepentant, her voice rich with challenge. 'Go on then. Hit women and childer, why don't you? Show us what a fine man you are.'

The constable looked into those blazing, beautiful eyes and hesitated.

'Well, what are you waiting for? Let's see just how brave you are.'

A hush fell upon the entire street, broken after a long, paralysing moment by a loud commanding voice. 'What's going on here?'

All eyes swivelled in its direction, watching in awe as the chief constable himself strode towards them. Even before he had uttered a word, people began to melt away, the crowd quietly to disperse. Ruby could almost smell their alarm. Only Bart remained where he was, thumbs in his waistcoat pocket, standing before them as the baron, voice of the people. What a man, proud and defiant as always! Just watching him brought a rush of unexpected emotion to catch her by the throat.

Giles Pickering was politely requested to withdraw, which he did with obvious reluctance, going to stand at his own front door in an aggressively defensive stance.

The chief constable turned to Bart and addressed him in quiet, reasonable tones, clearly bent on calming a dangerous situation. 'Don't think I'm unaware of your activities, Stobbs, despite your efforts to disguise the true purpose of these dangerous antics. It is not my place to take sides but this is yet another example of your coming perilously close to breaking the law. My men have been keeping a watch on you and your fellow agitators for some considerable time. You've been lucky today. This demonstration, as you call it, could easily have turned into a riot. I want no illegal...'

Bart interrupted him. 'Peaceful trade union meetings and demonstrations are perfectly legal, despite the efforts of the judges to destroy us through bankruptcy.'

The chief constable looked irritated and confused. 'All right then, if not exactly illegal I'll not have unofficial trade union activities on my patch, however worthy you may believe them to be. I'll give you five minutes to clear this street, or I'm taking you in for creating a disturbance. Move. Now!'

Bart remained steadfast for another half second, and then politely doffed his bowler hat and smiled. 'I thank you, sir, and your officers here, for your exemplary patience. We will peacefully depart, as I believe our point has been made. Good day to you, sir.' And bowing slightly to the chief constable, he cast Pickering a last, withering glance before swivelling on his heel and striding away. The street, by this time, was completely empty.

–

'Why didn't you tell me you were a union man?' Ruby considered confessing to negligence over her assigned duties but her courage failed her at the last moment.

'You never asked, having already made up your mind about me. Besides, admitting to union activity only invites trouble in today's unsettled world.'

'And what was all that about judges and rules you needed to fight?'

Bart took a long draft of his wine to cool his anger. 'You wouldn't understand.'

'Try me. I'm not stupid.'

He considered her with a wry smile. 'No, Ruby McBride! No one could ever accuse you of being stupid. Well then, they've decided that although unions may be legal, strike action is not. It's all a result of a strike last year by the employees of the Taff Vale Railway Company. They were blamed for loss of profits. As a result the company brought an action for damages against them. It bankrupted the union.'

'Why ever did they take such a risk in the first place?'

'Their cause was just, in their opinion, and they thought themselves protected by the Trade Union Act. When it came to court, however, the judges decided otherwise. It's a decision that rebounds upon us all, Ruby, putting the power back into the hands of the employer.'

'Into the hands of men like Giles Pickering?'

'Yes, sadly into the hands of men like him. If he thinks he can squeeze a bit of extra profit by underpaying his workers, he will do so. I'm seen as a socialist dissident and so, growing tired of constantly being picked on by the police and taken in for questioning, let's say I deem it politic to adopt a change of appearance once in a while.'

She looked at him keenly, seeing him for the first time in a different light. Could he be more honest than she gave him credit for? Could she trust him? 'There's more to it than that, surely? What about those other occasions, like the trick on the pawnbroker, when you actually took money which didn't belong to you?'

'However true though that might be, in theory, his interest charges were extortionate and the money rightly belonged to my men. More often than not they had paid through the nose without the item they were attempting to redeem being returned to them. We – *I* – decided to do something about it.'

Ruby gave a brittle little laugh of disbelief. 'What are you then, some sort of Robin Hood? Or Saint George slaying the dragon?'

'A happy notion, Ruby, but although much of the money goes to the poor, to those in most need, I am neither folk hero nor saint. Would that I were. I can say no more.' He leaned closer, the whisper of his breath caressing her skin. 'Remember, so far I haven't trusted you any more than you have trusted me. Perhaps you were right to criticise, but aren't you glad I'm not quite the devil you once imagined me to be?'

Chapter Thirteen

A few days later, Ruby woke to find Bart dressed in frock coat, wide silk tie with a stiff collar, figured silk waistcoat and top hat. His appearance had been completely altered with the addition of false whiskers and a droopy moustache, which obscured his mouth. Again he wore the padding about his stomach that turned him into a paunchy, mature figure. Ruby almost laughed out loud, so ludicrous did he appear, but then recognised the challenging glitter in his eyes and thought better of it.

'Who are you today? Some posh gent off to the opera?'

'The name is Joshua Parker, engineer to the Manchester Ship Canal Company board. Not that it's any business of yours, you young chit. I tell you what you need to know, as and when you need to know it.'

'I've noticed. Is that Sir or plain mister?'

He chuckled. 'Good idea Ruby! Let's make me a Sir, shall we?'

Ruby turned her back on him and stalked away, head high, not wanting him to see the laughter in her eyes. What a card he was. Which poor soul was going to suffer today? she wondered.

After a breakfast of kippers and toast, he instructed her to put on her best dress, bonnet and shawl. She never failed to feel a huge relief at no longer being obliged to wear the dreaded uniform which had so loudly proclaimed her to be at the bottom of the heap, so far as status in the community was concerned. He'd taken her to visit the Flat Iron Market, bought fabric for her to make herself up two frocks, a warm brown one that she wore every day, and a navy blue serge for Sundays. In addition, the baron had provided her with this very plain bonnet and shawl, boots and thick woollen stockings, all of which he happened to have already in his metal chest. Ruby didn't investigate too closely how he'd come by them, she was simply glad to have them. But to wear her Sunday frock in the middle of the week was unheard of, and made her shudder to imagine what he was up to now.

On this particular day they didn't walk through the city streets, as they normally did, nor even take the tram to wherever it was they were going. Instead, he hired a rather smart little gig and, despite her misgivings, Ruby was entranced by it, feeling mighty important and grand to be sitting up so high and looking out at the world over the back of a fine bay mare. She was less thrilled as they ventured out into the hurly-burly of the traffic with the baron weaving his way, at what seemed to be breakneck speed, between omnibuses and electric trams, bakers' carts and carriages of all sizes, nearly knocking over one crossing sweeper in the process.

'Hey, where's the fire? I'd like to get there in one piece, if you don't mind. Where are we going in such a tearing hurry?'

'There and back, to see how far it is.'

'Oh, very droll!'

He didn't slow the pace until they were well out into the Cheshire countryside, by which time Ruby felt sufficiently relaxed to loosen her grip on the handrail. But he offered no further explanation until they approached a lodge house by a set of gates, with a glimpse of a large mansion set at the end of a long drive. For one dreadful moment Ruby thought he was taking her to another reformatory or convent school and she almost leapt out of her seat. 'I'm not going in there! You said I was done with all of that.'

He seemed to find her reaction so amusing that he laughed loud and long, the first sound he'd made throughout the entire journey. But he drew the horse to a halt and finally turned to address her. 'You remember the name I told you?'

'Sorry, *Sir* Joshua Parker,' Ruby obediently repeated, well used to this routine.

'And you are my fiancée.'

Ruby accepted this fact without argument and tucked her wedding ring into her purse, out of sight. 'What is my name?' Her gaze upon his was steady, resigned and yet alert, anxious not to make any mistakes.

He was smiling down at her, giving her the impression, as always, that he could actually read her thoughts. 'You can keep your own name, Ruby, along with your virtue, so long as you recognise that we are soon to christen this very practical marriage of ours, hopefully by the time you reach nineteen in July. A twelve-month wait is long enough, I reckon.'

'Thanks for the warning.' She wasn't concerned. Not for a moment. A lot could happen before July.

They were admitted into the house without hesitation. The bay mare and gig were attended to by a groom in the yard while Bart and Ruby were shown into the library where the lady of the house, a Mrs Jessica Pickering, welcomed them with outstretched hand, charming smile firmly in place. Ruby recognised the woman's surname instantly. It was the same as the man's at the demonstration in Byrom Street. No wonder the baron was in heavy disguise.

She knew that the men at Pickering's Wharf had called off their strike and backed away from further confrontation, despite heated arguments with Bart long into the night. He'd grown angry at their decision, accusing them of being lily-livered cowards.

'Nay, we've no money, so how can we risk it? We can't let us childer starve.' Sparky had told him, and in the end Bart had claimed to wash his hands of the whole lot of them. Ruby knew this to be a lie, as did the men who'd walked away, shoulders hunched with despair. The baron would rise again and save them, they knew it. They had to believe in him, for who else cared?

Had this trip today any connection with the men's reluctance to strike? she wondered.

Mrs Pickering offered them each a glass of sherry before they embarked upon a tour of the property and for the first time it became clear to Ruby how it was they'd so easily gained entrance. The house was for sale and Bart was pretending to be a prospective purchaser. She'd no notion of the extent of his finances but couldn't imagine them stretching to buy this place, an Elizabethan manor house of some distinction. He had evidently seen an advertisement in the *Manchester Guardian* and had written to make an appointment for a viewing.

Ruby was introduced as his 'beloved wife-to-be' with comments on how fortunate he was to capture such a young beauty at an age when he'd believed himself to be a confirmed bachelor. Ruby became the object of much polite interest and speculation about how she thought she might take to life as the wife of a talented engineer who had worked on this marvellous new project, "the big ditch", as the Ship Canal was affectionately known. This amused her no end.

So that was who he was supposed to be, she thought, smiling and nodding as if charmed by the whole idea.

The lady of the house redirected her attention to Sir Joshua, whom she clearly found far more interesting. 'Perhaps you know my husband, Giles Pickering? He has a business in the canal basin, and has done rather well with it.'

'Indeed? I am acquainted with the name, though it is a vast area – Salford Docks, the Canal, and Trafford Park. One cannot know everyone personally.'

'Of course not! But when you first walked in the door I was quite certain we must have met before.' She smiled at him, a slight frown puckering her brow.

'Perhaps at some function or other?'

'Perhaps so.'

In no time Bart had taken control of the conversation and was well into his stride, smoothing the droopy moustache as if it had always flourished there. He sipped sweet sherry while postulating grandly about the development of Trafford Park, claiming to have satisfied even the shareholders in the end, despite a poor showing thus far. He sounded almost as if he knew what he was talking about. He then progressed to outline their plans for a summer wedding and a honeymoon on the Isle of Wight. The woman simpered and gushed, addressing him constantly as 'my dear Sir Joshua', finally offering a convoluted explanation of her reasons for moving, which involved an 'incompatibility with the countryside' and a necessity to seek softer climes.

'My health is so delicate, don't you know, that my doctor has advised Italy or the South of France.'

'I'm sure that would be most wise.'

'I am not nearly so young as your young lady here, nor as robust as you undoubtedly are, *dear* Sir Joshua.' She fluttered her eyelashes extravagantly at him, clearly hoping for a denial. She was not disappointed.

He took a monocle from his waistcoat pocket and examined her quizzically through the eyeglass. 'I beg to disagree ma'am. I am sure you must have all the young beaux queuing to sign your dance card, and once the kinder climate of the continent has brought back the colour to your cheeks, I am quite certain you will set the whole place on fire with your beauty.'

His smile was dazzling, as if he truly were captivated by her charms while the woman appeared riveted, hanging upon every word of this supposedly rich and titled gentleman. Ruby nearly burst her sides with stifled laughter at the performance. She had to admit the woman was attractive, if a year or two older than the baron in actual fact, did she but know it, being probably in her mid-thirties. Bart played the middle-aged roué to perfection while flirting outrageously with her!

'And what does your husband say to all of this? Is he happy to decamp to the continent?'

'*Dearest* Giles spoils me dreadfully. This was the house he shared with his first wife and understands how dreadfully that depresses me. He also owns a small town house close to the wharf, though I loathe staying there even more. So many odours from the canal, most unpleasant! He is to build me a new mansion. One convenient for the city, without being in the rough and tumble of it, and also a home on the continent.'

'A most generous man.' Bart's words came out sharply through gritted teeth and Ruby glanced up, puzzled. Jessica Pickering giggled girlishly, and went on to give a good many more details about the fragile state of her health, her need for company – of the right sort, of course – and the generosity of her husband. Ruby stopped listening and wandered off to look out of the long casement windows on to a formal rose garden. This was a fine house. Why would anyone want to leave it? Imagine having the money to own and live in such a property. How was it some could have so much while others, like Ruby's own mother, never had anything they could call their own? No wonder she'd died of consumption after all the damp, awful places they'd lived in. Didn't seem right somehow.

Finally, Ruby heard the woman say, 'Oh dear, I really mustn't twitter on any further, nor presume any longer upon your good nature, dear Sir Joshua. I'm sure a busy man, such as yourself, has a great many more calls upon his time. Perhaps you would like my butler to show you around now, without further delay?'

'That would be most kind.'

'Would it not be inconvenient for you to live here? It is rather far out,' she said with a slight puckering of her smooth brow. 'Did you say that you worked at the dock office by the canal or in the company office on Spring Gardens?'

'It would be ideal,' Bart assured her, without answering her question. 'I have been fortunate enough to be left a legacy. Of modest proportions, you understand, but sufficient to provide my dearest beloved with, shall we say, more appropriate accommodation than can be found in the city centre.'

'Oh, how very splendid! Indeed, splendid.' She quite perked up at the mention of a legacy, clearly hoping it was not too modest and could stretch to the price she had in mind. 'Shall we proceed?' she trilled.

'Indeed. Perhaps we could begin with the study?' Bart swung around, indicating a heavy oak door set in the corner of the room.

Jessica Pickering looked surprised. 'How did you guess that was my husband's study?'

For the first time, Ruby saw confusion on his face, as if he'd been caught out in some mistake, and wondered anxiously if the woman would notice but then he brushed the awkward moment aside with a dismissive bark of laughter. 'Seemed logical. A gentleman knows these things, ma'am.'

'Of course.' Seemingly unconcerned, she sailed before him into the room, and Ruby followed more thoughtfully.

The tour seemed to go on indefinitely, with Ruby trailing along behind, attempting to look suitably impressed and even, at times, enchanted by the delights of the property he was promising to purchase for her. Afterwards they were offered luncheon, which Bart reluctantly declined due to yet another board meeting he must attend that very afternoon, he ruefully explained. He promised to be in touch soon, via Mrs Pickering's solicitors, and courteously took his leave. To Ruby, the whole thing seemed to have been a complete waste of a morning.

'What was all that in aid of, all that rubbish about board meetings, a summer wedding, and a honeymoon on the Isle of Wight?' she asked, as they bowled back into town. 'Got a bit carried away, didn't you?'

'Perhaps I did, but I became quite engrossed by the whole notion of a honeymoon, Ruby. Perhaps we should consider it. Why not?'

She chose to ignore this comment. 'Have you ever been in that house before?'

His hand tightened on the reins and Ruby knew that he lied when he said, 'No, of course not. Whatever put such an idea into your head?'

'Only that you seemed to know where the study was.'

'Such rooms are generally found off the main living room, are they not?'

Ruby hadn't the faintest idea where a study might be found, since never in her life had she been in such a grand house before. Judiciously, she let the subject drop. 'Thought any minute you'd be describing what the bridesmaids would be wearing.'

'Perhaps that's because I was engaged once before but it ended tragically so I was hoping for better luck this time, that we could perhaps achieve a happy marriage.'

The smile slid from Ruby's lips. 'Happy marriage, don't talk daft! Look, you can stop this game right here. We're on our own now. You're talking to me, Ruby McBride, not Lady Muck in there.'

'It's no game, Ruby. It's true. Give me the chance, and I'll do my best to make you happy.'

'What happened to her then, your fiancée?'

It was some moments before he answered and then it was in a hushed, quiet voice, barely above a whisper. 'I was very young and recklessly, heedlessly, in love. Tragically, she went into a decline and the wedding was called off.'

'What sort of decline?'

'She became depressed over the fact that our respective families were against the match, which finally resulted in some sort of breakdown. After months of ill health her doctor advised against marriage, saying she was quite unsuited to the sort of demands it would impose upon her. It was all pretty dreadful. I was utterly devastated and swore I would never allow myself to love again. Which is how I came to acquire the barge. I needed a fresh start, a new beginning.'

For a moment Ruby couldn't speak, surprised by these revelations as it was the most she'd ever learned about his past and she itched to know more. But seeing him with his mouth compressed and shoulders drooping, she guessed that for once he might well be telling her the truth, and that it pained him to do so. 'So why did you want to wed me?' she asked instead.

He slowed the mare to a walk before cocking his head sideways, so he could consider her in all seriousness with his brandy-coloured eyes. 'Perhaps I was attracted to your sharp brain.'

'You married me for me *brains*? I've never heard anything so daft in all me life.' A gurgle of laughter bubbled up in her throat and Ruby simply couldn't resist laughing, swaying backwards in the carriage so that her body arched unconsciously in provocative abandonment while, unnoticed by her, his eyes slid lingeringly over the curve of her throat and breasts. After a moment, Ruby wiped the tears of laughter from her eyes with the flat of her hands. 'More likely you picked me 'cause you fancied me. But you can stop slavering because you ain't going to get me.' There was steel behind the camouflage of humour, which he duly recognised. Yet he had the grace to smile.

'It's true, I did fancy you from the first moment I set eyes on you. But then you aren't simply pretty, Ruby, you're beautiful. Didn't anyone ever tell you?'

'Sister Joseph certainly didn't, that's for sure. Nor did anyone in the reformatory, no,' Ruby drily remarked. 'But then there aren't many good-looking fellas in there, and what chance have I had to meet any out here, with you watching every move I make?'

'I like to keep an eye on what belongs to me.'

'I don't belong to no one,' she snapped.

'Yes, you do, Ruby. You are mine. Exclusively. Make no mistake about that. My reaction to you certainly came as a surprise, particularly in the circumstances. However, having decided that I wanted you, I had every intention of getting you. I'm not a man who takes no for an answer.'

'I'd noticed.'

He gave a lazy smile. 'I can understand your resenting my forcing you into marriage. How was it Miss Crombie described you? Ah, yes, as having an "individual and determined nature". But I think you will come to see that our arrangement is for the best.'

Ruby made as if to interrupt at this point, wanting to protest that surely she should be the one to choose what was best for herself, but he held up one hand to silence her.

'It will be worth it in the end. I shall see that you want for nothing, a house, a carriage of your own, servants, and I'm a man of means, Ruby. I've kept my promises thus far, have I not? Not laid a finger where I shouldn't. Provided you with a home and employment, food in your belly and clothes for your back. Perhaps it's time we sealed the bargain. Time you gave me something in return for my generosity. I haven't even kissed you or tasted any of your charms, and I am your very own, loving husband after all.' He reached for her and she slapped his hand away, her voice filled with loathing.

'*You*, keep your promises?' she sneered. 'Pull the other leg and see if that's got bells on it. I told you, you don't touch me till I say you can, which will be when hell freezes over and not a day before.'

'Whatever the weather in heaven or hell, Ruby, I mean to have you.' The glitter in those liquid eyes was ominous as Ruby returned his glare with loathing, yet there was a tremor of excitement within her that she didn't quite understand. She was breathing fast and furious as she desperately strove to stem the tide of panic, which was surely all she was suffering from. Could he be serious? How much longer could she hold him off? She did not ask herself how she would react if she failed in that task. She dare not.

'What about our Pearl? You promised you'd give my sister a home too, if I behaved myself. Which I have, so when are you going to do something about that?'

'You drive a hard bargain, Ruby. It would be a shame if we were to have a falling out, when we've been getting along so well.'

She edged away from him on the narrow seat, making sure no part of her dress touched him. 'Not for one minute do I believe all this fanciful talk of fine houses, and I've seen little sign of respectability or security. I'm living on my nerves here with all your nasty goings on.'

He seemed to consider this remark for some time before answering in softer tones. 'What does a chap have to do to win your heart, Ruby?'

'Try going straight.' Seeing his eyes narrow dangerously and feeling again that tremor akin to fear, she deliberately adjusted her tone, attempting to lighten it, even managing to smile flirtatiously up at him. 'A bit of honesty wouldn't go amiss for a change, now would it?'

'Why do you always see the worst in me? That is so sad. When you smile at me so enticingly, I melt inside. I'm a man with a heart, Ruby, like any other. What was it that Shakespeare said? Something along the lines of, "If you prick me, will I not bleed?"'

Ruby snorted her disdain. 'Who's he when he's at home? We didn't do no Shakespeare in the reformatory, and I'll believe you have a heart when I come across a pig what can fly.'

'Perhaps I have good reason for what I do, have you considered that?'

'Aye, to make your pocket fatter.'

'I mean, you didn't know about my union involvement, did you?'

'Is that what this is all about? Is that the whole reason why you steal and play tricks on folk? Is that what this morning's trip was about, union business?'

He sadly shook his head and she slumped back in her seat, eyes blazing with triumph. 'Thought not.'

'But maybe you don't know everything about me, even now. Maybe there are a few more layers still to peel off, rather like an onion.' He smiled as she lapsed into confused silence, then clicked the reins, urging the mare to a brisker trot. 'As for that other, more personal matter between us, my patience will not last forever, Ruby McBride. You'd best start expecting a visitor one night to that chaste cabin of yours. And don't think you can keep me out by locking the damned door. I've my own key. Make no mistake about that!'

Ruby gasped, this thought never having entered her head. 'Drat you... I'll have a bolt fitted on the inside.'

'The panels are not robust. I can easily take the door off at the hinges once I'm ready to come to you. Oh, and I almost forgot, you may have these as a wedding gift.' Dipping into a pocket, he pulled out a pendant of sparkling gems, which he laid in her lap. 'It's a ruby I believe. Appropriate, don't you think? Not such a wasted morning, after all, eh?'

–

She had thought herself so clever, imagined she could hold him off, even persuade him to go straight by working hard with the tug and the barges, and then he'd handed her the pendant. Ruby realised, in that moment, that she had absolutely no control over what he did with her, and never would have. Her desire to reform him, suddenly seemed foolish, her efforts at obedience in order to win his assistance in finding Pearl utterly naive. What a soft fool she'd been to imagine he'd even listen to her. Oh, but she was in a proper pickle this time, that was for sure. Escape from the baron would be nowhere near as easy as her previous attempts at flight. He was surely an expert in utter ruthlessness.

She'd been appalled by the gift. Never, in all her life, had she knowingly performed a dishonest act, no matter what the authorities might accuse her of, nor had she any intention of starting now. Ruby refused, absolutely, to accept the pendant, arguing that he should never have stolen it in the first place, and should take it back, which he seemed to think most amusing. 'Are you accusing me of stealing it?'

'I'm not stupid, as I know you stole it. You must take it back this instant.'

'And what would I say to her, Ruby my love? "Well, would you believe it, missus? This ruby pendant fell into me pocket, just as I was being shown around your lovely house. Fancy that!"'

Ruby thought about this for a moment. 'You could ask for another viewing, and slip it back when no one was looking.'

'That wouldn't be appropriate.'

'Why wouldn't it?'

'Because I say so. My skill lies in discretion and speed. Once having formulated a plan, I move in quickly, carry it out and leave with equal speed. Not even that hawk-eyed butler saw it go, now did he?'

'Soon as they realise it's missing, they'll guess it was you what took it,' Ruby warned.

'What good will that do? How can they find Sir Joshua Parker, when he doesn't exist? I never return or use exactly the same disguise twice. Besides, she can afford it. Did you see the emeralds dangling from her ears? Made of money, she is. Won't miss the odd trinket here and there. And for all you know, she may not have come by it honestly herself.'

Ruby gave up. It was impossible to reason with someone who clearly had his own twisted sense of morality.

Chapter Fourteen

The second gin had gone down much quicker than the first, nicely lifting the chill off her stomach. But then it was warm anyway in the tavern, with the press of all the sweaty bodies around her. It stank of coal dust, beer and body odour, but that didn't trouble Pearl in the slightest. She probably ponged a bit herself, but then who would care or even notice? These men, factory hands and tradesmen of all sorts, were more interested in the contents of their glass and the need to wash the day's dust and tiredness from their throats.

All told, Pearl decided, life was pretty good. She'd just enjoyed a substantial dinner of roast beef and Yorkshire with one of her clients, with a couple more lined up to while away a happy and profitable afternoon which would pay for her supper, as well as contributing towards the rent on the room she'd found for herself here in Rochdale.

The young seaman who had started all of this weeks ago, in Pearl's estimation had done her a favour. He'd chanced along at just the right moment. This was the easiest, most pleasurable way of making a living anyone could imagine, and one she might never have considered had she not found herself in such dire straits. Pearl felt as if she were in clover. Since then, of course, there'd been a whole stream of men, young and old, in need of a bit of comfort, whom Pearl was more than willing to oblige. She took great pride in her work, made sure her customers were given the kind of care she felt they needed. Everybody deserved a bit of loving after all. She certainly did and, so far, touch wood, she'd had no trouble from any of them.

'Now then, Pearl. How you feeling?'

'Champion, thanks.'

'Are you working today, lass?'

She smiled and twirled her empty glass. 'I'm allus working, love. But I'm busy this afternoon.'

The man took the glass from her with a grin. 'Can I see you later then?'

'I always find time for you, Tommy.'

'Aye, yer a grand lass! Do you need a top up of gin?'

'Ta, love.' That was another thing! She had friends and folk who talked to her like a human being, instead of a number.

Tommy came to her in the early evening. 'Just a quick one, chuck, before supper.'

He was old and it didn't take much more than a kiss and cuddle to keep him happy. He just loved to touch her young, firm flesh. Pearl sent him off a happy man, tucking away the shilling he'd given her in the pocket she'd stitched into her skirt. She'd no intention of finding herself on the brink of starvation ever again, nor up the duff. She'd learned ways to stop that little problem happening again. How could she afford to keep a child when she could barely afford to feed herself? She was only sixteen, after all. Her childish plumpness had been replaced by a newly voluptuous figure, one which men appreciated. Her cheeks were rosy and pink, and her dandelion-yellow hair had disappeared beneath a liberal application of henna.

'I'm a survivor,' she told herself, countless times in a day. She was back in the tavern the next day, and the one after that, it being her favourite place for picking up clients. The rest of the time her pitch was a stretch of road near the gasworks. But it must be carried out with discretion. Not for the world would she risk the rozzers getting wind of her activities since they took a somewhat narrow-minded view of soliciting, as if sex were an activity reserved exclusively for the legally married.

Pearl kept well away from Salford and Castlefield, the canal basin and the railway arches, because she still had bad memories of Sister Joseph on the prowl down there, the sound of police whistles and Billy screaming the place down. Gave her the shivers just to think of it. And not for one moment did she imagine that the old dragon would be dead, not after only seven years. What's more, the woman would have a long memory and be short on sympathy for Pearl's situation, her being a nun.

It was one evening as she sat enjoying a drink, between clients as it were, that a fight broke out. Pearl paid little attention. Bar-room brawls were commonplace when drink got the better of the men who packed this place to the doors night after night, usually finishing off in the street with a jeering crowd to cheer them on, bets being placed on the likely winner. This one was no different, or at least it seemed not to be, until she heard a familiar voice.

'I'll beat yer bloody brains in, if'n you call me that again.'

'Nay, it's true enough. Thou art scum. Nothing less. You were scum when you went into the reformatory, and scum when you came out.'

Curious to check on her suspicions, Pearl picked up her glass and wandered over. One man was sitting astride the other who lay prone beneath him on the floor. The one on top had his fist raised, preparatory to knocking his opponent's brains out.

Pearl bent over for a closer look, eyes wide with surprise. 'Kit?'

She would have known him anywhere. The slouch cap was still miraculously in place at the back of his head, the thick crop of shaggy black hair, the brilliant blue eyes. The only difference was that his face was now more mature, the lines at each corner of his mouth seeming to harden and sharpen the sunken planes of his face. The once pale skin was now dark and swarthy, no doubt from years spent working on the deck of the reformatory training ship. It was the face of a man who was a youth no longer, a man who had looked into the jaws of his own personal hell and somehow survived. Pearl recognised this in him instantly, and welcomed it as a form of kinship.

She grinned, lifted her glass and winked. 'It's me, Pearl, remember? I was ten when you saw me last, but I've grown up now.'

He paused, fist suspended in the air, the other still clutching the collar of his victim as he glanced up at her with a puzzled air. 'So you have, Pearl. So you have.'

'How about buying me a nip o'summat, by way of a reunion?'

'Aye, why not?' Kit Jarvis flung aside the man whose brains, moments before, he'd been about to beat to a pulp, as if he were of no consequence. He took off his cap, smoothed back his hair, then replaced the cap again exactly where it had been. 'What'll it be? Same again?'

As she handed him her glass, a man paused as he passed by, placing a hand on her arm. 'Are yer working, lass?'

'Not just now, Ted. Happen later.'

'I don't think so,' Kit interrupted. 'I reckon she might be busy later an' all.'

–

Ruby attempted to bury her concerns in hard work and, perhaps so Bart could prove that he was a hard worker after all, life settled into a routine with the pair of them working together on the barges. To her surprise, she enjoyed it. They carried cargoes of tobacco to a bonded warehouse on Chapel Street, sisal and alpaca to Liverpool where Ruby scented the salty tang of the sea for the first time in her life. They transported cotton to Blackburn, and regular loads of coal to the various factories linked to the canal basin, often having to break the ice on the surface of the water as they went along so that great shards of it would stack up, one on top of the other, making progress difficult.

They would pass from the canal basin, crowded with tugs, barges and narrow boats, through the docks with ships displaying flags of every nation. It seemed a miracle to Ruby that these great vessels could sail right into the heart of the city.

Within no time they'd be over Barton swing bridge which carried the Bridgewater Canal over the Ship Canal, water leaking from the corners of the aqueduct gates. When the big ships came through this would move first, followed by the swing of the road bridge, its arches supported by massive steel girders. Ruby would look out for the man in the peaked cap who operated the gates to stop the traffic, and the children standing on walls and railings to watch the spectacle. She'd feel their excitement as they waited for the big ships to pass through, often accompanied by a tugboat or two; share their amazement that water, a whole stretch of the canal, could be contained and moved on a bridge, in addition to a road normally bustling with traffic. In no time Ruby would be looking out upon open countryside, where cows grazed in flowered meadows. It was like another world, far removed from memories of destitution and the harshness of the reformatory. It gave her the first glimpse of how it might feel to be free.

The work on the boats, and Bart's constant scheming, continued as normal and then one day he took her to another house, this time situated in a terrace on Quay Street, one among a hundred others of similar ilk.

'There you are,' he announced. 'Didn't I say I'd do right by you, Ruby? It's modest, admittedly, but I trust you won't turn your nose up at this.'

Ruby was stunned. She walked wonderingly through the dusty rooms, touching a broken chair, stroking the blackened surface of the stove, pulling away a tangle of cobwebs. The house was filthy, had the usual dank smell of neglect and vermin, but it was spacious with three bedrooms above, a kitchen and parlour below, and a private yard at the back complete with their own privy. Far grander than anything they'd lived in with Mam. She could make something of this house, given the chance.

But what would agreeing to live here with him cost her? She'd come perilously close to breaking the law on a number of occasions and very much doubted the police would be prepared to consider her an unwilling accomplice if he ever got caught, not as an ex-reformatory girl with a history of absconding. If they ever swooped on the baron, she'd be done for. They'd throw her in t'clink and toss away the key. Wouldn't it be better just to get as far away from him as possible? And yet it was her responsibility to think about Pearl. 'What about me sister?'

'I've asked around. Nobody has heard of her.'

'I don't believe you. Why would you even bother?'

'You know why.' With his eyes narrowed, it was well-nigh impossible for her to read his thoughts behind those lowered lids, though she could guess them since he'd made no secret of his desire for her. His soft chuckle sounded harsh, edged with the stirrings of anger or passion, Ruby wasn't sure which. 'There is, admittedly, a part of me that wonders why I should bother. You are my wife after all, and I could simply claim my rights here and now. It would be perfectly legal.'

Ruby swallowed the lump, which must be fear that had lodged in her throat. She really mustn't antagonise him too much. Intimacy with Barthram Stobbs was the last thing she wanted, wasn't it? 'If *I* were to find her, would you have any objection to her moving in?'

'So long as your sister helps with the chores and keeps out of my way, can't say fairer than that, can I? Have I fulfilled all the criteria you require, Ruby? Here, at last, is your own home. Cleaned out and furnished, it'll serve for weekends. During the week we will remain on the boat, naturally. And you can have your sister with you, if that's what you wish. Now, don't I deserve a little reward for such generosity?'

He pushed her gently back against the wall as he stroked her face, the skin of his hands hard and rough against the satin softness of her cheeks, catching in the silky tangle of her hair. Ruby was breathing hard, desperately trying to quell a surge of panic. And yet, somewhere deep inside, she felt the stirrings of some other emotion, one she didn't care to put a name to.

'No! Not till I've found our Pearl. That was the agreement.'

'Oh, Ruby! What an unfeeling wench you are. Won't you even give me the slightest nibble, just a taste of what you have to offer?' He put his lips against hers, brushing them lightly from side to side, a delicate overture to further plunder. The effect was startlingly sensuous and Ruby found herself instinctively lifting her mouth to his, her hands creeping up to grip the lapels of his jacket, her own body betraying her by its need. Hard on its heels came a kickback of guilt when she thought of Pearl, and she shoved hard at his chest, pushing him away.

'I told you, no! I need to find our Pearl first.'

'Don't you care about my feelings at all?'

Ruby tossed her head with defiance. 'Why should I? Nobody ever cared about mine.'

'Oh, Ruby, that's not true. Have you found nothing in my treatment of you that would count in my favour?'

'Not that I've noticed.' There was such a heart-rending sadness in his tone that she felt compelled to turn away, unable to bear to look at him in case she weakened. He didn't give a toss about her. Nobody ever had, so why should Barthram Stobbs be any different? She certainly had no intention of dropping her guard.

Ruby put all her energies into cleaning the house. She was thrilled to be permitted to buy a few pieces of second-hand furniture then set about scrubbing and black-leading the Lancashire range till it shone. She even stitched some lace curtains to make it look homely, something she'd never had in her life. This was the nearest she'd had to a home and Ruby was entranced by it. All she needed now was for Pearl and Billy to share this good fortune with her, so she could give them the love they'd lost when their mam had gone into the sanatorium.

Her siblings had never known the privilege of a normal childhood, and even Ruby's hopes for a new life, following the years in the reformatory, had been stifled by the reformers' zeal. She'd been married off to a stranger, a thief and conman whom she hated. Yet she was confused. If she loathed him so much, how was it they could work so well together? Why did the touch of his hands turn her insides to water? Was she a wanton, a wicked woman with no morals? Ruby dreamed of taking a ship to Canada to find Billy, yet if she were honest, she could not quite bring herself to walk out the door. Not just yet.

–

Late one night, instead of Sparky coming to talk to Bart as he so often did, it was his wife Aggie who turned up. Ruby recognised her as the woman who had stood at the back of the crowd on the day of the march and told Pickering that it was easy for him to talk, with money coming in regularly every week. Never rosy-cheeked, her pale face looked even more haggard tonight, her ragged dress and shawl hanging from her too-thin frame. Ruby hurried to her side, full of concern.

'What is it Aggie? Has something happened?'

'Aye, you could say so. Our Sparky has been sacked.'

'Sacked? Why? Not for taking part in that demonstration surely?'

Aggie gave her head a sharp jerk. 'Is he in?'

'I'm afraid not. He's off on one of his jaunts some place. Can I help?'

Aggie looked deflated, chewed on her lip for a moment before answering. 'Tell him I can't pay into the burial club this week, what with our Sparky being laid off. Once he gets taken up again, I'll catch up somehow. I like to keep up.'

Ruby gravely promised she would pass the message on. She knew well enough how important a burial club was to the people of Salford and Castlefield. A penny or two a week was a good deal of money to find at times, but it bought them peace of mind. Ruby's own mother had feared, perhaps more than anything, one of her children succumbing to the many childhood illnesses and her not having the wherewithal for a decent burial. Yet, in the end, it had been Mam herself who'd died and been buried as a pauper. She'd be turning in her grave at the shame of it.

But what Ruby had not known was that Bart operated such a club. She wondered who he acted as agent for. Insurance societies and trust funds didn't seem quite in his line.

Aggie was so upset she was repeating her tale all over again. 'Tell him I'll catch up. I will, I will. I'm that sorry.'

'Don't worry, Aggie. You won't be in need of it for years yet.' The remark, meant to console and comfort, sounded false and fatuous and Ruby bit down on her lip, wishing she could find something genuinely useful to say, like she knew where Sparky could find another job, for instance, so that his family wouldn't be in any danger of starving to death. 'I'll put the kettle on. You'll have a cuppa with me?'

But Aggie stood up, all bustle and energy now that she'd delivered her message. 'No, no, I have to get back t'childer. See you tell him, that's all.' And seconds later she was gone in a flurry of skirts and anxiety.

Ruby delivered the message the moment Bart got back, while he was barely halfway down the ladder. She carefully explained how upset Aggie had been, how anxious to keep up to date with her books, presumably one for each of her several children as well as herself and Sparky.

'You say Sparky was sacked?' Bart didn't seem to be listening to Ruby's message about the burial club so she repeated it. He silenced her with a peremptory, 'I heard you the first time. Are you saying that Sparky has been *sacked*?'

Wordlessly, she nodded.

'Damnation, the man is a heartless boor!' Bart swung about and began to ascend the ladder even more swiftly than he'd come down it. 'Don't expect me home till late. I have business to attend to.'

Ruby didn't ask with whom. She rather thought she could guess. This response was typical of her husband, just as the women of the cut had told her. Nothing was too much trouble for the baron where they were concerned, and she felt a surge of admiration and pride that he should care so much. Yet a part of her felt neglected, resentful and jealous even that as kind and giving as he was to everyone else, he showed no such concern for her, save for wanting a bit of the other. What about her problems? She was his wife after all. Didn't that count for anything? If only he would put as much effort into helping her to find Pearl, his own sister-in-law. She may still be locked up in the reformatory, or suffering at the hands of some mill owner or cruel employer. Awash with unaccustomed self-pity, Ruby sat on her bed, put her face in her hands and wept.

The world was an unkind and cruel place. She had little hope that her sister would be happily enjoying life somewhere. Ruby was quite certain that Pearl would be in dire need of care and attention and it was her duty, as she'd promised Mam, to provide it.

–

Pearl and Kit lay in bed, sated from their lovemaking. He was an exciting and demanding lover and she had no regrets about moving into his rooms above a chip shop in Rochdale, for all the stink of hot fat and old batter was a bit overpowering at times. 'It's only temporary,' he told her. 'Just till I get meself sorted.'

Neither of them could find employment: Kit, because young men who'd spent years on a reformatory training ship were not welcomed with open arms by prospective employers, despite the claims of the reformers to the contrary; Pearl, because she didn't even bother to look. She was more than content with her life as it was, and meeting Kit had only made it better.

'I must say, I appreciate the enthusiasm you put into your work,' Kit told her, a teasing light in his blue eyes as he untied the ribbons of her grubby camisole, not having had time to remove it earlier in his urgency to get at her.

'What a cheek! If you call this work, then you can pay me for it.' Her breasts spilled out when the fabric parted but as he greedily reached for her, Pearl slapped his hands away and swung herself out of the bed, flouncing off and falling into a sulk, as was her wont. 'Trouble with you, Kit Jarvis, is, you're never satisfied. You always want more, and with not a word of gratitude or appreciation.' She was already halfway into her blouse and pulling on her skirt while he was filled with regret for the loss of these delights.

Kit had discovered early on that it was easy to offend Pearl. 'Aw, I do appreciate you, really I do. There's none better than my lovely Pearl at turning tricks. And don't I deserve some reward for providing you with free accommodation, as well as so many well-paying clients?'

'Aye, but you're happy enough to help me spend whatever they pay me.' Pearl paused in pulling on her stockings to glance provocatively back at him over her shoulder, pouting her soft full lips. Ooh, but he was that handsome she wanted to eat him all up.

'That's the deal, love, and I believe in looking after my own, you know that.' He drew her back on to the bed, peeled off the stocking she'd just put on, and stroked her thigh before cupping her with his hand. 'We suit each other nicely, don't you reckon?'

Pearl fluttered her eyelashes with enticing allure. 'Till summat better comes along, you mean.'

He adopted a mockingly sad expression. 'Pearl, that's a sorry reflection on my loyalty. Are you saying that you don't trust me?'

'I'm saying this isn't no flippin' love affair, I'm not as green as all that. It's in your interests to have me around, since I'm earning good money.'

He'd already removed her blouse, now he slid off the skirt she'd only just put back on. 'And it's in yours to stick by me for the protection I can offer. There are some weird characters out there, love. Like I say, you need someone to keep an eye out for any likely trouble. We can look out for each other, right?'

Now he was on top of her again, desire hot in her as only he knew how to stir her senses to fever pitch. Pearl quite liked it when they argued, and if she let him win occasionally, it was only in her own best interests. She was quite happy for him to act as her protector, so long as she was the one secretly in control. 'I allus thought it was our Ruby you fancied,' she gasped, arching her body so he could take one nipple into his mouth.

Kit chuckled as he pushed back her arms, easily holding both her wrists with one hand while he eased himself into her with the other. 'You were only a child when I last saw you. How was I to know you'd grow into such a stunner?'

Pearl purred with pleasure, not only at his words but at the sensations he was creating within her. Besides, she knew well enough how much Ruby adored Kit Jarvis, which pleased her all the more. Serve her sister right if Pearl had got to him first.

Chapter Fifteen

Ruby's worries over Pearl, her constant grieving for the loss of Billy, and her longing to meet up again with Kit, her childhood sweetheart, were not in any way diminished by her sense of contentment in working the boats. Rather, the placid routine of her life filled her with a sense of guilt. How could she be so content when her brother and sister were not?

Nor was she consoled by the fact that she now accepted there was more to Barthram Stobbs than had at first been apparent. He might have his generous side, particularly when it came to seeking justice for his fellow workers, but he showed precious little towards her, preferring instead to keep her firmly in her place.

It was a strange, almost hostile relationship they had. Even now that he'd provided her with a lovely little house to live in for a part of each week, he was rarely in it. Said he felt confined, suffocated by four walls. Ruby suspected he couldn't bear the thought of sleeping alone, aware she was in the next room having rejected his advances. But how could she live in a marriage without love? And didn't she deserve to make her own choices in life?

One day in early spring, Ruby finally plucked up the courage to retrace her steps to Kit's old home. So many times she had ached to look for him but had never done so, and she knew why. To her mind, he represented her one hope of happiness. Yet if he rejected her – and he had every reason to do so since it was because of her that he'd been caught and sent to the training ship – then her last hope of finding Pearl and of escaping Bart's tyranny, would be gone.

It took an age to find the tenement block among a dozen others, and when she was finally satisfied that she'd found the right one, enquiries proved that Marie and her children no longer lived there. No one had heard of her for years, or had any idea where she might be living now. Ruby hadn't realised, until she experienced the keenness of disappointment, how very much she'd been counting on Kit being there, or at least on finding his mother who would surely have known where he was. She longed to turn back the clock and find him still fetching stale bread and broken biscuits for his brothers and sisters.

It was as she was walking away, head down to hide the tears that washed over her cheeks, arms wrapped about herself in abject misery against a brisk north-east wind, that she heard the voice. She would have known it anywhere.

'I just happened to come by it. Must be worth a bob or two. What d'you reckon?'

Ruby jerked up her head, swung about to stare hard at a tall, gangly youth who was leaning against a lamppost, just a few yards away. He was holding something in his hand that he was proudly showing to a mate.

'*Jackdaw!* I don't believe it. Still up to your old tricks then?'

He turned round to glare at her, a fierce expression in the dark eyes that peered out from beneath the jauntily placed slouch cap. But gradually they seemed to focus more keenly, narrowing as if in deep thought, and then opened wide with surprise. 'Ruby? As I live and breathe, is it really you?'

'Last time I looked it was.'

'By heck, you're a sight for sore eyes.' Then he was lifting her off her feet to swing her round on a whoop of joy. 'Where have you been hiding all these years?'

'Where d'you think?' She was laughing too, and holding him tight in a fierce hug of delight, so pleased was she to see him. It was like discovering an old friend, and she hadn't many of those these days.

He bought her a mug of tea from the stall under the railway arches and they stood about in the raw cold of a March day, stamping their feet to keep warm as they sipped the scalding brew, recalling old times and laughing like drains.

'I remember getting all filthy scrounging for coal.'

'And rummaging through dustbins for anything to sell, or even eat, if it hadn't gone off.'

'Where is Pongo?'

'He's still around. Got himself a wife now, and a couple of kids. Right proud of them, he is. Works down the docks. Nothing but the best is good enough for his childer. I remember your Pearl falling in the River Irwell when we went gurdling for fish.'

Ruby laughed. 'I never managed to catch any either. No wonder we near starved when we left you lot.' Which inevitably turned their thoughts to Kit.

The laughter swiftly died and Ruby gazed at Jackdaw with mute appeal in her eyes. 'Where is he? Have you heard from him?'

Jackdaw shook his head. 'Not lately! I know he's been released from the training ship. I heard they gave him a bad time. Got the birch once. Admitted as much to me once. It was for trying to escape, apparently.'

A wave of sickness washed over her at the thought of Kit being whipped, and her knees went all funny so that she sank down on to a low stone wall to catch her breath.

Jackdaw crouched down beside her. 'I know how you feel, Ruby. Gives you the bleedin' shivers, don't it? And I remember you was allus fond of him. It made me mad when I heard. What had he ever done to deserve such treatment? Only try to feed his family, that's all. Which was more than anybody else was prepared to do. There were rats on that ship, sweatshop labour, bitter cold and sickness, beatings and bullying. No wonder he tried to escape. Them places aren't fit for human consumption.'

They both fell silent, as images of what Kit must have gone through on board the reformatory training ship, filled their minds.

At length Ruby said, 'I thought I might find Marie. Who better to know what happened to Kit, than his own mother?'

'We haven't seen hide nor hair of her in years. Or the rest of the family.' Again a short silence. 'How about your Pearl? How's she doing?'

Ruby cradled the fading warmth of the mug in her hands as she began to tell her own tale: of the harsh, unfeeling world of Ignatius House with the nuns, the bullying of Billy and their desperate bid to find their mother, although sadly far too late. She finished off with the grim years in the reformatory, the riot, and Pearl being incarcerated in solitary confinement in a padded cell.

'As if she were a flippin' lunatic. Where she is now I have no idea, assuming she's still sane. She might be working in a factory or skivvying some place. Oh, but I'm desperate to find her. Billy too. I gave my permission for him to go to Canada and now I wish I hadn't.'

He gave a harsh laugh. 'They didn't need your permission. They'd be telling you what they meant to do, not asking.'

'You're probably right, but I do so want us both to go to Canada and find him. It's all I can think of, to make things better for them both. They've had such a terrible start in life. Nobody to love them or look after them properly, not like Mam would've done. For all we were poor, she had so much love and fun in her, you know?'

'Aye lass, I know.'

'That's all we ever wanted, a bit of love and food in our bellies. You wouldn't think it too much to ask, would you?' Tears were welling up in her eyes, threatening to overflow. Jackdaw put an arm about her shoulder and gave her a comforting hug as they both considered this seemingly impossible dream.

'But you loved them, eh? Your Pearl and Billy allus knew that.'

'Look at me. What a mess! It must be talking about it again, and you giving me all this tea and sympathy that's turned me into a wet lettuce. Oh, but I do hope they knew that I loved them. I do hope so.'

Clearly embarrassed by having caused this emotional outburst, Jackdaw stood up, suddenly all brisk efficiency. 'Hush now. I can't be doing with a lass who cries. I know what we'll do. We'll ask Charlie and Clem. There's nowt goes on these parts that they don't know about. If Kit's around, one or other of them will have heard.'

'That would be marvellous!' Ruby's spirits rose and fell again in an instant. 'Oh, but I can't go just now. Not today.' She was suddenly all of a fluster. 'I have to get back before Bart misses me.'

Even as she flung the words at Jackdaw, explaining in short, breathless sentences where she lived and why, that she would come again, she was running from him. She was anxious not to bring the wrath of the baron down upon her. It would never do for him to suspect what she was up to.

Jackdaw stood and watched her go, mouth agape.

–

Ruby met Jackdaw regularly after that, and each time he would shake his head, gloomily relating his lack of success. After several weeks with no progress, Ruby gave up hope. What had possessed her to imagine for one moment that Kit would want to see *her*, who'd landed him in all that trouble, even if he were still living in the neighbourhood, which was highly unlikely after what he'd been through?

Jackdaw, however, never gave up hope, or relinquished one jot of his cheerful optimism. 'I've put out the word, and I keep asking around. We'll find him in the end, never fear.'

And then suddenly there he was. She arrived at their usual meeting place one day to find him waiting for her, a grin on his face as if they'd parted only yesterday, Jackdaw bouncing beside him like a delighted puppy.

'Kit!'

Ruby ran straight into his arms, felt them tighten around her in a big hug before he set her down to examine her face.

'Hey, lass. How're keeping?'

'Oh, why did you never write to me?'

He looked startled by the question. 'Never got chance.'

'I kept looking for a letter, and hoping.'

'Wasn't easy.'

'Oh, Kit, I'm so glad to see you.' She knew her eyes must be shining out her love for him. She felt dazzled, confused, overwhelmed by the mere sight of him, the masculine scent which brought back memories of her first heady encounter with love. Wasn't he her first sweetheart, her only one? And ever would be if she'd any say in the matter. From the first moment she'd set eyes on him as a thirteen-year-old girl, she had been utterly smitten, and now here he was, standing right before her. Ruby put a hand to his cheek, unable to resist touching him as if to prove this miracle was true, wanting him to touch her, disappointed when he made no move to do so. But then he'd always been reserved, rather shy of showing his feelings.

He smiled down at her, hands in pockets, the slouch cap as audaciously placed as ever. How she loved that in him, his sense of independence, that he was his own man and would make a move only when he chose. Besides, she was content simply to drink in the glorious sight of him, remind herself how beautiful he was, how utterly irresistible.

'Jackdaw told me about what happened on the reformatory ship. It must have been hard.'

'It was no picnic, that's for sure.' His face darkened, and Ruby realised that mentioning the ship had been a mistake. She quickly attempted to retract.

'S-sorry. I didn't mean to distress you.'

'I don't like to talk about it.' His voice was cold and hard as he turned to glare across at his mate, who instantly fled.

'Don't blame Jackdaw, I made him tell me.'

An awkwardness had sprung up between them, one Ruby wasn't sure how to bridge. She felt suddenly uncertain. Kit seemed different somehow, but then weren't they all? And she'd no wish to lose him again. Not now, after all the time it had taken to find him. She must be patient and not throw herself at him like a silly schoolgirl.

Jackdaw reappeared with a mug of tea for each of them, mumbled some sort of apology then quietly withdrew. They sat together on the low wall to drink it while Ruby haltingly filled Kit in with the details of her life, and how it had been no easier for her. When she reached the part about being forcibly married off by the Board of Guardians to the baron, he lifted his head to look at her more keenly.

'You're married to the baron?' He didn't sound particularly surprised, or even disappointed, merely interested. But perhaps Jackdaw had told him already.

'Not willingly, and in name only.' It was important to Ruby that she got this fact across. 'He took a fancy to me but it's done him no good. You can take a horse to water…'

He gave a harsh little laugh. 'Ever the rebel, Ruby, so good for you.'

They grinned at each other then he sipped his tea before continuing more thoughtfully, 'I hear he's well placed, with a string of barges as well as a house that he actually owns. You've landed yourself a rich husband there, girl.'

Ruby dismissed this as of no interest to her. 'He's got a couple of barges, that's all. Hardly a string, but he's not the man I would have chosen for a husband. You know who I would've chosen, Kit, if I'd had my way.'

He smiled into her adoring eyes, seeing her transparent love for him, and knew, in that instant, that his decision to meet her had been right. The minute Jackdaw had told him who she was wed to, he'd known he could use this to his advantage. 'Aye, lass, I feel the same.'

'Do you? Do you really?' The thrill of his words almost made Ruby swoon with delight. She could hardly believe it. As he put his arms about her to hold her close, she felt as if all her dreams were coming true at last. She stayed with him far longer than she should have done but couldn't seem to tear herself away. It was more than an hour later when she stood up to go. 'Can I see you again, Kit?'

'You're my girl, Ruby, same as always, husband or no. Isn't that right?'

Joy burst inside her like the fireworks on the day of the old Queen's jubilee. It was almost too much happiness to bear. 'Oh, yes, Kit. Yes, I am.'

Then his lips were on hers in the way she had so longed for during all those long lonely years in the reformatory. Ruby swayed in his arms, weak with emotion, overcome by the miracle of finding him again.

But just as her eyes fluttered closed, she caught sight of a movement in the shadows beyond. On a jerk of fear she recognised a familiar figure approaching, striding towards them across the quay. The anger in him was all too evident in the grim expression on his face, and in the rigid set of his powerful shoulders, let alone on the waves of rage that seemed to wash towards her.

Breathless with sudden fear, she thrust Kit aside. 'Go! You must go, Kit. *Now!* He's here. Lord help me! I'll never get the chance to find our Pearl and Billy now.'

—

Much to her relief, Kit managed to slip away unnoticed while Bart was grabbing poor Jackdaw by the collar and shaking him till his teeth rattled. He must have thought this was the man she'd been embracing. Had she not caught sight of the poor lad's ashen face, she might have laughed out loud. Ruby was filled with pity for him for who wouldn't be terrified of such fury? No one defied the baron's wishes. Except for her.

'How dare you follow me! You've no right to spy on me.' Characteristically, it took Ruby no time at all to recover her wits and summon up her usual truculence. It was the only way she knew to protect herself. She confronted him, hands on hips, every line of her body flaunting her defiance.

Bart couldn't help but feel a surge of admiration, knowing that he could never settle for a compliant wife. Yet deep inside he remained angry, and more hurt than he had any right to be. Certainly more than was good for him. His tone was harsh and uncompromising. 'Just as well I did, since you and your fancy man here were all wrapped up together like a Christmas parcel.'

To his great annoyance she threw back her head and began to laugh, a deep-throated sound that made him want to stop it with his mouth, to punish her with kisses. Why did she continue to resist him? The thought of some other man's hand in her hair, caressing her cheek, unbuttoning the cotton bodice of her gown where the soft outline of her breasts strained the fabric, made his blood run cold. The image was unendurable.

She wiped tears of laughter from her eyes with the flat of both hands. 'Jackdaw isn't my fancy man, though there might well be one.' Ruby sent her old friend a warm smile of reassurance that she'd do her best to protect him.

Bart looked as if he might kill Jackdaw anyway, just for the hell of it. But if what she said was true then the other had taken to his heels and fled. And still needed to be found. 'Who would he be then? Some childhood sweetheart, no doubt.'

'Wouldn't you like to know?'

'I shall put a stop to this nonsense, Ruby.'

'How? What could you do about it, eh? Nowt!' She spat the word at him, tipping up on her toes so she could reach him better. 'I'm your wife in name only. Nothing more. I never asked you to wed me. In fact, I seem to remember that I'd no say in the matter whatsoever, which doesn't mean you can rule me, or dictate every damn thing that I do.'

'Watch your language. I'll not have a woman of mine use foul language.' He grabbed hold of her wrist and started to drag her away.

Ruby gasped, pummelling his unyielding shoulder with her free fist as she attempted to resist. 'Drat you,

Barthram Stobbs, I'm no woman of yours and never will be.'

She might as well have been a fly battering on walls of granite for all the impression she made. He simply strode on, jaw rigid, making no concession to the fact she had to run to keep pace with him.

Jackdaw chased after them at a safe distance, brandishing a fist. 'Don't you lay a finger on Ruby. She's done nowt wrong. We was only talking over old times.'

Bart ground to a halt and whirled about, golden eyes blazing with wrath. 'I'd stay out of this lad, if I were you. While you still have a head on your puny shoulders.' And ignoring Ruby's pleas and cries for help, he strode away, dragging her ignominiously behind him.

He didn't pause till they reached the tug, then he swung her up in his arms and carried Ruby on board as if she were no more than a parcel of rubbish he'd picked up off the quay. Ruby fought like a cat with teeth and claws, kicking her legs in a lather of temper, but to no avail. He strode into her cabin and dropped her on the bed, where she lay gasping for breath, nut-brown hair falling loose from its pins and tumbling over her face and shoulders.

'It's time you learned to do as you're told. Any more rebellion, and I'll consider it mutiny, the punishment for which does not bear thinking about.' His tone was harsh, jagged with fury.

'You daren't do anything to *me*.'

'Oh, I'd do anything, Ruby McBride. Make no mistake about that. What I want you to do now is wash your grimy face and get ready for bed. I shall go and make myself, and my cabin suitably presentable for a lady. When I am ready, I shall come for you.'

There was triumph in his tone of voice, a terrifying glitter in his searching gaze, then he removed the key from the lock, slammed shut the cabin door, and as Ruby heard it turn on the other side, she screamed out her frustration in an explosion of rage.

'*Drat you!* I shall *never* come willingly. Make me walk the plank if you must. Flog me with a cat o' nine tails. But you can't ever make me into *your* woman!'

The sound of his soft laughter filtered back to her through the panels of the door. 'Oh, but I can, Ruby. I rather think that I can.'

–

It was half an hour later when she heard the key in the lock a second time and her heart leaped into her throat on a surge of apprehension. She still had not washed her face, or removed a stitch of her clothing. Nor would she. Ruby had no intention of giving herself willingly to any man other than her beloved Kit, certainly not this one, husband or no. If he insisted on taking her, then it would have to be by brute force. A prospect that despite her brave thoughts, made her shudder with foreboding.

He stood in the doorway, quietly looking down upon her. 'I see you have not taken me seriously.'

He was dressed in the silk robe he had worn that first night, except that beneath it she guessed he was quite naked, and her heart fluttered, although not with foreboding this time. His commanding presence seemed to fill the tiny cabin, making him seem taller, more muscular, more strikingly handsome with his tousled, red-gold hair, than she'd ever seen him before. Ruby felt diminished by his power, and by some emotion inside herself she had no wish to examine too deeply.

There seemed to be only two ways of dealing with this. Either she surrendered willingly, or he took her without her consent. Neither prospect appealed. Why did it have to happen now, just when she'd found Kit and had scented happiness at last? She could cry at the unfairness of it all.

'Perhaps a little night-cap, to relax you?'

She snatched at the offer, then saw how he clenched his teeth in fresh annoyance when she chose cocoa. Alcohol was quite out of the question. She needed to keep her wits about her. Nevertheless, he made the hot drink without protest, watching in silence while she drank it. Ruby made it last as long as possible, sitting in the main living area of the barge, all too aware of the open door to his spacious cabin through which she caught a glimpse of a rumpled bed with a green silken coverlet. She could feel the beat of her heart in her breast, slow and rather breathless.

He did not drink, which surprised her. She'd expected him to take a nip of whisky or rum which he did some-times of an evening. Instead, he sat looking quite relaxed, hands loosely clasped, elbows on knees as he watched her, his gaze unfathomable. What she could see of his legs beneath the robe were strong and muscled, and bare. She averted her eyes. The tension in the room was palpable, her breath now caught in her throat as if she did not dare to expel it.

At length, he calmly removed the empty mug from her hand. 'I've been a patient man long enough, Ruby. Too patient! I've done everything in my power to make you comfortable, to provide you with a home, food on the table every night, as well as keep you safe from harm.

I've even spared you from danger in the very important and essential work that I do. But I am a red-blooded male and you are my wife. I can wait no longer. Most women seem to find me attractive. I cannot understand why you continue to resist. Do you imagine that I'll hurt you? Have I given you cause to think so?'

'You still haven't found Pearl.' Her voice sounded weak, the excuse feeble, even to her own ears.

His reply was soft, and tinged with sympathy. 'I know, and I'm sorry about that. I'm sorry too if my irritation on the subject has alarmed you, but I swear I have made several enquiries and will do everything in my power to find her. Come.' He held out a hand for her to take.

He tried not to show the vulnerability he was feeling, emotions he was not accustomed to experiencing let alone reveal to others. If she rejected him now, Bart hadn't the first idea what he would do. His passion for her had driven him to the edge of madness, the heat of his desire made his loins ache. How he had managed, in all this time of living at such close quarters with her, not to take her, he would never know. It spoke volumes for the effect she had on him. Above everything he wanted her, and yet respected her right to refuse him, not only because of the nature of their marriage but also because of the high esteem in which he held her.

Something she couldn't seem to grasp.

But was he capable now of asserting these rights he spoke of so glibly? Did he believe for one moment that such an act would win her? He did not want to lose her. Still she held back, resisting every appeal he made. And then it came to him, on a blinding flash of understanding.

'Dear heaven, you're still a virgin. Is that the way of it? Has no man ever touched you?'

Ruby did not answer. She could not. She felt a tightness in her chest, a breathlessness at her own vulnerability. She'd hoped and prayed to give this precious gift to Kit Jarvis and now this man, this hated man, was to rob her of that pleasure too. One by one he had destroyed all her dreams, but she would not allow him to destroy her. Ruby's chin came up, fists clenched as she leapt to her feet.

'Why should that surprise you? Did you take me for some sort of harlot, just because I was brought up in the reformatory? Well, maybe I am. Maybe I have more experience than you think.'

In one fluid movement of defiance she ripped open the buttons of her dress, pushing it back over bare shoulders to let it fall to the ground. She stood before him in her short cotton shift, her breasts revealing the outline of dark nipples beneath the thin fabric.

He watched, mesmerised by her beauty as she turned from him and strode away, slender and graceful, into his cabin.

Quietly, he followed her, and closed the door.

Ruby turned to face him, giving no indication of the inner turmoil she was experiencing, save in the way her eyes flaunted her contempt and in the bravado of her words. 'I'll not make it easy for you.'

'I very much hope, Ruby, that you will enjoy this as much as I.'

If she did, she made every effort not to show it. Ruby bit down hard on any cry which he might mistake for ecstasy, for all her fingers clung tightly to his broad shoulders. And although she did not offer up her mouth for his kisses, when he claimed it anyway her lips seemed to open for him of their own accord, very much against her will. Even her skin seemed to flare with desire at his touch, causing her to react with a shameful wantonness, to beg him for more.

He made no concessions to her innocence but took his fill of her, meaning to staunch his need once and for all, only to find, after that first climactic exorcism, that he could not resist loving her all over again. His greater gentleness the second time, was her final undoing. Ruby McBride, that stalwart of stubborn pride and fierce rebellion, crumbled beneath the onslaught of this tender passion and wept as he cradled her in his arms.

Chapter Sixteen

Bart stood on his soapbox on the quay before his normally stalwart and loyal supporters, feeling close to exasperation. His carefully rehearsed speech on how he, together with a select band of workers, would approach Pickering and demand that he acknowledge the union and concede to at least some of the men's requests: showers and lavatory facilities, safety procedures put into place, and a decent rate of pay, had been listened to with close attention. There'd been mumbles of agreement all round, rousing cheers at times. Some had been sufficiently stirred by his passion to call out the odd, 'Hear! Hear!'

But when he'd asked for volunteers to accompany him, it was as if they shrivelled before his eyes. Their faces seemed to close up, and they looked anywhere but into his eyes. Some sloped quietly away, leaving others hesitantly to express their appreciation of the baron's efforts on their behalf but explain how they personally couldn't do anything to help, for one reason or another. Their wife was sick, there was a child on the way or some relative had died. Less than half the excuses were genuine for not one of them was willing to be a member of this select band, or to take up the cause on behalf of their colleagues. Some offered no apology at all, but simply denounced the idea out of hand.

'A waste of time as we'd get nowhere.'

'Aye, and look what he did to Sparky.'

'How can working men take on employers? It isn't reasonable to ask.'

'He'd probably refuse even to talk to us.'

'It's not like there are other jobs we could go to,' said Tom Wright. 'All employers are as bad. And there's a score or more chaps waiting every morning for work down at the docks. Maybe six'll be taken on out of a long line of hopefuls. And every day it gets worse. The foreman always picks his favourites. You only need to get yourself a reputation as a troublemaker, or worse, a union activist, and that's it. You're done for.'

The men all looked at Bart in aggrieved silence and he could guess what they were thinking: that it was easy for him to talk. He had a bit of money in the bank, and he wasn't the one in danger of losing his job. Bart had offered Sparky some work on his own barges, which he'd finally accepted, once convinced it wasn't out of charity and that he was genuinely needed. Bart suspected Aggie had had something to do with this change of heart. But it wasn't in his power to give work to them all.

It was Sparky himself who broke the silence, which threatened to undermine the entire meeting. 'Much as we might like to deny it, Tom's right. Bosses hand out the work and we're the ones who need it. There's nowt we can do, and they know it. They've got us over a barrel.'

Bart protested that this kind of defeatist talk would get them nowhere, but the argument continued to range back and forth, going round and round in endless circles, the most prevalent response being that everyone thought it a good idea to wring better conditions out of the bosses, so long as they weren't asked to be the ones to do it.

One man even insisted that it wouldn't be patriotic to take any risk which might result in a strike. Most, however, were simply too hungry or too afraid of losing the work they did pick up in Pickering's Wharf, however irregular, to risk it.

Giles Pickering owned one of the largest carrying companies in the district and though he could never be accused of philanthropy, there was no question that he possessed power. He was an important employer, rivalling the Ship Canal Company itself, far too big for any of them to take on.

Their fear was palpable. It hung on the evening air like acrid smoke which Bart could almost taste in the back of his throat.

Nevertheless, he persisted. 'You should at least try. Can't you see that? Don't expect the government to solve your problems. Certainly not this Conservative government.'

Tom, ever cautious, refused to accept this. 'They're holding a Royal Commission on Trade Disputes and Combinations. They mean to sort it all out. All we have to do is hang on to us jobs in the meantime.'

'They'll fudge it, as always,' Bart argued. 'They haven't appointed one single union member to serve on it. Where's the resolution to improve conditions for the working man? How is it that the wealthy employer is allowed to pay money into clubs and political organisations of which he is a member, but is not permitted to contribute through his own union to the political party of his choice? It's intolerable. If you want unions to be accepted and taken note of, and your working conditions improved, you'll have to do it yourself. First on a local level and then nationally as there's no other way. The truth is, if you don't fight, you won't win.'

'And what about our childer?' one man, known as Flitch, called out. He was a big, burly chap who worked as skipper on a Pickering-owned pair of barges. 'They need an education, same as town childer do. What about his promise to get us a school for them?'

'What good did schooling ever do anyone? Our childer need to know how to manage a boat to be sure of a safe future. What more do they want?' Sparky countered.

'We could all be out of work tomorrow if the Ship Canal doesn't start making more profit,' Tom warned. 'So we have to tread carefully.'

'But we could at least have some proper privies on the canal bank.'

They were off again on another tack of grievances, more concerned now with the plight of their wives and children who travelled the canal system with them, moving from one local authority to another – Manchester, Cheshire, Liverpool, Leeds – so that no local inspector could quite catch up with them to check on how much schooling their children were getting, if any at all. And nothing got done to improve their lot.

Bart listened with patience till they finally ran out of steam, then he held up his hands for quiet. 'It's no good grumbling when you insist on taking your entire brood with you in overcrowded, unsanitary conditions on board your boats. But if you want better provision for your families, decent lavatories, laundry, showers and washing facilities, which is all very laudable, you have to do something about it. So what is your decision? Do we send a deputation to Pickering, or sit back and take what he throws at us? Isn't it time you aired these grievances directly to him?'

A long and uncomfortable silence, then Flitch stepped forward, wiping his hands on the back of his grubby trousers. 'We all reckon it would be best if it came from you. We're good at shifting stuff about, shovelling and lifting and managing our boats. You're the one who thinks and talks well.'

'You never thought before you spoke in your entire life, Flitch,' Sparky yelled good-naturedly, and the big man grinned.

'That's what I mean. Not my line of country, thinking. I leave all that brain work to the wife.' He glanced about at the other men who were nodding, just as if they had held a debate and come to an agreement. Bart could guess what was coming, and braced himself for it. 'We'd rather you spoke up fer us. We reckon as how Pickering'd be more likely to listen to you. You're one of his kind like. So we wants you to be our spokesman.'

'You want me to tackle Pickering on my own?'

'Aye. With our backing like, but – aye – on yer own.'

The brave words faded into silence and Bart knew that they'd lost. Whatever argument he personally presented to their tyrannical employer, would be instantly rejected. They couldn't have picked a worse representative for their cause.

–

Bart's request for an interview was turned down, not simply once but on three separate occasions. Finally, some six weeks after the meeting with the men on the dockside, Giles Pickering finally agreed to receive him.

The two men confronted each other in the plush interior of Pickering's office and it seemed for a while that neither was willing to be the one to broach the subject they were clearly there to address. The older man ostentatiously drew out his pocket watch to indicate that his time was precious and there was a limit to how long he was prepared to tolerate this imposition. Uninvited, Bart drew up a red velvet, button-backed chair and sat down, spreading his long legs as he reclined in comfort upon it.

'As arrogant as ever, I see.'

Bart offered his crooked smile then leaned forward, resting his elbows on his knees. 'Is it not possible for us to have a civilised conversation for once?'

'That is entirely up to you, Barthram. You are welcome in my office at any time, as you well know. I'm sure I've never intended to cause offence by my actions.' And in complete contradiction to these words Pickering continued, 'Where are your lackeys, your mates from the docks? Don't tell me they are trusting you to solve their petty problems?' The mockery in his tone was unmistakable but Bart held on to his patience, albeit with difficulty, grinding his teeth together and clenching his fists in the effort required to stop himself from marching out of the door or, better still, planting one of them in the other man's face and knocking that sardonic expression to kingdom come.

'Lackey' was precisely the sort of word Pickering would choose. That or slave, minion or underling. He was a man who considered himself without equal. The cold, ascetic face with its trim beard and neatly clipped moustache, slick black hair which gleamed in the shaft of sunlight from the tall Georgian window, and the expensively tailored three-piece suit, broadcast loud and clear his good opinion of himself.

'So get on with it. I can't stand about here all day.'

By way of reply, Bart pulled out a sheet of paper from his inside pocket, unfolded it and laid it on the desk before him. 'Our list of demands.'

'That sounds very like a threat.' Pickering opened a humidor and took out a cigar. He did not offer one to the younger man. As he went through the business of clipping and lighting it, he scanned the paper before him. 'Preposterous! Only a fool would agree to such demands. Schools? Showers? Safety precautions? By heck, it's a load of namby-pamby nonsense.'

'It may have slipped your attention but this is a new era, a new century in fact. The Victorian age is gone.'

'Aye, and with it any sense of decency.'

'These people are poor. If you, as their employer, can improve their living and working conditions, it behoves you to do so. They deserve better.'

Giles Pickering blew out a cloud of noxious cigar smoke. 'It behoves them to improve the state of their morals. If they're in difficulties, it's of their own doing. It's not the responsibility of the state or employers to correct those evils, but themselves. Less profanity and drunkenness and happen they'd be better able to put a bit by.'

'Out of what you pay them, don't make me laugh?'

Pickering grew red in the face. 'I had to make my own way in the world, so I don't see why I should pity them what squanders their wages.'

'You succeeded by being utterly ruthless and stepping on anyone who got in your way.'

'It worked, didn't it? Not that it stopped you behaving like some sort of plaster saint.'

Bart stood up, thrusting back the chair as his patience came close to snapping point. 'I knew I would be wasting my time. When have you ever listened to anyone's point of view but your own? When have you ever cared who you hurt so long as you get your own way, in business as in everything else?'

Pickering's face creased into tight lines of fury. 'So we're dragging up old history now, are we?'

Bart planted two tightly clenched fists on the desk as he leaned closer. 'What you did to Alice was despicable! As for my mother...'

'Get out! I'll not be vilified in me own office.'

Bart strode to the door, pausing with his hand grasping the brass knob as he recalled the real purpose of his visit. This wasn't the moment to pursue personal vengeance. He must save all of that for later. The time would come. What mattered now was his mission, his promise to the men. He took a deep, steadying breath and again turned to face his adversary.

'All these men are asking for is a fair rate of pay and decent conditions for themselves and their families. It doesn't all have to happen overnight, but some sign of goodwill on your part might help to prevent further trouble in the future.'

The older man's face grew florid and blotched with temper. 'Don't you threaten me with talk of your bloody strikes. I'll sue anybody who damages my business. If men aren't hungry, why would they work? That's all I have to say. Nothing more!'

'And I have nothing more to say to you, Father. Nor ever will have.'

—

Kit had never expected the baron to be an easy quarry. Somehow or other, no matter what the risks involved, he needed to devise a workable plan, one that rid them of Barthram Stobbs but kept his working boats. Kit could make good money out of those barges. He said as much to Pearl night after night. Not that she listened.

'Who cares about a few boats? Money is far more useful. Hasn't that sister of mine managed to get her hands on any yet?'

Frowning, Kit explained the difficulties: that although Ruby was eager enough to leave her husband, she was less keen to rob him.

Pearl gave a derisive snort of disbelief. 'Don't tell me your charms are failing? I'll accept that sister of mine always did have a mind of her own, but you should have had her eating out of your hand by now. I've been waiting all year for that bright new start you promised me. The fancy frocks, a place of our own, money to jingle in my pocket, so how much longer do I have to wait?'

'Not much longer, Pearl.'

'The waiting won't be worth it if all we get at the end is a pair of bloody barges. A string of working girls to earn us brass would do us more good, so's I don't have to turn tricks any more. Mind you, I'd be that sorry to pack it in. I take pride in me work, and you aren't the only chap what fancies me, Kit Jarvis, don't think you are. Happen it's time I came out of hiding and tackled Barthram Stobbs meself. I'm good at squeezing a bit of cash out of a bloke.'

'No, Pearl, it's too soon. The minute Ruby finds you she might simply take you to live with them in that poxy little house on Quay Street. There's nothing she'd like better than having you under her thumb again, all safe and sound. She talks of little else, spends every minute she can searching for you when she's not working on the boats.'

'And I'm sick of not daring to go out and about as much as I'd like. She's stubborn is our Ruby, and if she keeps on asking for me, she's bound to come upon one of me gentlemen sooner or later. Then the fat will be in the fire.' Pearl shrugged her shoulders, nearly bare in the flimsy nightgown she wore, and sauntered over to the dressing table to pour herself a tot of gin. 'Mebbe I should let her find me. I could happen get my hands on the money a lot quicker.'

Kit sat chewing his nails, annoyed with her for stating the obvious, a fact he was well aware of and worried him constantly. The last thing he wanted was for Ruby to find Pearl too soon, let alone discover how she earned her living. She'd consider it her duty to save her sister. And Kit's need for the money Pearl earned him was far greater. It was the reason he insisted she stay indoors as much as possible, at least until he had his hands on something more substantial and long-lasting, like those barges. Even Pearl's beauty wouldn't last forever. But she was right, they couldn't go on like this for much longer. One day their luck would run out. But first, he had to work out a plan.

'He's a slippery character is the baron, and no fool. He'd be sure to get suspicious if you suddenly turned up out of the blue and then started wheedling him.'

Pearl tossed back the gin and refilled her glass. 'We have to do something. We can't afford to hang about.'

'I know. I know. I've never missed a trick yet, and don't intend to start now. Not after everything I've gone through, and all because of your sister. She owes me good and proper, I'll tell you that for nowt. All we have to do is put our brains to steep and come up with some way to lighten the baron of enough of his wealth to see us in clover, without him ever suspecting he's been robbed.'

'And how do we do that? Strike him deaf, blind and dumb first?'

'Why not? Happen I should just knock him over the head and have done with it.'

'He'd see you coming a mile off. From all accounts he's wily as a snake.'

This, of course, was the crux of their problem. The baron was far too intelligent and well versed in methods of fraud and trickery to be easily conned. And he'd be utterly ruthless if it ever came down to fisticuffs between the two of them. Kit had no appetite for a fight, yet no matter how many ideas he came up with, none seemed workable or even feasible.

His only hope seemed to be to work on Ruby. Perhaps he could persuade her to help.

Chapter Seventeen

To Ruby's everlasting shame she could not help herself from responding to her husband's lovemaking. Most nights she was in his bed early, eagerly waiting for him to come to her. On that very first morning when she'd woken to find herself alone, she'd lain in a daze of guilt and yet felt reluctant to rise, wanting only to languish in his bed and go over and over the events that had forever changed her from a girl to a woman. So much passion, and many delightfully unexpected discoveries! The night with Bart had been a revelation.

She did not wonder why he had not chosen to take her during the years they'd spent together on the tug, despite his strongly professed desire for her. Nor did she give him any credit for making her first experience of lovemaking particularly enjoyable. Ruby was far too preoccupied with blaming him.

He had denied Kit the most precious gift a girl could give to the man she loved. Wiping the tears of misguided self-pity from her eyes, Ruby vowed that she would never, *ever*, allow it to happen again.

She consoled herself by the thought that it was only her body which had betrayed Kit, the romantic sweetheart of her lost youth, that she could at least still give him her heart. In a way, she loathed Bart all the more for tempting her into these sinful pleasures. She had been young, a virgin still. What hope had she of refusing? He had taken advantage of her, for which she would never forgive him, she told herself.

But at the end of that first day, Ruby cooked supper as always and when the time came for them to go to bed, he simply jerked his chin in the direction of his cabin, telling her that was where he expected her to sleep in future.

And to her intense shame, a pulse of excitement began to beat low in the pit of her stomach. Ruby had obeyed without protest, her mind a blur of confused emotion, a furious resistance mixed with desire. She told herself that she could do nothing to prevent what was about to happen as he possessed complete control over her.

Yet later, when he came to her, his glorious golden body as naked and strong as she remembered, she was more than ready for him, greedy for whatever he had to offer.

–

Following his failure with Giles Pickering, Bart was moody and bad-tempered for days, hardly saying a word to anyone. The men were largely philosophical about his lack of success, although there were a few grumbles. Plans for a strike fizzled out. Men still slipped in and out of the cabin for discussions of an evening, but Bart went out and about with them less frequently. He seemed to spend more of his time working the boats, which was what Ruby loved best. She didn't ask him why this was so. Nor did he offer any explanation.

The year progressed at its own pace, the days long, sometimes twelve or more hours at a stretch, and often cold and wet. The routine grew familiar to her, filled with activity and interest whether it be loading crates of pottery or rolls of cotton, negotiating locks or making rope fenders. Yet the work was hard and unrelenting, Bart himself equally so. Once, she slipped on the wet boards of the deck and cut her chin. He staunched the bleeding but allowed her no time off work to recuperate, despite a raging headache as a result of the fall.

'I'm worn out. I need to rest up a bit.'

'You can't demand that I turn my hand to honest endeavour and not pull your weight.'

Ruby was outraged. 'Of course I pull me own weight. Are you saying I'm trying to skive off? Flippin' cheek!'

'Don't turn soft on me, Ruby McBride. I can't stand a woman who expects to be cosseted all the time. Real work is much harder graft than pulling the odd con trick.'

She didn't dispute that, and because an honest, safe life was what Ruby craved, she gritted her teeth against the pain, mopped the blood from her injured chin and battled on, worrying whether the cut would leave a scar.

In the bitter winter months he gave her a thick overcoat to wear, known as a 'duker's rough', and taught her how to wrap strips of hessian around her legs to keep them dry. Some days Sparky might be working with them, perhaps at Number Three Dock where the Irish ships berthed, or Number Four for the London ships, or carrying wheat from the Canadian ships. Ruby would always pay particular attention to these, half hoping she might see Billy. Hadn't he said how one day he meant to go on a big ship?

And in all the time she worked with her husband, Ruby rarely had any money of her own, save for the few coppers he gave her now and then to buy herself a pie or mug of tea when she gossiped with Aggie and the other women. She would complain that it wasn't enough, that she deserved to be properly paid, just as Sparky was.

'Why do you? I buy the soap, candles, paraffin, tea and provisions. I provide coal for the fire, clothes for your back, what need have you for more?'

'It would show that you value me. I deserve it, for the sake of my pride if nothing else – a need for my own independence.' And he would snort with laughter, as if she had made some sort of joke.

'I thought you believed in the rights of workers?'

'I do, but apparently that only proves I'm soft in the head. Besides, if I gave you money, Ruby, you might take it into your head to run away. You're still my wife, but your reluctance in the role is all too evident. If I gave you too much independence you might be tempted to abscond, as I believe you have done before, more than once.'

She hated him even more when he was right. But mostly for his control over her, and did not hesitate to tell him so. 'You can't treat a woman as if she were a chattel, a horse or dog that you happen to own.'

'Indeed not. A horse is a damn sight more useful, although maybe a woman can supply other benefits.'

Then he'd pull her into his arms and begin to make love to her till she was purring with pleasure and had quite forgotten the thread of her argument. It shamed Ruby that despite her love for Kit, this man could still make her shiver with need. He had only to put his hand on her thigh and her pulses would start to race. She must be a wanton, a loose woman, to have such strong physical cravings for a man she professed to loathe.

Spending time with Kit, Ruby told herself, was all that kept her sane. Though wary of taking unnecessary risks, they continued to meet secretly. Whenever she had a little free time she would run to him, eager for his kisses, his assurances that he still loved her. Were her husband ever to suspect that she had a lover, albeit a chaste one thus far, she knew his rage would be incandescent.

There were times when he seemed to watch her ever more closely, and she feared all might be lost, but then the moment would pass and Ruby would dismiss the idea from her mind. Discovery was a frightening prospect. Bart would be unlikely to believe in her innocence, nor take kindly to the idea of being cuckolded, even if, strictly speaking, it were untrue. And he was not a man to cross.

But surely her love for Kit rose above such base concerns. He was her romantic ideal, a boy who had suffered as she had suffered throughout a punishingly short and difficult childhood. They were soul mates. Unfortunately, because of the clandestine nature of their meetings, she couldn't entirely relax or give him what he asked.

'I couldn't, Kit. I'm still his wife, it wouldn't be right,' she would protest, whenever he begged for more.

'Why would it matter if you did betray him?' Kit would demand to know. 'Isn't he the much-hated baron, a husband you loathe?'

She really couldn't explain, even to herself. Ruby seemed to be in a state of total confusion about what was right and what was wrong, let alone understanding her own confused emotions.

'Lovemaking, in the purely physical sense, is unnecessary to prove the depth of our love,' she told him. And, to be fair, he finally seemed to accept the situation with remarkable aplomb which, perversely, irked her all the more. How could he be content to allow matters to go on in this way indefinitely when she was in a constant agony of suspense? Wilful and contradictory as ever, she longed for him to sweep her off her feet and run away with her to Canada, to fulfil her dream.

'We'll be together soon,' she promised. 'We won't always have to skulk about in back alleys, content with a few fumbling kisses. As soon as we can find our Pearl and get away from this place, everything will be different. We'll be together for always then.'

'It takes a deal of money to get to Canada,' he would say, fondling her breasts and wondering if he could ever hope to persuade her to change her mind. She was a handsome piece of goods was Ruby, not so luscious as Pearl, nor so yielding, but a fine woman all the same. He always hoped that today might be his lucky day. 'There's little point otherwise, is there? We need a bit of cash put by, as well as being safe from that tyrant of a husband of yours.'

'I've told you, I have no money of my own, and I'll not steal a penny piece off anyone, not even off him.'

'But he owes it to you, Ruby. For back wages if nothing else.' Drat the woman. She was too damned stubborn.

So many times over the weeks and months following, this conversation would be repeated in various ways, but always ended the same. Kit would appeal for her to take money from the baron, reminding her of the difficulties of living rough, that he still hadn't found himself a job despite looking for one from dawn to dusk.

Ruby would listen and her soft heart would go out to him, full of love and sympathy, and yet she would obstinately refuse to rob her husband of anything, not even her own fidelity.

Months slipped by and nothing was resolved between them. Ruby, blithely ignorant of the dangerous undercurrent of Kit's resentment, felt riddled with guilt at seeming to fail him. She believed in him utterly. Yet she enjoyed her life with Bart working the barges, and the passion-filled nights, details of which she never divulged to Kit, or even allowed herself to dwell too closely upon the feelings they evoked in her.

She had her little house, which she loved, but her dream of gathering her family about her seemed as far distant as ever.

Bart had taken great care not to make her pregnant, for which she was thankful. Lately, though, he'd begun to talk of them starting a family together, a prospect which filled Ruby with a strange mix of excitement and dread. This loveless marriage surely represented everything that had gone wrong in her life. She needed to escape before it was too late, before he'd given her a child and tied her to him forever. The father of her children must be her beloved Kit. Hadn't he loved her for years? Hadn't he sacrificed his young life, suffered the punishment of the reformatory because of his great love for her? Ruby knew that no man, not even Kit, would be willing to take on another man's child. If she got pregnant, she might well lose him for good.

Yet neither could she risk letting Kit have his way with her. Not yet, or how would she explain a child to Bart? Oh, what a muddle.

She lay in Kit's arms by the canal towpath and urged him to find a solution to their problem which, so far, he'd been quite unable to do. Even if they couldn't be together all the time, at least being with him here, now, was more pleasant than lying awake night after night worrying over the matter till her eyes were red-rimmed through lack of sleep and she was too exhausted to work properly the next day.

'There must be an answer, Kit. We just have to find it. I do mean to leave him. I *must*! I can't breathe living this way. I shall tell him that it's you I love, that we need to be together.'

He thrust her from him, gave her a little shake as if to bring her to her senses. 'For goodness sake, Ruby, if he ever found out we were seeing each other, he'd kill me. He might throttle you an' all.'

Kit was appalled by this possibility, which seemed very real. He was keen to keep Ruby sweet and committed to him, yet anxious for her not to lose patience and leave her husband – not till he'd managed to work out a way to get himself a good slice of the baron's assets. As his wife, Ruby had access to riches beyond his imagining; the kind of money Kit could never save in two lifetimes.

He just needed a little more time to persuade her to get her hands on it. Dissatisfaction was growing. Rumours were circulating around the docks that the baron had failed to help the workers' cause because he hadn't tried hard enough. Word had it that he'd actually sided with the management and done nothing more. Kit had no idea whether this was true or not.

What did surprise him was that little was known about Barthram Stobbs, except that he'd come to the canal basin mere months after the Ship Canal opened. He would like to know more about his past, such details were often useful, but everywhere he asked, he'd come up against a blank wall. No one knew anything about him except that he was a rebellious young man with a chip on his shoulder. It couldn't be as big a chip as his own, which was why he spent so much of his time sweet talking Ruby with practised persistence.

'As you said yourself, pet, you're still his wife and, as such, you should demand your share of the profits.'

Ruby was shocked. 'I couldn't. I really couldn't.' She meant that her pride wouldn't allow her to ask, yet couldn't bring herself to admit as much. She'd certainly no intention of breaking the law and stealing it.

'Aye, you could, Ruby. He doesn't own you. He robbed you of your freedom, of your youth. Ask him for a proper share of the money. Demand it as your right.'

'I ask him all the time but he just points out that I'm well provided for, and laughs at the idea of my wanting money of my own. He says he's saving it for me. Anyway, I've told you, Kit, I don't care about money. I just want you to find our Pearl, then we can be off.'

She pressed herself closer in his arms, lifting her lovely face to his, her eyes, lips, fingers, every inch of her pliant body begging him to understand her dilemma. 'Bart hasn't been cruel to me. In fact he's quite considerate in his way, I suppose, so far as he's capable. Some might say he's a good husband, quite kind and considerate.' She thought about this for a moment, privately admitting it was true, at least more true than it used to be. 'But I'll not rob him of what rightfully belongs to him. What I object to is the way he controls every inch of my life, every thought and decision I make. I just want to be free, free to be with you, and our Billy and Pearl. I can't bear to be apart from you any longer.'

Kit swallowed his irritation as he smiled down at her. 'Then do something about it. You owe me that much, surely, after what I went through for you. Think of some way to make him compensate for how he's robbed us of our happiness.'

Ruby looked into his eyes and felt her heart clench with fear and guilt. He was right. What hope did they have of ever finding Pearl without money, and she had no wish to fail in that, or to lose Kit. Hadn't he always been her soul-mate? Just because Bart had softened slightly in his attitude towards her, now that he wanted a family, didn't make what he had done to her right. And hadn't she always been able to stand up for herself?

'All right Kit.' She almost dragged the words out, but it felt the right thing to do, before she was trapped with a child. Yet even as she spoke the words something broke inside her, and a new fear pounded in her heart. 'I'll ask him, as you suggest, but I'll never steal from him, so long as that's understood.' The prospect of being caught if she ever tried such a thing, of the reformatory and prison loomed too large for her ever to change her mind over that. But it was up to her to break the impasse. 'I will do what I can, I promise.'

'There's my sweetheart.' And he began to kiss her till her head spun.

Recognising the effect he had upon her, Kit felt an unexpected surge of pity, for he'd absolutely no intention of ever giving up his life here in the canal basin to follow this cock-eyed dream of hers, or of swapping one sister for this one. He'd had a good life once, with nice little earners

215

in place. Then she'd come along and ruined everything. If he'd never got involved with her childish escape from Ignatius House in the first place, he'd never have been caught and sent to the reformatory training ship; never have been forced to endure the birch, the sickness and the sweat box conditions amidships.

Neither would his family have suffered as they had, following that dreadful day. Without his support, and the care he'd taken to keep them fed and provided for, his mother had faded away and died. Largely, Kit believed, of starvation since she would always give her last mouthful to her beloved children. His orphaned brothers and sisters had been put into children's homes every bit as dreadful as the one Ruby had fled from, and he'd never set eyes on them again. A part of him appreciated that it wasn't all Ruby's fault. She was as much a victim of the system as he himself had been, yet she owed him big time. And if there was some way that money could be made out of this unlikely marriage of hers, he was more than willing to take advantage of it. When had he ever turned down an opportunity to make a bit of brass?

Chapter Eighteen

It was a bitterly cold day and the tug was passing by Trafford Park, which had somehow managed to hold on to its rural character despite the encroachment of new manufacturing industries springing up where once children had played, families had picnicked or rowed boats on the lake. They came to Waters Meeting, where a branch of the Bridgewater Canal went off to the left over the Barton Aqueduct until it ultimately joined the Leeds & Liverpool. Keeping to the main canal, the *Blackbird* continued on its way, slowing when they reached the stretch of canal where the coal barges from Worsley were moored.

'Nip on board, Ruby, and grab some. We're running a bit low. I've been afraid to light the stove in case we ran out altogether before nightfall.'

'I will hell as like.'

'Why ever not? You've done it before often enough.'

This was true, though under protest. She had in fact grown quite nimble at jumping on to passing coal barges and tossing a few cobs of the stuff on to the deck of the *Blackbird*. It reminded her of the scrounging she'd done with Kit on the slag heap. So on this day, as always, she consoled herself it was no worse than that. Not stealing exactly, not from anyone who couldn't afford to part with a bit. And it was pitch dark for all it wasn't yet seven o'clock, so who would see? The coal barge had been anchored for the night and the skipper and mate were no doubt either fast asleep or in the pub. And she and Bart were nearly out of coal and freezing cold.

She tucked up her skirts so that they did not impede her, tugged the cap she wore to hold her hair in place well down and got herself positioned ready to jump. She made it in one agile leap, graceful as a deer, and heard his soft chuckle follow her over the water. Ruby gathered up a few of the largest pieces she could find and tossed them one at a time over onto the *Blackbird*'s deck. As quickly as they fell, Bart picked them up and dropped them into a sack he kept handy for the purpose.

'That'll do, Ruby,' he called quietly across to her.

'Just one more.' She scrabbled about, found one, then another, too tempting to resist as she thought of their need for a warm cabin that night, and the stew she would prepare. When she'd filled his belly and got him all nice and cosy, she'd make her demands clear. No more lovemaking. She deserved, and should be given, proper financial recompense for her work. And as she schemed and picked coal, all the while the *Blackbird* was moving alongside the stationary coal barge, albeit slowly. 'Quick, Ruby! We're nearly past.'

Again gathering up the hem of her skirts which were trailing loose, she ran along the edge of the Worsley coal barge and flung herself into the air in a flying leap. She missed the deck by mere inches. Her fingers, grappling for purchase, failed completely and she fell with a resounding splash into the murky waters of the canal. Fear hammered in her breast. She was wearing so many clothes against the cold: the heavy greatcoat, thick socks, boots, the hessian strips wrapped about her legs, and several layers of clothing beneath her dress. Ruby could feel them dragging her down, pulling her under so that she choked as water filled her mouth.

Then something hit her shoulders: a rope. A voice shouted, ordering her to grab it. Somehow, she managed to take hold and Bart pulled her up, finally grasping her by the shoulders and heaving her on board.

As she lay floundering on deck gasping for breath and shaking with cold, he said, 'Are you going to lie there all day? Go and put some dry clothes on and get that fire lit. I'll be wanting my supper soon.'

'Damn you, Barthram Stobbs, you get worse. You're the nastiest, most ungrateful man I ever…'

'Bedded? I hope I'm the one and only, Ruby, dear. Supper. Now, please?'

Dripping water everywhere, she stalked past him, head held high. 'And I hope it chokes you.'

Later, when she was stripped off and rubbing herself dry by the stove, he climbed down the ladder, lifted the pan from the heat and took her to his bed where he completed the process of warming her with his own body. Ruby did not protest. Her demands for compensation would have to wait until tomorrow.

–

There was no time the next day for talking, nor the one after that, as they had a new load of cotton to take on board and transport to Liverpool. A few days after that, it was Bart, as always, who startled her by demanding that she take part in another of his schemes. It came as a bitter blow. Ruby refused, absolutely, to have anything to do with it. 'Have you taken leave of your senses? I thought you were done with all that.'

'This is the last one, I promise.'

By the time he'd finished explaining his plan, she was slack-jawed with shock. 'You must be mad if you think I'd agree to waylay a fella in an alley. D'you take me for some sort of trollop?'

'No, I don't think you're a trollop, Ruby.' He smiled placatingly at her, in a manner she'd come to know well. 'You needn't let him actually do anything to you. Besides, I shall be nearby to see that he doesn't. I want you to make certain that he makes the suggestion. Or, if necessary, you offer and make damn sure he accepts.'

'There you are then, you do want me to be a tart.' She was outraged, and deeply hurt that he should think so little of her.

'It is only a trick, Ruby.'

'And I know the sort of tricks you're talking about.'

'No, I've told you, I shall be standing by to step in and confront him the moment he walks into our trap. He won't lay a finger on you. I just need proof that Giles Pickering uses women much as he treats his workers, with callous contempt. I need to find some sort of lever so I can prise out of him what the workers deserve. I want to unmask him as a ruthless, social-climbing, cold-hearted womaniser who doesn't give a damn who he treads on, so long as he gets what he wants.'

There was such loathing, venom in his voice, and Ruby was stunned into silence for a whole half-minute. She cleared her throat, asking the next question in a quieter, more rational tone.

'And how will that help you get better pay and conditions for the dockers?'

'Give me the ammunition and I can fire the bullets, believe me. He'll be a lot more compliant once I can knock him off that self-erected pedestal of his.'

'You mean blackmail?'

'If you wish to call it that.'

'Why do you hate him so much? What's he ever done to you?'

'What indeed!'

Bart walked away, his back turned towards her as he considered his answer, and although she couldn't see his face when he spoke, Ruby was in no doubt of his feelings on the matter. 'He once hurt someone I cared very deeply about, and I mean to make him pay for that. I mean to take from him all that he holds dear, just as he took it from me.'

She was shocked. 'Who was this person? Was it a woman. Tell me. What did he do?'

'The details needn't concern you, Ruby.'

'They do if you mean to get me involved.'

But his only answer to that was a closed door. He had gone.

–

Ruby ran to Kit to beg him to help her. 'What am I to do? I daren't even imagine what horrors might befall me if I agree to this. How do I know he'll bother to save me? I could be raped, murdered, anything, in that back alley.'

'I'm sure that's unlikely,' Kit told her, even as his brain furiously turned over the possible implications of the baron's plan, and any advantages it might bring to his own cause.

'You don't understand. He's utterly ruthless. I've only his word that he'll save me, and I really don't trust him as far as I can spit.'

Desperate to make Kit see her difficulties, Ruby told him how Bart had made her steal coal, and how unsympathetic he'd been when she'd fallen in the canal. It didn't seem to occur to her that there would be even less sympathy from a young man who had himself taught her the art of coal scrounging years ago. She excluded the part about them falling into bed together at the end of it all, preferring to eradicate this guilty memory from her mind.

'Now he means to turn me into a prostitute in a nasty attempt at blackmail. I can't bear it. We have to go to Canada. Now! Together. We must make one last effort to find our Pearl, then we can all have a new beginning in a new country. I'm quite sure I could find our Billy, if only we could just get on a ship to take us there.'

Kit struggled to hide his irritation. 'Nay, lass, don't talk soft. I've told you, it takes a deal of money to emigrate, and we haven't a bean between us. How could we get on a ship for Canada, even supposing we could find your Pearl?'

He did not say that he knew already where her sister was: that at this precise moment she was no doubt dealing with one of her regulars, earning them a crust if not exactly an honest one, nor one with much butter on it. A state of affairs they meant to change given a decent plan and the right sort of co-operation. Sadly, no such plan had emerged from their endless arguments and discussions and Pearl, as well as Ruby, was growing fretful.

In truth, Kit felt under siege from both sisters and was near to throwing in the towel and giving up on the whole deal, when Ruby suddenly said something which caught his attention. 'What was that? He gave you what?'

'I said, I do have something we could use to make a fresh start in Canada. Not money, but a pendant that he gave me once. He'd stolen it from this woman who was showing us round her house. Not a house that he could afford to buy, mind, but one he was pretending to…'

'What sort of pendant?' Kit interrupted, his head aching with the effort of restraining himself from shaking the information out of her.

'A ruby pendant,' she admitted. 'He said it was highly appropriate.'

Kit beamed, all the anger seeping from him. 'And so it is, Ruby, my love. So it is.'

–

Ruby looked surprisingly convincing in her disguise. She'd grown somewhat taller than when the idea of passing herself off as a cabin boy had first occurred to her, but she was still slender enough to get away with dressing as an ordinary seaman, or so she hoped. She'd suggested that they might both try to get jobs on board. Kit had disagreed.

'Why should I work when I can go for nothing? Anyroad, they'd be unlikely to take me on, with my record. And I wouldn't like you to cut your hair, Ruby.'

'Why not? It'll grow again.'

'I don't like women with short hair. Not ladylike. You can wear my slouch cap.' He made her tuck up her hair into a knot, then pulled the cap over it. 'Perfect.'

They were testing out the gear for their plan at the entrance to the tunnel down by the Roman fort, the only place they could think of away from prying eyes. It was cold and damp in there since the tunnel led almost as far as Duke's Lock at the junction to the Bridgewater Canal. Ruby had no wish to go too far along it in case she should come across the baron waiting at the other end. Even being here, so close to the water, made her feel anxious and jumpy. She kept glancing along it, half expecting him to appear out of the gloom.

It was Kit who decided that they would stow away in one of the lifeboats. 'No one will think to look for us there.' Ruby's disguise, he explained, would come in useful once the ship was underway and they needed to venture out from time to time to look for food. 'There must be scores, if not hundreds, employed on a big freighter like that. Most of them won't even know each other. We can just mingle with the other blokes when we need to for meals and such like, and vanish when we don't. No one will suspect a thing.'

Ruby sincerely hoped that was true, but it all seemed much more dangerous than her fanciful imaginings had led her to believe. Yet hadn't she grown used to taking risks over these last few years? Surely, it was worth the gamble to get away from the baron, go to Canada, and find Billy. 'I really don't want to go without our Pearl.'

Kit laid a finger to the side of his nose. 'Ah, now, I've been asking around again, and got word that she's working in a pub Rochdale way. I'm going over there this evening, s'matter of fact, see what I can find out.'

Kit had decided that she might never hand over the pendant if he didn't offer up Pearl in return.

Ruby's face came alight with joy. 'Really? Oh, Kit, you are so clever.' She let out a great sigh of happiness. 'Do you really think you can find her?'

'I do.'

'Oh, what would I do without you? I really don't know how to thank you.'

'That's easy. I quite fancy you in those trousers, so maybe you could start by considering actions rather than words.'

He pulled her roughly into his arms, clenching the soft curve of her buttocks and pressing her hard against him. Ruby felt his arousal and chuckled as she shook her head, the fronds of thick brown hair whispering over her flushed cheeks. She pushed his hands away, while at the same time lifting her face to be kissed, almost bubbling over with excitement as she laughed up at him. 'Not yet, Kit. Not till we've left these shores far behind and there's no further danger from my tyrant husband. Till then, you have to behave yourself. You must see that.' She playfully tapped his hand away from where it lingered at the buttons of her waistband.

'You're a lovely lass, Ruby, but hard on a chap. A tease, nothing less.'

He wasn't pleased by her refusal, she could tell. But then the growing impatience in his face was more frequently evident these days. She arched a provocative glance at him from beneath her lashes. 'It'll be worth the wait in the long run.'

He might well have been tempted to persist to try his luck, were he not wholly satisfied with Pearl's offerings in that direction. Besides, he had other, more important matters on his mind. 'You'd best give me the pendant, pet. It'll be safer with me.'

'Why?'

He smiled pityingly at her, as if she were half stupid. 'Now how would you defend yourself, a skinny little thing like you?'

'Defend myself against who?'

Kit could feel the tension in his jaw, just as if his teeth were clenched for all he was actually smiling at her. 'Theft. Against whoever tried to rob you. It happens all the time on ships. We'll need eyes in the backs of our heads once we get on board.'

She smiled brilliantly at him. 'But I shall always have you beside me, Kit. I've nothing to fear. Don't worry, the pendant is tucked away nice and safe. Go on, go and fetch our Pearl. I can't wait.'

Swallowing his fury, he spoke through gritted teeth. 'I'll bring her to our meeting place at the end of the tunnel next Thursday, an hour before sailing.'

Ruby frowned with disappointment. 'You won't let me down, will you? You'll have her with you?'

'When have I ever let you down?'

As he swaggered away, leaving her to pull her frock back on over the trousers so that Bart wouldn't suspect what she was about, Ruby wondered why, deep inside, she felt the slightest bit sick, as if something wasn't quite right. Was it the excitement of being about to see Pearl again after all these years? Or was it fear for the risks they would take, the hazardous journey they were about to embark upon to a new land, because the thought of making love to Kit Jarvis suddenly seemed like a betrayal of sorts?

'You daft ha'p'orth,' she told herself as she strode away through the tunnel. 'Now you *have* lost your marbles. How can you betray a man you never asked to marry in the first place, and don't even love?'

As she swung around the corner out of sight, a soft voice echoed in the darkness behind her. 'How indeed, Ruby McBride? How indeed.'

Chapter Nineteen

Ruby lay drowsy in the glowing warmth from the coals, filled with languor after their lovemaking. Beside her lay the long, hard body of her husband. If she wished, her fingers could stretch out and stroke his naked, gleaming flesh. The very thought set her imagination racing, recalling the shameful pleasures of the last hour, reawakening that hunger in her which never seemed to be quenched. The merest butterfly kiss from her fingertips and he would turn to her, filling that aching need once more. She did no such thing, of course. Wouldn't that be a true betrayal of her beloved Kit? This man didn't give twopence for her, his own wife. Kit, on the other hand, had sacrificed his life and suffered untold privation and punishment on her behalf. That was the difference between them, the evidence of their love.

Yet she could not sleep.

This was proving to be the longest night of her life. Ruby lay, tossing and turning, agonising over whether she was doing the right thing, whether Kit really would manage to find Pearl, and whether she would be willing to drop everything and come with them to Canada at a moment's notice. It was a great deal to ask of anyone, and her sister had ever been self-obsessed. She might have a good job in that pub, friends, a lover, even a husband. For the first time, Ruby realised that she'd given no consideration to this possibility.

'Are you awake, Ruby?' Bart's voice came to her out of the soft dark.

'I'm restless,' she admitted, wanting to blame him for her sleeplessness.

'Shall I soothe you?' He lifted the heavy curtain of brown hair, smoothed it back from her hot brow. 'You are over-warm. Are you sickening for something?'

'More like we used too much coal on the flippin' stove.'

'Are you happy, Ruby?'

'Why would I be?'

'You gave every impression of it just now.'

She fell silent, unsure how to respond.

'Have you yet forgiven me for making you marry me?' His teeth glowed white in the light from the fire as he grinned down at her, wickedly sensuous in the gloom.

'I certainly haven't forgiven you for the risks you've made me take, most of them for no reason.'

'For every reason. The work I do is vital for the dockers. I've explained all of that.'

'You've explained very little. Who is this Giles Pickering you seem to have it in for? Why him, and none of the other employers? Why not the Ship Canal Company, who likewise have a long way to go to make life easier for their workers? Why always this Pickering chap?'

'If I tell you, Ruby, will you keep it a secret? Just between the two of us?'

She looked at him, puzzled, his eyes glittering in the semi-darkness. Was that with anger or passion? She couldn't quite decide. Even after all these years, he was still an enigma to her.

'I know how to keep a secret.'

'Very well. Giles Pickering is my father.'

Ruby was stunned into silence. This was the last thing she'd expected.

He abruptly sat up, rested his arms on his knees as he stared into the flickering flames. He began to speak, his voice hollow and bleak with remembered pain. 'He was the one who disapproved of the girl I was to marry. She was called Alice, the sweetest, gentlest, prettiest creature you could ever imagine.

'But her father was a grocer. In trade. Not good enough for the snobbish tastes of my father, even though he himself came up from nothing. A self-made businessman. I believe he spoke to her, went on and on about how she'd be "dragging me down", although she never admitted as much. The pressure made her ill and drove her to call the wedding off. In the end…' He paused, as if fighting to control his emotion. 'In the end she killed herself.'

'Oh, no! How?'

'Her family took her on holiday to Torquay to recuperate, and she flung herself off a cliff. I shall never forgive my father for that. Never!'

Ruby took some moments before answering. She wanted to ask him what sort of father could consider it beyond the pale for him to marry a grocer's daughter, and what his mother had had to say on the matter. But somehow, with a man like Bart, it felt like prying. Then, without thinking, she crept closer and wrapped her arms about his hunched figure. 'Revenge only hurts them what harbours it. It solves nothing.'

'That's easy for you to say, Ruby.'

'No it isn't, as a matter of fact. There's been nothing easy about my life. I understand the feeling right enough.' Sensing the tension in him, she smoothed a hand over his naked back, soothing, comforting. 'There have been people I would've liked to get me own back on. Sister Joseph for one, not to mention that lot at the reformatory who were far worse. And I could have killed you stone dead once over, without a second's thought.'

'Once over?'

'Well, still could, given half a chance, I suppose.' She felt the vibration of his laughter and chuckled along with him, still stroking his back, but it didn't occur to her to wonder why her threat sounded so hollow.

'You make me quake in my shoes, Ruby McBride.'

'You said you'd stop calling me by that name, once we were – you know – man and wife proper.'

'Ah, but we're not exactly, are we? It takes more than mere coupling to make a proper marriage, don't you think?' He turned to see her face, and Ruby nodded, her mind a turmoil of confused emotion. How was it he could tug so at her heartstrings?

'Anyroad, you should stop and think before you do anything you might regret. You don't really want me to play the whore with your own father, do you? Not just so you can blackmail him. What good would that do?'

He gathered her into his arms, holding her close. 'How very sweet and caring you are all of a sudden, Ruby.'

'Oh, I'm a proper little angel, me, when I want to be.'

'I prefer it when you play the devil.'

Pulling her beneath him, he pushed her back on to the bed to spread out her arms, capturing her hands in his. But he didn't start to make love to her as she expected, half hoped that he might, nor even to kiss her. He simply looked deeply into her eyes. Ruby found herself gazing back: a long, serious, thoughtful look, assessing, appraising, evaluating, as if each was seeing the other for the first time. Never had she known him to divulge so much information about himself, or for him to be so tender towards her. She felt sure he must sense the slow, hard beat of her heart, read her inner thoughts and secrets, her plans to leave him. It was this last awesome prospect, which brought her from her trance.

'I thought I'd go early to the house, at the end of this week.'

He looked momentarily surprised, as well he might since the change of subject had been startlingly abrupt. Ruby could have kicked herself, but didn't attempt an explanation for fear of making it worse.

'Is there any particular reason?'

'Not really, only I need to rinse those net curtains through. I'm ashamed to have them on show.' The talk of net curtains in the midst of all this intensity of emotion seemed incongruous, almost laughable. She could see the shutters coming down over his rugged features, fixed firmly back in place before he coldly responded.

'Of course. If that's what you would like, Ruby.'

'It is. And you'll come on Friday, as usual?' By which time she would be long gone, heading west to Canada. Strangely, she felt a tinge of regret.

–

Over the following days Ruby became increasingly jumpy. Each morning she half expected Bart to put his blackmail plan against Pickering into effect, yet he did not even refer to it. This gave no relief, however, since she was far too concerned about her own reckless plan. Escaping from Sister Joseph seemed mild by comparison with the agonies she was now experiencing.

When Thursday evening finally arrived, Ruby stuffed a few belongings in a carpet bag, just as if she were really going to their house on Quay Street, as she'd claimed, and cheerily waved goodbye.

'See you tomorrow,' she called. 'Goodbye, Bart.'

Perhaps it was the unexpectedly formal farewell which alerted him, but he looked up from where he was cleaning the decks, narrowing his eyes as she leapt from the tug on to the quay, her movements as graceful and fluid as ever. There had been moments in recent weeks when he'd fancied that he might be reaching her but in this last day or two she'd grown oddly distant again, rarely speaking to him and yet jumping in a startled sort of way whenever he spoke to her. He didn't attempt to detain her now, merely remained on deck, a thoughtful frown creasing his brow as he watched her wave and smile, and stride away. Something wasn't right. He couldn't put his finger on what it might be but watching her walk away, some inner instinct told Bart that, in spite of all his efforts, he had lost her. Or more accurately, he'd never quite had her.

Glancing back, Ruby saw him standing on the tug, a breeze ruffling his red-gold hair, feet astride. He looked rather as he had on that first day he'd brought her here, when he'd waited for her to choose. Not that she'd much of a choice to make, either to go along with the inevitable, or starve.

Now he stood watching almost as if he knew this was the last he would ever see of her. A fanciful notion, she told herself, since how could he know? As she strode away along the quay, Ruby felt a sudden and unexpected lump come to her throat. How would he manage without her? Who would cook his meals and wash his clothes? Who would occupy his bed? For goodness sake, what was wrong with her? This was no time for sentiment. What if they had known a few moments of pleasure? He was still the man who had forced her into marriage and controlled her ever since, making her take all manner of risks which could well have landed her in jail, and all to further a campaign for revenge against his own father. The very idea.

Would he succeed? She wondered. Would he find a lever to use against the man? Was it possible to force the all-powerful Giles Pickering to recognise the unions and improve the pay and conditions of the men on his payroll? Somehow, she rather thought that it might be. The baron was not one for giving up, not until he got what he wanted. For all he'd been the bane of her life ever since she'd first clapped eyes on him, Ruby had to admire his tenacity. But then neither was she a quitter, and wouldn't she soon have what she'd always wanted?

When she had vanished from sight around the struts of the bridge, Bart set down his cleaning rag and reached for his coat.

–

She hurried through the quiet streets, past Coal Wharf, under the viaduct and out along Chester road, constantly glancing back over her shoulder, anxious in case he should choose to follow her. She jumped at every shadow, her fancy making her nervy. She almost leapt from her skin when once a dog ran across her path, another time as a youth stepped out in front of her before sidling guiltily off, clearly up to no good. But she saw no one.

Not until a pair of figures loomed out of the mist that hung over the water.

'Pearl?' Ruby stopped in her tracks, unable to quite believe her eyes. Could this be her little sister? This voluptuous beauty with the craziest of red hair, a sweeping feather in the broad brimmed straw hat, a jacket and skirt in the loudest purple and maroon stripes imaginable. Where was the plump, pretty girl with the dandelion mop whom she had loved so dearly?

'Goodness, you've changed. Is it really you, love?'

'Last time I looked it was.'

Ruby's eyes filled with tears. 'Oh, I'm that pleased to see you. It's been so long. There've been times when I thought I'd never find you. I can't really believe it even now. Oh, come to Ruby, pet. I've missed you so much.' And she held out her arms, just as Mam would've done ready to soothe the prodigal child, to offer love and comfort to her sibling. After a moment's hesitation, Pearl stepped forward and allowed herself to be hugged.

Ruby saw at once that her little sister had indeed changed, that something about her had gone forever. But then, was it any wonder after what she'd been through? Heaven alone knew what had happened to her after Ruby had no longer been there to protect her. She'd been damaged already, even before her elder sister had left the reformatory. Her mood swings had been increasingly erratic and she'd found it hard to trust anyone, ruthlessly disposing of friends, always leaving them before they left her. Perhaps she blamed her sister, as well as her mother, for abandoning her. It would take time, Ruby guessed, to restore that confidence.

She stroked back the garish red locks and smiled into the pale face. 'It'll be all right, chuck, don't worry. We're together now and nobody is ever going to part us again.'

Pearl said nothing, having had it forcibly impressed upon her by Kit that she mustn't start to argue, blame or contradict her sister the minute they met. It was vital, he'd told her that they all get on that ship together, or how else could he get his hands on that dratted ruby pendant? Thinking of this, she managed a tremulous smile.

'Has Kit told you the plan?' Ruby asked, glancing anxiously back over her shoulder, checking they hadn't been followed, wondering how they were doing for time.

'Yes.'

'And are you willing to come with us, to find our Billy and start a new life?'

Pearl nodded, and, suddenly overcome at the prospect of all her dreams being on the brink of coming true, Ruby squealed and grabbed her close in a suffocating hug of delight. 'Come on then. Let's get on with it.'

–

Getting on board was laughably easy. Such men as were still working on the loading were concentrating far too much on the job in hand to pay proper attention to what was going on behind their backs. Their minds were fixed firmly on the welcome beer that would be waiting for them, once the ship was underway.

'In here,' Kit hissed, and lifting the tarpaulin that covered a lifeboat, he urged the two girls to climb inside. They did so, crouching in the bottom of it, hardly daring to breathe in case anyone had heard them, for what may have been hours. It certainly felt like it.

'I don't know what I'm doing here in this dratted boat, messing up me best frock,' Pearl complained, quite unable to keep quiet any longer. 'Only you, Ruby, could come up with such a daft notion.'

'This is a new beginning for us all,' Ruby whispered. 'I can't tell you how thrilled I am. I've dreamed of this moment for years.'

Pearl dusted some flecks from her gown. 'If you'd ever considered anyone other than yourself, you'd've come looking for me sooner, instead of settling down all comfy with that rich husband of yours.'

'Don't start, Pearl. Bart isn't rich, and from now on I shall no longer consider him to be my husband. I never did really, since I'd precious little say in the matter if I was ever to get out of the reformatory and escape jail. As for searching for you, I've tried and tried over the years. How Kit managed it, I shall never know, but I'm so grateful he did.'

Pearl gave a loud snort of derision. Kit quickly intervened before she was tempted to blurt out the truth: that they'd been living together for months. 'Have you brought the pendant?'

Ruby smiled. 'Don't worry. Everything is taken care of. I have it safe.'

'It would be safer with me. I'm the man after all.'

Pearl said, 'He's right Ruby. You shouldn't be in charge of something so valuable.'

'It's *my* pendant.' She paid no attention to the peevish note in her sister's voice. That was just Pearl, being Pearl.

'Yours, is it? And you say your husband isn't rich?' Again she gave a puff of contempt, which Ruby duly ignored.

Kit held out his hand, as if implying Ruby should hand the pendant over without delay. It looked faintly green in the dim light of their strange surroundings and she stared at it, confused, uncertain what to do.

She could feel the weight of the ruby pendant nestling between her breasts, pricking the soft flesh. If anyone got their hands on it tucked down there, she'd have far more to worry over than a flippin' pendant. She was so delighted to have found Pearl at last, and to be with her beloved Kit. At the same time, that didn't mean she must abandon all responsibility and allow others to take control over her life. Not ever again. Wasn't this the moment of freedom she had always longed for? She'd no wish to fall out with Kit, who was only trying to take care of her, after all, but he needed to understand that she was perfectly capable of managing her own affairs. She'd grown up a lot since last he'd known her.

'I'll show it to you soon as we get to Canada,' she said with a smile. 'In the meantime it's safe enough where it is.'

Even in the dim light of the lifeboat she saw his frown. 'Don't you trust me?'

'Of course I trust you, Kit. Only I am quite capable of looking after it myself.'

'Oh, Ruby,' Pearl said crossly. 'Why do you always have to stubbornly argue and rebel?'

'Hush, what's that?'

'Don't tell me to hush,' Pearl protested loudly.

'But I heard something.'

'I think we're moving!' Kit said.

Just as their nerves seemed stretched to breaking point, and their patience well-nigh exhausted, they felt, rather than heard, the unmistakable vibration of the ship's engines starting up, heard the churning of water as she prepared to leave her berth. Led by a pair of tugs the great vessel would be turned about in the central basin before making her stately progress out of Manchester Docks towards the sea and a new future for them all.

'Quickly, give me the pendant, Ruby, then I'll stow it safely in the pouch on my belt. If anyone tries to get it, they'll have to kill me first. You know you can trust me with your life.' And Kit pulled her close to kiss her, smoothing one hand over her cheek.

A quiver of longing ran through her. For years Ruby had dreamed of this moment, when she and Kit could slip away and begin a new life together, when she'd find Pearl and go looking for Billy. Now it was all coming true and it was so exciting. Pearl was right, she really mustn't spoil it with her usual display of rebellion, not after all their effort. She unbuttoned the top of her frock and drew the silver chain of the pendant over her head. Holding it out to him, it spun around in her hand, its normally fiery sparkle dulled to a deep purple in the eerie gloom beneath the tarpaulin.

And then it was as if the whole world exploded into light. Ruby cried out, put her hands to her eyes to shield them from the sudden brightness.

'Who goes there?' Someone was shining a powerful torch right into the lifeboat. 'I know you're in there.

I heard you talking. Let's be having you.' And then the tarpaulin was ripped aside and Ruby knew that everything was lost. She'd never get to Canada now. Never find Billy.

Chapter Twenty

The pendant lay on a table in the dock manager's office. Guarding it was a bulky policeman, while beside Ruby stood Kit and a weeping Pearl. All three of them were in handcuffs. Ruby could feel Kit's nervousness and her sister's fury despite the tears and protestations of innocence. Their resentment was palpable. They hadn't yet spoken a word to her, but it was as if they were accusing her of letting them down yet again. It seemed pointless to remind them that if Pearl hadn't started the argument, the seaman would never have discovered their hiding place; that if Kit hadn't insisted on Ruby handing over the pendant, they wouldn't now be accused of trying to steal it.

'You're trying to make us believe that this valuable ruby pendant was a present?'

'Yes.'

The policeman and dock manager exchanged disbelieving glances. 'More likely the lawless life of the street proved too tempting for you to resist. Incorrigible, that's what you reformatory hooligans are.'

It did not surprise Ruby that they should brand her a liar. It had taken no time at all for their respective histories to be revealed and who would ever credit ex-reformatory inmates with telling the truth? It was well known that such unfortunates were constantly picked up by the police at the slightest provocation and many lost heart, finally being driven to steal for lack of any alternative way of making a living. Ruby reminded herself that despite the mistakes she'd undoubtedly made in her desperate need to care for her family and find happiness, she still possessed more stamina than most, and was innocent of this particular crime. She lifted her chin. 'The pendant was given to me by my husband.'

'Your *husband*?' This declaration was greeted with hoots of laughter. The policeman nearly lost his helmet as he put back his head and roared, while the manager wiped tears of mirth from his eyes. 'By heck, that's a good one, that is. Best excuse I've heard in a long while to try and wriggle out of being sent to the Bridewell.'

'It's the truth.'

'Trouble is, love, who'd this rich husband be who's daft enough to spoil a no-good ruffian like you with such a fabulous gift?'

'Me.'

All eyes swivelled to the door. The manager was so startled, he half rose out of his chair before falling back into it in stunned disbelief. 'Barthram Stobbs?'

'As I live and breathe.'

Ignoring the policemen completely, Bart walked over to Ruby and put his arm about her. 'Up to mischief again, my love? I thought I had tamed that adventurous spirit of yours.' Smoothing a hand over the nape of her neck, he commented drily. 'You haven't lost that pretty pendant I gave you, have you, my dear?'

He looked enquiringly across at the manager, now flushed with evident embarrassment, and his eyes lighted upon the pendant, its rose-red depths sparkling like fire on the grimy office desk.

'Ah, there it is. What a relief.' Bart picked it up, hooked it back around her neck and smiled at the now silent pair opposite. 'Family heirloom was my dear mother's, but she's now sadly departed this life. Do I take it that there has been some mistake, and my wife is now free to leave?'

Nobody moved for a long breathless moment. Then the manager cleared his throat and, finally finding his voice, burbled on about how they had assumed the pendant was stolen because why else would three people be hiding in a lifeboat on board a ship bound for Canada? 'It's against the law to attempt to stow away.'

'A youthful adventure, or misadventure, whichever way you look at it. Nothing more. Are you challenging the honesty of my wife?' The arching of his brows only emphasised the cold anger in Bart's face.

The manager was huffing and puffing in furious protest while the constable volunteered the information that reformatory lads and lasses generally re-offended, in his experience.

'Indeed? I wasn't aware that my wife had ever committed an offence, before today, that is. Being in the reformatory does not, in fact, brand her a criminal. You have some problem with the fact that she was an orphan, and poor? Destitution is not, or certainly should not be, against the law.'

The police constable blustered his way into silence but the manager ploughed on, determined on using the hapless trio as an example to anyone else who might consider attempting to board one of his ships illegally in the future. 'Reformatory hooligans are nothing but trouble. These other two aren't even in employment, so are clearly up to no good.'

'Perhaps they are desperate to leave the country for that very reason, because they are unemployed. Have you never been desperate, with your back to the wall? Then you are a most fortunate man if you have not.'

The silence this time grew ominous. It was Bart who broke it. 'Well, unless you have any other evidence against my wife, perhaps you wouldn't mind releasing her, together with her ruthless accomplices? I can vouch for the fact there will be no further assault on your vessels, Canadian or otherwise.'

As the police constable reluctantly unlocked the handcuffs from the miscreants' wrists, the manager continued to issue dire warnings of the fate awaiting anyone who ever stepped unauthorised on to his dock again.

Bart merely smiled, tucked Ruby's arm safely into the crook of his own, and led her away. Kit and Pearl followed meekly behind.

–

Ruby had never known him to be so cold towards her. His reaction seemed deeper than anger, like a skein of steel about to snap. He'd taken her attempt to leave as a personal rejection. Grateful as she was for his intervention which had again saved her from jail, inwardly she grieved for the loss of her dream. There would be no adventure, no trip to Canada to search out her lost brother. In the time it took for Bart to march her back to their house on Quay Street, ungraciously offer her sister a bed for the night, and close the door in the face of her 'new friend', Ruby had come to see that she'd lost everything. Whatever show of tenderness there had been between them the other night, there would be no more. All she could think to do now was to hand over the pendant, and give it up forever. Even the feel of it against her skin scalded her with shame.

Bart accepted it without protest and slid the gem into his pocket.

Ruby blinked back tears which, for some reason, were threatening to fall. She cried not for the loss of the pendant but for something indefinable, and far more precious. She had never asked for love from this marriage, nor expected to feel any in herself, but his faith and belief in her she had taken for granted. Now, Ruby realised, all of that was gone.

His expression showed only scathing contempt. 'Is that really what you wanted? Why Canada, for heaven's sake? What did you hope to achieve by running off so far?'

'A new start for Pearl, and to look for our Billy, of course.'

'Have you any idea of the size of Canada? You have as much chance of finding your brother as you have of locating a flea on a dog's back.'

'We found Pearl, didn't we? Or rather Kit did.'

'We'll come to your friend in a moment, though doesn't it strike you as rather odd that he should suddenly be able to locate her just before the ship sailed? A remarkable coincidence, do you not think?'

A matching anger was rising in her, soaring upwards from the depths of her misery in order to counteract a ridiculous sense of guilt that she had in some way disappointed him. She ripped off the slouch cap Kit had made her wear, letting her nut-brown curls tumble anyhow about her flushed face, glorying in the sudden spark of need that lit in his eyes at the sight of their wild beauty. 'You're bound to see only the worst in him.'

'Because he is sleeping with my wife? Now I wonder why that should trouble me? You would do well to remember, Ruby McBride, that you *are* mine. Never doubt it.'

'Damn you to hell, Barthram Stobbs!'

They sat at table that evening in total silence, the only sound in the room that of the loud ticking of the clock on the mantelshelf. Upstairs, they could hear Pearl pacing the floor, alternately weeping and railing with fury. She had refused to share their supper; even so, Ruby half expected her to come tearing downstairs at any moment and blame her for everything going wrong, as she always had in the past. Pleased as she was to have Pearl here, safe and sound, she'd never quite forgotten how utterly self-obsessed her sister was.

Bart tore at his bread with white, even teeth, drank his soup with one elbow propped casually on the table, and throughout the meal never took his eyes from her face. His stare was unnerving and left Ruby simmering with a rage that she dare not express. When the silence became almost insurmountable, he finally spoke, his voice calm and strangely matter-of-fact.

'Have you never wondered why it was I wished to marry you, Ruby McBride? Why I was so anxious to share my life with you? Have you never considered that it might possibly have been more than a fancy I felt for you, or that what I feel now might well be akin to jealousy?'

The pounding in his head which had tormented him ever since he'd found her with that ruffian seemed to intensify with each passing moment as he waited, in vain, for her response. Images of the pair of them together would, he knew, produce unendurable torture the instant his head touched the pillow. Yet what could he do to avoid it? He was as trapped as she claimed to be, with no hope of escape. Even now, though she craved physical intimacy between them as much as he did, he was no nearer to possessing her. Ruby McBride was very much her own woman and if it was his misfortune to love her, he must live with the consequences. Where was the point in denying it? Perhaps in admitting his vulnerability, he could in some way exorcise this need for her from his soul, reduce it to a physical necessity.

'I was captivated by you, by your beauty, by your strength, and by your resolution to hang on to your individuality despite having spent years in an institution. That was no mean feat, Ruby, and it shone out of you like a beacon. I admire that courage in you still, that sense of fiery independence. This woman, I thought, is one who deserves a chance in life. She needs to be cherished.'

She laughed at that, tossing back her brown curls with haughty disdain. 'You took advantage of my dire circumstances. I was still a young girl who'd never tasted freedom, and you robbed me of that chance. I don't need cherishing, certainly not by someone who has kept me prisoner as an unwilling wife for years.'

'The door is unlocked, Ruby. It has ever been so.' He indicated the general direction with his crust of bread. 'Where would you run to this time? To your lover?'

Ruby's gaze was riveted upon his mouth as he chewed, as if reminding herself of every intimate detail of it. 'He is *not* my lover! It's true that I *do* love him, have always loved him, but we never...'

Bart stood up, pushing back his chair so violently that it fell backwards on to the stone-flagged floor with a crash. 'Spare me the sordid details. I believe I've heard enough excuses for one night. Go and tell that sister of yours to stop that infernal din and then get to bed.'

'I will do no such thing!' The thought of making love with him on this night, the one she should have spent with her beloved, gloriously handsome Kit, albeit stowed away in a lifeboat, was more than she could bear.

Bart grasped her by the wrist and thrust her before him up the stairs, informed a startled Pearl to shut her noise, and in one fluid movement swung Ruby into their room and shut fast the door.

She turned upon him with the ferocity of a tiger. 'Lay one finger on me and I'll scratch yer bleedin' eyes out!'

'I think not, Ruby. You will undress and get into bed like a good, obedient little wife.'

'I will not!'

He sighed deeply. 'I do not believe you are in any position to argue.'

'Because yet again I face possible arrest? Is that the only way you can keep a woman, Barthram Stobbs?' Ruby saw the impact of her words made him reel, almost as if she had physically struck him, and felt a burst of shame at her own cruelty. What in heaven's name had she become?

A heartbeat later he stepped forward, his face so contorted by ice-cold rage that for one dreadful moment she thought he might strip the clothes from her back and take her there and then on the rug, against her will. Instead, by some supreme effort, he managed to control himself and, stretching out a hand, traced the outline of her cheek with the tips of fingers that trembled. His latent fury seared into the heart of her, causing it to melt at his touch.

Ruby strove to maintain a denial of her need, to keep her eyes wide open, her heart stony with defiance as he slowly removed the boyish waistcoat, unbuttoned the blue shirt and slid the braces that held up the seaman's trousers from her slender shoulders. Yet in contradiction to her own wishes, her traitorously weak flesh responded to his touch. It was as if he had lit a fire in her, one that burned and smouldered and could only be doused by him. As she swayed, giddy with need and might well have fallen, he lifted her easily in his arms and dropped her on to the bed.

He took her then as he never had before, with a force that declared his supremacy, his dominance over her. He punished her perceived betrayal with the power of his body but when she cried out, it was with desire not defiance, with passion not agony. The sound was wrenched unwillingly from the depths of her soul for no matter how much she might deny him in the cold light of day, in the secret dark of the night, Ruby knew that she belonged to him entirely.

–

Over the following days and weeks the rain seemed never to stop. It swept the rubbish from the streets, filled the gutters and lashed the decks of the tug and barges, making them dangerously slippy under foot.

The weather suited Kit's mood exactly, adding to his all-pervading sense of gloom. He could scarcely take in the cataclysmic effect Ruby McBride had had upon his life. Wherever he walked, whatever he did, he kept coming across that same police constable who had confronted them in the manager's office. Kit was quite certain the man was keeping a beady eye on him, eager to prove him guilty of some offence or other. He popped up around every corner, tenaciously determined to find Kit up to no good so that he could throw him in jail and toss away the key. His constant presence cramped Kit's style, for one step out of line and he'd be a goner.

Ruby McBride and that so-called-baron had ruined everything. Not only had he been deprived of the opportunity to enjoy her undoubted charms, and access to her husband's wealth, now he had a copper permanently on his tail. He'd also lost Pearl and the convenient comforts she freely offered, not to mention a most useful source of income.

Not for a moment was he prepared to allow them to get away with his. Hadn't Ruby McBride done enough damage to his life already? Once again he felt used by her. She'd strung him along all this time yet must have said something to warn Barthram Stobbs of their plan. She no doubt gave some indication of what was afoot, or how would he have known to find them in that blasted office? Kit suspected she'd either spilled the beans, or made it so obvious by her behaviour that she was up to something that he'd followed her. Perhaps had been doing so for some time. And after all his patience, all the trouble he'd gone to. Never trust a bloody woman!

There was nothing now that Kit wasn't prepared to do in order to exact revenge. He needed to redress the balance. He felt driven to the limits of his endurance. One way or another, he'd punish them both.

–

'You are not my mother.' Pearl's strident voice rang out for the umpteenth time as it had done throughout those first few difficult days and during the endless miserable week that had followed.

'God rest her soul,' Ruby quietly added. They were walking along Deansgate, a blustery wind making Ruby glad of the shawl wrapped about her head and shoulders. Pearl was struggling to keep control of her ridiculously wide straw hat with the sweeping green feather. Bart had generously provided them with funds and they were looking in shops, trying to find something more appropriate for her to wear than the maroon and purple skirt and fitted jacket she wore constantly. 'What about this lovely grey twill? It's both smart and practical.'

Pearl curled her lip with contempt. 'I'd look like a schoolmarm in that.' She marched over to another mannequin swathed in pink satin. 'Now this is more my style.'

'You'd look like a tart in that.' Ruby started to giggle. 'You'd set tongues wagging if you walked about the canal basin in pink satin and no mistake.'

'Happen I wouldn't wear it in the canal basin. Happen I won't be stopping in Castlefield.'

Ruby looked at her askance. 'Where else would you go?'

'Wherever I want. Back to Rochdale probably. I'll live where I like. Dress how I like. Like I say, you're not me bleedin' mother.' She picked up a wide-brimmed hat, swathed in blue spotted net and masses of silk flowers, and placed it on her head as if to prove her point. 'You're only my *sister*! You can't tell me what to do.'

'I'm your older sister. And didn't I promise Mam that I'd take care of you?' Seeing a floor walker approach, Ruby snatched the hat from Pearl's head and put it back on its stand, swiftly apologised and hustled her out of the store. 'Someone needs to see that you're properly looked after.'

'Why? That promise only held good till I was old enough to take care of myself, which I am, so you can stop your preaching. I'll decide what's right for me, not you.'

Oblivious to the passers-by who jostled them, they stood on the pavement locked in combat, Pearl fighting for her independence, Ruby desperate to carry out her self-imposed duty to the letter.

'And what *is* right for you, Pearl? What's so special about Rochdale that you're so determined to go back there? Or that pub? There are pubs in Castlefield in need of a barmaid, I'm sure.'

'I'll please myself what I do, and where I go. Stop bossing me about, I'll not have it.'

Ruby gazed with sadness upon her sister. 'Aren't you pleased that we've found each other again, our Pearl? Don't you want us to be friends?'

'I want you to keep your interfering nose out of my affairs, that's what I want. Where were you when I needed you months, years ago? Living the life of Riley with your rich husband, that's where. Don't think you can just swan back into my life, pinch Kit off me and turn my life upside down. It won't wash.'

'Pinch Kit? What are you talking about? You and Kit aren't – are you?'

Realising suddenly what she'd said, that she'd gone too far and Kit would be furious with her, Pearl attempted to backtrack. 'Well, no, n-not in that way. But he was my friend, and now he's *yours*. He's dropped me completely.'

Ruby reached out and gave her sister a comforting hug, chuckling softly as she did so. 'What nonsense you do talk. Your obsession over friends always wanting to leave you has to stop, Pearl. Believe me, it is possible for a person to share friends. Oh, Pearl, love, you've had a hard time. It's going to get better from now on, really it is. Just give us a chance. Why don't we go and have an ice cream in Kendal Milnes, eh?'

But even this treat didn't mollify Pearl in any way. She kept on and on about how she missed her friends in Rochdale, how she had a little room there, and money of her own to spend.

'Well, if that's what's troubling you, you have your own room at Quay Street, and you can earn some brass helping on the barges. There's enough work for two of us there.'

'Swabbing decks in the bleedin' cold, not on your nelly?' They argued all the way back down Deansgate, all through the dinner they ate standing at the counter of a tripe stall at Campfield Market, and were still squabbling when they arrived back at Quay Street with no purchase to show for their morning's effort. Pearl had disliked everything Ruby had wanted her to buy, and vice versa. They had disagreed on everything and achieved nothing.

Back in the house, Pearl snatched up the carpet bag she'd brought with her for the much hoped for escape to Canada and made to leave without even pausing to take off her hat and coat or have the pot of tea Ruby was offering. 'No, thanks, I'm off back where I belong. I'd a nice comfy little number going for me there.'

Ruby felt as if her heart were breaking. 'Oh, Pearl, I'd so hoped we'd get on better, now that we're all grown up and have been apart for so long. Which pub is it? How will I know where to find you?'

'Don't you fret. I'll pop over to see you from time to time, seeing as how I know where you live now.' She paused at the door to issue her final shot. 'It's too late to try to play mother or even big sister to me now, Ruby. You should've taken better care of us years ago. We might never have lost our Billy then, if you had.'

After she'd gone, Ruby sank to her knees and wept, for surely Pearl was right.

Chapter Twenty-One

'I'm seeking a job and I reckon you owe me one.'

Bart stopped plaiting the rope fender he was repairing to find Kit Jarvis standing beside him, every bit as cocky and arrogant as he'd appeared in the dock manager's office. 'How do you work that out? Seems to me I saved you from the nick, not so long ago.'

'But if you hadn't recklessly given Ruby that valuable pendant, I'd never've been accused of trying to steal it, would I?'

Bart deliberated over this upside-down logic for a moment. 'You were intending to steal it, weren't you?'

'No, only to keep it safe for her.' Kit slammed a fist into his other hand on a burst of exasperation. His distress sounded so genuine, he could almost believe in his own innocence. 'That's my point exactly. You think the worst of me, as does everyone else. And because of your interfering, yours and Ruby's, that copper has never been off my tail since. No one'll ever give me work while he's hanging around.'

Bart eased himself into a more comfortable position, eyes narrowing as he considered this unexpected request. 'Since you were running off with my wife, why the hell should I offer you a job? I'm more inclined to take a horse whip to you for your presumption.'

This threat was issued in the mildest of tones but Kit was not fooled. The sincerity behind the words was indisputable, and he'd no wish to put them to the test. Nor did he attempt to deny the charge, rather he acknowledged it with a sly smile.

'You should happen wonder why she was prepared to leave you, and come with me.'

'Perhaps you applied undue pressure, in the shape of a suddenly resurrected sister and the ludicrous promise to find her brother. Ruby is vulnerable where her family is concerned. If I find you taking advantage of that vulnerability, I'll strip the skin from your backside and hammer it to the decks here.'

Kit swallowed, taking extreme care not to allow his very real fear to show through the veneer of bravado. 'At least if I'm here every day, on the tug, you can keep yer eye on what I'm up to.'

The slightest of pauses, and then Bart slowly inclined his head. 'An excellent point. Now why didn't I think of that?'

–

Telling Ruby that he'd agreed to give her lover a job so that he could keep a better eye on him was the hardest thing Bart had ever done. He chose to announce his decision as they prepared for bed in the cabin one night. She'd deliberately kept her distance from him as she hurriedly undressed and slid into her nightgown, keeping up the pretence that she didn't come to him willingly, but only under protest as her wifely duty. Bart couldn't believe that he'd got himself into this situation, and wasn't in the least surprised when she didn't believe his tale. No wonder that she looked at him as if he'd completely lost his reason. Perhaps he had.

'He's not my lover.'

'I shall make damn sure of that fact in future, my dear. That's why I gave him the job. Always best to entertain the enemy in your own front parlour, then you can see what he's up to.'

Ruby tossed back her hair in that haughty way she had when she was displeased. She sat at the end of the bed and began to tug a brush angrily through nut-brown curls that tumbled down around her shoulders, the vigorous movements making the neck of her nightgown gape at the throat as she lifted her arm, revealing enticing curves of soft white flesh.

The thought of some other man caressing her slender form made his stomach clench, and Bart wondered if he could go through with this apparently civilised deal. Having Kit Jarvis on board had, at the time, seemed like a sensible idea. But he was already having second thoughts. How could he bear it? Bart knew he would be constantly on the lookout for the exchange of loving glances between them, secret notes passing from hand to hand.

He took the brush from her hand, and standing beside her began to brush her hair himself. It sprang to the brush as if with a life of its own and he felt a quiver run through her. Her nightgown slid down a fraction more and he placed a caressing hand on her bare shoulder.

'What would I do if you left me, Ruby? When you planned to run off on this wild goose chase of yours, didn't you wonder how I would manage without you?'

The stroke of the brush massaging her scalp was setting off strange little pulses of longing deep inside her, making it harder for her to concentrate. 'Why should I?'

'Have you not forgiven me yet for spoiling your little adventure?' He laid the brush aside, his breath soft against her cheek as he turned her into his arms and pushed her back upon the bed. Held close against him, Ruby could actually feel the beat of his heart. Instinctively, she tilted her chin so that her mouth was bare inches from him, feeling a surge of excitement as she saw how his gazed fixed instantly upon it.

'If I did, it was to assume that you'd quickly replace me with another reformatory kid, some other innocent girl who'd be happy enough to fill your bed and do your bidding, probably more willingly than me. I know about men, you see. My own mother warned me how they chase every bit of skirt that crosses their path.'

'Oh, Ruby, what a sad indictment upon our marriage, have you seen me chasing other girls?' He kissed the tip of her nose, nibbled the soft curve of her lower lip. Ruby did not allow herself to respond.

In truth she'd never seen him so much as glance at another female. Not in her presence, anyway. But what did that prove? You couldn't trust men. You only had to let down your guard once, and they'd be off with the next rain shower. Mam had said so a score of times. And what did he expect her to say? That she was sorry for trying to run off to find their Billy. Well, she wouldn't say such a terrible thing, and a few kisses and cuddles certainly wouldn't win her round. All this pretence of affection didn't move her one bit.

As her breathing quickened under the skill of his caresses, Ruby struggled to maintain her composure. Deliberately adopting a scathing tone, she continued, 'No doubt you think you can bribe Kit into helping with your nasty schemes and con tricks because he's a reformatory kid too. Isn't that the real truth behind this apparent show of generosity?'

He had the gall to chuckle, as if he found the suggestion amusing, his eyes moving over her face as he tucked a glossy curl tenderly behind her ear. The tips of his fingers lingered over her cheek, capturing her chin and smoothing them over the firm line of her throat. 'Not a bad idea! I should think Kit Jarvis would make a much better associate in crime than your own sweet, self, Ruby. If there is one thing you couldn't accuse your friend of, it is honesty.'

She tried to push him away but his hold on her tightened, his body pressing hard against hers as his hands moved slowly up and down her back, along the length of her hips and legs, awakening in her that oh-so-familiar need. He drew off the cumbersome nightgown, slid easily out of his own dressing gown and there was nothing now to prevent the touch of flesh upon flesh.

Ruby fought to keep her breathing even, to remain detached from whatever it was he was doing to her, but he was not to be denied. He kissed her: a long, slow plunder of her mouth, taking his time and sending her emotions haywire, revelling in his power over her. Try as she might, she could not resist him. She could feel her own body lifting instinctively to his, her hands slide up around his neck, gripping his hair, pulling him close against her, wanting him to physically devour her, to make her a part of him.

Their loving was unusually sweet and fulfilling, a lingering exchange of sensation, each giving the other physical pleasure perhaps in recompense for the bitter words, the harsh reality of their fractured relationship.

When it was over, Ruby found herself so overwhelmed by this unexpected display of tenderness that she couldn't think straight. Her brain seemed to have turned to jelly, and she was shaking like a schoolgirl. Was that out of regret? Because, deep inside, they both felt certain that this might be the last time they made love? That they could no longer maintain this farce of a marriage and must either make their peace, or part.

Or was it simply because she was suffused with shame by her own response, at the raw need he awakened in her?

–

They lay side by side in the bed, not touching, not speaking, perhaps each wondering what the other was thinking. Was he regretting this coupling as some sort of display of weakness on his part? Was he thinking that he should never have followed her, that he should have let the ship sail with her on board? Perhaps he regretted ever having met her in the first place, ever having come to the reformatory seeking an assistant for his nefarious purposes. He'd ended up getting more than he'd bargained for.

So had she, by agreeing to stay with him that day. Yet Ruby remained utterly fascinated by Barthram Stobbs, her husband. Since their inauspicious start, Ruby had come to respect and admire him. Even, and this she found hard to admit, close to liking him. Far from doing her harm, he'd done his utmost to protect her, in point of fact. For a moment she toyed with the notion of abandoning her dreams, and of staying with him.

Could she settle for being his wife for always? To become Ruby Stobbs instead of Ruby McBride? And then she thought of her lovely Kit, ever faithful, patiently waiting year on year. She couldn't let him down. How could she, after all this time, after all they'd meant to each other? She was suffering from sentiment and guilt, nothing more.

When Ruby could bear the silence no longer, she brought his attention seamlessly back to their earlier discussion, her voice consciously cool and detached. 'You're falling into the same trap – calling Kit a criminal just because of his background. Kit is a good man. He has stood by me all my life.'

Bart turned on his side to study her pensively for some long moments before he answered. When he did, the crispness of his tone was pure steel, almost as cold as his eyes. 'You only imagine he has stood by you, but you'd be wrong in thinking so. In point of fact, he is concerned simply with saving his own skin, and may well have been up to no good with another member of your family.'

Ruby felt all the colour drain from her cheeks, then rush back in, flagging them to a bright fury. She sat up in bed and, snatching up her nightgown, dragged it back over her head. 'That's the cruellest remark I've ever heard you make. I'll have you take it back this minute.'

He said nothing, merely lifted his eyebrows in that sardonically mocking way of his.

'There are times, Bart Stobbs, when I could swing for you!' Whereupon she left him and returned to her own cabin, but for once he did nothing to stop her leaving.

–

Bart found little to amuse him in the situation. He was incensed by the way in which events had turned out. Annoyed with himself for having been foolish enough to reveal something of his own vulnerability in his lovemaking, and furious that he was in serious danger of appearing to have gone soft over Jarvis.

He began to make plans and decided it would be a good idea to find out more information about the fellow. He set Sparky on the job, issuing instructions for him to seek out this Jackdaw character who'd helped Ruby to locate Kit in the first place.

'I reckon they were mates when they were boys, so he must know Jarvis's background well. Find out where he hangs out when he's not here. I want to know everything about him, most particularly when and how he found Pearl.'

And since Sparky owed Bart a favour, he set about the task with relish. There was nothing he liked better than a bit of high drama, and this tale bore all the hallmarks of such.

Within days Sparky returned to his boss with the information that Pearl McBride was working as a prossy at a certain tavern in Rochdale well known for such goings on. She was apparently very popular with her clients.

Bart felt as if he'd been kicked in the chest. He could almost feel the pain this would cause Ruby, and he didn't relish being the one to break the news. In Ruby's eyes her sister Pearl was one step removed from the blessed Virgin Mary herself. He must make sure the tale was correct before he embarked on a course of action, whatever that might be. 'Thanks, Sparky. Keep this under your hat for now, will you? I have to work out how to handle it.' And since it was made worth his while to hold his tongue, Sparky gladly agreed to do so.

The next day, Bart followed Sparky's careful directions which led him to the tavern tucked away in a back street behind the gasworks in Rochdale. It was packed to the doors, it being a Friday, stinking of sawdust and beer, either freshly poured in huge tankards or spilled on the floor, all overlaid with the sweet-sour odour of stale sweat and vomit. None of this troubled Bart. He strode in, ordered a pint of bitter and as he quietly sipped it leaning against the bar counter, glanced interestedly about him, as if he were a regular in the place and was just checking to see if any of his mates had turned up.

The place was so busy he thought he'd be lucky to find Pearl, but almost at once, he spotted her. She was sitting on the knee of a plump, middle-aged bloke, playfully tugging his beard while he groped down the front of her dress. Bart watched this performance for some moments as he drank his beer. She didn't see him, didn't even glance his way, and after about ten minutes, Pearl and the man, evidently a client, went outside together. 'Give me another, landlord, and one for yourself.'

'Fancy a bit o' company, mister?' A girl lolled against him, her old-young face clown-like with its scarlet lipstick and garish cheeks.

'No, thanks.' He cast scarcely a glance in her direction, so deeply absorbed was he in his own thoughts, and she wandered off, disappointed at failing to pull this handsome gent.

Bart knew it could be fatal to make the wrong move. Should he confront Pearl with what he'd just discovered, or go to Ruby, tell her straight and let her sort her sister out? Though why would she take his word against that of her precious Pearl? She'd be unlikely to believe him without proof. He could always go and bring Ruby here, let her see Pearl at work with her own eyes. Such a prospect made him cringe. Far too cruel even to contemplate. My God, loving that woman was turning him into a mindless milksop. He had to get his life back in order, and Ruby's too, before it was too late.

Perhaps the only way forward was to offer Pearl the golden path of redemption. Grease her palm with sufficient silver and she might well take it.

–

'Thanks, chuck, I allus like the cash up front.' Pearl gave her client a playful wink as she shoved the florin he'd paid her down between her full soft breasts where it would remain, firmly lodged with one or two companions. Then she lifted her skirts up about her waist and quietly smoked a cigarette while he got on with the business, the first of many such encounters this evening. And she didn't expect to get home until the early hours when she would finally strip off, wash herself all over and go to bed. Alone.

This was the one part of Kit's Grand Plan of which she did not approve. The fact that she was on her own most nights of the week now that he slept on board the tug, if not exactly with Ruby, then certainly close by. Pearl found it infuriating how things always turned out right for her blessed sister, and wrong for herself.

'Ooh, yer so strong, Jimmy. You really get me going,' she whimpered, embellishing her words with a few groans and gasps of supposed pleasure.

Although Pearl was strong on self-pity, she did not allow it to stand in the way of business. It was early and trade would be good tonight, it being pay day. She was about to tell her client that he'd had his money's worth for one night when it dawned on her that someone else was in the back alley, watching them. Surely they weren't queuing for her favours now?

'What's your game mate? I won't have no peeping Toms watching me.'

The reply came out of the darkness, softly menacing.

'I'm so sorry to interrupt, Pearl, when you're working but I thought it time you and I had a little chat.'

'Eh?' As his face emerged from the shadows, Pearl's heart seemed to stop beating and she gazed up at him in horror. Being discovered 'on the job' as it were by Barthram Stobbs had not at all been part of the plan. Kit would kill her for this. As for Ruby… It didn't bear thinking about, really it didn't. Flustered and thrown off balance she shoved her client away with very little consternation. 'Buzz off, Jimmy. We'll finish this another time, eh?'

Pearl made a feeble, if ineffectual, protest when Bart grasped her by the arm and led her away down the back alley, though she soon abandoned the effort when she realised how fruitless it was. Barthram Stobbs was tall and strong, and his hold tenacious. For the first time, Pearl began to doubt the wisdom of embarking on her chosen profession.

He, on the other hand, seemed blithely unconcerned, almost relishing his discovery. 'This won't take long, Pearl, and I don't mind paying you for your time, if you feel it necessary. But it is essential that we have a little chat, don't you think?'

Chapter Twenty-Two

'I take it Ruby knows nothing of this little sideline of yours?' Bemused, Pearl shook her head, garish red hair blazing like a ball of fire in the light from the gas lamp.

'I thought not. Then answer my questions and she won't hear anything of it from me. How long have you known Kit?'

Still she said nothing.

'It would be in your best interests to co-operate. I've no more wish than you for Ruby to learn the truth about her innocent little sister, but I need something in return.'

'Like what?'

'Information. I want to know all about Kit Jarvis. How it was that he found you so easily, when everyone else had been searching for years.'

'That were just chance.'

'I very much doubt it. I think that you and he are in this together. I believe you only became interested in Ruby's rather naive dream to run off to Canada and look for Billy after she'd foolishly told you about that pendant. She did tell you, didn't she?'

'Not me she didn't, no. She might've mentioned it to Kit.'

'And which he fully intended to steal from her.'

'That was nothing to do with me.'

'If it was Kit's idea, why not admit it? You know I don't like him, and I certainly don't want him hanging around my wife. I need him to sling his hook, to vanish out of Ruby's life for good. You're the only one I can think of who is capable of achieving this seemingly impossible task. Come on, Pearl, you must know of some way to persuade him to change his plans and leave her in peace. You want him for yourself, after all. Admit it.'

Pearl gave a snort of disbelief. 'Nobody ever persuades Kit Jarvis to do anything he don't want to. He's the stubborn sort. Even the birch don't tame him.'

Bart considered this piece of information with serious interest. 'Hmm, rather the reverse, I should imagine. Is that why he's such a bitter young man? Does he blame Ruby for landing him on the reformatory ship?'

When Pearl merely shrugged, he nodded, just as if she had spoken her thoughts out loud.

'Well then, you must know of some way I could scare him off, something I can use against him. I need to protect my marriage, do you see, Pearl? It's important to me.'

'Why should I help you? Or care a toss what happens to your so-called marriage? I might vanish myself, or stop on and live with me sister in your fancy house. Ruby's said I could, if I choose to.'

'But you don't choose to, do you, Pearl? You prefer the thrill of the chase, or is it control over men's appetites that you enjoy so much? Having a bit of fun without any sort of commitment, is that it? No, don't look daggers at me. It's your choice and I can honestly see the attraction in such a philosophy, if not the way you choose to carry it out. But I'm not moralising here. From what I've seen, you evidently give good value for money.'

She smirked at him. 'Fancy a bit yourself then, do you?'

'I don't think so, Pearl, thanks all the same. Just tell me how I can get Kit Jarvis off my back? Otherwise, I shall be forced to reveal the truth about you to Ruby, which wouldn't be pleasant for any of us, now would it?'

'You rotten, twisted, nasty piece of...' She hissed at him, angry as a spitting cat. 'You think I'm scum don't you?'

'Misguided perhaps. You've had a hard time of it, Pearl, and if you're looking for a way out of this hole you've got yourself into, I can help you do that too.'

Hands on hips, she tossed back her cascade of hennaed hair and laughed, a loud and raucous sound. 'Hark at you! Never thought the baron himself would turn into Preaching Pete. Right bleedin' saint you are, to hear you talk. Well, I'm not the only one with skeletons in me cupboard.'

'I'm sure you aren't, Pearl, but which cupboard, in particular, are you referring to exactly?'

'Don't pretend you don't know who I'm talking about.'

He lifted his brows in polite enquiry. 'I'm sure you're going to tell me.'

'What about you and that Pickering woman you visit so regular? Her what lives in the big fancy house. Oh, aye, our Ruby told me how you went a-calling there once, pretending to be interested in buying it. You've called again since, haven't you? Several times in fact.'

'I was interested in the property at one time, yes, unfortunately the owners decided not to sell.' His eyes narrowed consideringly. 'How do you know all of this?'

'Kit decided to follow you. He wanted to find out more about your background, who you were, like, and where you come from.'

'And did he succeed?' The tone was sharp, interrogative.

'Keep yer hair on! He found out about the woman.'

'Nothing more?'

She chuckled throatily. 'Isn't that enough? Oh, we haven't been idle this long while. Aye, you're right. I've been with Kit for a year or two now. We suit each other very well. No ties. No fuss. Our Ruby may have landed herself a big fat fish with loads o' brass, but it were allus Kit she wanted and *I* was the one to catch him, so she lost out, didn't she? Not that you care, since you have yer own bit of comfort, eh?'

'Comfort? What sort of comfort would that be exactly?'

'Aw, don't play the innocent with me, I know all about her, that secret mistress of yours.' Pearl began to feel more confident at the surprised look on his face. 'Thought no one knew, eh?'

'Pearl, I haven't the first idea what you are talking about.'

'Nay, don't play the innocent with me. You know well enough. Like I say, we've been watching you, where you go, who you see. Kit and me decided we all deserved a share of your loot, being family like, and considering all we've been through, especially since we didn't manage to get the pendant.'

'The pendant wasn't yours to keep.'

'Maybe not, but we reckoned we deserved it. Don't you think that's fair? According to our Ruby you don't

270

even pay her what she's entitled to, no wages, nothing. Just think how she'd react if she knew you were tossing brass she'd worked hard for into another woman's skirt. She's not the vindictive type our Ruby, but even she has her limits. She'd strip you bare of everything you own. So, you scratch my back, and I'll scratch yours. Make it worth my while and I'll say nowt to her about your visits to your fancy woman up at the big house. I'll even persuade Kit not to make you pay for our silence.'

He put back his head and laughed loud and long. 'I'm afraid you've got it all wrong, Pearl.'

She was unconvinced by this display of casual indifference. 'I don't think so. Like I say, Kit saw you, more'n once. He reckons you'd pay him quite a lot to keep his mouth shut, if only because you need to keep your end up with the workers. You didn't reckon you were the only one to enjoy her favours up at that posh house of hers, did you? Eeh no, she has quite a few gentlemen callers besides yourself. All from t'top drawer, I'm sure.' Pearl had adopted a mincing voice in parody of the lady in question, and was delighted to see how his eyes had widened, how she'd shocked him at last with this latest piece of information.

She blithely continued. 'According to Kit, who's done his homework proper I may say, she was called Jessica Ramsden before she wed that Pickering chap. And she was a high-class whore even in those days. A leopard don't change its spots, eh? She's no better than me, not underneath. She does tricks, and her clients pay for the privilege. They just pay more, that's all, for the frills and furbelows.'

Pearl seemed to have finally run out of steam and stopped, waiting to judge the effect of her words. That'd show him, making himself out to be some sort of plaster saint, when all the time he was no better than any of them. But instead of looking furious, as she'd expected, he was actually smiling, as if she'd said something that had pleased him.

'Pearl,' he said at last, 'you've opened my eyes this evening, you really have. You've no idea how pleased I am that we've had this little chat.' Then he turned on his heel and began to stride away.

Pearl ran after him. 'Hey, do we have a deal or not? You don't tell our Ruby about what I get up to here, and I'll keep mum about your secret visits to your lady friend. That's fair, isn't it?'

He paused to cast an eye over her tousled charms, his gaze searingly intimate and yet starkly critical. Pearl found herself flushing, tidying a stray curl, buttoning her gaping bodice and preening herself before his scrutiny. 'Well, how about it?'

'You could be so much more, Pearl. So much more.' There was sadness in his tone, and in the expression on his handsome face. As he walked away, she silently watched him go, smarting at his superior attitude, and at the pity in his tone.

It was only as she flounced off through the puddles, making her way back to the tavern that the significance of his lack of an answer came to her. He'd made her no promise, no vow of silence. None at all.

A sudden shaft of fear struck her. She'd told him that Kit had been spying on him for months, that he'd found out about his visits to that mistress of his, Jessica whatsit.

Oh, Lord help her, what had she done? She'd really cooked her goose this time. Kit would near kill her for this. And what would the baron do to Kit? He'd looked far from pleased at having his background investigated.

Pearl turned on her heel and began to run. Heaven help her but she must find Kit and warn him before he carried out whatever mischief had brought that shining light of purpose to his golden eyes.

—

Giles Pickering was every bit as intractable on this occasion as he had been years ago. Then, as now, Bart had stood in this very same study, with the same overwhelming scent of leather, beeswax polish and acrid cigar smoke filling his nostrils, while accusing his father of driving his fiancée to suicide. A state of affairs that he'd bluntly denied. Today he again refused, absolutely, to accept responsibility for any of it: the devastation he had brought to his son's life, to that of his own first wife – Bart's mother – or to his employees in his obstinate refusal to recognise their union or improve their working conditions. In his own eyes he was outside the normal standards of human decency. He was Giles Pickering, self-made man of affairs, and therefore could do as he pleased.

'I will not discuss what is in the past and cannot be altered. I did what I thought was right at the time, and there's an end of the matter.'

Bart was livid. As always, when confronting his father, he felt a great sense of futility, as if he were desperately swimming against a tide of self-interest, which would ultimately overwhelm him, no matter how hard he floundered and fought against it for every last breath of air. He felt again like the schoolboy he had once been, who his father had loved to criticise and bully, and insist he try harder to make something of himself.

'What *you* thought was right, and to hell with everyone else. That's just typical blast you! You've never given anyone else decent consideration in your entire life. Look at the way you treated Mother, no wonder she went into a decline and died before her time.'

'You know nowt about it. Whatever went on between me and your mother is none of your goddamned business!'

'You think it didn't affect her, you sneaking off to see this Jessica Ramsden woman? And *she*, I have learned, had something of a reputation. Was that part of her attraction? Were you one of her clients?' He smiled as he saw his father pale. 'Oh, yes, I've heard all about it. Though I'm sure you'll say that's none of my business either.'

'Damn right I would!'

'It would never do for such information to be spread abroad, would it? For either yourself as a respectable businessman, or for dear Jessica. You know how people do love to gossip.'

Pickering stabbed out the butt of his cigar with furious jabbing motions into a silver ashtray. 'Damnation, are you out to ruin me, boy?'

'No, of course not, Father. I'm no longer a boy, but perhaps a less trenchant stance might be called for. What do you think? A little give and take, perhaps? Some open discussion with the men at the docks could well prove fruitful.'

'Over my dead body! How dare you come in here, ordering me about, telling me what to do in my own house, mischievously accusing me of causing the death of that gold–digging little tart you once fancied marrying…'

Bart clenched and unclenched his fists. How he would love to plant one on that arrogant, smug, self–satisfied face. But this was his father, for pity's sake! 'You'll take that back! Dear God, what kind of man are you?'

Pickering smirked. 'The kind who holds all the damned cards, and you son are nobody. Never will be.'

Bart swallowed his contempt. Every nerve ending was crying out for revenge, yet it was vital he keep in mind the true purpose of his visit: to use this new information for the benefit of the men, not his own personal vendetta. If he didn't, then this dratted tyrant of a father of his would have won again. He drew in a deep, steadying breath. 'I'm not talking about me. What about the men in your employ? Don't they deserve better consideration?'

The older man snorted his derision. 'They're paid well enough, considering all the time they spend hanging around the docks doing nowt.'

Bart ground his teeth, striving for patience. 'They don't want to spend hours on end hanging around the docks, doing nothing. They should be given new orders the minute they've finished unloading, not be left to travel empty. If you ran your wharf in a more efficient manner, they might not have to.'

'And happen if my son would come and work *with* me, instead of against me, I might just manage that.'

They glared furiously at each other, neither prepared to back down one iota, though in his heart Bart recognised this as a fair point. His future had at one time been assured: to become a partner in his father's business and, in the fullness of time, take it over completely. All that had been lost to him with the death of Alice. How could he ever work with such a man again? Bart calmly continued speaking, reining in these straying thoughts. 'As for hours, most of the slow-boat carriers start work at five or six in the morning and are still working at eight or nine at night. They need at least one day off a week.'

'If I were to give them Sundays off, we'd lose the momentum at the end of the working week when most goods are ready for shipping, and even more loads would go on the railways. We're fighting for our lives here, a losing battle some say. I've had to take the house off the market, put my plans to semi-retire on to the back burner for now. I've no time to concern myself over the grumbles of the men. I'll not buckle under your threats, so spread what gossip you like about Jess. It'll not touch us. We're well thought of round here. In any case, we've heard it all before. We can ride whatever dirty waters you stir up.'

To his great chagrin, Bart realised that this was probably true, that he too was fighting a losing battle. Now, he strode from his father's house rigid with fury but forced to accept that he had failed yet again. No concessions were to be granted. He had achieved nothing for the men, in spite of all the hours of negotiations, the endless meetings, the talking, the arguing, even this futile and pathetic attempt at blackmail. It was a hard pill to swallow and as he took his leave, he swore never to return.

'You've seen the last of me, Father, I swear it.'

'Then good riddance!' Pickering called after him.

–

Pearl had failed to find Kit, so he was unprepared for the torrent of rage that strode on to the tug in the shape of

Barthram Stobbs. 'Right, the game's up. I want you off this tug immediately. And if I catch you hanging around in future, or within half a mile of Ruby, you'll live to regret it.'

Kit jerked as if he'd been struck. For whatever reason, Bart was raging back and forth, ranting like a mad man. 'What're you talking about? I thought we had a deal.'

'I've changed my mind. I'll make no deals with you. I've spoken to Pearl and she's admitted that you and she have been living together for months. Did you imagine you could get away with it? I know now that you probably cooked this whole plan up between the pair of you.'

'What plan?' Kit blustered, aghast at this turn of events. What had the silly fool admitted to?

'To rob Ruby, or rather use her to get *your* hands on some of my assets. I assume your motives to be pure greed. And though you may pull the wool over Ruby's eyes, you can be absolutely certain that you have not succeeded so far as I'm concerned, so leave quietly, before I decide to enlighten her about your dishonourable intentions.'

Kit was not sure who to be most angry with: Pearl, for having been stupid enough to spill the beans, or Bart, for being clever enough to ask the right questions. 'You've no proof. You're surely not going to believe Pearl, to take the word of a...'

'Don't say it! Whatever misfortune or inadequacy has led the poor girl down that particular path, she is not well served by friends such as yourself, who clearly take advantage.'

'Are you accusing me of acting as her pimp?'

'I'd say that's a pretty good description, yes. If you'd left her to Ruby's care, she might well have had a chance.'

'Never. She was always a lost cause, was Pearl.'

'How would you know, you arrogant bastard? And what were you planning to do in Canada? Dump Ruby, once you'd stolen the pendant from her? Oh, I know all about your long-held resentment against my wife – how you blame her for your being put in the reformatory training ship and losing your family. I'm sorry that happened to you, Jarvis, but it wasn't Ruby's fault, and you'd no right to blame her. Yet you were willing to rob her of what she treasured most, and leave her to search for a long-lost brother in a strange country all on her own. That's always assuming she survived the voyage, of course, and you didn't take your revenge there and then.'

'You're just saying all of this because you can't face the fact that Ruby prefers me to you.' There was a sneer on Kit's face, triumph in the glitter of his brilliant blue eyes. 'You can't bear to think she's sleeping with me, that she's let me have what you thought was all yours.'

'By God, I'll make you take that back,' Bart roared, and launched himself at Kit with clenched fists. The young man dodged the blow and Bart struck again, this time landing a crack on his jaw, knocking him sideways. Kit was back on his feet in seconds to come charging back at Bart like a steam train. The next blow missed completely as Kit ducked and punched him in the stomach, making Bart gasp. The pair pummelled and pounded till blood spurted from noses, knuckles were red raw and purple bruises stained aching jawbones. As exhaustion began to set in, they fell to wrestling, one moment hanging over the side of the tug as Kit held Bart in a stranglehold, the next sprawling on the deck in their combined effort to land a punch on the other. For once, Bart, by far the larger and less agile of the two men, was the first to get to his feet and it was at the precise moment his fist connected with Kit's jaw that Ruby came on deck. She flew at Bart desperately trying to intervene, yelling at them both to stop.

'What are you *doing*? Leave Kit alone. For goodness' sake, *stop it*!'

'Tell her,' Kit shouted, as Bart held him by the collar preparatory to socking him again. 'Go on, tell her, and see if she believes your accusations.'

'What accusations? Let him go. Stop that this minute, Bart. Let him go, I say!' Ruby was slapping at Bart's hand, wrenching his arm, quite certain that he was about to beat Kit to a pulp. 'Stop it! Stop it! You'll kill him!'

'I wouldn't do him the favour.' Bart flung Kit to the deck in a gesture of contempt, and turned to Ruby. 'He's filled with bitter resentment against you and had every intention of robbing you of that pendant, *and* me of my livelihood, from the start. He's been planning this for months, with Pearl.'

Ruby looked at Bart with a dazed expression in her eyes. 'Rob me? Kit and Pearl? Don't talk daft. Anyroad, how could our Pearl know anything? Kit has only just found her.'

Kit said, 'Go on, why don't you tell her the rest of your daft theory?'

'I don't want to hear. You're making all this up out of a fit of jealousy. Well, it won't wash.' Ruby half turned towards Kit, anxious to help him up, but he brushed her hands away and got to his feet unaided, his gaze riveted on Bart. 'Go on, finish it why don't you? See which one of us she believes.'

'I'm listening,' Ruby said, resigned disbelief in her tone. 'I'll hear you out, but if you think I'd ever believe that Pearl, my own sister, would want to hurt me, you are sadly mistaken.'

Bart glowered down at the man he loathed, still snivelling like a coward, and then across at Ruby, the girl who had come into his life on a whim. He'd gone looking for an assistant with a sufficient lack of scruples to be useful in his deals and instead had found himself a bride. He'd fallen for her like some sort of besotted fool, and had been punch drunk with love ever since. Even now as she gazed at him with that defiant, dark-eyed gaze, his heart ached for her. What he wouldn't give for her to love him in return, as fiercely as she seemed to love this no-good piece of scum. But how could he ever hope to convince this supremely honest, this right-thinking, fiercely protective, rebellious, gloriously lovely girl that the beloved young sister whom she'd been seeking for years was now one of the lowest of the low? That she was totally bereft of both morals and scruples. He simply couldn't do it.

'Well?' Ruby folded her arms, a hint of triumph lifting her voice, as if by his silence he proved his own guilt.

Again he felt the urge to explain his feelings to her, to convince her how very much she meant to him, but she was already turning away, a look of mocking disbelief on her lovely face.

'Ruby?' He took a step towards her, impatient to make one last effort to capture her attention. The blow came out of nowhere and caught him full on the nose and chin. He saw an explosion of light, heard the crack of bone, felt the spurt of blood that tasted like rusty metal in his mouth. Rage soared through his veins on a burst of adrenaline as he pivoted about to retaliate. But then just as swiftly it drained away, leaving an amazing sense of release as he seemed to be flying through the air. As a cold dark wetness enveloped him, Bart found himself sinking into an all-pervading peace.

Chapter Twenty-Three

Ruby could hardly take in what had happened. Fear cascaded through her. One minute the two men had been fighting, the next Bart had fallen backwards off the tug and splashed into the murky depths of the canal. Or had Kit hit him? She'd half turned away, hadn't quite seen what had caused him to fall. And thus far, he hadn't yet surfaced.

She ran frantically up and down the tug, wild with distress, praying that at any moment she would see him come rising from the depths, spluttering with rage. But all Ruby could see in the dim light of dusk was a spiral of ripples, like a huge black mouth that had swallowed him up. She whirled about, grabbing hold of Kit, her voice raw with pleading. 'You must go in after him.' He didn't answer and she began to shout, shaking him by the collar of his jacket to make him listen and respond. Kit made no move to do anything. He just stood, apparently mesmerised by the swirling black water beneath. Perhaps he was himself injured, Ruby thought, or in shock. And there was really no time to be lost. 'If you won't save him, then I must.'

She ripped off her boots, snapping the laces in her haste, and without stopping to remove her work dress she scrambled up on to the rim of the tug and prepared to leap in. The action must have brought Kit from his daze for he grabbed her just in time and pulled her safely back, holding her fast in his arms for a moment before giving her a little shake of irritation. 'Don't be a damned fool, Ruby. You could drown in there. There's oil, filth, dead cats, weeds and rubbish, all sorts in that canal. There's nothing you can do for him now, Ruby. He's a goner.'

'*Nooo!*' It was a cry from the heart, from the very depth of her soul. 'Don't say that.'

She was crying, sobbing, distraught in her distress as she furiously fought him, desperate to break free from his hold. Kit held her fast, his arms wrapped tightly about her till the hysterics finally abated and she grew calmer, if still weeping against his shoulder as if her heart was broken.

Why didn't the silly woman see this was the golden opportunity they'd both longed for? Kit thought. They were rid of Barthram Stobbs at last. And they still had his tug and pair of barges.

–

By morning it was clear to Ruby that Kit was right. All night Ruby had watched and waited with hope and fear in her heart but Bart had not emerged from the water. At one point she'd slipped past Kit, who was snoring his head off in the chair, and made her way along the towpath, swinging a lantern, desperately hoping she'd come across Bart sitting in a sulk somewhere.

'If you're trying to frighten me, Barthram Stobbs, you've succeeded,' she called, but only the echo of her own voice came back to her over the cold slap of water. At last, chilled to the bone with the damp and a grey, early morning mist spreading over the city, Ruby crept back to bed and cried silently into her pillow.

She'd hated him, loathed him, hadn't she? They'd fought from the first moment she'd set eyes on him, yet never in a million years had she wanted it to end like this. She felt bereft, her world suddenly empty, as if she could see the horizon stretching into eternity, pale and featureless, without hope.

She must have slept in the end for she woke with a jerk to discover bright daylight, the awful events of the previous night flooding in upon the instant, which no doubt accounted for the heavy sense of depression she nursed deep inside. It seemed there was nothing left to do now but to wait for his body to float to the surface some-where. Perhaps when the tide had come up the Irwell, and washed the Ship Canal clean and retreated again, he might be taken with it, deposited in some lock or beneath the struts of a quay or bridge along the way. All of this was described to her with painful clarity by Kit, who carefully explained how the accident had occurred, how Bart had slipped on the rope fenders he'd been making earlier in the day, lost his balance and fallen overboard.

'I know we were having a bit of a barney, but I never meant him any serious harm, Ruby. There was nothing I could do. It all happened too quick.'

She looked at him in blank acquiescence. How could she believe otherwise? The alternative was unthinkable. Not for one moment did she imagine Kit capable of deliberately knocking Bart overboard and leaving him to drown. That would be murder, and Kit was certainly no murderer.

'We must tell the authorities, his friends. Sparky will need to be told. And Flitch, and…'

'No!' Again Kit gave her a little shake of exasperation. 'You'll tell no one, d'you hear me? No one's going to believe it wasn't deliberate. If they hear we had a fight, they'll be sure to think the worst, then they'll blame me. Next thing you know they'll be stringing me up on the gibbet.'

'Oh, goodness me, that must never happen.' Ruby was appalled at the very idea.

'Why would they believe in my innocence, an ex-reformatory lad? Nay, Ruby, you know well enough how it is. I'd be done for.' Kit placed a finger against her lip. It smelled of tar and coal dust but she made no protest, mesmerised as she was by the urgency of his gaze and the fear in his voice. 'You say nothing. Is that clear? Bloody nowt!'

She swallowed, fighting for breath, and for some sort of calm in her head, but she seemed to be incapable of a single rational thought, could find no voice, nor anything to say.

He gripped her chin between finger and thumb. 'I'd never hurt you, Ruby. He got that all wrong, jumping to conclusions just because of my past history. He thought the worst, same as they all do. You believe in me, pet, don't you? You understand how it is.' There was an edge to his panic, which finally penetrated the cloying layer of mist that separated her from reality.

'Yes, Kit. I understand. And of course I believe in you. I swear I'll not say a word.'

His shoulders sagged with relief as he gathered her in his arms. Ruby was weeping again, this time out of an indescribable sense of loss.

Ruby was so afraid for Kit that when anyone asked, she said that Bart had had to go away on urgent business. She made no mention of the fight. Kit slipped quietly away that very first morning before dawn and kept out of sight. They agreed not to meet again until the weekend when he would come to the house on Quay Street. He promised to bring Pearl with him.

Day after day Ruby walked the canal towpath, her frozen body wrapped in a shawl. She felt numb, as if she were standing outside herself, watching herself search every clump of weeds, every turn in the canal, every strut beneath the railway arches. When Sparky appeared, as usual, ready for work, she put him off, telling him there was no work just now and that Bart had gone away for a while. He looked dumbfounded, as well he might. Ruby was filled with pity for him.

'No work?' he'd repeated, looking shocked. 'Nay, lass, that's a bit of a rum do. Me and Aggie depend upon the work we get from t'baron. Are you saying I have to look elsewhere?'

'It might not be a bad idea Sparky. Just till Bart gets back – from – wherever it is he's gone.'

'Eeh, it's a bad job is that. I can't afford to lose work.' But he didn't argue, just hunched his shoulders with philosophical resignation and turned away. Then a thought struck him and he turned back to her. 'It hasn't anything to do with that bit o' business I did for him the other day, has it?'

'What bit of business was that, Sparky?'

'About your Pearl.'

'Pearl? What about our Pearl?'

A shadow crossed his face as he suddenly remembered his promise to say nothing. 'Aw, nowt important! I forget now, exactly, but I'm sure the baron knows what he's doing. He generally does.' Then, brightening, he said, 'Tell you what I'll come back next week. How will that do? Happen he'll be back by then.'

'All right, Sparky, happen he will.' She couldn't bear to let poor Sparky down, nor his wife and children, yet how could she tell him the truth and risk a fate even more terrible for poor Kit?

After Sparky had gone, Ruby gave no further thought to whatever bit of business it might have been that concerned Pearl. She'd learned long ago not to take Pearl's little dramas too seriously. It would be nothing. And Sparky himself was ever one to make a mountain out of a molehill. Nor did she hang around waiting for him to call again. Seeing as there was nothing more she could do to find Bart, she fled to the house on Quay Street.

Here she lit the range, the day being cold and drizzly with rain, and did what she always did when she was upset, she began to clean. She'd already cleaned the tug from stem to stern in the last few days of endless waiting, now she set about the little house with equal energy. Taking each room in turn she turned out all the furniture, scrubbed floors, beat carpets, dusted, swept, even washed the net curtains all over again. Only when everywhere was spick and span and the washing line crowded with blowing clothes, did she brew herself a pot of tea and stop to take stock.

What now? She couldn't go on cleaning, or playing this game of pretence and denial forever. Everything had changed. Bart had gone, and she couldn't quite work out how she felt about that, or what she should do about it. The terrible accident seemed too incredible to have any connection with the stark reality of her life. She kept expecting him to walk through the door at any minute, an expression of mock triumph on his face, pleased to have scared the wits out of her.

'Aye, you've certainly done that,' she would shout at him. Oh, she'd give him what for, she would really.

Ruby stooped to poke the fire and riddle the coals, a task she'd performed only a second before. But then she still couldn't seem to get any warmth into her bones. She felt ice cold inside, even as her nerve endings tingled as if they were on fire. She paced backwards and forwards in the tiny living-kitchen, arms wrapped about herself in utter and complete misery. She wiped the already clean slop stone, dusted the spotless mantelshelf before wandering into the front parlour to tweak a tapestry cushion, or twitch a curtain. Then she padded upstairs to smooth the green silk coverlet on the great double bed where so often Bart had made love to her.

She recalled his explosion of jealousy over Kit some weeks ago, the night he'd 'rescued' her from the ship. And the last memorable occasion, a more tender coupling, almost as if he'd known it was a farewell.

For some reason this brought a rush of tears to her eyes and, in despair, Ruby put her hands to her face, desperately trying to shut her mind to the memories crowding in. Her cheeks were wet with tears and she wiped them away with the flat of her hands. Without realising it, she'd been quietly weeping while she worked. Wearily she went back downstairs to brew herself a fresh pot of tea, the other having gone quite cold.

She'd barely taken a sip when there came a knocking on the front door. Ruby flew to answer it, hoping against hope it was him only to discover Pearl standing on the doorstep. She was prettily, if garishly dressed in a king-fisher blue crepe silk dress with an emerald green bolero and matching hat. And if Ruby momentarily wondered how her young sister could possibly afford such magnificence, she pushed the thought aside. She was so delighted by the sight of her sister's dear face that she burst into noisy, gulping sobs.

'Oh, Pearl, I'm that glad to see you.'

The two sisters embraced awkwardly then Pearl settled herself comfortably in the only easy chair in the kitchen while Ruby refreshed the tea with scalding hot water. Pearl seemed fidgety and nervous, affected by events, no doubt, as they all were.

'I've heard about the accident. How did it happen?' she wanted to know. 'Kit says there was a fight. Did you speak to him – to Bart, I mean, not Kit? Did he say anything?'

'About what? There wasn't much time for conversation. He'd been out all day, and it all happened so quick.' Ruby set a mug of steaming tea in Pearl's hand. She sipped at it quickly before setting it to one side and leaning forward, her face tight with concern.

'So what was the fight about? Were they having a row? Why were they arguing? It wasn't about me, was it?'

Ruby finally lost patience. 'For goodness' sake, Pearl, you may find this hard to believe but the entire world does not revolve around *you*! We don't spend our entire lives talking about you, or looking for you or even thinking about you, let alone fighting about you. Some of us have problems of our own to worry over.'

Seeing Pearl's face crumple and the tears well, Ruby momentarily closed her eyes as if silently praying for strength, then setting down her mug of tea untouched, she went to put her arms about her sister. 'I'm sorry, love. Take no notice. I'm not meself today. Proper crosspatch I am. Well, look at you, pretty as a picture. Where are you off to, love, somewhere nice?'

Ignoring the question, Pearl continued, 'You'd tell me if there was anything – particular – you were worrying over, wouldn't you, our Ruby?'

Ruby studied her sister's face, struggling to damp down the fresh burst of anger that rose in her chest like a hot balloon, swelling and expanding till it threatened to explode at any moment. Could she really be asking such a naive question? What was it about Pearl that forever brought Ruby to the limits of her patience, despite loving the bones of her? But where was the point in allowing it to consume her? Nothing would ever alter her sister's self-absorbed view of life.

Even so, there was a trace of bitter irony in the tone of Ruby's reply. 'No, Pearl, there's nothing in particular I'm worried about. Oh, maybe the fact that my husband has fallen overboard into the canal, and probably knocked himself out and drowned. Kit could well be accused of his murder as a result. But apart from that, no, I'd say there's nothing to worry about at all.'

–

Kit came on Friday, as promised, although he came alone, declaring that Pearl couldn't come, as she was otherwise occupied.

Ruby groaned. 'She hasn't taken offence, has she, over what I said the other day about the world not revolving around her?'

Giving a snort of laughter, Kit shook his head. 'Hide as thick as a rhinoceros, our Pearl. Why, did you have words?'

Ruby pulled a face. 'Just a few. Sometimes I could wring her neck for being so flippin' selfish, even if she is my own sister. Our Pearl is quite incapable of seeing any other problem beyond her own. She was like that as a child, but she gets worse as she gets older, not better.' A thought struck her. 'Did she call at your rooms to tell you she wasn't coming over?'

'No,' Kit hastily fabricated. 'I popped in the pub.'

'What is it she does there, serve behind the bar?'

'Aye, that's it. Pulling pints all night she is. They keep her pretty busy.' And then he added as an afterthought, 'She sends her love.'

'Aw, bless her, she does have a sweet nature you see, underneath.' Ruby's eyes filled with a gush of tears, as they were wont to do these days, now that the first shock was receding. She'd felt proper queasy this morning when she got up first thing, though was it any wonder after all that had happened?

'I know we were always at odds. Me and Bart, I mean. I never asked to wed him, and he wasn't your normal sort of man. He was a bit of an eccentric, full of more secrets and schemes than I cared to know about. But he never hurt me. In his way, he was good to me. He took me out of the reformatory, fed me, clothed me, gave me the opportunity to work with him on the barges and...'

Kit interrupted this flow of what he considered to be maudlin babble, brought on no doubt by an idiotic sense of guilt. 'Speaking of the barges, what are we going to do about them?'

'Do? What do you mean – what are *we* going to do about them?'

He poured himself a glass of stout and settled in the easy chair, taking pleasure in assuming rights over the baron's property. He'd enjoy more than the use of his chair, if Kit had any say in the matter. 'Ruby, you have to get your wits together. You were the baron's wife, now his widow. So the tug and barges will belong to you.'

'Oh, but how could I claim them, or even admit that I'm his widow when we daren't tell anyone that he's dead?' These last two words echoed over and over in her head. *He's dead. He's dead.* The concept was too difficult for her to comprehend so Ruby pushed the thought aside. Barthram Stobbs was far too full of life. How could he possibly be dead? 'I can't do anything about the barges, not right now,' she repeated. 'He might come back at any second. You never know.'

'He isn't coming back, Ruby!'

'Don't say that!'

'Why not, it's true.' Kit took hold of her wrist, pulled her on to his lap and slid his arms about her, fondling her shoulders and neck, stroking her cheek. 'Now I don't want you worrying your head over this. I know it came as a shock to you, to us both, but it's over with now and we have to get on with life. He'd want you to be properly looked after, and isn't this a big chance for us? A new beginning? As we always wanted.'

Ruby was staring at him perplexed, hearing the words he uttered but unable to put them into any sort of logical order in her mind. They simply didn't make sense.

He kissed her gently on the mouth, savouring the taste of her sweetness. 'Listen, love. Why don't you leave it all to me, eh? I'll see your all right. I'll look after the barges for you. When has good old Kit ever let you down? You and me were meant for each other. Pearl might think she has prior claim, but you and me know different.'

'Pearl? Prior claim? I don't understand.'

'Well, you know how she is. As you said yourself, Pearl allus thinks she's the star, the one and only. Just because I was the one what found her, she thinks it's her I fancy, but you understand that there's never been any other girl for me but you, Ruby.' He eased her blouse out of her skirt and pushed his hand up over her cold flesh to cup her breast. His mouth was nuzzling at her throat, nibbling her ear. 'Come on, love. I've been patient a long time. How about it?' His hand was on her leg now, sliding under her skirt. Ruby stopped its progress with the sharp dig of her elbow.

'Not just now, Kit, all right? I want us to be together. I've longed for this moment, really I have, only I can't think straight. I've got a terrible headache and colly-wobbles in my stomach. I feel sick. Maybe I've eaten something that disagrees with me. Or else all this mess and worry has made me feel ill. I just need a bit more time, that's all.'

'More time? Nay, Ruby, I've waited months for us to be together. And you're not wed now. Your husband's gone, so where's the harm?'

Ruby pushed him away and scrambled to her feet. 'Not now, Kit. I've told you, I'm tired. Besides, I want our first time to be more romantic than this. I think it would be best if you go.'

He half laughed as he stretched back in the chair, clasping his hands behind his head as he made himself more comfortable. 'Go where? Nay, lass, I'm going nowhere. I'll stop here tonight, and every night from now on. Everything that once belonged to the baron is now mine, including you.' Seeing the bemused expression on her lovely face, he hastily softened his tone. 'Isn't that what you wanted?'

She *must* be feeling poorly if the prospect of belonging at last to her beloved Kit didn't fill her with the joy she'd expected. After all, hadn't he been her childhood sweetheart? Hadn't she pined for him year after year in the reformatory? Hadn't she hated Bart for robbing her of the chance to be with him? So why didn't she respond with more enthusiasm? Why was her heart racing, but not with excitement? It must be shock after the accident. What else could it be?

'Yes,' Ruby placated him. 'Of course it's what I want. But all in good time, eh?'

'Never mind about all in good time, what we waiting for?' He made a grab for her, but she was saved from an unseemly tussle by the front door banging open and Pearl marching in.

'By heck, I'm fair starved, what's for supper? Has anybody got the kettle on?'

Ruby was so pleased to see her sister at that moment, she actually laughed out loud. 'That's our Pearl, popping in and out at all hours and demanding sustenance, just as if she owned the place.'

An hour later she was behaving very much as if she did. It was Ruby who cooked supper, despite being the one grieving. Pearl launched into a long-drawn-out description of a yellow striped frock she'd tried on in Kendal Milnes, wondering if she could increase her charges at the pub to allow her to buy it. Ruby said nothing, not being in the mood for Pearl's ramblings right now. Her head was throbbing and she slipped quietly off to bed, leaving the pair making themselves very much at home: Pearl chattering twenty to the dozen and Kit pouring himself yet another glass of stout.

Chapter Twenty-Four

Following the drowning Kit made no effort to leave, and Pearl too decided to move in, returning to Rochdale only for the odd evening's work at the pub, or so Ruby believed. At first she was pleased. Hadn't this been what she'd dreamed of for so long? But she'd forgotten how much mess her sister created, how she expected to be waited on hand, foot and finger, and never thought to help with the cooking or the washing up.

Having Pearl live with her was not at all as Ruby had imagined it would be. The house was small, and the tug, where the three of them spent much of the week while they worked on the carrying, was smaller still.

For three people it meant a degree of tidiness beyond the norm if everyone was going to get along, and tidiness, along with consideration for others, was a skill Pearl had never acquired despite her years of discipline at Ignatius House and in the reformatory. Though she may have little in the way of clothes and possessions herself, perhaps because of this sad fact she felt free to use other people's at will.

Ruby did her best to be understanding if she found her best dress lying in a crumpled heap on the floor, or her one and only pair of decent boots soaking wet after Pearl had borrowed them for a late-evening stroll.

'Where was it that you had to go so urgently, and so late at night, that you must wear my boots?'

'Are you saying that you begrudge me a pair what don't leak?'

'Certainly not. But it's only good manners to ask permission first.'

'You sound like Sister Joseph. I hadn't realised you'd got so particular and so toffee-nosed. I'll apply in writing next time, shall I?' And she would flounce off in a huff, leaving Ruby feeling the guilty one.

She longed to pursue the matter of where exactly it was Pearl went to of an evening when she wasn't at the pub, but knew she must tread warily because of her sister's oversensitive nature. As she was fond of saying, whenever Ruby did attempt to broach the subject: 'I've a right to me own life, haven't I? And to me own friends?'

'Of course you do. It's just that I worry about you.'

'Well, don't. I've looked after myself all my life and I can manage to go on doing so without any help from you, ta very much.'

'Oh, Pearl,' Ruby sighed, wondering if her little sister would ever give her credit for at least trying to protect her as a child, both from starvation and the cruel menace of Sister Joseph whose evil Pearl had continually under-estimated. 'You know how much I care. Haven't I always tried to make it up to you for not having a mother?'

'I know that you abandoned me in the end, just like she did.'

'Mam didn't abandon us. She put us in a home because she was dying of consumption.'

'Same thing.'

Ruby stifled a weary sigh, and gave up.

Pearl also openly flirted with Kit. They would often cast each other sidelong glances, and Pearl was always ready to serve his dinner, offer to help him take off his boots, fetch his coat or newspaper for him, like some sort of adoring slave, even as she did nothing to help Ruby in the house. And she would seek any opportunity to be close by his side where she could frequently touch his hand or shoulder, and laugh at his jokes.

Whether in the tiny house, or the close confines of the cabin, if he tried to squeeze past her to fetch something for Ruby, she would block his path so he had to brush up against her, or she would bat her eyelashes up at him in that enticing way she had. On the rare occasions she was inveigled upon to make supper, she always succeeded in soliciting his help, as if she were incapable of so much as boiling an egg or peeling a potato without his manly assistance. But then what man could resist her sister's abundant charms?

Watching this naked attempt to captivate him, and Kit's response to the seductive teasing, Ruby found, to her great surprise, that she felt not the slightest prick of jealousy.

Living at last with her beloved Kit should have been a dream come true, but something was wrong. The free-and-easy chatter between the pair of them made her feel very much the outsider, an interloper in her own home. She couldn't help but compare their teasing good humour with her own daily communication with Kit, confined to practical topics related to the barges. No intimate words or shared thoughts were ever exchanged between them.

And her desire for him physically seemed to be diminishing by the day. Instead, she kept recalling Bart's lovemaking, to which she had once so eagerly responded and now sadly missed.

Ruby was feeling utterly miserable and increasingly unwell. Not a day passed without her thinking of Bart. It surprised her how much she missed and grieved for him. She would lie in the quiet dark of the night, tears sliding from the corners of her eyes, a band of pain clenched tight about her heart. Could she possibly have felt more for him than she'd realised? Surely not. She'd hated him, hadn't she? Yet she ached to see his handsome face again, for things to be as they once were, and to feel his arms about her. Ruby was filled with longing for him, and still often returned to the canal to search, half fearing what she might discover as there was little hope of finding him alive after all this time.

—

Having Pearl around at least helped to deflect gossip from nosy neighbours. Rumours about what exactly had happened to the baron were rife, and many uncomfortable questions were being asked, not least by Sparky. He came to the tug one morning when she was swilling down the decks.

'Have you heard anything yet?' he asked.

Ruby shook her head, not knowing quite what to say by way of a reply.

'I reckon there must have been an accident?'

Her heart gave a loud thump. 'Why do you think so?'

'It isn't like the baron to stop away this long. He promised me regular work. And he'd've told me if there was a problem.' As if to add weight to his words, he started to coil rope too heavy for Ruby to manage.

'You know Bart, he's his own man, and likes to keep things close to his chest. But you can still have work, Sparky,' she promised, suddenly realising that this was the answer to at least one of her problems. 'I need you now more than ever.' And she did, for who else had the knowledge of how to operate the barges? It wasn't often that women took on the role of captain, and those who did were usually widows, like herself. And she surely owed it to Bart to keep his business going.

'What about that other chap I've seen hanging around? Are you employing him, an' all?'

'Kit Jarvis? Yes, I suppose I am.'

'He's one of your Pearl's chaps, isn't he? Is she stopping on with him?'

'For a bit, yes.' Ruby decided it might be better if the general opinion was that Kit and Pearl were a pair.

'Given up on that other line of business then, has she?' And he gave a lopsided sort of smile, almost a smirk.

Ruby frowned. 'What line of business would that be, Sparky?'

He shuffled his feet and looked quickly away, recalling how dependent he was upon Ruby for a weekly wage coming in, if the baron was going to be away for a while. Wouldn't do to be too nosy and upset her. 'Serving drinks behind the bar in a Rochdale pub, I heard.'

Ruby smiled. 'Oh, she still goes there occasionally, though she claims it's only to see her friends. But really she loves to have a bit of money of her own, never having had any before.'

'Aye, right.' He nodded, eyes narrowing as he tried to puzzle out whether this remark meant Ruby understood perfectly what it was her sister got up to in that pub, or was completely ignorant. Knowing her as he did, he decided on the latter. That little lass too sweet and trusting for her own good! Now he cleared his throat, preparatory to what was obviously going to be a difficult question. 'I was wondering, if you don't mind me asking like...' He stopped, chewed on his lower lip for a moment then started again. 'I mean if he's going to be away for a while what'll happen to the burial club? He hasn't taken it with him, has he? It's not me what's worried about it, you understand, but there are some as are asking questions.'

Ruby hastened to reassure him. 'No, of course he hasn't taken it with him. The money is quite safely invested, and the books of reckoning are all here, in this metal box.' She felt a constriction of emotion block her throat as she remembered the care Bart had taken over administering the burial club for the water folk. 'Yes, I can see that they would be concerned. What d'you suggest we do about it, Sparky?'

'I could ask around. Find someone reliable to take it over like.'

'That would be wise,' and they looked at each bleakly, for this decision was tantamount to admitting that Bart hadn't simply gone away for a short time, but may not be coming back at all.

–

The reason for feeling unwell soon became all too clear to Ruby. She was pregnant. A quick calculation in her head gave her the answer, and the tenderness of her breasts and feeling sick each morning confirmed it. She was carrying Bart's child. It made her weep all the more to think how happy such news would have made him. How he would have rejoiced. Time and again he'd talked of starting a family, as if doing so would turn her into a true wife and make her love him. Yet she'd always managed to talk him out of the idea, besotted as she was with Kit, her childhood sweetheart. And now that it was actually about to happen, she felt grief and excitement in equal proportions. What on earth was wrong with her?

She kept her condition secret, wishing to sort out these confused emotions before she divulged it, but then one night Kit came to her room and tapped on the door.

'Let me in, Ruby love. It's long past time you and me got together. What do you say? It's cold and lonely in that back room on me own. Let me in.'

Ruby lay beneath the green silk coverlet in the big double bed, where Bart had taught her the meaning of passion, and knew in her heart that she had no wish to take Kit into her bed, not just yet anyway. Why she felt this way she couldn't quite fathom, not after wanting him for so long.

Slipping across the room on bare feet she silently slid the bolt in place, then crept back to bed. Minutes later the tapping came again, and the door handle turned. But finding it locked, and presumably deciding that she must be asleep, Kit lost patience and gave up. When she heard his steps fade away along the landing Ruby sighed with relief. The next night he came again, and the one after that, loudly rattling the handle, as if in a fury.

'Let me in, Ruby. You know you want this as much as I do.'

Ruby flung open the door, smiling kindly as she saw his face light up with hope. 'I knew you'd come round in the end,' he said, looking pleased with himself.

302

'Kit, I'm sorry but this has to stop.'

'What d'you mean? Why should it stop?'

'Please leave me alone. It's too soon. I'm not ready. Perhaps I'm still grieving for a lost husband.'

'Never, I don't believe it! You hated him. You and me were meant for each other. Let me in.'

'Not tonight, Kit. Not just yet, I'm sorry.'

Turning on his heel he strode away in a huff, clearly angry, as she quietly closed the door, preparatory to going back to bed. Then Ruby heard the tapping again, this time on Pearl's door. Startled, she held her breath, listening carefully as she heard the door open, a few hushed words exchanged, then it closed again.

There was no further sound of receding footsteps on the landing.

In the days following, Ruby expected to feel devastated by the fact that Kit was probably sleeping with her sister. He and Pearl were more than likely a couple before today, as Bart had once suggested. But she was surprised to find that she really didn't care. Why was that? She was, however, irritated when, night after night, Kit continued to tap on her bedroom door. Did he think her deaf, dumb and blind to what was going on before her very nose? She decided she'd really had enough.

The next morning she made her feelings crystal clear. 'No more tapping on my door, Kit. Do you understand? I should think you have enough on your plate with our Pearl.'

A flush of guilt suffused his cheeks, yet his belligerence remained. 'Pearl's not important, not by comparison with you.'

'Well, she's important to me. She's my sister and I'd prefer you to treat her with proper respect, at least.'

'Respect? Pearl?' He laughed. 'I'll tell you about your Pearl if you like...' Ruby didn't allow him time to finish.

'Are you listening to what I'm saying? It's over between us. You've made your choice, now live with it.' And she closed the door on his shocked face.

–

Five months later Ruby's child was born. It was a boy, with glorious, sandy-brown hair and brandy-gold eyes. Kit was not pleased. Any lingering desire to persuade her into marrying him so that he could claim ownership of those barges, instantly died. He instinctively knew that he had no wish to take on another man's child.

But the baby's presence was yet another thorn in the crown of his resentment.

With difficulty he managed to keep these feelings to himself, anxious to convince Ruby that he adored the child, at least until he'd won complete control over the barges. But to his intense irritation she remained stubborn over the issue. Even throughout the long, tiring months of her pregnancy she'd insisted on working, as usual. The business, by rights, should be his. He was the man of the house, after all, and the one who had taken all the risks to rid them of the baron. She insisted it wasn't hers to give away, just as if the stupid bastard might return from the dead to claim it any day.

But Ruby doted on the baby and Kit was convinced that it was only a matter of time before she lost all interest in the barges, in carrying coal and cotton up and down the canal system, and gave her full attention to her child. That's what women were best at in his opinion.

Ruby called the baby Thomas and welcomed little Tommy, as he quickly became known, into the world with pride and joy. She'd been unprepared for the rush of love she'd felt for him at first sight. It quite overwhelmed her. Pregnancy had been a trial, endlessly tiring and blighted by backache and a vague sensation of sickness throughout. All due, she was quite sure of it, to tensions at home. Not simply with Kit, who she guessed hugely resented the fact that she wouldn't allow him to take control of the barges, but also with Pearl.

The evenings, when they were all in the house together, were the most difficult to cope with. It soon became apparent to Ruby that what Pearl hated most of all was to be ignored. She craved attention, though even then it must be on her own terms. If Ruby was fully occupied feeding the baby, Pearl wouldn't think to offer to make the supper, grumbling loudly should Ruby ask her to so much as peel a few potatoes!

'I'm not yer bleedin' skivvy.'

And she was fiercely jealous of the slightest attention Kit might give to her, quite unnecessarily so. If, when he came in, he went straight over to Ruby as she fed the infant, Pearl would watch the two of them smiling and cooing over Tommy for mere seconds before jumping up from her chair to squeeze between them. 'Isn't it time you made supper, our Ruby? I'll finish Tommy off with the bottle, shall I?'

Perversely, if Ruby had fed the baby early for once and was at the stove when Kit came down the ladder into the cabin, he might hover at her side as she stirred the stew to see what was cooking. At which point Pearl would suddenly discover that little Tommy needed changing, and she really didn't know how to do it, or for no reason at all the baby would wake up and start to cry.

Often her sister would do one of her disappearing acts for a few days, returning only when she was quite certain that Ruby would be miserably worrying over her, eager to placate and welcome her back with open arms. Which Ruby did, time after time, if only for the sake of peace.

Ruby's resolve to be a surrogate mother to Pearl, and to help her make a good start in life, sometimes drained her of all energy. Then she'd remember her mam saying, 'I'll not lose my sparkle,' and she'd smile and struggle on. But with the best will in the world she found her sister's moodiness an increasing source of irritation, preventing her from enjoying being a mother to little Tommy. Living with Pearl was becoming a trial.

She constantly complained about any work she was asked to do on the boat, and yet protested vigorously should Ruby suggest that she might like to go out and look for another job elsewhere.

'Want rid of me, do you, so's you can have Kit all to yourself? You're just jealous of him preferring me to you.'

'I promise you that's not the way of it at all. I'm happy for you.' Ruby was beginning to wonder what she had ever seen in Kit Jarvis, wishing she'd never met him in the first place. She kept remembering how Bart had warned her against him, and how she hadn't listened. 'I've told you, I don't want Kit. You're welcome to him, but perhaps you and he would be happier some place on your own.'

'So you'd throw him out of work too, would you? Selfish cow, you just want everything for yourself.'

Ruby simply couldn't win with Pearl.

–

The main joy in Ruby's life was, without question, her child. He represented her future, her reason for living. She took little Tommy with her everywhere. When she was working on the barges, Ruby would prop him up on cushions where she could keep an eye on him and his eyes would follow every movement she made, as if he couldn't bear to let her out of his sight.

When all the chores were done, Ruby would devote all her attention to the baby's needs. She would bathe him each night in the small white basin she'd bought specially for that purpose, laughing as he kicked and splashed her with his sturdy young limbs.

'Cheeky boy,' she'd tease him. 'You're smacking that water at me deliberately.' Then she would tickle his tummy, making him squeal with delight and giggle entrancingly. Oh, how she adored him. He was her treasure, her delight, her utter and complete joy.

Afterwards, she would powder and dry him, cuddle him close and breathe in the sweet baby scent of him as she lay him in his cot beside her bed, and settle him to sleep. She'd lie on her side so she could watch him breathing, promising that nothing would ever be allowed to hurt little Tommy. He was Bart's child, and one day the tug and the barges would belong to him. They were his inheritance. His right. And it was her task in life to keep Bart's son, and that inheritance, safe.

'I shall build us a fine business, Tommy lad,' she would say. 'One that you can take over one day – that would have made your daddy proud.' And he would listen with close attention, his brandy-gold eyes bright and knowing. Sometimes, it almost felt as if Bart were still with her, so like him was his young son.

The thought of never seeing Bart again, never having him make love to her, never again feeling his mouth move against hers, or his touch that could rouse her to a tempestuous passion, brought an unbearable pain, as if her heart truly were breaking in two. But why should she feel this terrible anguish over losing him? It wasn't as if she'd ever loved him.

But then, what exactly was love? She'd loved Kit Jarvis for years, hadn't she? Ever since she was a girl, he'd been the one she wanted above everything. So why didn't it trouble her that he preferred her sister? And quietly, out of the darkness, the answer came all too clearly.

Because she'd made a terrible mistake. She'd imagined herself in love with Kit Jarvis because she was young and vulnerable, desperate for someone to care for her. But he wasn't the love of her life at all. Barthram Stobbs was. All those years of being in love with a dream, a child-hood memory, instead of being in love with the man who already occupied her bed. The bitter irony of this discovery was heartbreaking.

Oh, how cruel of fate not to allow her to discover her true feelings until after he was dead, when it was far too late.

Chapter Twenty-Five

Learning her trade proved a difficult challenge for Ruby. There were times when being a woman was a definite disadvantage; at others it worked in her favour. There were some who claimed she'd be a danger to herself and to others, that she'd be hopeless at steering, and that the work was unwomanly. This made Ruby laugh. In all her life she'd never done the least little thing that could be considered 'womanly', save perhaps for the laundry work she did at the reformatory. And she knew where she'd rather be. Here, on the boats, out in the fresh air. True, she felt tired after a long day working on the tugs and barges, yet invigorated, glowing with health.

She felt she owed it to Bart to make the business successful. Admittedly he had never been as obsessed with the boats as she was, being more interested in his scams and schemes and union activities. Nevertheless, the boat and the pair of barges had belonged to him, and in a way were his legacy. Ruby meant to put into practice all he'd taught her, and justify the faith he'd once had in her.

The work was frustratingly unreliable and irregular, affected as it was by the weather, and by delays often of a day or more waiting in a bottleneck of other craft for the barges to be unloaded, or for a fresh load to be taken on. The worst part was travelling empty, hoping to pick up a load. They needed five or six longish trips every fortnight in order to be economically viable. Because this rarely happened, the boats sometimes going for days with no work at all, on other weeks she'd take orders thick and fast, going for long spells without a day off or a glimpse of her little house.

Life with Kit and Pearl did not improve. He spent more and more time with Pearl, and Ruby often wondered if they would even notice if she simply vanished into thin air and never returned.

Rather as Bart had done.

If it hadn't been for Sparky, Ruby doubted she'd have managed at all. Kit, although always so full of talk and plans, insisted on working only a few days each week, because he claimed to have 'other irons in the fire', as he put it. He wasn't prepared to give those up until she handed control of the barges over to him, as he thought she should, since he was a man and she a mere woman.

Strangely, the more he grumbled about that, the more she resisted. The business was hers, and would remain so.

'Well then,' he'd say, his tone hard, 'since you refuse to share it, and I'm not your husband, nor even the father of your flaming child, I'll do as I please.' And he and Pearl would go off, arm in arm, Pearl with a smug smile on her face.

Sometimes they would stay away for days, off on some mysterious personal errand. On these days, Ruby employed Jackdaw, who proved to be an absolute treasure. He and Sparky got on famously and worked well together: one so full of life and good humour, always quick to spot a load in need of transport; the other methodical and painstaking, if constantly on the lookout for bad weather or a leaking boat.

And the pair were very protective of her. Not that Ruby minded. She accepted the rules they set without too much argument. They wouldn't allow her to help haul the barges by hand through the locks, though were happy enough for her to operate the mechanism, and even let her steer once in a while, if never at night.

Ruby was always scrupulously fair with them, as Bart had been, often adding a bonus whenever they'd worked over the odds, so that they proved to be able and willing hands. She didn't exploit them, and unlike many, they wouldn't have dreamed of pilfering cargo. Not that they'd have got away with it under her sharp eye, but she trusted them utterly, knew they would never try as they were scrupulously honest and supremely loyal, partly because of their respect for Bart, but also, Ruby hoped, for herself too.

Traditionally money for transporting a consignment of cotton, coal, pig iron or whatever, was handed to the captain, according to tonnage or trip rates. Therefore it was Ruby's responsibility to pay her team, to which Kit vociferously objected.

'I should be the captain, as the man of the house and your partner in the business. I should be the one to dole out the wages.'

Ruby sighed. 'That's not the way it's done,' she tactfully pointed out.

'It's the way it should be done.'

'Maybe, in certain circumstances, but generally speaking this method works quite well. And you're not my partner, Kit, you're my sister's lover.'

'Only because you're too selfish and stubborn to share. And I know why. You want everything all for yourself, and to cut Pearl and me out. Yet you know it's not normal for a woman to be captain.'

'Eeh, I don't know about that,' chipped in Sparky. 'There were Annie Heap, down Bolton way. She were a right tartar! Her first mate once come back drunk and she...'

A warning glare from Ruby made him clamp his jaws shut on whatever it was Annie Heap had done to her first mate, and Sparky scurried away about his business.

She was ashamed of how long it had taken her to see through Kit; before her suspicions as to the true nature of his relationship with Pearl had finally crystallised in her head. And if it rankled just a little that the man she'd once believed to be the love of her life hadn't turned out to be quite as she'd expected, perhaps the situation was entirely her own fault.

She should never have indulged in those foolish dreams. She'd believed with the optimism of foolish youth that what she'd felt for Kit Jarvis was love, when it was nothing more than the desperate cry of a child in need. Had she not been so stupidly blind, she might never have lost Bart. He would never have fought with Kit on the boat and he'd still be alive today.

This was a mess of her own making, for not being satisfied with what she had. So what right did she have to complain?

–

Outwardly, she tolerated Kit's demands, his grumbles and moans, Pearl's constant prattling and dedicated selfishness,

312

and continued to care for them both as if they were children, and not a pair of adults at all.

She wasn't jealous of their close friendship, only curious and a touch resentful perhaps that they should use her so, without even a thank you or any sign of appreciation, let alone love. Everyone needs love and privately, in her heart, Ruby continued to grieve for Bart, the father of her child. She thought she could cope, and go on in this way indefinitely, but perhaps she underestimated the effect of all this inner anguish and heart-rending emotion. One day, while working on deck with Sparky, she fainted. One minute she was swabbing and scrubbing away grime and muck; the next she'd keeled over, and was, in Sparky's words, 'out like a light'.

'I knew summat were wrong with you,' he said, wafting some air in her face with his cap minutes later when she finally came round. 'You've been looking a mite peaky for weeks now. Months! You work too hard, Ruby, and them two selfish gits do nowt.'

'Don't! Don't say it, Sparky. I'm a fool, I know I am. But what can I do?'

'You could tell 'em to fetch and carry for themselves.'

'Oh, I couldn't do that. Pearl is my little sister. She needs me. Mam is dead, you see, and Pearl depends upon me. I'm all the family she has.'

Sparky gave a sad little shake of the head. 'Nay, lass. That's no excuse and you know it. You wait on them two like a chap wi' three hands. You can't go on like this. Summat has to give. They don't even appreciate what you do for them – off on the razzle every night.' He helped her to her feet and they sat on a coil of rope together, sharing a tot of rum.

'It'll warm your belly on a raw night like this.'

Perhaps it was the alcohol that loosened her tongue but suddenly Ruby was asking questions, the words spilling out of her mouth as if of their own volition. 'This pub in Rochdale where our Pearl works... what's it like? They never seem keen for me to go with them.' She made an attempt at an exasperated laugh, as if this were some silly foible of theirs. But a sideways glance at the expression on Sparky's face, like a trapped rabbit caught in a beam of light, told her that he knew more than he was saying.

'What is it, Sparky? I'm a grown woman. You can tell me.'

Gloomy by nature he may be, but never had she seen him look more miserable. 'Nay, it's nowt to do wi' me.'

'But it *is* something to do with me, and I thought you were my friend. You've just shown your concern, for goodness' sake. Whatever it is that you know, I've surely earned the right to be told properly, by someone I can trust.'

'I promised the baron...'

Ruby was instantly alert. 'What? What did you promise him? You must tell me, Sparky. You can't leave it like this, hanging in the air. What is it that you promised the baron? For God's sake, he isn't here to know that you've broken your promise, is he?'

'Happen not, no. Eeh, can I ask our Aggie? She'd know what to do for the best.'

'No, tell me now, Sparky, if you know what's good for you.' It was cruel of her to bully him, but whatever it was, Ruby needed to know the truth.

He began his tale haltingly, going off at tangents, stopping in tantalising places to sip his rum or make excuses that the details had slipped his mind, but in the end his meaning was all too clear. Kit and Pearl had known each other for a long time, far longer than they'd let on. Sparky finally admitted that the baron had asked him to make some enquiries, and he'd discovered that they'd been living together, as a couple, for at least a year before ever Kit had brought Pearl to the ship that night. Ruby felt as if she'd been kicked in the stomach. 'Are you saying that all the time I was asking him to find Pearl, he was already living with her?'

'Aye, that's right. He were one of her chaps.' Sparky could have bitten off his own tongue. He'd nearly blabbed too much. He started to back away, even as he nodded his agreement, desperate to escape and get back to his work before she started asking any more awkward questions, the kind, which would lead to even more uncomfortable facts coming to light than were good for her.

'And he didn't let on because he wanted that pendant, didn't he?' The pendant had been yet another bone of contention between the three of them. Kit had wanted her to sell it and use the money to buy more barges, another way for him to wheedle his way into the business. Ruby had refused. The pendant had been the only gift that Bart had ever given her, and nothing would make her part with it.

'You're so selfish!' Pearl had said.

Kit had brutally echoed her sister's words. 'That's right, Ruby McBride, you think of nobody but yourself.'

She was glad now that she'd held on to her resolve. She understood everything now, how she'd been duped. No wonder Bart had been furious. He'd been trying to protect her, and she hadn't realised.

As often as possible the pendant still hung about her neck, though during the week when she was working on the barges, she stowed it away in a secret place beneath a floorboard in her bedroom in Quay Street. She'd hate to lose it overboard. The single ruby was a reminder of what now, looking back, seemed to have been happier days. It broke Ruby's heart that she hadn't realised it before, that they'd wasted so much of their time in passionate argument. But then that had characterised their entire relationship. Passion.

Only at the end had there been any true sign of tenderness, but she'd still been too obsessed with her dreams to notice. And even then she couldn't be sure of the significance of that tenderness. Was it out of love for her, or pity for her childish infatuation for Kit?

She could accept Kit and Pearl's casual disregard for her property, but coming to grips with the realisation that they'd been betraying her all along was hard to swallow. The mere fact of Kit pretending he had no idea of Pearl's whereabouts, when all the time she was probably occupying his bed night after night, was more than she could reasonably take in at one go.

Ruby thanked Sparky for his honesty, assuring him she didn't hold him in any way responsible for not telling her earlier about all of this. It had been up to her to ask, not for him to decide what she needed to know. He'd kept his word to Bart, and that was important.

All that day she thought about what he'd told her, and during the long night. Throughout the rest of the week she watched Kit and Pearl and saw how close they were, how she was excluded from this private world they shared.

Even then, Ruby was reluctant to confront them, to face the truth about how long this situation might have existed.

She decided, in the end, to do nothing and, apart from having to deflect some puzzled looks from Sparky, life continued very much as before with Kit and Pearl going out every night like a pair of giggling children. As usual, Ruby stayed on board to look after the boat, deal with the washing and housework, mind little Tommy, and cook all the meals. She was utterly exhausted but had no wish to upset the apple cart of her dreams entirely. She'd waited years to have Pearl back with her. How could she deprive her sister of the first decent home she'd ever had? It would be too cruel. Didn't she deserve a little mothering at last?

But then Ruby recalled what Sparky had told her, about the pair having known each other for a long time, and suddenly it seemed as if the whole plan must have been calculated from the start.

But how could it have been? Wouldn't that mean they'd intended all along to dispose of Bart? Ruby's mind balked at the thought. Now she really was allowing her imagination to run away with her. Kit might be foolish and selfish, he might be a weak male where Pearl's charms were concerned, but that surely didn't make him guilty of premeditated murder?

–

Kit was heartily fed up. He'd lost all patience with waiting for Ruby to come up with the goods. She seemed stubbornly determined to hang on to everything herself: control of the barges, the house they lived in, the baron's possessions, even that flaming pendant which could bring in a bob or two. She also had the cheek to pay him a wage, as if he were no more than an employee and not an equal partner. Kit hated the feeling of being beholden to anyone, least of all a woman. That hadn't been his plan at all. He'd expected her to go along with his schemes, as she had done when she was a girl. Selfish, Pearl called her, and he was beginning to think she might be right. At first he'd argued that Ruby was only suffering from a sense of guilt, that she was simply being overcautious, absolutely certain he could win her round in the end.

But she was turning into a veritable nag, constantly asking him questions. Where was he off to tonight? Which pub was it? When was it, exactly, that he'd first met Pearl? He was beginning to grow tired of being interrogated. Worse than the rozzers she was. Anyone would think she didn't trust him. It came to him one day that perhaps he'd been too patient. She was having him for a fool. He had a right to his fair share of the baron's business, which she wouldn't have had at all were it not for him.

He knew where she kept the pendant. He'd secretly watched as she hid it away, just as if she were afraid someone might steal it. Kit prised up the board and lifted it out. He smiled to himself. Well, somebody just had. Never miss an opportunity, hadn't that always been his motto?

With a swagger of self confidence at his own cleverness, he took the gem to Samuel, the pawnbroker on Liverpool Road. The old man refused to touch it.

'How would you come by such a gem honestly? It must be hot.'

Kit took it to another shop further along the road, and another, and the one after that. The reaction was always the same. Either they wouldn't handle the jewel at all, or they offered him a derisory sum, far below its true worth, to offset the risks involved. Kit was annoyed and excited all at the same time. Pleased that it was genuinely valuable, but irritated and frustrated when he couldn't find anybody to touch it.

It was a mate of his who, quite inadvertently, offered a solution. Kit had idly asked him where he would go if he'd come by an item of some value which a normal pawnbroker wouldn't take. And he'd given a harsh little laugh and said, 'The only one with any brass round here is Pickering. Sell it to him, whatever it is. If he can't afford it, nobody can.'

Chapter Twenty-Six

Dressed in his cleanest trousers and jacket, with his Sunday bowler clutched respectfully in his hand, since he didn't want to be mistaken for anything less than an honest merchant or artisan fallen on hard times, Kit stood in Pickering's office, acutely aware of the weight of the pendant in his pocket. The great man himself was seated behind his mahogany desk, a fat cigar clenched between his teeth and a sour expression on his bony face. 'I hope you aren't intending to waste my time, young man. I've better things to do than sit here listening to the likes of you prattle on over some misconceived complaint or other.'

'Oh, I reckon you might be interested in what I have to show you,' Kit remarked, and laid the pendant on the blotter before him. Pickering's reaction was astounding. The cigar fell from his mouth, and had to be rescued before it set fire to his trousers. His face turned every shade of purple, his lips going almost blue.

'Where the blazes did you find that?'

'I didn't find it. It belongs to a friend of mine. She's been left a widow and this is the only item of any real value left to her by her husband.'

'Don't lie to me, man. I'm no fool. If you've stolen it, I could have you arrested.' Not that he would, Pickering thought. Hadn't he long dreamed of holding this pendant in his hands once again?

Kit was blustering, showing outrage at the very idea he might have stolen it. 'I never did no such thing,' he lied. 'I told you, her husband give her this trinket, and now he's a goner. Dead as a door nail. Hard cash would've been more useful since she has a kid to think of, and I've promised to deal with the matter for her.'

'This is no trinket.' Pickering reached for the pendant and held it tenderly in his hand, as if half afraid to touch it. It might have been Dresden from the delicate way he handled it. He considered it worth dealing with a common thief, just to have it in his possession at last, after all these years. He turned it this way and that, allowing the light to catch the fire in the ruby. 'She has a child you say?'

'Aye, a boy.'

'Name?'

'Tommy, just a babby he is.'

'I meant the woman.'

'Oh, Ruby McBride, at least that was her name afore they wed.'

Pickering was still examining the pendant. 'That must be hard for her, having to cope with a child so young. And you say her husband is dead. When and how did he die? Does she have regular employment or other assets to help maintain her? I would be interested to know—'

Growing impatient with all the questions, Kit interrupted. 'There's others I could take it to if you're not interested.'

A soft chuckle came by way of response. 'But you chose to come to me. I wonder why?'

'I thought as how you would be the sort to appreciate classy goods.'

'How right you are.' Then he looked Kit full in the eye. 'How much are you wanting for it?'

Kit couldn't resist a smirk of satisfaction. His mate had been right. This was the chap to make things happen round here. 'As much as it's worth.'

Pickering gave a brittle laugh, as if Kit had said something amusing. 'Some items are beyond value. Name your price.'

Kit drew a deep breath, inwardly warning himself that this was his best chance yet, possibly his only one since no one else would touch it. 'Enough to set me up with me own pair of barges,' he said, rather breathlessly.

'Done!'

Minutes later he was outside of the office door with the money in his hand, in a state of numb disbelief. His only regret was that he hadn't asked for more.

–

It was a day or two later and they were back in the house on Quay Street for their day off. Kit and Pearl had gone off for the evening, as usual, and again, as usual, Ruby had stayed behind. She was no nearer to making a decision. Ruby had half decided to do nothing at all about the information she'd gleaned from Sparky. Where was the point in raking up old grievances? Bart was dead. She'd no wish to lose Pearl too, even if Kit hadn't turned out quite so well as she'd hoped.

She found solace in working the boats, and of course she had her child – Bart's child. Tommy was growing into a sturdy, delightful little toddler. She also found comfort in her memories and each night would lift the piece of broken floorboard, pull out the pendant from its hiding place, and go to bed with it about her neck. She lifted the board now, her heart aching with need. How she missed him. More than she would ever have imagined possible. No matter how hard she tried to adjust to her new life, she couldn't seem to fill the dark, gaping hole left by his absence.

Ruby slid out the piece of flannel in which she kept her treasure safely wrapped and to her utter shock and disbelief, found it empty. The pendant had gone. So stunned was she that she frantically examined every crevasse, every crack it might have slipped through, unwilling to believe the evidence of her own eyes. It was nowhere to be found. Kit wouldn't have taken it, surely? Not without her permission. But then, if he could keep quiet about Pearl's existence, the sister she'd been seeking for years, how could she be sure of anything?

Perhaps she'd forgotten to put it safely away, though this seemed unlikely. She was always most careful with it.

Ruby searched the house from top to bottom, including going through Pearl's things, just in case her sister had decided to borrow it. Of course, she might be wearing it even now. She felt sick at the thought of her careless sister wearing her beautiful ruby pendant in a pub in Rochdale. Who knew what might happen to it in such nefarious company? No matter how Bart had acquired it, whether it were a genuine gem or not, it held a very special meaning for her and the prospect of losing it made her feel ill. But there was not a sign of it anywhere in the house.

If what she suspected were true, then the moment had come to have it out with them both. They really had no right to borrow her personal things without permission. It was long past time to settle the matter.

Ruby sat in her chair by the fire, her son safely asleep upstairs, and waited impatiently for Kit and Pearl to return. She had gone over and over it in her mind, and could find no other explanation. The pendant was gone and who else but Kit could have taken it? Hadn't he demanded it off her once before? And hadn't she denied the truth long enough? She'd been a fool to trust him.

As Ruby waited, her frustration and anger mounted with each passing hour. It was not until the clock struck one o'clock in the morning that the pair finally came rolling through the door, smelling strongly of beer and propping each other up as they listed to starboard. Kit was surprised to find her still awake.

'What's this? Waiting up with the rolling pin now, are we?'

'Where is it?' Ruby came straight to the point.

'Where's what?'

'You know full well what I'm talking about – my pendant. What's happened to it? It isn't in its hidey-hole under the floorboards where I keep it safe while I'm working. It's gone.'

There was a small, stunned silence, mainly because Kit hadn't expected her to realise it was missing, but he soon rallied. '*Your* pendant and hidey-hole! While *you* are working! There are three of us here. Why does it always have to be about you?'

'For goodness' sake, you're sounding like an echo of our Pearl, picking up all her bad habits.'

Kit sniggered. 'Not quite all of them! There's a few I wouldn't care to pick up, thanks very much.'

'And what's that supposed to mean?'

Pearl dropped into a chair, lifted her head and regarded Ruby with unfocused, bloodshot eyes, very much the worse for the gin she'd consumed that evening. 'Get off yer high horse. You're the one what's disposed of her husband, so you can sleep with another man. Only it didn't quite work out that way, did it, since he's *my* man, actually.'

Ruby jerked as if she'd been slapped while Kit gave a mocking laugh. 'Oh dear, Pearl love, now look where your big trap has taken you.'

Ruby knew she had to remain strong, and take time to make it clear she knew everything. 'I didn't know at first, as I certainly do now, that you and Kit were a couple. I never planned on anything terrible happening to Bart. I've grieved for him every single day since. I wanted only to find you, Pearl, and our Billy, to find a new life for the three of us, in Canada. A foolish dream, as it turned out.'

Kit laughed. 'Poor little innocent Ruby. So naive and trusting that in order to achieve that 'foolish dream', you believed every damn thing we told you.'

'Is there any reason why I wouldn't?'

'There happen is where your Pearl is concerned.'

Ruby ignored him, took a deep breath. It was now or never. 'Sparky has told me that you knew all along where Pearl was, that in fact the pair of you had been living together for a year or more. Is that true?'

Kit put back his head and laughed. 'Good old Sparky. Well now, why not ask your loving sister how long we'd been together before we pretended to find her? Go on, she'll no doubt sing like a flamin' canary, given half a chance. And while yer about it, ask her what it is she really does in Rochdale. Go on, ask her.'

'Shurrup, you! You were happy enough to spend me ill-gotten gains, so don't put all the blame on me,' Pearl protested, swaying drunkenly on her feet.

'Don't I deserve decent recompense, considering the number of clients I find for you. You'd be lifting your skirts at the end of the tunnel with the other working girls, if you didn't have me to look after you.'

Ruby went cold. She could feel herself start to shake inside, though she did her best to disguise it. 'Lifting your skirts? Clients?' The conversation had taken an unexpected, not to say unpleasant turn, not at all in the direction she had expected. And if these words meant what she thought they meant, then her worries over a single pendant were as nothing by comparison. 'Pearl, what is he saying? Tell me it's not true.'

'Mind yer own business.'

'I believe it *is* my business. I promised Mam I'd look after you.'

Pearl flopped back in the chair with a loud groan. 'Not that old chestnut again.'

'Oh, Pearl, I don't know what to say, I really don't.'

'Then don't say anything. I'm me own boss, not beholden to anybody.' She hiccupped gently and lolled back, eyes drooping.

'But is it true? Pearl, wake up.' Ruby shook her, trying to keep her awake. 'What have you done, for goodness' sake? You aren't really a...' Ruby couldn't bring herself to use the word. The very idea of her little sister selling her body for money, or worse, some perverted sort of pleasure, was foul beyond belief.

Instead, firmly closing her mind even to the possibility that this might be true, she switched tracks. 'Were you deliberately hiding from me? If so, I'd like to understand why. I've dreamed of little else but us getting back together again, as a family, finding our Billy and starting afresh, to make up for the troubles of our past. Now I hear that you knew where I was for ages, and did nothing about it. Can you imagine how much it hurts me to learn that?'

Pearl regarded Ruby with an almost clownish expression of surprise on her face. 'Canada was *your* dream, Ruby, not *mine*. We never had a cat-in-hell's chance of finding our Billy. Everyone knew that but you, though we'd've been happy enough to give Canada a try, see where it got us. Nor are you responsible for me. You're the one living in the past. So what if I do spread me favours a bit? I earn myself a crust off me own wits, without being bossed about or bullied by anyone.'

'On your back, you mean.'

'So what if I do?' Pearl giggled. 'I'm me own boss, just as much as you are. And I'll thank you to keep your nose out of my affairs. Affairs... eeh, that's rich, that is!' She began to giggle, a raucous, drunken sound far louder than the pun warranted.

Ruby, on the other hand, found that her eyes were awash with tears. She felt as if she'd failed, that she'd let their mother down. She must not have looked after Pearl properly, though Lord help her, she'd done her best. What more could she have done? 'Have you thought what you're doing? Have you ever considered the consequences?'

'If you mean a babby, I did for all that years ago when I had an abortion.'

Ruby felt sick, and knew in that moment that all was lost with Pearl. The silly girl was her own worst enemy and no one could save her unless she wanted to be saved. Perhaps the reason was that a certain person had far greater influence over her than a nagging sister could ever hope to have.

She turned again to Kit, remembering the reason why she'd started on this conversation in the first place. 'So where is my pendant? Have you taken it?'

'What if I have? If you insist on treating me and Pearl like we come off the muck heap, don't we deserve to look after our own needs once in a while?'

'If you've borrowed or pawned it, I'll…'

'What will you do, eh? What will you bleedin' do? If you must know, I sold it. Got a good price for it. In a day or two I'll buy me own train of barges and take you over, or put you out of business, whether you like it or not.'

She ignored this last threat. 'Who did you sell it to? One of your mates in the pub, I suppose?'

'S'matter of fact, it went to a good home. I sold it to Giles Pickering, would you believe? Since he has plenty of dosh. That's a laugh, eh?' He was highly amused to see all the colour wash from her face, so stunned was she by this revelation.

'Giles Pickering?' Ruby could hardly believe it. It seemed cruelly ironic to sell her precious pendant, the only memento she had left of him, to Bart's own father. Not that Kit was aware of the true nature of their relationship. Nobody was, so far as she was aware. Bart had taken great care to keep this fact quiet. And who would ever suspect any connection between the baron, content to live on his tug, and one of the most powerful, wealthiest men in the city? But then he'd been an eccentric had Barthram Stobbs, a one-off. Ruby certainly had no intention of revealing his secret.

Kit was rubbing finger and thumb together, to indicate money. 'He has plenty of the readies, d'you see. You'll not get it back off him, so there's nowt you can do about it.'

'You don't know what I might do.'

'Don't make me laugh. What can you do? Tell me that!'

What Ruby did was to order Kit Jarvis, whom she'd once believed to be the love of her life, to leave that very minute. 'Get out of my house, and don't ever attempt to come back on to my boat. There'll be no work for you there. Yes, it's my tug, and I'm asking you – nay, telling you – to leave. *Now!* I've had enough.'

'*You've* had enough?' He gave a loud snort of disdain. 'What about us, me and Pearl here? We've waited years to get our hands on these boats and some of the baron's money. If it hadn't been for Pearl's earnings, we'd've starved. Then, when I finally got rid of the flamin' baron, you decide to turn stubborn and not share your spoils. Pearl's right, you are selfish.'

Ruby could feel herself going hot and cold all over from a mixture of anger and shock. She was sure that at any moment she might actually throw up. 'If you don't leave my house this minute, I'll fetch the police.'

'If Kit goes, I go with him,' Pearl yelled.

'Fine. Good riddance to the pair of you.'

And so they left, packing their goods and chattels in a flurry of fury and taking half of Ruby's stuff with them as well. Not that she cared. Ruby sat in her chair shivering, despite a blazing fire in the hearth, until they had done, and only as they reached the door did she add one more thing.

'That door's always open for you, our Pearl. Remember that. As for you, Kit Jarvis, you can go hang yerself for all I care.'

'Fortunately, Ruby girl, you made sure that I wouldn't, so I reckon I'll survive.'

–

As before, Ruby buried her pain in her work. Sparky's wife, Aggie, became a great friend, sometimes travelling with them on longer journeys, with all her brood on board. Ruby loved them as if they were her own family. And it did at least solve the problem of someone to mind little Tommy.

'What would I do without you?' Ruby would say as Aggie brought her a cup of tea and offered to put the little fellow to bed. 'I'm exhausted.'

'And soaked to the skin, by the look of you. Get yerself out of them wet clothes. There's a stew bubbling. When I've put these babbies down, we'll get some of that inside you. We have to keep our lovely boss healthy and strong, eh?'

'Oh, Aggie, what would I do without you?' She reiterated the oft-repeated phrase, and both women would laugh.

Ruby loved having them all on board. The children were noisy and full of fun, as ready to buckle to and help with the work as race around playing games in a field during a stopover.

Aggie was a dark haired, steady-eyed, handsome woman, far more cheerful and outgoing than her husband, though having his family about him lifted Sparky's natural gloom wonderfully. He was almost a different man. Almost! To Ruby's great delight, she saw that Aggie very much wore the trousers in that family and her word was law. So there was also less drinking on board when she was there, and consequently the work got done quicker. But it made space even more at a premium since every spare inch was taken up with cargo, a necessity if they were to survive.

Aggie was also a Trojan worker, never still for a minute, and they all grew used to dodging the line of washing flapping over the decks by seven every morning, all because she'd been up at four using the canal-side tap. Not that there were many of those about. The canal companies were ready enough to provide money for the church or chapel but less forthcoming when it came to washing and lavatory facilities. Bathing the children was always a problem and if a tap wasn't handy, they'd have to take a dip in the canal, assuming a clean stretch could be found.

'Failing that, we has to rely on a lick and a promise,' Aggie would say, scrubbing each of their grubby faces with a loofah and carbolic soap.

'If they survive that treatment,' Ruby would laughingly remark, 'they can survive anything.'

'Oh aye, canal children are tough. Have to be. This is where they get their education, not at school, even supposing we stopped long enough in one place for them to attend. And the teachers allus picks on canal children, making them sit on their own, away from all the rest, as if the others might catch summat off them. Waste of time schools are, teach them nowt of any use. They learn everything they need to right here.'

Ruby didn't argue, her own memories of schooling being similarly blighted.

Sometimes, though, she went along to meetings to express her concern over the lack of welfare, or even a doctor for the women and children. She held little hope of anything being done as it was the same old story, the employers leaving it to the voluntary bodies to provide welfare, as they themselves were only interested in profit. But she remembered how Bart had fought for the canal folk, and so would she.

Business went from strength to strength and Ruby was not only holding her own, but at times earning more with her train of barges than many men. Aggie introduced her to the other women in the canal system and most accepted her, despite the lingering gossip and rumours about the baron's fate.

From time to time there were hints that Bart had run off because he had some dark secret, which Ruby always furiously refuted. She hated the thought of people prying into his affairs, even after his death. Ruby handing over all the necessary papers, record books and details of bank accounts to his successor quickly silenced the nasty rumours about his absconding with the burial club funds. But the whispers persisted. No one quite knew what to believe, and she had no answers to give. Not without endangering Kit's safety, and however much he might have betrayed her, that didn't make him a murderer, only an opportunist, as he had ever been. He and Bart had after all been fighting. They were surely equally to blame, and it had simply been an accident. She'd no intention of allowing rumour to rule, or to be panicked into hasty action.

But then one morning, she was woken early by Sparky hammering on her cabin door, shouting that the tug was taking in water. Ruby hurriedly threw on some clothes and joined him on deck. It had been a calm night with no rain and very little wind. Now, as dawn approached, the sky was tinged with soft pinks and blues, promising a lovely day ahead.

'She's been holed, and it must be deliberate because she were nice as ninepence when we tied her up last night.'

'I didn't feel anything. How could anyone bump into us and we not feel it? It couldn't be the weather, could it?'

'No, but it could've been done with a spike, nice and slow like, levering out a plank till there's a gap wide enough to cause a leak. Whether it's splintered or not I won't know till I take a look. I'll kill 'em when I find out who did this.'

As Sparky desperately shouted to Jackdaw to start pumping while he went underwater to check the extent of the damage, Ruby thought she might know who was responsible.

Chapter Twenty-Seven

In the days and weeks following there were similar incidents, some more dangerous than others, such as other unexpected leaks, a cargo loosened or even goods tipped into the water. They once found a dozen or so frogs in their water barrel, more of a nuisance than anything as it had to be refilled, but Ruby began to feel unsafe. It gave her the feeling that they were being followed, and could no longer leave the boat unattended, or who knew what might happen?

They set a watch, taking turns to sit up at night and keep an eye out for whoever the vandal was. Without exception they'd decided it must be Kit, but had talked it over and decided nothing could be done without proof.

Their suspicions seemed to be confirmed when they heard that he'd bought a tug and train of barges of his own, and was undercutting everyone. The word was that he was picking up a lot of orders as a result, that he and Pickering were working hand in glove. Ruby said she could well believe it and admitted to having thrown him out of the house.

'He took something of mine. I've no wish to go into details, but this is his revenge. And there were some problems with our Pearl.' She looked away, flushing slightly, as she'd no wish to air her family's dirty linen in public. Sparky came to her rescue.

'I don't blame you for throwing him out. He's a wily monkey, that one. But there's no point in tackling him till we can catch him red-handed. He'd only deny it.'

'I could get him seen to,' Jackdaw offered, for although he had once been Kit's firm friend, he had long since changed his allegiance.

Ruby swiftly put a stop to that idea. 'Goodness, whatever we do must be proper and above board. We're not going to be the ones put in the wrong.' She came to a decision. The very next time they took on a load from Pickering's Wharf, she'd ask to have a word with the great man himself. It was surely up to him to make sure that competition was fair, and help her put a stop to these reprisals.

—

Ruby sat opposite Giles Pickering, striving to catch any likeness in him to Bart. She failed utterly. This man's face was tightly set, cheeks sunken, with deeply etched lines drawn from a narrow, bony nose to the corners of his mouth. This gave him a spiteful, sour demeanour, not helped by the dullness of his pale brown eyes that held none of his son's golden glow. There were streaks of dull brown amongst the grey hair, not a sign of Bart's red. She concluded that perhaps he'd taken after his mother. If so, she must have been a beauty.

Ruby was instructed rather than invited to sit, and a plump, bustling woman, no doubt Mr Pickering's secretary, poured tea, handing her a cup with what might pass for a sympathetic smile before quietly withdrawing. Ruby was impressed by such hospitality. She couldn't imagine Pickering entertaining all the independent carriers he used in this way, albeit he largely depended upon them to transport his goods. She wondered what this politeness was all in aid of.

It didn't surprise her that he came straight to the point. 'Now, young woman, what is it exactly you want from me? I'm a busy man, so say what you've come to say and look sharp about it. If there's one thing I can't stand it's shilly-shallying about.'

'I shall try not to waste your time,' Ruby drily remarked, her smile warm. Lancashire bluntness didn't trouble her one bit. She thanked him for the tea and sipped it gratefully, hesitating not out of fear but uncertainty as to how best to proceed.

She'd rehearsed various versions of her tale, different ways to approach this man, from a vague description of the vandalism done to her tug and barges, accompanied by a polite request for assistance, to a more detailed explanation. The first sounded as if she was simply whining, which might lead him to assume she was unable to cope because she was a woman. The second touched on matters she'd much rather keep to herself.

Much as she might regret the fact that Kit had sold Pickering her pendant, Ruby had no intention of asking for it back. Where was the point? He'd no doubt bought it in good faith, and for all she knew it may well have been nothing more than tinted glass. He could very well accuse her of being in league with Kit, of trying to get it back so she could play the same trick on someone else. Besides, she didn't imagine for a minute that Kit would have admitted how he came by it.

She was taken aback, when Pickering interrupted her thoughts with the question: 'I suppose you want it back?'

'I – I beg your pardon?'

'The pendant! I suppose you've come to try and get it back. You are Bart's widow, aren't you?'

Ruby swallowed and bleakly nodded.

'I thought the name was familiar. And you asked that chap of yours to sell it for you. Well, I gave him a good price, more than he deserved, so if you've spent the money already, that's your bad luck. So far as I'm concerned that's an end of the matter. You can whistle for it.'

'I didn't actually expect to get it back,' Ruby began, thrown into sudden confusion by the viciousness of his tone. 'What I mean is, I never asked him to sell it for me. I just thought you might—'

'Be persuaded, so you went along with it, eh? And now you think it might be worth seeing if I'm good for a bit more where that came from. Well, you can think again. I know about you money-grabbing boat people. Never satisfied. And don't think you'll be in my will either, just because you wed my son. I may be well off, but I've a good few years in me yet, and when I do get to the stage of pushing up the daisies, there'll be nothing coming your way.'

During this long diatribe he'd got to his feet and begun to pace about the room, his face like thunder, spittle flying as he vented his spite upon her. Ruby sat astonished, struggling the find the words to explain that nothing of the sort had ever entered her head, when he leaned over his desk and hissed, 'I suppose you do know that Bart or the baron as you no doubt call him, was my son?'

'Yes, I do know. Bart told me.'

'And no doubt he also told you why he'd left home, and that we'd not parted on the best of terms.'

'He said something of the matter, yes, but I'm not sure that it is any of my business. I only came to—'

'Too damn right it's none of your business! None whatsoever. By heck, but he had poor choice when it came to women. First a piddling grocer's lass and then you. Which bush did he drag you out from under?'

Ruby could hardly believe what she was hearing. She certainly had no intention of pretending to be what she wasn't, but she met his accusing gaze with as much dignity as she could muster. 'As a matter of fact, he found me in the reformatory.'

Giles Pickering snorted his derision. 'Aye, he would. That's typical of him, that is. Daft bugger. Always did have a soft heart when it came to a pretty face. For all I know you could have stolen that pendant from Jess. We'd assumed a sneak thief had got into the house. She was proper cut up about it when the police failed to catch him.'

Now Ruby was on her feet too, indignant colour flaring upon each cheek and the pair faced each other across the mahogany desk, open animosity on Pickering's face, a mixture of defiance and dismay on Ruby's. 'I never did anything of the sort. Bart took it himself, if you want to know.'

In that moment everything finally slid into place. Bart had taken the pendant from the dressing table because it had once belonged to his mother. No doubt he believed that he'd more right to it than the woman who had supplanted her. Jessica must have been his father's second wife, perhaps his mistress before his first wife died. No wonder Bart had known where the study was, and that he'd been careful to wear a disguise.

'Even my rapscallion son wouldn't be so soft as to give away his mother's heirloom. He worshipped the ground she walked on. And you can kiss goodbye to any hopes you might have had for that son of yours. Oh aye, I know all about him. Tommy, isn't it? Well, so far as I'm concerned he's no relation to me. He's no doubt a by-blow of that no-good piece of rubbish who came to sell me the piece in the first place.'

Ruby's mouth dropped open. 'He's your grandson!'

'Not unless I say he is. And I don't say any such thing. He's nothing to do with me. Not my responsibility, and neither are you.' He wagged a finger at her. 'So if you think you can smarm your way in here and have me grease your palm with silver, you've mistaken your man this time round, madam. I suggest you take yourself off home, before I call the constabulary.'

'Don't worry, I'm going.' Ruby marched to the door, pausing with her hand on the brass knob. 'I came here for your help because Kit Jarvis, that no-good piece of rubbish, as you call him, is making my life a misery as well as damaging all the other carriers by undercutting them. I can see now that *you* probably put him up to it. Which means your grandson's livelihood is at risk, but clearly you don't care about that either. I didn't come here for any of your money. It never entered my head, and as for the pendant, I never thought it particularly valuable in the first place. I just loved it because Bart gave it to me. And now he's dead, so...' She could say no more. Her throat closed, choked with emotion, her eyes filling with tears. Ruby valiantly drew breath and finished what she had to say. 'I can see now why Bart left home. You're a nasty, mean, selfish old man who deserves to be left all alone, even by your own son. And I certainly don't want mine anywhere near you. Good day to you, sir.'

She was vastly proud of the fact that she didn't even slam the door.

As Ruby walked briskly home, ignoring the tram in the hope that the fresh air might help to cool her temper, she suddenly began to laugh as she recalled how the woman, Jess, had flirted with Bart, not recognising her own stepson. But then the laughter changed to tears.

Bart had given her the pendant. The fact that it had once belonged to his beloved mother somehow made the gift infinitely more precious, and even more painful that she had lost it. Did that mean that perhaps he had cared for her a little, after all? Oh Bart, if only we could start all over again, she thought. She had lost more than she'd realised that day. A love that could never be regained!

–

The Friday following her visit to Giles Pickering, they suffered yet another 'accident', on a return trip from Liverpool. A load of timber broke free from the strap securing it, and a third of *Blackbird*'s cargo was lost, not to mention a good deal of time wasted before they managed to make the rest of the load secure. Nor did they catch the culprit. Jackdaw heard running feet and gave chase, but could see nothing in the darkness.

The following morning as they tied up at Trafford Wharf, Kit strolled over. 'Dear, dear, having problems, are you?'

'As if you didn't know,' Ruby drily remarked.

'You should take more care. The canal system is a dangerous place for a woman. Anything can happen.'

Ruby spoke through gritted teeth. 'Is that some sort of threat?'

'As if *I* would threaten you when yer like family to me, being Pearl's sister. No, I just wondered if you'd like me to ask around for you, and see if I can get wind of who's causing all this trouble?' His face was a picture of innocence as he smiled at her.

'No, thanks, I can manage.' She walked away from him, determined not to get involved in an argument. But to her great annoyance, he followed her.

'Make it worth me while and I'd see you were safe in future, Ruby.'

'Oh, and how would you achieve that, I wonder?'

He grasped her by the elbow, pulling her to a halt. 'Whatever you've suffered so far is nowt to what could happen. Believe me, life could get pretty nasty for a woman alone on these waters.'

'Ah, but I'm not alone. I have Sparky and Jackdaw with me at all times.' She tried to pull her arm free, but he was holding her so tightly there was no hope of escape.

'Lot of good they'll do you. You know, of course, that there are some nasty rumours doing the rounds about what exactly did happen to your husband? It wouldn't do your business any good at all were they to get wind of the truth – that it was you who pushed him overboard.'

Ruby gasped. 'You know very well that's not how it was.'

He gave a sad little shake of his head. 'Aye, but since there were no witnesses, who's to say? Then, having got yer hands on his boats, you sent me to sell that pendant.

Now, having spent all of that money, you're now after the insurance money on the tug and barges, which no doubt your careful husband was astute enough to take out, which would nicely compensate for these so-called "accidents" to your boat.'

'Dear heaven, you're trying to blackmail me!'

'Now that's not a nice word, Ruby.' He chuckled softly as he drew her closer. 'I'm trying to help you, pet. All you have to do is hand over them barges to me, which is only right and proper after the fuss and bother I went to. Oh, we'll make it look as if I've paid you a fair price, on paper that is. Not what you'd get on the open market, of course, but then you're not in a position to dictate terms, are you? What with your business going down the sewer after all these careless mistakes you've been making. Everyone knows that.'

Ruby was gasping. 'I don't believe I'm hearing this. I haven't made any mistakes. You're the one deliberately damaging my vessels, and I'll see that everyone knows it.'

He looked sadly at her. 'They'd never believe you. They'd only think you were trying to prevent yourself, a reformatory girl, from being accused of murder.'

'And why would they believe you, a reformatory lad?'

'Oh, there'd be some who wouldn't, I'm sure you're right. But you wouldn't want to take any risks by arguing the toss, now would you? No, Ruby, I'd say that, all told, your best bet would be to get out of the carrier business altogether. Otherwise things could get very nasty. Very nasty indeed.'

The barefaced cheek of the man was almost beyond belief, and Ruby told him so, in no uncertain terms, using the kind of reformatory language she hadn't used in a long while. He simply laughed, finding her fury amusing.

Finally, she managed to wrench her arm free. 'You'll never get your hands on my business. Never! It's my son's inheritance. And don't you *ever* come anywhere near my boats again. If, as I suspect, it's you who's damaging my cargo, then make no mistake, we'll have the police on you.'

He chuckled as he turned to leave. 'You have to catch me first. Remember what I've said, Ruby. Give in gracefully or it'll be the worse for you.' And with an arrogant smirk on his handsome face, he stuck his hands in his pockets and strolled away.

Three nights later they were all asleep in their cabins, save for Jackdaw who was on watch, when Ruby woke to the smell of smoke and pandemonium all around her. A window had been smashed and a ball of burning, oily cotton waste thrown inside the tug. In the seconds it took her to grab her coat, the fire had already taken hold in the main cabin. Children were crying, Aggie was having screaming hysterics, and poor Sparky was doing his best to get everyone up and tackle the blaze all at the same time.

'Tommy, Tommy!' Ruby was frantic to wake her son. Gathering him into her arms, she fled, almost falling into the water in her terror.

The minute the other children were all safely ashore, Ruby left him in their care and was back beside Sparky, beating at the flames, Aggie and the older children were filling water buckets from the canal for them to throw. But they could see from the start that it was hopeless. They were fighting a losing battle. Nothing could save the tug. It was more than an hour later that they found Jackdaw, lying unconscious on the tow path, a pool of blood spreading beneath his battered head. The shock made the loss of the tug and Ruby's income seem small by comparison.

They believed that Jackdaw must have heard a sound or spotted something moving in the darkness. With his keen senses, he was always the most effective on watch. It was clear that he must have gone after whoever it was, and this had been the result.

Ruby saw red. She left Aggie and Sparky tending to him and, unable to bear the sight of the blackened ruin of her precious boat, she marched off down the towpath, head held high and war in her heart.

Perhaps it was the very depth of her anger that saved her, the fire alight in her now so that nothing would quench it. This matter had to be settled once and for all. Certainly nobody she met on the canal bank that day was in any doubt that she meant business, and every single one of them offered their assistance, which she politely, if somewhat brusquely, refused.

'I can deal with my own troubles, thanks all the same.'

And she did. She found Kit, as expected, skulking in the messiest pair of barges she'd ever had the misfortune to step aboard. Ruby stepped over one man prostrate on the deck, presumably the worse for drink, and strode the length of the barges with practised ease. The first mate looked on, goggle-eyed, evidently enjoying the show.

Hands on hips she confronted her enemy. 'So, you're up to your old tricks again? Not content with cutting the wire on my timber and losing me half my load, now you've resorted to arson. Well, let me tell you, Kit Jarvis, this is your last warning. If you ever come within a hundred yards of my tug again, it'll be your throat that is slit, from ear to ear. Do I make myself clear?'

He was foolish enough to snort his derision.

'Oh, don't think I can't. So far I've been very patient. Too patient perhaps. But don't forget, I'm a reformatory girl too with friends in the right places. Jackdaw was always on at me about being too soft before it all got out of hand. Now he's the one who has suffered the most because I refused to heed his warning. That was a bad mistake, Kit, attacking your one-time friend. If Jackdaw wasn't such a hard nut to crack you'd have done for him. It's a miracle he survived.' She allowed herself a small smile as she saw uncertainty creep into his blue eyes. 'I'll certainly be hard pressed to hold him back now. But then, why should I care what he does to you? You're not the only one who can take revenge. You and Pearl had best watch out.'

'Huh, I haven't seen Pearl in months.'

For a moment Ruby was thrown off her stride, but quickly recovering she continued, 'Be that as it may, my sister must make her own way in the world, as she insists that's what she wants. What she does with her life is no longer any of my concern. And what you do with yours is your business too. But interfere with me and mine, and you'll wish you'd never set eyes on Ruby McBride.'

'I already do,' he grumbled sourly.

'Good. Then you'll think twice before taking me on again. Do your worst, Kit Jarvis, if you dare. Tell your sordid little tale and I'll tell mine, and we'll see who they believe. I'm willing to call your bluff. And don't forget, if anything were to happen to me, Jackdaw and Sparky would know well enough where to come looking for you. Believe me, there'd be no holds barred. And just to show you that I mean business, how about this for starters.' Whereupon she picked up the long pole used for hauling the barge through tunnels, and stabbing him in the chest with it, pushed him into the canal. He gave a yell of surprised fright as he toppled backwards into the filthy water. 'Now why don't you tell everyone that I shoved you overboard, because that bit would be true, wouldn't it?'

She left him spluttering and swearing, not least cursing at his first mate who was roaring with laughter.

Chapter Twenty-Eight

24 June 1911

The man standing amongst the motley gathering of dockers was tall and with a powerful build that would make him appear dominant in any crowd, despite his evident desire to stay well back and not be noticed. He wore rough working clothes like everyone else, and a slouch cap pulled well down over his eyes, allowing him to glance to right or left unobserved. He was only half listening to the irate debate, taking place amongst the dockers who, having finally lost patience with being ignored, had come out on strike. The rest of his attention was centred upon a young woman. She stood on the fringes a few yards away from him, holding tightly to the hand of a child: a boy, of around three or four years old at a guess.

Only yesterday the people of Manchester and Salford had been celebrating the coronation of George V. The streets were still decked with paper bunting, Union flags, and dusty-looking banners wilting in the heat. It had been one of the hottest summers on record, trade was booming and any visitor to these shores, come to revel in the majesty of imperialistic glory, must have thought it a fortunate land indeed.

But Bart, like many another union man, knew that all was not as it appeared. Underneath the pomp and circumstance festered an open sore of discontent.

A voice rang out, echoing his troubled thoughts. 'A chap shouldn't be at risk of losing his job just because he's joined a union. The bosses have their combinations, why not we men? We should have the right.'

Murmurs of assent rippled through the crowd, though one man shouted out a warning. 'Take care who you say that to lad. A bloke at Pickering's Wharf got sacked the other week for just such a remark.'

Bart recognised the speaker as Flitch and smiled to himself. Big he may be, but never foolhardy, not where his livelihood was concerned. The same could be said of most of these men. Good, honest men who asked only for someone to listen to their problems, offer some sort of security, and at the very least provide decent working conditions. He understood their frustrations and felt a nudge of guilt because by doing his disappearing act, he felt he'd let them down somehow.

He'd spent the last few years working on the docks in Glasgow, physically hard labour for a low wage, but sufficiently taxing to allow him to sleep at nights. Now he was back and dockers, carters, railway workers and union men everywhere were making their voices heard up and down the land, here in Manchester as much as anywhere.

The trouble was there were too many unions: small, regional groups with too little power or muscle to use against the employers, who rarely managed to agree with each other let alone join forces and work together for the benefit of all. Owners and managers were every bit as stubborn, and often refused even to speak to a union man, let alone employ one. Madness!

The syndicalists might speak with passion of their dream for creating one big union that would tailor the share of power in society to suit all, but there was little chance of their succeeding in this over-optimistic aim. Unlike his father, Bart had never seen them as an evil and sinister force, out to destroy the very people who provided them with work, and found it hard to hold his patience with such an attitude. Though in truth he believed the real answer lay in seeking a middle ground, one less radical but fair.

'You can't teach an old dog new tricks,' his father would say. 'The world is changing too fast for me. Join forces with me in the business, if you care that much.' Yet Bart had always refused, knowing the cost of such an action would be high. Swallowing his pride for one thing. Learning to work with his father for another. Quite impossible!

And now his father was gone. Giles Pickering had died of a heart attack less than a week ago. Bart had returned for the funeral, and now had some hard decisions to make. Did he stay, and take responsibility for his heritage, or return to Glasgow and anonymity?

It surprised him that he'd even been given the choice, but the solicitor had called him into his office and outlined the terms under which he could take control of Pickering's. And there were indeed conditions. No unions had been one. He must take his proper place in society and stop denying his background and heritage for another; also recognise that his stepmother could continue to live in the house for the remainder of her lifetime. Bart had listened carefully and then walked out of the door without giving his response. Even in death his father attempted to control him. But Giles Pickering could not halt the progress of history.

'I got the push last week for being an agitator,' one man cried out, 'though I'd only attended a couple of meetings. I'll show 'em agitating! They won't know what's hit 'em, once I get started.'

'Don't talk so daft. We're wasting our time. The union will never be recognised.'

'It will if we keep faith. We have to hold fast to our beliefs.'

'Aye, and stick to our demands for a wage above star-vation level.'

'How can we hope for that when employers want things all their own way.'

The argument raged on but Bart's attention was again distracted by the woman who was moving away. She had her head down as she talked to the boy, and a swathe of nut-brown hair fell forward over her cheek. He ached to go over to her, push back the hair and kiss her, as he might once have done without a moment's thought. Though would she have welcomed such a kiss even then? He thought not. There were times, in the privacy of their bed, he'd felt he'd come close to possessing her, yet even that may well have been an illusion.

They'd got off on the wrong foot from the start. He shouldn't have bullied her into marrying him. He prob-ably would never have done so had not that pompous chairman of the Board of Guardians been so determined to have her locked up for inciting a riot. The prospect of that lovely girl being incarcerated in a stinking cell had been more than he could stomach, even then, and he'd put forward an alternative suggestion without hesitation.

And not for a moment, a second, had he regretted it. He loved her now even more than he had loved her then. He froze as he saw that she was walking towards him, heard the clear tinkle of her laughter, and his heart clenched into a ball of pain deep inside. He should walk away now, before she spotted him, but somehow his feet wouldn't respond. He stood transfixed, paralysed by the sight of her.

Discovering she had taken Kit Jarvis as her lover had nearly broken him. He'd followed her because he'd been unwilling to believe it could be true. For a time, after he'd saved her from that crazy escapade on the ship, he'd thought he'd finally won her. But Kit Jarvis had put him right on that one, and the fight, coming as it did on top of the argument with his father and his failure to help the men, had well-nigh finished him. His whole life had suddenly seemed useless, without value or purpose. It had been touch and go for a while at the bottom of that filthy canal but even after he'd finally come up, some distance from the tug and gasping for air, he'd felt no urge to return.

Looking back, he didn't regret taking advantage of the fight and his plunge into the canal, cold and unpleasant though it had been. He'd been right to leave. Look at her now, with living proof of her betrayal. The child was dressed in a spotless blue shirt, buttoned at the cuffs but open at the neck, and knee-length grey trousers. The child looked healthy and robust, with rosy cheeks and a large floppy beret pulled down over his head to protect him from the sun.

She was wearing a blue linen, ankle-length dress that moulded to her figure as she walked. It suited her, contrasted well with her colouring. Her hat, he noticed, was a golden straw with a matching blue ribbon. She'd taken it off in the heat and was swinging it idly in her hand.

She was less than ten yards from him now. Were she to glance up, she might look straight into his eyes. Fortunately, she was utterly absorbed in the child who was playing with a diabolo, trying to make the bobbin spin in the limpid summer air.

'Toss it, Tommy. Go on, don't be afraid, just roll it along the string then up it goes.'

The child was concentrating hard but didn't quite have the necessary dexterity. The spinning bobbin flew from its string well enough, its painted colours glittering in the sunlight, but did not return as expected. Ruby laughed uproariously as she chased after it.

Their fingers closed on the toy at the same moment. 'Oh, thank you. My son dropped it, he...'

She stopped speaking and every vestige of colour drained from her face as she looked up into his eyes. Then she put her hand to her mouth, shook her head slightly as if in disbelief. Bart handed her back the bobbin, tugged the neb of his cap and gave a cool smile.

'He looks a fine boy, ma'am. His father must be proud of him.' Then he turned smartly on his heel and strode away.

–

Ruby found that she was shaking so much her knees buckled. She staggered to the low stone wall that ran along the quayside and slumped upon it. Perhaps she'd dreamed it. Perhaps it was simply her imagination playing tricks. How could it have been Bart, he's *dead*! They all knew that. She'd seen him fall in the canal with her own eyes.

But what if he wasn't? At the time she'd found difficulty in believing that he could simply vanish off the face of the earth. And his body had never been found. Since that terrible day the baron had become a legend. Many people believed that he'd been murdered by political opponents who disapproved of his union activities, while others rumoured that he'd gone back to his wealthy family somewhere, when he'd failed to establish a union at Pickering's Wharf.

Ruby didn't know what to think. She knew only that her world had changed forever on that dreadful day. When he fell from the tug she'd lost the one man she could ever love, for she loved him still. She'd loved him all along and hadn't realised it until far too late. Had she lost him, or was he still alive?

She jumped to her feet, shading her eyes against the sun as she scanned the jostling crowd, now dispersing with nothing having been settled. The dockers' strike was spreading, and involving thousands of seamen, firemen and miners as more men came out in sympathy with their fellow workers. Her carrier business was in jeopardy with precious little in the way of orders coming in. No conclusions had been reached today, save to call another meeting, at some other time. Yet now her livelihood didn't seem important as panic filled her breast. What had she been thinking of? Why hadn't she run after him, grabbed him, fallen into his arms with a cry of joy? Oh, drat! Why did she always do the wrong thing?

'Are you all right, Mummy?'

'Yes, love. I'm fine. It's the heat, just give me a minute.'

'I'm hot too, Mummy. Can we have an ice cream?'

She smiled at her son. He was a good boy, her right hand man she called him. 'Why not?' She followed him, laughing, as he ran excitedly after the ice cream barrow. He jigged up and down beside her while she bought them each a licking dish of ice cream.

'Here you are, darling. Strawberry, your favourite.'

It probably hadn't been him at all, just her fevered imagination. How many times since he'd disappeared had she thought that she'd seen him. No doubt it was simply a man who looked like him, no more than that.

When they had finished their ice creams she wiped the rim of pink from his small mouth, took off the floppy beret and mopped the beads of perspiration from his brow, pushing back the tousled red-gold curls with her fingers. Then she replaced the hat, and once more the vibrant colour was banished from sight.

What if it had been Bart, and he'd thought Tommy was Kit's child? Had her son not been wearing the beret, it would have been all too plain that was not the case. Ruby began to laugh, even as tears rolled down her cheeks. She'd put on the hat to protect his head from the sun, had she as a result lost the only opportunity to be reunited with Bart? No, hadn't she just decided it was the heat, and her own desperate longing to see him again that had conjured him up. But Barthram Stobbs was dead.

—

'Forty thousand people idle,' cried a passing paperboy. Ruby gave him a couple of pennies for the *Evening News* and quickly scanned the contents. It was now August, almost September, and the situation was growing worse by the day, with winter just around the corner. There was no coal, no fresh supplies, factories and shops were closing, and no manufactured goods were being transported. She screwed the newspaper up and struck out across the square.

A few strike-breakers, protected by police, were making an effort to shift some goods, coal and food mainly. A futile attempt as pickets created blockades. But what choice did they have? They weren't asking for charity, only what was just and fair.

But then who said that life was fair?

She called to her dawdling son. 'Hurry up, Tommy, love. We haven't got all day.'

'I want to watch the ships.'

'Sadly, there are no ships going anywhere today, darling.' Countless stood idle in docks the length and breadth of the land, including the Ship Canal. She went to take his hand and drag him away. 'Come along, it's time to go home.' He looked crestfallen, as well he might. Didn't all little boys love big ships?

She remembered her brother Billy watching them on the day the Ship Canal had been officially opened. How long ago that seemed. Like another lifetime, a different world. Even at eleven Ruby had sensed the change in the air, knew something was about to happen, yet she'd held on to her dreams, her promise to Mam to care for her brother and sister. Too long perhaps! Ruby had no time these days for dreams. She was far too busy dealing with reality. The lack of orders had hit them hard. Jackdaw, Sparky and Aggie were suffering along with her but, much as she loved them as if they were her own family, how could she pay them money she didn't have?

But then things had been hard ever since the fire. Bart had indeed been far-thinking enough to take out insurance cover. Kit had been right about that, if wrong to predict that anyone would believe her capable of firing her own boats in order to claim it. Everyone knew Ruby McBride was incapable of such trickery. They'd had the boat rebuilt, held on to the business by the skin of their teeth. But she never forgot how much she owed Bart, nor how much she missed him. There wasn't a day passed when she didn't think of him, and yearn for him.

'We'd rather have your dad here with us any day than his boats, wouldn't we, love?' she'd say to her son as she sang him to sleep each night. 'But that's what we've got, so we have to make the best of it, eh?' And he'd nod, and look sad for a father he'd never known.

Ruby wiped a tear from her cheek with the flat of her hand. What good did weeping do? She'd learned that too, over the years: learned it even as a child, and at a hard school.

Now, just when they'd been getting back on their feet again, they had the strike to contend with. Like many another, they were running up debt in order to recover and do whatever was necessary to survive. But then most people were living on t'tick, as they called it, till even the corner shops put up their shutters and said: '*No more credit.*'

Other shopkeepers were more generous. Ruby had seen butchers doling out bowls of soup to a whole queue of women and children, grocers tossing stale loaves of bread into the street for the desperate to gather up. Most of these men had no union pay to help them through the strike.

Everyone was expected to survive by their wits and they'd been hanging on for weeks, all through the long, hot summer. Many were growing perilously near to destitution, Ruby along with them. She'd been in this sorry state before so knew well enough what to expect. Coronation or no coronation, people were more interested in bread to feed their children than frippery and penny bunting. It had been almost a relief when it had been ripped down, and the streets of Salford and Castlefield had again lapsed back into their more workaday sheen of dusty grey.

Over the weeks, she'd watched the haunted expression creep over Aggie's face. Miraculously now it was Sparky who kept their spirits high as he and Jackdaw spent hours scouring the docks and wharves, determined that if there was any work going, they would be the ones to find it.

It had been Jackdaw who came to tell her that Giles Pickering was dead; that word was out he had a son somewhere and everyone was wondering who he was, and if he would take over the family business.

Ruby had made no reply, knowing that Bart's stubborn pride and determination to be one of the men and not classed as the enemy along with the father he so despised, had all been for nothing. How could he ever take his rightful place now? He was dead. She thought of the man she had seen on Salford docks the day after the coronation. He seemed like a mirage to her now, a touch of sunstroke. Aye, that was it. Too much sun. She'd quite convinced herself that he couldn't have been Bart at all, simply a figment of her imagination; a resurrection of her longing for him, not the man himself.

Aggie would say to her as they sat together in the *Blackbird* trying to make a watery cabbage soup stretch to six children, not forgetting a drop left over for themselves, 'You should marry again. You can't stay a widow forever.'

Ruby would give a hard little laugh. 'Who would have me?'

'Plenty would. You're still young, and a handsome woman. Time you took things a bit easier.'

'Why, for heaven's sake? I need to keep busy, don't pension me off yet.'

'I said you deserve someone else to do all the worrying, and all the labouring. You need a man to love, and to give you more childer.'

'And pigs might grow little pink wings and fly.' Ruby laughed, though there was an echo of sadness in the sound. She got to her feet suddenly anxious to get back to work before any more unwelcome advice was given. Aggie saw her face, and gently touched her hand.

'I only want what's best for you, chuck. We all do.'

'I know. But I couldn't bring myself to marry again. It wouldn't seem right somehow.' Tipping the remains of her soup into Aggie's near-empty bowl, she smiled. 'Here, I'm not hungry.' She put up a staying hand when she saw the beginnings of protest in the other woman's face. 'Don't fret, I'll have something later. And don't worry about this strike. It won't last forever. It'll be settled soon, and we'll win too, if only we hold on. Mark my words, even if the baron himself has to rise from the dead to see to it.' And a voice at the back of her mind wondered if perhaps he had.

Chapter Twenty-Nine

It was the following afternoon as she took a short cut down a back alley that she first sniffed trouble. Ruby had been to see one of the factory owners who had a standing order for her to transport his goods. This time the response had been no more than a sad shake of his head, but on the way back she heard of a load of cotton waste needing disposal and decided to go and investigate. It would be better than nothing. She was halfway down the alley when she caught sight of a crowd milling past, the clatter of their clogs loud in the late summer heat. Some broke away and started to run towards her.

'Run for it!' they yelled to her. 'It's the rozzers.'

But Ruby didn't run. She'd done with running away from trouble years ago, now she met it head on. Once out amongst the throng she was aghast by what she saw. There must have been thousands taking part in the procession, many of the women carrying babies in their arms.

The demonstration, one of many during the course of that summer, reminded her very much of the one she'd experienced all those years ago, on Byrom Street, with Bart. Here again were the same grey faces, the weary bands of loyal women, the same placards bearing the same pleas for a living wage, and a more poignant *Give Us Each Day Our Daily Bread*. But numbers now were massive, the resolve of the strikers to win through stronger than ever. They'd suffered too much, for too long, to countenance the possibility of defeat.

There were shouts and rousing cheers. Some women fainted in the heat while others starting singing 'Hearts of Oak', in tune with the brass band which was leading the procession. Police and infantry were everywhere. There seemed to be hundreds of them. A whole army of troops facing up not to the enemy in Africa or India, but to their own people: women and children, men like themselves who wanted only sufficient food to fill their bellies.

The charges seemed to come out of nowhere. One minute all was peaceful and orderly, the next came the sound of those dreaded whistles that still had the power to chill Ruby's blood. Batons were swung, clogs thrown, great lines of police linked arms and surged into the crowd, herding them together like cattle in the pitiless heat of the sun.

Ruby couldn't simply stand there and watch. All her rebellious spirit bubbled to the surface and she pitched in along with all the rest. Grown men cowered in doorways, desperate to protect themselves, as their heads were hammered senseless by truncheons. She saw a woman knocked over; Ruby managed to catch her child as it fell from her arms, seconds before it hit the ground, thereby saving the infant from being trampled underfoot. Not till the dazed woman was on her feet again did she hand the child over and move on.

It was a tragic day for Manchester. Ruby thought she'd seen everything, witnessed the lowest a man could sink to, and then she spotted a dearly familiar figure. He stood in a doorway some distance away, and she could tell, even from this distance, that he was sorely afraid. She'd thought he was safe with Aggie, but he must have escaped in the mayhem, and come looking for her.

'Tommy!' she screamed, and then the crowd surged forward and he was gone from her sight.

'Tommy!' Ruby screamed his name again. She ran out into the crowd. Heedless of her own safety, she pummelled and fought her way through the throng, the frightened pounding of her heart loud in her ears, all other sounds fading away to nothing. She heard no other cries but her own, saw nothing and no one as a red mist of fear swam before her eyes. She would have been ploughed down underfoot had not a hand pulled her away from a line of baton-waving troops at the very last moment. She fought furiously against it. 'Let me go! Let me go! I must reach my child. Tommy!'

'It's all right. Ruby. I have him. He's safe.'

And there her son was before her, looking suitably chastened and subdued after his fright. His knees were bloodied, his little shirt torn and he'd lost his beret. The red-gold hair shone like a blaze of sunshine in the dull, grey street.

Bart looked down at it and then at Ruby. 'Is it true? Could he possibly be...?' He didn't finish the sentence as he stared in wonder at his son.

Ruby was struck speechless, unable to find any words at all, not even to chastise Tommy for running away from Aggie and venturing out into the thick of the demonstration against strict orders. She could only gaze up into Bart's face, drink in the glorious sight of him standing there before her, so solid and normal, and *alive*! Or perhaps she had flown up to heaven and met him there. Ruby would not have been the least surprised were this the case, and did think for a moment that perhaps she had. But then he spoke again.

'I've shocked you. I think perhaps we'd all better get out of this fracas, don't you?' He put one arm about the boy, tucked Ruby under the other and led them, under his protection, through the throng and down a side alley, to relative safety. He didn't stop even then, but hustled them along till the shouts and cries and screams faded in the distance behind them. They turned a corner and Ruby recognised, through the mists of her confusion, that they were in Byrom Street.

In no time it seemed a door had been opened, and Ruby and Tommy were led inside, ushered into a cool, shady parlour and offered refreshment.

'There's cold lemonade for the boy. Would you like a glass yourself, or something stronger?'

'A double brandy might be more appropriate, 'ceptin I don't ever drink the stuff.' She could feel herself starting to shake, a reaction no doubt to the shock.

Bart addressed a young maid servant. 'The child needs some attention given to his knee. Will you see to him, Mary? Then get him some lemonade and a plate of cook's best ginger biscuits.'

Mary beamed at Tommy as his eyes lit up. 'Don't you worry, sir. I'll look after the little lad.'

When they'd gone, Bart settled Ruby in a comfy chair and poured her a small shot of whisky. 'Get that down you. Medicinal purposes only, and it'll bring the colour back to your cheeks.'

It did more than that. It made her weep. The tears rolled unchecked as she sat staring up at him, bemused, her mind a turmoil of unexpressed emotion and a million and one questions.

Bart sat opposite her, a frown of concern on his face as he urged her to take another sip. 'It's so good to see you, Ruby. There was a time when I thought I might never see you again.'

Any minute now he'd ask her how she'd been keeping, and she'd say that she was just fine and dandy, ta very much, save for the excessive heat. Just as if it were but a month or two since they last saw each other, and not nearly four years. Ruby couldn't believe this was happening. She felt as if she had stepped outside of herself, and was watching this little scene played before her eyes while she hovered somewhere near the ceiling. Perhaps she had indeed snuffed it and this was what heaven was all about.

'Is it really you?' There, she'd said it.

'Yes, Ruby, it's really me.'

'You're not dead then?'

The foolishness of the question brought not a flicker of a smile to his face, and she loved him for that. 'No, Ruby, I'm not dead, though there were times during these long empty years when I've wished that I was, rather than suffer the pain of losing you.'

'Why did you? Why did you leave? And why didn't you tell me where you were or ever come to see me?' Having now started to ask questions, she couldn't seem able to stop.

'Why did you take a lover? Why did you betray me?'

'I didn't! I told you that at the time.'

'Oh, Ruby, don't lie to me ever again. Surely I deserve the truth after all this time.'

'Kit Jarvis was never my lover. Not even after you were dead, or when we thought you were a goner.'

He gave her a quizzical look, eyes narrowing in that familiar, assessing way he had. 'But he told me that you were.'

'Huh, he'd lie on his own mother's grave, that one!'

'You wanted him to be your lover though, didn't you? Which is almost as bad. Even though you bore my child – my son – at least I assume that he is mine, with such hair? Nothing I said or did could prevent you from loving Kit Jarvis, your childhood sweetheart, rather than me, your husband. It sent me out of my mind with jealousy.'

Ruby gazed up at him, contrite. 'That was all a bad mistake. I didn't really love him at all. He was just a silly young girl's fancy, part of a childhood dream when I'd no one in the world to care for me, not even a mother. Oh, Bart, I realised what a terrible mistake I'd made the minute I lost you. I've asked myself a million times since why did I have to lose you before I discovered it was really you that I love.'

He was regarding her with a deep, impenetrable frown and Ruby had a sinking sensation in her heart that told her it was too late. That whatever she said now could never convince him she was sorry, that he was the one she loved.

'Why did you sell the pendant I gave you then?'

'It wasn't me, it was Kit.'

'At your instigation, no doubt! Once before, I seem to remember, you handed it over to him while stowing away on a ship. Your love for me can't amount to much if you would give away the one gift I ever gave you to mark the sincerity of my feelings for you. A jewel that in fact belonged to my mother.'

'So I believe.' Ruby was filled with remorse and shame. 'But I didn't know that at the time, did I? Kit stole it from me in the end, and I couldn't get it back.'

She explained then, how it had all come about. She told how Kit had taken it from its hiding place, about her interview with Pickering and how his father had accused her of being after the family inheritance. 'I told him it wasn't true, that I didn't want your money. I didn't then, and I don't now. It was you I wanted, Bart. Only I found that out too late because I was dazzled and hoodwinked by that no-good piece of rubbish.'

He was looking at her now with an expression of cautious wonder, alight with fresh hope. 'Is this true? I must warn you, Ruby, that I'd not take kindly to being betrayed a second time.'

She slid on to her knees before him and, reaching up, stroked the firm line of his jaw. 'I love you, you daft ha'p'orth. Always have, though I was too stupid to realise it. But then, if you'd talked to me properly about this jealousy of yours instead of just going off in a huff in that overly dramatic way, we might have saved ourselves a lot of bother, don't you reckon?'

'Oh, Ruby, I loved you too much to dare risk challenging you about it. I was convinced he was your lover. That's why we had the fight.' Then his arms were tight about her, as if he never meant to let her go, not this time.

'We were both too damned stubborn, eh?'

'I think we must have been.'

He asked her gently about Pearl, and Ruby said she knew all about what her sister had been up to but could do nothing about it. 'In any case, Pearl has gone, and I've no idea where.'

'I did so not want you to find that out.'

'Aye, well, what can't be cured must be endured, as my mam used to say.'

He smiled sadly. 'I wish I'd known your mam.'

'I wish you had too. Oh, but she was a lovely mother to us all. Poor though we were, we were never short of her love. It would have made all the difference to Pearl if only she'd lived.'

He put a finger to her lips. 'Don't! Things are as they are. Your mother did her best for her family, and so did you. Let it rest, Ruby.'

—

It was much later, as they lay between the sheets in his great bedroom, having reminded themselves of the original source of their attraction to each other, now confirmed and sealed with a deep and lasting love, that he explained why he'd come home, and how he'd agreed to take over the family business.

'My father set a number of conditions, which was typical of him but nothing I can't agree to.' He explained to her what they were.

'Oh, so you're ready to admit to everyone who you really are, at last?'

He smiled. 'I have no reason not to now. I shall keep his conditions, save for the one about no unions. In any case, I believe Asquith will shortly resolve that problem for us all. The strikes will be over soon and the dockers will win their demands for union recognition and better pay, I'm sure of it. Perhaps I can do my part by helping to bring new harmony to the Ship Canal and in particular to Pickering's Wharf. The only question is, will you stay with me and help me do it?'

'There's one other question I'd like you to answer first?'

He smiled at her, his brandy-coloured eyes intoxicating her with their dazzling warmth. 'Name it.'

'Can I keep the boats?'

'Not the pendant?'

'That too.'

He laughed. 'You don't ask for much, do you, Ruby McBride?'

'I don't want the boats for myself. I'd like to give them to Sparky and Aggie and Jackdaw. I don't know how I'd've managed without them. They've been like family to me. Oh, and there's one more thing.'

He was smiling at her in a way that told her he knew already what she was going to say. 'If I can supply it, it is yours.'

'My name in future, just so as you don't forget I'm your proper legal wife, is Ruby Stobbs, or should that be Pickering? Stobbs was your mother's maiden name, I dare say.'

'You'll always be Ruby McBride to me.'

–

Three years later, just a month after Britain declared war on Germany following their invasion of Belgium, Ruby was down at Salford docks seeing Sparky and Aggie off in the tug, pulling two pairs of barges behind them. Being six months pregnant with her third child, she'd been banned from accompanying them on this trip, which she still loved to do from time to time, given half a chance.

'You'll be welcome to come with us some time, once this babby is born, like always Ruby,' Aggie told her, and added, as she did times without number. 'Where would we be today without your generosity?'

'Where would I have been without you?' And the two women hugged each other.

Sparky interrupted. 'Come on you two, we've a living to earn.' And they all laughed at his grinning face. He certainly suited his name better, now that he was captain of his own tug. There were never any unexplained accidents these days. Jackdaw, captain of a second train of barges, would by now be on his way back from Liverpool, fit and well and quite his old self again.

Ruby had heard some time ago that Kit Jarvis had sold his boats, having found himself in a tight spot owing money to the bookies. It didn't surprise her. He hadn't been seen in the area since, which was a great relief. She certainly had no wish to be reminded of her youthful foolishness by seeing his face popping up again.

The day was cool, a weak sun peeping out only occasionally from behind a blanket of grey cloud. It reminded her very much of the day she'd stood at this very spot to celebrate the opening of the Ship Canal by Queen Victoria. Ruby well recalled the excitement of that day, her mam in her Sunday best, Billy with his sailor hat on, and Pearl with her doll.

Out on the wide expanse of water, ships were lining up, not for the Queen on this occasion, but in preparation for war. No hawkers plied their wares, sold toffee apples, monkeys on sticks or little flags today, as they had done all those years ago. But Ruby felt the same warm sense of pride at such a fine sight, coupled with a flicker of fear at what the future might hold for them all.

Posters adorned walls everywhere, calling on young men to join up as their country needed them. There was just such a man now, a young soldier dressed in his smart new uniform, the peaked cap tugged well down over his face. He was standing talking earnestly to a young woman, no doubt his sweetheart. They had their heads close together and were deep in conversation, oblivious to the world around them. Ruby's soft heart went out to them. How dreadful to be saying goodbye to your young man, to stand on the docks and see him go off to war, perhaps never to return.

Bart had assured her that he wouldn't have to go as he had an important job to do here in the Ship Canal. She trusted implicitly that he was right. In the three years since he'd come back into her life, he'd never let her down once. Ruby had found a happiness she'd never believed possible, marred only by her continuing concern for Pearl and Billy. Yet despite the uncertainty of what the future might bring, Ruby felt sure that they, at least, would win through. She just knew it in her heart.

She waved to Sparky and Aggie as they drew out into midstream and then started for home, banishing all worries from her mind. Wasn't she the most fortunate of women to be so well blessed? They had a little sister for Tommy now, their precious Opal, and a proper little madam she was turning out to be, though where she got it from Ruby couldn't imagine.

Ever since the strike, things had gone smoothly for them. Bart had been right about that. The dockers had won their demands, thanks to the support of Asquith who'd tackled the bosses on their behalf; not only winning recognition of their union and decent pay, but also the promise of disappointment money on days when they'd been taken on and were then not used. Since then, Bart himself had indeed brought new harmony to Pickering's Wharf. It was one of the happiest places to work in the entire canal basin.

Ruby smiled as she saw the young woman take her soldier boy's hand and begin to pull him along the quay. They were heading in Ruby's direction, walking quicker, as if suddenly in a tearing hurry. The girl had yellow hair, with a tiny hat perched on top of her curls. She was dressed quite plainly in a sensible grey dress and Ruby guessed that she might work in a shop or office. She scolded herself for being so curious and looked away to carry on walking. If this was their last day together, they didn't want nosy strangers staring at them. And then she heard the trill of the girl's laughter, and something in the sound of it made Ruby turn her head. It couldn't be, could it?

The young man standing next to the girl suddenly took off his cap and waved to her. 'It's me, our Ruby. Don't you recognise me? I'm back from Canada, come to fight in the war.'

There was a roaring in her ears, and her heart seemed to burst with pride and joy. 'Oh, my God, it is you, our Billy? And I can see that must be Pearl with you, if I live and breathe.' Then Ruby began to run towards them both with her arms open wide, eager to hold her little brother and sister close. For weren't they her beloved family and all together at last?

A Salford Saga

Ruby McBride
The Favourite Child
The Castlefield Collector
Dancing on Deansgate